I0843011

wandering closer

BOOK ONE OF THE WANDERLAND SERIES

ETTA LANE

To the ones who saw the red flags, and stayed anyway.
Don't settle for less than you deserve.
You are enough.

playlist

The Touch - A Tale Through Audio
She Lit A Fire - Lord Huron
Fallingforyou - The 1975
The Way That You Were - Sleep Token
Breathe - Lo Spirit
Think I'm In Love With You - Chris Stapleton
Labour - Paris Paloma
Power Over Me - Dermot Kennedy
Runaway - AURORA
Somewhere Only We Know - Keane
Home - MGK, X Ambassadors, Bebe Rexha
Die With A Smile - Lady Gaga, Bruno Mars
Ocean Eyes - Billie Eilish
The Love You Want - Sleep Token
Trouble - Never Shout Never
The Only Exception - Paramore
Hold On - Chord Overstreet

lily

I knew this drive would be long, but I didn't expect it to be so cathartic. The further I get, the more the tension in my chest seems to dissipate. I wouldn't call it running away, I wouldn't even call it an escape. It's a fresh start to find myself; to feel alive again. The cabin I bought two weeks ago is small and in need of some serious love, but it's all mine. Michele, the real estate agent I worked with, informed me it was fifteen minutes from downtown Cedar Ridge, a small town she called "dreamy in the winter." I've never been to Washington, but I've been dreaming of lush mountains since I was a kid. A small cabin in the woods, far from people–or, more specifically, far from Arizona–is precisely what I need.

I've been on the road for eight hours today with just one more to go. I rub my hand over Marge's dash, my old Jeep Cherokee, encouraging her, "We're almost there, girl." She's loaded down with everything I own, but she's chugging along like a trooper. I'm grateful for her all-wheel drive because looking around at the towering evergreen trees in the surrounding hills, I know I'll need it to navigate the snowy roads in about four months. In the last two days, I have driven through three states, but the surrounding sights right now are the best I have seen, bar none. The stunning mountain peaks as the backdrop for endless forest is what I have always dreamed of seeing. Waterfalls cascade down tall rock formations along the roads, while the odd creek runs alongside the highway. It's incredibly verdant, with a wider array of greens than any hardware store paint aisle could offer. I cannot wait to see what it all will look like as it changes colors in the fall, and is covered with snow in the winter.

Despite the breathtaking scenery around me, the cramped confines of Marge has me yearning for some fresh air. My back is aching, and my voice is a little hoarse from all the singing I have been doing to make the time go by faster. Thankfully, I seem to have chosen the best real estate agent around. When I called Michele this morning to ask where to pick up my keys, she told me they would be under the mat, and my fridge and pantry would have enough food to last me a few days while I settled in. I'm so grateful to her, and I'm really looking forward to finally meeting her face-to-face.

I did some research on this quirky town, but as I drive down the main street, I'm surprised by the eccentric storefronts. The stores are all alpine-style and fit into the Bavarian inspired theme of the town. Even the grocery store is quaint and fits the style, with pretty arches and painted cornucopias on the front. I follow my GPS as it guides me off the main street and out of the town center, further up the mountain and deeper into the woods. It's pretty clear Michele did not steer me wrong and my neighbors are few and far between, exactly as I asked for.

Turning right onto the gravel of Alder Avenue, I spot three mailboxes at the end of the street. All three of us have long driveways surrounded by thick forest, so none of the cabins are fully visible from our gravel road. I pass a driveway on the left, mine is a little further up on the right, and the last is straight ahead. As I pull up my driveway, the trees clear, revealing the small A-Frame cabin. It has a covered front porch, a bright red door, and the cutest little circle window near the top where I know the bedroom is.

Stepping out of my car, I take a moment to breathe in the crisp mountain air around me. It's what I imagined it would smell like, with a blend of damp earth, pine needles, and something slightly sweet, like wildflowers. I fill my lungs with the heady scent and breathe out the stress and anxiety of the last few days.

Grabbing only my purse, I retrieve the key from under the mat and step into my new home. The sunlight streams into the space, illuminating the expansive windows along the back. The entryway is small, with a coat closet and laundry closet to the left, and stairs leading up to the bedroom to the right. Beyond the entryway is a large open room housing a kitchen to the left with a small island and an adorable breakfast nook. The bathroom is to the right, and while it needs a deep clean and some updates, it's a decent size and functioning, so there's no room to complain. The rest of the open space along the back of the cabin is the living room. It has a large fireplace in the center with glass doors to the right and floor to ceiling windows to the left.

After setting my purse on the island, I head back to the stairs to check out the bedroom. There's a queen size bed on a side wall with two small side tables facing the opposite wall with two doors leading to small closets and a built-in dresser in between. This house is a complete contrast to my modern Phoenix condo, but it suits me beautifully. It's the view outside the glass door beyond the bed that made me fall in love with this cabin. I flip the lock and walk out onto the small balcony. It's the perfect size to fit a cozy chair and a small table to put my coffee and laptop.

As the sun filters through the trees, an hour before sunset, a sense of tranquility washes over me. Aside from some far off birds and a creek, it's utterly silent. Looking down, I can see the large back porch with two old wicker chairs in the center that I do not trust to hold me. There's a small yard surrounded by a mix of grass, weeds, and wildflowers that leads straight to thick forest. God, it smells so good out here–I know this is where I am meant to be.

After I emptied my car, ate a small meal from the pantry, and put away what I could, I called Andrea before going to bed. She's my publication manager and one of the few people who knows I bought this cabin and moved out here.

She picks up on the third ring, "Hey Lily, did you make it there alive?"

"I thought I was supposed to be the dramatic one, seeing as I'm the writer. But yes, I finally made it about three hours ago, and I'm exhausted."

Her deadpan tone is obvious, "If you weren't in such a rush to get out there, you wouldn't be so tired. No sympathy from me. Is it everything you hoped and dreamed of, or did the realtor sell you a run-down piece of shit?"

I roll my eyes, but I appreciate her blunt honesty in everything she does. It's what drew me to her out of the four publishers that wanted to work with me. Some see her as harsh, but I know it all comes from a place of love. She truly loves what she does and is brilliant at it. There is nothing she wouldn't do for her authors, and she has become a friend because of it.

"Loving the optimism. Honestly, it needs some small renovations and updating, but it's all in working order. It has cozy vibes and I haven't even decorated yet. The partial furnishings are saving my butt right now, but I can feel the creative juices flowing already. My next book will be done in record time."

"That is exactly what I want to hear. Send me some pictures and updates. I would love to have at least ten chapters in the next month, but take some time for yourself, too. You deserve it, that's for damn sure."

I couldn't agree with her more. "Thanks. I'm probably going to crash for a solid twenty hours, but I will keep in touch. Talk soon." Sleep was already beckoning to me before I even put my phone down.

The sun is blazing through the windows when I finally open my eyes. Curtains will have to be added to my list of items to shop for this week. My body still feels exhausted, but my bladder and the prospect of coffee drags me out of bed. Grabbing my phone on the way downstairs, I tap the screen to see it's already almost ten. Not quite the twenty hours of sleep I joked about, but the most sleep I have gotten in the last few weeks.

There's an old coffeemaker on the counter that I fill with the grounds from what looks like a local coffee shop. While that is busy brewing, I head to the bathroom for a quick shower. I should have showered last night, but since I slept in a sleeping bag because my new sheets needed to be washed, I don't feel so bad. The pipes creak as I turn them on, and water sputters out for a minute before a steady stream starts. A new shower head will also be added to the list of things I need. As I step into the shower, I see more than a few cracked tiles; okay, so maybe a whole shower reno would be best.

Despite the crumbling shower, I take my time washing the road trip grime from my body. With my hair wrapped in a towel, I head back into the kitchen for my freshly brewed coffee, the delicious scent spreading through the small space. To my surprise, there's vanilla creamer in the fridge. The woman is a god-send for supplying me with local coffee and creamer, let alone enough food to get me through the week. I put on a David Kushner playlist as I make myself some eggs for breakfast. When done, I hung my towel back up in the bathroom before taking my plate and coffee to the back porch to take in the late morning sun.

The chairs look as sketchy as I first thought, with holes and cracking wicker throughout. Instead of risking a broken tailbone when I inevitably fall through, I take a seat on the top step of the deck, letting my feet feel the warmth of the grass a few steps below. The peace I felt last night still radiates through me as I eat my breakfast to the tunes from my phone while the birds chirp around me. Setting the empty plate next to me, I stroll around the yard, sipping my coffee. It was recently mowed, but I will definitely have to find a lawn service or add a mower to my ever-growing list of must-haves. Making my way back to the deck, I notice quite a few of the boards are rotting and warped and need to be replaced soon.

My type-A brain is spinning with a need to get these lists onto paper before they fall out of my ears. Grabbing my plate, I head back into the cabin to write everything down. I find lists very calming, and I'm sure I'll cover the dining table with them soon. First things first:

1. Go to town and look for more furniture and paint
2. Make Michele a thank you basket and deliver it to her
3. Make another list of must-haves that will need to be ordered
4. Get cleaning supplies to give the cabin a thorough deep clean
5. Make a list of things to repair and renovate
6. Find maps and information on the best hiking around
7. Write your next amazing novel

That seems like a decent start. Michele left me a guide of her favorite places to eat, shop, and buy furniture, so I decide to start there. I brushed my teeth and threw on one of my new summer dresses with sandals and sauntered out the door.

The drive back into town is easy, and I roll down my windows to make the most of the fresh mountain air. There's one main street through the town that holds hotels, restaurants, and activities, and a parallel side street full of little shops with restaurants and bars placed in between. Everything is utterly adorable, and I can already tell this town at Christmas will be a Hallmark movie dream.

After visiting the hardware store for paint samples, I meandered to a few furniture stores. For my little balcony, I picked up a cute Papasan chair and side table that barely fit in the back of Marge, then quickly realized whatever else I found would need to be delivered, so I put furniture shopping off for another day. Next, I found a local coffee shop, where I grabbed more of their local blend that was in my cabin for both Michele and I. At a local boutique, I nabbed a cute tote bag and some fun earrings as well as a stack of amazing smelling candles. My last stop in town was the grocery store, where I stocked up on basic items and the entire aisle of cleaning supplies.

With Marge loaded down, I head to the address Michele gave me for her office. The tote bag filled with the goodies I found sits in the seat next to me as my thank you. I'm surprised to find that her office is a converted garage that sits next to her beautiful home. It is painted a deep hunter green with white accents and flower pots around the entrance.

Throwing my purse over my shoulder, I grab the tote and head through the french doors in the front of the office. The walls inside are a pale pink that coordinates with the green outside, creating a warm and inviting atmosphere. Michele shoots up from behind her desk, recognizing me immediately. Nine video house showings and countless video calls going over paperwork will do that.

She's dressed in a white flowy top and wide leg navy pants that fit her curves beautifully. Her light brown hair flows around her shoulders, framing her face that I have come to know well. I never got to see her outfits on the camera, but I love her style.

"Lily! You're finally here. It's so good to meet you in person." She wrapped me in a hug I wasn't expecting as I stood there awkwardly, arms trapped at my side. "Sorry, I'm a hugger, and I feel like I know you already. How was the move? Do you love the cabin?"

"It's okay, you just caught me by surprise. People don't hug much where I'm from." Her lips purse down at that, her nose wrinkling. She was very expressive in our video chats too, never one to hold back how she's feeling. It's what made me trust her judgement as she walked me through each home, telling me exactly what it looked like, smelled like, and what desperately needed fixing.

"The cabin is everything you said it was and more. It needs a day's worth of cleaning and some updates, otherwise, I am so in love with it and the area already." I hand her the tote bag. "Here's some small things as a thank you. I really appreciate all you have done for me."

"You are so sweet, but it's not necessary. I love doing things for people, it's why I love this job. Have you had any time to explore? Most of the locals live a bit outside of town, leaving the homes in town to renters and the tourists. We like to keep our little slice of the woods separate and clean." She moves to sit on a little couch in the corner, waving me to sit with her. Michele has this magnetic energy that radiates warmth, drawing me to follow and sit with her.

"Besides a few stores in town today, I explored my backyard. I'll need to get some good hiking boots and trail guides. I want to get lost in the woods without actually getting lost in the woods, you know?"

"You should head to the park ranger's office next time you are in town. It's small and has funky hours, but they have endless safety information and trinkets for not getting lost. There's also a local furniture maker in town who creates beautiful pieces if you need some new stuff. I'll write down his website for you, but he is terrible at keeping it updated, so texting or calling him is best. You'll love Jake, and he would make the most incredible outdoor set for you. I saw the horrendous state of those wicker chairs out back," she chuckles. Michele might be the nicest woman I have ever met. It's nerve wracking being in a new place with no friends, but I absolutely want to be friends with her. Her wealth of knowledge on the area and the people doesn't hurt to have either.

"I would love his information. Do you know anything about my neighbors? I would like to make them muffins and introduce myself." I lived in my condo for four years, and while I may have said a 'hey' in passing, I didn't know a single other person. I don't want to live like that again. I want to meet people and make a life for myself here.

"You may not want to make muffins for the Campbells. They are the cabin on the left and use it as a vacation place. Maybe leave a note in their mailbox introducing yourself? The neighbor on the end is a bachelor and a really nice guy. I went to school with him and his brother. He would probably love muffins. Also, he is a total babe, if you're in the market," her eyebrows raise playfully. My cheeks heat under her playful stare. I am nowhere near being in the market. I might have sworn men off for good.

I hum in agreement and move the conversation along. "I am itching to get back and start on the deep clean, but I would love to get together for dinner or coffee next week if you're available?"

"Yes! I would love that. I will look at my calendar and we will set something up."

With a plan to meet next week and a business card for Anderson's Fine Furnishings, I head back to my cabin. I am already feeling more at home here than I ever did in Phoenix. It's nice to feel like I'm not alone here. I have acquaintances and old colleagues back in Phoenix, but none I would realistically keep in touch with. My parents are retired and living in Florida, and we don't talk all that much. Andrea is the closest thing I have to a friend, but she also writes my paychecks, so I'm not sure she fully counts. Settling back in at home, I unload everything from Marge, make a small dinner, and sit on the porch to enjoy the quiet before going to bed early to prepare for a day of deep cleaning.

thoren

The incessant jingling of the back door bells drags me from my dreams. Peeling my tired eyes open, I mutter, "I'm coming." I slide my feet over the edge of the bed and trudge downstairs in my boxers, silently cursing myself for teaching Shadow to paw at the bells when she has to potty. Read the puppy training books, they said. It will be worth it, they said. Worth it, my ass, when it means that bells are my wake up call most mornings. I unlock the door, giving her a head scratch on her way out, then head to the coffeemaker to start a pot.

I haven't been sleeping great since I took over the Search and Rescue team while they look for a new department head. The number of calls they get this time of year to 'check on hikers' is insane. It all falls on me now if one of those hikers is actually lost and can't be accounted for. To add to that headache, it's my day to work at our office in town. I normally love what I do, but sitting in that office just hoping someone calls or walks in for eight hours slowly kills my soul. It's not our big office that we share with the Search and Rescue and Wildfire teams, but a small storefront in town to make us available to locals and tourists alike. The only bright side is that Shadow gets to come in with me.

After a quick shower, a travel mug of coffee, and a breakfast burrito to go, I load Shadow into my truck and head to the office. For one day every other week, one of the park rangers has to hang out here to be available to the public for information on the local wildlife, hiking, camping, laws, and any general questions they may have. Since we took over the small space two years ago, I have had maybe twenty people come in on my time, hence the soul-sucking boredom.

Shadow and I are having a tug-of-war battle on the floor around noon when the front door swings open. Shadow bounds out around the desk before I can stand up and get a warning out to the patron. I hear her squeal of delight before I catch a glimpse of the woman in front of me. Long dark brown hair falls around her face as she plops right to her knees, giving Shadow love. When she finally notices me standing here, her eyes travel up my body until brilliant blue eyes land on mine. Her naturally tanned skin and brown hair so dark it almost looks black is at a complete contrast to the stark eyes that have rendered me speechless. Shadow nudges her hand, which has now stalled with the pets as we take each other in. My brain and mouth connect before hers do as I stammer out, "Hi, can I help you?"

The woman before me stands so I can fully take her in, my mouth drying at the sight. She's short and petite in a pretty dress paired with ankle boots and a jean jacket. Her smile is bright, her cheeks flushing.

She giggles as Shadow weaves around her legs, trying to get more pets and attention from her. "Hey, I'm new to the area and was hoping to get some info on the hiking around here. My realtor mentioned you might have a list of supplies that would be good to have any time I venture into the woods. Also, if this is your dog, can I take her home with me?"

"Shadow, sit." She does immediately, but right at the woman's feet. "While she seems to be happy with that idea, I could never part with my traitorous best friend. But I can absolutely help you with all things outdoors in the area. Do you have any experience hiking or are you looking for safe, easier hikes? Do you know much about the local area and what to expect in the way of wildlife and plants to avoid?"

Her hands trail through Shadow's short fur on her head as she talks. "Think of me as a complete novice in it all. I'm from Phoenix, and while there are hiking spots around there, they are nothing like this. I was raised a city girl, and I rarely did anything outside of work."

Just what we need around here, another transplant that will last less than a year when they experience the rough winter and move right back out. The last type of woman I need to be checking out, but I can't help myself. She radiates pure kindness.

"I will take any and all advice you have for me. I'm Lily, by the way, it's nice to meet you." Her small hand reaches out, and I take it in my own, giving it an easy shake. Her fingers feel delicate, soft, and so warm. My rough, calloused hand dwarfs hers, but I don't want to let go.

"Nice to meet you, Lily. I'm Thoren and you've obviously met my sidekick, Shadow," I say, letting her hand drop slowly. "What made you decide to move here?"

Her sapphire eyes shutter as her gaze darts away, and she fidgets with her hair. "I've always dreamed of getting out of the city. I hit a point in my career where I could do it, so I did." Her voice is quieter, more reserved, and I hate that I made her shut down. I want to know the real reason, not the clear lie she just told me, but that would be an overstep, so I change the subject instead.

"Let's get you set up with everything you need to make the most of your time here." I walk behind the desk, grabbing one of the 'Bigfoot Vacations Here' totes we sell. "I'm going to fill you up," I mumble out as my cheeks immediately heat, registering what I just said. "Umm, not like that.. Sorry… I meant this bag.. I'm sorry." Running my hand down my face, I take a deep breath, trying not to die of embarrassment.

Her awkward giggle is cute as she talks to my dog, "Is your daddy stumbling over his words? Yes, he is. It's okay though, we're all human." She snorts, then immediately covers her mouth with her hands. "Sorry. That was embarrassing. It's just, she's obviously not human." She points down at Shadow, her cheeks flushing again.

Apparently, I'm not the only one affected and fumbling with my words. "I'm putting a few pamphlets in here. They'll have pictures and descriptions of the local wildlife and plants. There's two maps I'm adding as well," I say as I continue filling up the tote. "A pocket guidebook, a compass, and I'll even throw in the holy grail."

I head back to my desk, grabbing my carefully curated list. "It's my personal list of everything I carry in my backpack when I go hiking. On the bottom is a list of the apps I have on my phone, and emergency numbers to know. Be careful because you won't always have service. It's better to be safe than sorry, and this list has been finely tuned over the years," I can't help but brag. I love my job and I love spending time in the woods even more.

Lily's fingers graze over mine as she takes the list from me, and I swear I feel a jolt of electricity run through my body. "Wow, this is extensive. I guess I have some more shopping to do." She grabs the bag I have outstretched, "Thank you, Thoren."

"You're welcome, Lily. If you ever need anything else, feel free to come back," I try to prolong the inevitable.

She leans down again, giving Shadow a kiss and some chin scratches. "See you two around."

With that, she's out the door and I feel the loss of her immediately. I should have asked for her number, or at least invited her to the group hikes I lead monthly. I shoot off a text to Jake, partly to brag and partly to get advice.

THOREN ⚒:

You missed out today, a beautiful new girl came in and spent half an hour with me.

I may have been the awkward lanky kid in school, but I have filled out since then. Unfortunately, I am still awkward in person until I get to know someone. Something about Lily has me intrigued, even though I know spending time with her would be a huge mistake.

JAKE 🪜:

Did you have to tie her up to make her stay? That's usually more of my thing…

THOREN ⚒:

I hate you. She said she just moved here - city girl type. The most mesmerizing blue eyes with dark brown hair. Total killer.

JAKE 🪜:

Not all city girls are the same dude. How hot are we talking? Like enough for me to stalk around town looking for her?

THOREN ⚒:

I said beautiful, not hot. Short, petite, olive skin. Rendered me speechless.

JAKE 🪜:

Damn I swear I better get a knockout when I'm stuck there tomorrow or I'm quitting.

THOREN ⚒:

Sure thing buddy, beers this weekend?

JAKE 🪜:

If you come out with me, you bet.

I'm not one to judge, but Jake has a reputation for getting around. Aside from college, I have never been a 'bar on the week-end' kind of guy, so he knows that's likely a no from me. We have been best friends since we were kids, but we are total opposites. I've always wanted stable relationships and a family, while he has enjoyed the playboy life. I'm a little more rugged around the edges, while Jake is the quintessential bad boy. Somehow, our friendship just works. We are both park rangers, however, he is only part-time until he can make his furniture business a full-time gig. He is a true woodworking master and makes stunning hand-crafted items.

No surprise, not a single other person came into the town shop today. I close up at four and head to our large office. I have a meeting with the search and rescue (SAR) team and our volunteers, so I'm bringing Shadow to help calm my nerves. It's my first meeting being in charge, and we need to plan out training scenarios, schedule who will be available for the next eight weeks, as well as discuss my expectations for the group until a new department head is found. While I have been a volunteer member since I turned sixteen, and am familiar with these woods and zones, this is still not my specialty.

At five, I glance around our conference room, sizing up the numbers we have. Four full-time employees, five volunteer fire-fighters, and twelve citizen volunteers. Not terrible numbers, and within that group, we have two nurses. For the next hour, we run through schedules, plan out future dates for three training exer-cises, and discuss how we can work best as a team through this transition period. Around an hour later, we all start packing up and heading out, Shadow posted by the door demanding her goodbye pets from everyone.

Sherry lingers in the room, taking her time packing up her purse which, for some reason, is now half spilled across the conference table. As the last person walks out with a pat on my shoulder, she finally makes her way over to me.

"Hey Thoren, I am so glad I can finally be a volunteer. How fun that we get to do this together," she purrs, standing too close for comfort. We went to high school together, but she wanted nothing to do with me then. The awkward, skinny kid wasn't her type. No, she went after the Jakes, the ones on the football and baseball teams. And my brother, she definitely went after my brother, surely seeing a track to money and fame. Now that I have a good career, and I've filled out from my lanky form, I seem to have caught her eye. I have run into her in town quite a few times since then and she's shown interest, even when I was with Jen. She's not my type, especially since it's clear her affection is based on physical and monetary aspects only.

"So glad you can be a part of the team, Sherry. It's nice to see more of the community involved," I say, taking a step back to grab my backpack from by the door and clip Shadow's leash back on. The hint goes over her head as she follows me closely, keeping the space between us at a minimum.

"I heard you were put in charge, and I just felt the time was right." Her voice grates my nerves as she lets her fingers trail down my arm. "I heard Jen left town. It really is a shame. She should have seen how good she had it."

That's my cue. "Yep, well, everything happens for a reason. I need to head home. I'll see you at the next training exercise."

I bound away from her and into my truck as fast as I can. Avoiding conversations about Jen has become like a sport, and she left eight months ago. I wish people would drop it already. Putting my truck in drive, I give my best girl a scratch under her chin and head home.

After dinner, I grab Shadow's running leash and set out to do a couple of miles. My two-car garage is half home gym, half actual parking for my truck. It's great for lifting and running in the winter, but there is nothing like a quiet run in the evening air the rest of the year. On our way out, I notice lights through the trees at Gary's old cabin. The rumors were that it finally sold, and it looks like the new owner has moved in. I was enjoying being alone on this street most of the time, what with the Campbells hardly here. I hope they don't mind Shadow running through the woods when she finds something to chase. None of our cabins have fences, so Shadow roams free frequently, but she knows to not venture too far and always comes back.

We completed a nice six-mile run, the lights still shining from the cabin on our way back. I debate stopping for introductions, but talk myself out of it. It's dark out and I don't want to freak out my new neighbor, plus I'm a sweaty mess. I make a mental note to try to catch them later in the week. It's pretty secluded up where we live, so I should probably know my neighbors for safety, at least.

I trudge back into the house and head straight upstairs to the bathroom, turning on the shower. While the water heats, I stretch out my muscles, trying to release the tension of the day. The meeting went better than expected, and I seem to have a solid team that knows I'm wet behind the ears in this leadership role, yet is supportive anyway. If only Sherry could have kept her mouth shut. It's been at least a month since Jen's name has popped up unbidden and I thought a new leaf was being turned.

It's not that I'm still hung up on her; more so, I'm tired of everyone else being hung up on her leaving me. I went through the anger and depression—even got the t-shirt. The bitterness is what is left haunting me. Bitter that I wasn't enough to make her want to stay in this small town. Bitter that while I was busy planning for a future with a nice home, a marriage, and babies, she was busy planning for 'something more'.

I take a quick shower, then head downstairs to let Shadow out one more time. While she does her business, I lean against my kitchen island, taking in all the work I have done to my cabin. It was run down and in need of serious TLC when I bought it, but I have turned it into my dream home. I stripped this place down to the studs, replaced all the old pipes, and crafted everything for what I thought would be a perfect family home. It's still my dream home. That dream just looks a little different now. A little lonelier.

Shadow and I trek back upstairs where she beats me into bed, claiming the center like the hog that she is. I give her some good night belly rubs before rolling over and attempting to sleep. My mind drifts to Lily, the gorgeous woman from this morning with sapphire eyes. I haven't been struck speechless in a long time, but she took my breath away and wiped my brain clean. My cock stirs at the thought of her, but I scold it, willing it to stand down. I roll over again, letting myself drift to sleep where those blue eyes meet me again.

lily

In the last week, I have scrubbed every square inch of the cabin, including refreshing every piece of furniture. While I have always kept a clean home, that was as far as my maintenance skills extended. Painting my bedroom upstairs was the first time I had painted outside of art class, and I am beyond proud of the results. The fresh coat of pale blue is the exact color of the sky as the sun rises behind the forest early in the morning. The downstairs still needs new paint, but I'm not set on the colors yet, so it will have to wait.

The completed bedroom feels cozy. Inviting. It feels like *mine*.

While the painting is a step in the right direction, I haven't started on any updates yet. I've never fixed anything in my life, and the thought of messing something up is daunting. My parents were not the 'do it yourself' types. If something broke or needed repairs, they called a professional to come fix it.

I want to be an independent woman who can do things for herself. There are online tutorials for everything nowadays; there is no excuse for me to not tackle projects on my own. I want to look around my home and see improvements I have made, or at the very least, helped with. I just need a little more courage first.

I jumped into working on my next novel instead, since it's a safer project to start. Andrea has sent gentle reminders this week to not fall behind on my writing, so I'm doing my best not to. The problem is, my brain fries every time I open my laptop. I have no motivation, no ideas, no inspiration. Just anger, deleted paragraphs, and empty pages.

That, in turn, has led to hiking explorations in the area. After meeting Park Ranger Thoren last week, I felt more confident in going out in the woods on my own. I dropped a pretty penny at a local outdoor store in town after I left his office and stocked up on hiking boots, a hiking backpack, and everything on his list of must-haves. That is, after I chugged an entire bottle of cold water to cool myself down.

Relationships, and men in general, are not in the cards for me at the moment... or ever. But I would have to be blind to not notice every striking feature that man has. From his golden tanned skin with a perfectly imperfect mess of brown hair cropped short on the sides, to the few day-old beard on his chiseled face and strong chin, and hazel eyes that looked so deeply into mine. His thick thighs that filled out every available inch in his work pants... and here I am, flushing again just thinking about him.

I shake out my thoughts and focus back on the beauty of the world around me. After a night of rain, the trail has an overwhelming scent of earth and pine, wet but alive. Moss-covered trees surround the small walkway while ferns and mushrooms litter the forest floor. I'm sticking with an easy hike this morning, only two miles, so I can try to do some writing before dinner with Michele tonight.

I can't remember the last time that I went out to dinner with a friend that wasn't a colleague. I interned all through college, so even then, my friends were co-workers. I'm not sure if I'm a little sad about that, or excited that things are finally changing. I'm only one week into living in this charming town, and I have a dinner date with a real friend.

This is the third hike where I haven't passed a single other person on the trail, and I love it. The solitude is healing. Freeing. The overwhelming feelings of embarrassment, anger, and failure don't feel so heavy out here. Unlocking my car, I throw my backpack in the passenger seat and take one more steadying breath. The drive back to the cabin is quick and I immediately head to my little balcony to write. Sports romance is my specialty, which is ironic, since I am the least sporty person around. I decided to try a baseball romance this time around, and set about doing as much research about the game as I can while I flesh out some character ideas.

Time flies as I get a basic outline for the book mapped out. Maybe being isolated out here will be great for my career. Closing my laptop, I head downstairs to shower and get ready for dinner. Michele said the restaurant we are meeting at is a local hangout and nothing fancy, so I throw on a maxi dress with a suede jacket and heeled ankle boots. I keep my makeup at a minimum, just a little liner and mascara. My hair always dries into place. It's boring and straight, but it saves me time since I wrote a little longer than I was intending.

The town is bustling for a Tuesday night, the streets lined with cars and people milling about. I snag one of the few open spaces and walk a few doors down to the RiverRoots restaurant. Michele is seated at a small booth, waving me down when I enter.

"Hey girl, you made it!" She points to the margarita pitcher on the table. "I may have gotten a little overzealous by ordering a pitcher, but I've had a day."

I slide into the booth across from her, setting my purse down next to me and shrugging off my jacket. "I will never turn down a margarita. Never." I grab the empty glass in front of me and fill it to the brim with the pink drink. "What flavor is this?"

"Watermelon, so sorry, I should have checked with you first. It just looked so good and refreshing," she says, taking another sip of hers.

I wave her off before swallowing down half of mine. The mix of tangy and sweet hits my tongue, settling my nerves for this dinner. The restaurant is cute and brimming with people. Long wooden beams adorned with string lights run across the ceiling, and the walls are plastered with photos of the mountain peaks and woods. "That is incredible. Tell me about your day. What's going on?"

"Stupid realtor things. I had a sale fall through due to lack of funds, and a buyer I've been working with for two years came by today. She has something negative to say about every home I show her. I swear, I will be working with her in ten years and still won't have a home to sell her that fits her list."

I scrunch my nose at the thought of that. I have patience, but I would hate that. "You're a better person than me. I would tell her to take a hike. Literally." The server stops by then, taking our orders and refilling our water glasses.

As he walks away from the table, Michele leans forward, her eyes filled with mischief. "I'm one of two realtors in town, so I'll put up with her and reward myself with margaritas. But enough about me. I need to hear everything about you. You're an author, right? What kind of books do you write? What made you want to move here from Phoenix?" Her tone is all no-nonsense, so I try to explain without oversharing.

"Writing has always been my passion, but I didn't pursue it right away. I was an executive assistant at a financial firm, but it wasn't my dream. So on the side, I started writing a hockey romance series. Here I am, four books later, with an amazing publisher and pursuing writing full time. I have a baseball romance series in the works next." I lightly spin my margarita glass in a circle, trying to brush off the next part. "It was time to leave Phoenix. It never felt like home to me, and here already does. It feels like the perfect setting to focus on my writing."

Michele remains quiet, so I slowly look up at her. Her head is cocked a little to the side in question, but whatever she sees on my face, she must understand because she nods her head. "I love a good romance book. Please tell me it's spicy. I'll read it immediately!"

Our laughs ring out as I take another sip of my drink. "Very spicy. Have you seen the stretches those men do on the ice?" I fan myself playfully. "Imagine how those skills must transfer to other activities."

She sighs wistfully, "I could use some of those other activities."

"I'm good performing on my own for a while," I giggle, then freeze, realizing I said that aloud. My cheeks heat beyond the flush I was already getting from the margarita. "That was an overshare, so sorry. No men around here have caught your attention?"

"Please, that was a boring overshare. Next time, at least make it good. And no, I've grown up with most of these men. I either struggle to see them as more than the stupid teens they used to be, or they don't want the same things as me. I want stability. A man who enjoys spending nights at home with me. Realtor hours can sometimes be crazy, and I want someone who is home when I get there. Someone to take care of, and who takes care of me in return, you know?"

Her words hit hard, because I do know. My voice comes out a little quieter than I intended. "I completely understand that."

Our meals come and we dig in, both of us seemingly in our heads. I wanted stability, too, someone to build a life with. Instead, I believed in a man who said all the right things, despite the red flags that I saw. I let myself be made a fool of, in the pursuit of happiness and a future. It was a mistake I wouldn't be making again.

"Did you get in touch with Jake?" Michele asks in between bites.

"Yes! He is bringing the pieces I chose tomorrow evening. He sent me pictures of some of the stuff he had on hand. He's not sketchy, right? Since he is coming to my house to drop it off?" I ask, setting my napkin on my empty plate.

"Not at all," she laughs. "He's around your age, looks a little intimidating sometimes, but ridiculously nice. My dining table, coffee table, outdoor set, and chairs around my firepit were all made by him. If you want the best, you get it from Jake."

"Everything looked so beautiful. I'm getting an outdoor couch from him as well, and a rocking chair to sit by the fireplace. It's clear this is what he was made to do."

She sets down her fork and stacks her empty plate on mine before refilling our margarita glasses. "How is everything coming along in the cabin? Have you made any changes yet?"

I can't keep the excitement from my voice. "I painted the bedroom and cleaned everything. I replaced some of the hinges on the doors that were rusted and even installed a new toilet seat. They may be small things, but they are major for me, and I am really proud. I think fixing the deck and updating the bathroom are the first major projects I am going to tackle."

"That's amazing, Lily. You're going to have that place transformed in no time. You should be really proud of yourself." She clinks our glasses in cheers. It's been a while since someone has told me they were proud of me, aside from when Andrea loves the chapters I send her. I think I heard it once at the firm in the almost six years I worked there. My parents told me when I graduated college with their desired degree for me. But lately? Lately I hadn't felt very proud.

Hearing it from Michele with such a genuine tone strikes a

chord. I hide the rush of emotion behind a big sip. "Thanks, that means a lot to me."

We finish off our pitcher, talking more about the town, the people, and taking on renovations as a single woman. Our time is filled with laughter and genuine enjoyment. Michele is easily my new favorite person because she exudes a confident, kind, and radiating light for life. When our last glasses run dry, we plan to make this a weekly thing as often as possible, and she promises to stop by my place soon to help me decide on paint colors for downstairs.

With a hug goodbye, one that still feels a little strange but welcome, we part ways and I hop in Marge to head back home. The roads darken the further you get from town. Streetlights become fewer and farther between; my headlights and the moon are the only things lighting the road. When I pass a man and a dog running on the other side of the road, I feel a small pang of jealousy. I was braving hiking solo, but walking alone in the evening out here is a bit of a stretch for me. How I wish it wasn't though; the evening air is crisp, and the quiet relaxing.

I slow as I pull down my street and dark driveway. I have to start remembering to turn on the porch light when I leave for the evenings, something I never had to think about in the city. With keys in hand, I trudge up my small porch and head inside. The light from the moon illuminates my living room and deck, making the small space really shine. A shiver races through me, bringing on the feeling of 'right'. Everything about being here, now, in my home, feels like I made the right decision.

With a lightness from the margaritas, an evening with a new friend, and a peace of where I am at in life, I head upstairs to bed and crash for the night.

Waking the next morning, I finally felt an itch to write. Not only that, I wrote for the whole day without even realizing. My fingers were flying over the keys as the words spilled from my brain. It wasn't until my stomach rumbled that I noticed it was four in the afternoon and I hadn't even had lunch. Setting my laptop down, I picked up my phone, seeing a text from Jake from over an hour ago asking if I was still good for him to drop off the furniture this evening. I shot off a quick message, apologizing for the late reply, letting him know I would be home.

Closing up my balcony, I plugged in my laptop and set it on my bed before heading down to make a small dinner and move the sparse furniture in the living room around so I can fit my new rocking chair. I am beyond excited for the outdoor couch. I plan to park myself on it for the next few months. The crunch of tires on my gravel drive alerts me to Jake's arrival right as I am plating up my chicken and salad, so I plop it in the fridge and throw on some sandals to meet him.

I'm anticipating a big intimidating man based on Michele's description, and the hulking man in front of me is not far off. He's walking up my porch as I pull open the door, and we both stop short. Jake is dressed in scuffed black work boots, dusty jeans that fit him like a glove, and a black T-shirt. Thick arms with tattoos all the way to his hands bulge from the tight shirt, and a shiver runs down my back as I take him in. It isn't until I make my way up to his face that I see his broad smile radiating warmth.

He takes another step forward, reaching his hand out. "Hi Lily, I'm Jake. It's nice to meet you." His deep voice is smooth and exactly what I expected. The kind sparkle in his eyes and the bright smile are at complete odds with the rest of him, but it puts me at ease.

His hand completely covers mine, but he doesn't squeeze hard as he shakes it. "It's nice to meet you, too. Michele has so many good things to say about you, so it's nice to put a face to a name."

His laugh is loud, his chest shaking with it. "Chele is a troublemaker, but she's good people. Plus, she seems to know all the gossip in town without ever being part of it. She's a good one to keep around. I'm glad she got you in here, this place has real potential," he says, nodding past me to the cabin.

"I'm really happy here already. It needs a lot of love, and lucky me, I have a lot of love to give. Can I help you carry the furniture?"

Jake turns and starts walking to the trailer hitched behind his truck. "Yeah, that would be great. The couch comes in two pieces. Do you think you can carry the chaise side and I'll get the other?" He pulls a tarp off the trailer, revealing the pieces and my rocking chair. "The couch is made with oak, the chair is maple. They've been treated and sealed, but it wouldn't hurt to cover the couch in the winter months."

They may be simple pieces, but I can tell they were crafted with care and love. "They are beautiful. If you can hand me the chaise, I can try to get it to the back."

He works quickly, unstrapping his ties and gingerly passing me the couch base. It's heavy, but manageable, and I shuffle to the backyard with it, careful not to trip and drop it. Jake is right behind me with the larger piece, and he sets it down with ease before helping me set mine down.

"I've got a drill in my truck to connect these, if you want to come back out front with me and grab the cushions?"

"Oh, I thought I would have to get my own cushions. How much do I owe you for them?" My little legs work in overdrive trying to keep up with his long strides.

Jake turns, his cheeks getting a pink tint. "Nothing. My mom likes to craft, so she sews cushions for some of my items when she has free time. She made a little cushion for the rocking chair, too, but you don't have to use it."

It's my laugh that rings out now. This big man talking about his mom crafting for him is entirely too cute. He opens the back door of his truck and starts stacking forest green pillows in my arms. He tucks his drill and some screws in his pocket, then grabs the rest and we head back to the deck. I pile up the cushions while he connects the pieces, and notice there are two throw pillows mixed in as well. They are the same deep green but with white leaves hand sewn into the fabric.

"You better be paying your mom for these," I say, as my fingers trace over the hand-crafted beauties. "These are incredible. I feel like I definitely need to pay more."

"Nah, I'll tell her you love them and that will be payment enough for her." He arranges the pillows and cushions carefully, and my heart flutters with excitement at the thought of all the time I will spend on it. "Do you want me to take these chairs to the dump?" He asks, pointing at the wicker monstrosities.

"Please!" I practically shout at him. "Those things are a death trap."

He laughs, picking up one under each arm. "No problem, I have some things I need to take there anyway," he pauses, taking in the view from my deck, before continuing back to the front again. "It's really peaceful back here."

"Yeah, it's my favorite. I spend every morning enjoying my coffee on the deck. Now I don't have to sit on the half-rotten boards, so thank you," I trail behind him.

He throws the wicker chairs onto his trailer before unloading the rocking chair. "Can you grab the cushion for this one? It's in the front seat. I'm assuming this goes in the house?"

"Yeah," I nod, grabbing the cushion. "I'll get the door for you."

I lead him into the house and show him the little spot in front of the fireplace where I want it. "Thank you so much for everything. I'll let Michele know she didn't lie about your furniture, and please don't forget to thank your mom."

"I'm glad you like it all," his honeyed voice says as he heads back out my front door. "It was nice to meet you, Lily. I'm sure I'll see you around." He says with a knowing look in his eye that I don't quite understand.

"See you around, Jake." I wave him off as he loads up into his truck, then head back inside. Now I have the perfect spot to eat my dinner in comfort.

thoren

It has been a long fucking week, and the beer in my fridge is calling my name. I know Jake is going to try to drag me out to the bar tonight, but no part of me wants to go. A beer on the porch while throwing the ball to Shadow sounds like the perfect evening. My truck rambles up the gravel driveway to find a black truck identical to mine already parked out front. I pull up next to it since he's blocking the side of my garage I can park in and he knows it.

Shadow is at my feet, greeting me with eager barks and kisses before I fully get out of the truck. "Hey bubs, are you being a good girl?" I ask, dropping a kiss to her furry black head as I scratch her back. She barks some more, leading the charge to my front porch where Jake is sitting, one of my beers in hand. As I sit next to him, he pulls another from behind his back and passes it over.

"Grabbed you one, too," he says, like he brought it and didn't steal them from my fridge. I pop the top and take a deep swig in acknowledgement. We have keys to each other's places and it's not unusual for me to come home to find him drinking my beer and playing with my dog. Not that I mind, I hate when I have to leave Shadow alone.

"If you're here, does that mean I don't have to go downtown with you tonight?" He tips his head back in laughter as Shadow jumps at his feet, waiting for him to throw the ball again.

"Hey Jake. Good to see you Jake. Thanks for playing with my dog Jake," he mutters, beer bottle to his lips. "No, we don't have to go to town. But just to be a dick, I don't even want to tell you what I'm doing here."

I look over, intrigued. "The trailer gave away that you were in the area dropping off furniture. What's special about that?"

"That girl you met in town. What was her name?" He asks, standing up to walk toward my door, so I follow him inside.

"Lily," I answer, as he pulls two more beers from my fridge and heads to the back door like he owns the place. "Why, did you meet her too?" I try to tamp down the jealousy that starts coursing through me. Not that I have a claim to her, but I saw her first.

Outside, we take a seat on the rockers on my back porch and he finally throws the ball he had in his pocket for Shadow. She takes off like a bat out of hell, launching herself off the deck and into the woods, chasing the ball. "Blue eyes, long brown hair, tiny little thing. That's your girl, right?"

"Yeah, that's her. You're killing me," I kick at his boot with mine. "What about her?"

"She's your new neighbor," he says nonchalantly, like he didn't just drop a bomb on me.

My eyes widen as I soak in what he said. "Lily is who bought Gary's place? You're telling me she's been right down the road all week and I had no idea?"

He looks at me over the top of his bottle as he slowly takes a sip like a jackass. "Yup."

Holy shit. I shouldn't get excited. She's a city girl, likely trying out the small town life just for fun, but I am thrilled. There was something about her, beyond her beauty, that drew me in. The way her eyes lit up as I told her about the area, the way her hands never left Shadow's fur as we talked, the way her cheeks tinged pink when I flustered my words. And I have her living right next door.

"Do I invite her over for dinner or something? Go introduce myself? Is she living alone? When is she home?" My brain runs through all the possibilities, trying to think of the best way to go see her again without being a creep.

"You think I asked for her life story?" Jake scoffs. "She said she has coffee on her back porch most mornings. That's about as much as I know. Oh, and she's out of your league."

I kick his ankle, but think that through. I could go over in the morning with muffins or something, but I don't bake. Shadow could 'accidentally' run through her yard. Yeah, that might be the one.

"You want dinner? I was going to grill some chicken."

"Yeah, that sounds good. Grab me another beer? I'm too tired to drive home tonight," he says, scrubbing a hand down his face. "Mind if I crash here? I will be out first thing in the morning. I've got two tables to make this weekend."

"Of course." I head inside to grab the ingredients from my fridge. I hand him a beer when I step back on the porch before setting my tray on the grill and firing it up. "Two tables is a lot to get done in one weekend, need any help?"

"Nah, I don't have any other plans, so I can get it done. The orders have been coming in faster though since I put some pieces in the showroom in Seattle. If it stays at this rate, I'll be making it a full-time business by the end of the year."

I plop back in the chair next to him while the grill heats. "Congrats, man, it's finally happening. You deserve all the success coming your way." Jake gives me a small smile, then finishes his second beer. He's the most humble dude when it comes to his business, which is at complete odds with his cocky personality. He could probably afford to quit now and pursue his business full time, but he secretly has been helping out his parents and he can't do that on just one income yet.

We enjoy the warm summer night, and eat dinner on the porch, both of us giving Shadow pieces under the patio table. Besides my brother, River, Jake is my best friend, and I love easy nights like this with him. I tell him about seeing Sherry and how things are going with the SAR team, while he tells me about the work he's doing on his bike and how his business is growing. I don't feel old most days, hell I wouldn't even consider 28 to be old, but when we both decide to go to bed at nine, I feel it.

When Shadow's bells pull me from sleep the next morning, Jake is already gone. There is no lag in my steps as I head down the stairs to let her out. I came up with the perfect plan last night to meet Lily again, and I am ready for it. Making a cup of coffee, I fill Shadow's dish with breakfast. When she comes back in to eat, I head upstairs and throw on some gray sweats but leave my shirt off. I may be rusty at flirting, but I know what women like.

With my coffee in hand, Shadow and I head back outside and tramp through the woods toward Gary's old cabin. "Okay, you're my wing woman this morning. I need you to find Lily, and stay with her, even when I call you." I give her a scratch behind the ear as the trees start thinning and I can just make out the cabin. "Go ahead girl, find Lily." She takes off at a run, bee-lining straight for the cabin, like the best girl that she is.

I wait around for a minute, sipping my coffee, until I hear Shadow's happy bark. I know she's found her now, so I wait another minute before I call her name and walk closer to them. She shows me again that dogs are a man's best friend by not coming when I call. Finally, Lily's back deck comes into view, and there she is.

Her long brown hair is thrown into a bun on her head, an oversized pink cardigan wrapped around her small frame, as she sits on a couch with a mug in one hand, Shadow's face in the other. I'm stunned just watching the sweet smile on her face as she talks to my dog.

Shadow is the first to acknowledge me, looking over and giving an excited woof, clearly proud of herself for listening. Lily's gaze follows and I stand still as her eyes trail up from the shoes on my feet, stalling a little on my bare chest, and finally up to my face. Her cheeks flush as we lock gazes, neither of us making a move.

Her melodic voice calls out, "Thoren? I thought I recognized this sweet girl." Her hand is still rubbing through Shadow's fur. Unease starts to cross her face as she seems to register I just appeared out of the woods. "What are you doing here?"

Shit, didn't think that part through. A big guy she met once appearing at her home out of nowhere. "I own the cabin at the end of the road. I'm so sorry, I didn't mean to scare you. Shadow caught the scent of something this morning and ran off and when she didn't immediately return, I came looking for her." I scratch the back of my neck uncomfortably, kicking myself for not thinking this through more. "It's nice to see you again, Lily. I'm really sorry about the intrusion. Come, Shadow." I pat my leg, ready to head back home and wallow in my mortification in peace.

"It's okay, I was just surprised," Lily's small voice says. She looks me over again, then seems to deem me not a threat. She points to the mug in my hand. "Do you need a top off for your coffee? I was just about to get some more."

The smile on my face explodes as I stride over to her. "That would be great, thank you." As soon as I step onto her deck, I feel the boards give under me. I glance down to see that over half of them are warped and rotting. Lily stands from the couch, her cardigan falling open to show a silky matching sleep set. I try hard not to stare, but she looks effortlessly sexy and I want to wrap her in my arms and enjoy the nice morning together.

She is oblivious to my ogling and wayward thoughts as she gently takes my mug. "Sorry about the rotting deck. It's next on my list of things to fix. Do you take creamer or sugar?"

"However you take it is fine, thank you." I watch her step into the house before taking a seat on the other side of Shadow, giving her a quick kiss. "Good girl, you get a big treat when we get home."

Lily comes back out and passes my mug over, taking her spot on the couch again. "How long have you lived next door?"

"Almost four years now. It was in rough shape when I bought it, but she's a beauty now. I did most of the work myself, so if you need help with the deck or anything, let me know. Do you like it here so far?"

"If you mean the area, I'm in love. Every bit of this town, the people, and the land around me is exactly what I was looking for. If you mean the house, ehhh," she takes a sip of her coffee. "It needs a lot of work. I'm eager to tackle the projects but also might be out of my depth. I just am ready for it to really feel like mine. Something I poured my heart and soul into and am proud of the outcome, you know?" She stares absentmindedly out at the woods, taking another sip before looking over at me.

"I do know." I really do, too. It's nice to know that someone else wants to put in the work to make something right. When I was with Jen, she wanted a modern new build home where she wouldn't have to lift a finger or do anything. She complained constantly about the time I was spending working on fixing up the cabin, but never once offered to come with or help. Lily seems to understand the joy and pride you feel when you put in the work yourself.

"I think I remember you said you moved out here for work. What is it that you do?" I ask, as Shadow finally leaves her spot between us to explore the yard.

"I'm an author. I wasn't before, I just wrote on the side. But I got picked up by a publisher and got a decent bonus to write a series. Since I can write from anywhere, I decided to do it somewhere I would love. Somewhere that I could find inspiration from the world around me."

"That's amazing, congratulations. What is your new series about? You seem too sweet to write thriller, so my guess is romance." Her cheeks turn pink, and the flush travels down her neck to her chest. "Ohhh, you write dirty romance, don't you?"

She lets out a choked laugh and adjusts the cardigan tighter around herself. "You hit the nail on the head, it's a sports romance. MLB specifically."

My hands clamp around my mug as my knee bounces anxiously. Do I tell her about River? Or does she know already, and maybe she sought me out. That seems crazy, plus I'm the one who found her this time. She's going to find out eventually, I might as well tell her now. "That's wild," my voice comes out a little hoarse. "My brother plays first base for the Seattle Rainiers."

Her mouth slowly drops open, eyes wide as she stares at me. Then a delighted screech leaves her throat, as she almost spills the rest of her nearly empty coffee on herself. It's the same reaction I always get, any interest in me is immediately overshadowed by having a famous brother.

"No way! Do you know a lot about baseball then?" she all but squeals.

"Uhh, yeah. A bit," I laugh awkwardly, scratching at my short beard.

"Can you teach me? Like about the positions, and maybe what

your brother's life is like? Sports and I are not friends, and despite my research, I still have so much to learn for my book," she says, talking a mile a minute. "Could you even tell me what his routine is, if his dating life is hard in the public eye? Did he go to college first or straight to playing for the Rainiers? Oh, I have so many questions for you." She finally looks over at me, and I'm not sure what she sees, but she quickly shuts her mouth. "Sorry, that was overstepping. You don't have to tell me anything."

I'm too perplexed to answer right away. She didn't ask to talk to him. She asked me to teach her, to answer her questions. Hell, she didn't even ask for his name, although she could look it up easily. My brain and mouth finally get on board together. "I am happy to help teach you and answer any questions that I can. Whatever I can't answer, I can ask him next time we chat."

She perks back up a little, but her voice is still reserved. "Really? You don't have to, you probably get that a lot, huh? People wanting things from you because of who he is. I'm sorry I asked."

"Sometimes," I huff out. She narrows her eyes at me, and I relent. "Okay, most of the time. I really would love to help you, but if you still feel you're taking advantage of me," I wink at her, "you can do me a favor, too. On the days I can't take Shadow to work with me, it would be awesome if you could stop by and say hi to her or let her out if you're home."

Shadow comes trotting back up to the deck and hops on the couch between us again at the mention of her name. No surprise, the traitor gives me her butt and plops her head in Lily's lap, where I wouldn't mind being either.

"I would be happy to do that! Does she like hikes? Could I take her on some with me? If not, I can walk her around here. Oooh, can she hang out here with me? I will be spending a lot of time holed up writing and would love to have her as company," she rambles again, but I find it endearing. "If you don't mind, that is. Just let me know the days and what you're thinking and I'm your girl."

My girl. Hell, I kind of like the sound of that. "How about you get my number, and I'll text you my schedule. We can go from there, and any time you can spend with her would be great. We can also pick an evening after work where you can ask me all your baseball questions?"

"Perfect," she says, plucking her phone from beside her and handing it over. "I will work on a list of them today. Thank you, Thoren. Moving and leaving everything I knew behind was terrifying. But finding friends like you has been amazing, and everything has been seeming to fall into place. Like everything I want in life is suddenly closer than I ever dreamed of."

Her deep blue eyes shine in the morning light, captivating me. I am a man that is meant to be in a relationship. I like caring for someone other than myself, providing for them, protecting them, being there for them; it's ingrained in me. I have missed not having that, even before Jen left me, I wasn't having that need to be someone's everything filled by her. Lily, though… I could see myself opening her car doors as those olive cheeks flush a deep purple. Having her over for dinner where she plays outside with Shadow while I grill us steaks. I could see myself stocking her shed with chopped wood for the winter and she would be so grateful for the little things like that.

I put my number in her phone, and hand it back to her. "I'm happy to help, Lily. Anything you need, I'm here. Shadow and I will let you enjoy your Saturday. Thank you for the coffee, I'll see you around." As I stand up, Shadow jumps down with me, taking off into the woods toward home already. I make a mental note of approximately how large her deck is, then follow after Shadow. I turn back to wave at Lily one more time, to get one more peak at her soft legs, and messy bun on her head, only to see her eyes on me already, lids lowered in appreciation. She gives a small smile in embarrassment and waves back. I can't wipe the grin from my face as I turn back around. In fact, it doesn't leave my face all day.

Bros & Hoe Group Chat

THOREN 🔨:

I got her number. Need some assistance later Riv.

JAKE 🪜:

Damn. I'm impressed.

THOREN 🔨:

Good because I need to borrow your trailer this week too.

RIVER ⚾:

Whose number? No surprise on the second part.

THOREN 🔨:

Fuck off, she's writing a sports romance book about baseball and has some questions.

JAKE 🪜:

She's going to be a freak in bed, all those book girls are. What do you need the trailer for?

THOREN 🔨:

Don't even try to sleep with her.

RIVER ✏:

WHO? Call me whenever and I'll answer what I can.

THOREN 🔨:

Lily. Thanks bro. I need to get some new wood for her deck.

JAKE :

I've got wood for you. *winky face* How long
has your deck wood been out of commission?
laughing face

THOREN :

Grow up, I'm picking it up Tuesday.

RIVER :

Who the fuck is Lily?

RIVER :

Hello?? You can't ignore me just because I'm
not there.

CHAPTER FIVE

THOREN:

Hey Lily, it's Thoren. Tuesday, Thursday, and
Friday this week Shadow will be alone if you
want to spend some time with her.

LILY:

Yes! Do you have a way for me to get her?

THOREN:

I'll leave the back door unlocked. Her harness
and leash are hanging on a hook next to it if you
need them.

LILY:

Sounds good.

THOREN:

Thanks again, we both appreciate it.

Saturday morning after Thoren left, I sat down and wrote two chapters, weeded the small flower garden out front, and mowed my yard when my new mower got delivered. My mind constantly drifted back to him, despite my considerable effort to not think about him. My god, those tattooed arms, thick with corded muscles, and abs that led to that deep v. I really tried to keep my eyes on his face, but the man had no shirt on and I'm only human. The way the muscles in his back moved and flexed from *walking*… phew.

To add to it, he has the thickest thighs. Those sweats didn't hide a dang thing. I don't know what he does to stay in shape, but it's working. Another man in my life is the last thing I need. However, I could use more friends here, and he seems like a great one. He was sweet, listened, and understood me instead of doubting and judging me.

I texted Michele and asked how well she knew him, which led to her showing up Sunday afternoon with a bottle of wine so she could tell me all about him and his brother. She told me he and Jake were thick as thieves as well. I looked up Thoren's brother, River, after he left and picturing those three men together… it's every woman's dream. There must be something in the water here because it's insane that three good friends are all that attractive.

While Michele was here she helped me pick out what color to paint the kitchen and living room. I made it my mission to go out Monday morning and get all the paint and supplies that I would need, and wrote out an extensive list of everything I needed to learn about baseball and about player's lives that would elevate my book. Each new day brings a sense of empowerment, gradually easing the pain and loneliness of my past.

I wrote the last question down on the list and hung it on the fridge for when I see Thoren next. With a Lord Huron playlist on my phone, I taped off the living room. Michele and I decided on a deep hunter green in here, to blend the outside with the in. She also may have been partial, since it's the color of her office as well.

As I'm taping up the last window, my playlist stops and my phone rings, Andrea's name flashing across the screen.

"Hello," I answer and hit speaker so I can finish my project.

"Hello my favorite author, how are things going?" she sings out. It is really nice to hear her voice. While I have made friends with Thoren and Michele, I am still isolated out here in the woods. Hearing Andrea's voice is comforting, and it makes me miss her, probably the only thing I miss about Phoenix.

"You say that to all your authors. It's going great! I will have the next five chapters to you by the end of the week. I found someone to help me with my baseball knowledge, so it should be even better than you were expecting."

"Your work never disappoints. Who is your special helper? Please tell me it's someone hot," she begs.

"He is ridiculously attractive, and get this, his brother actually plays for an MLB team. And to top it off, he's my neighbor, and he has a dog."

"A dog? Oh god, you're in love aren't you?" she jokes. She has three dogs and I may beg her weekly for spam of their adorable faces. I wasn't allowed to have pets growing up, so I seek out every dog I can. I can't wait until I can get one of my own, maybe after I finish this next book. "Also, I saw Tyler at a coffee shop this weekend and was curious if you had heard from him at all? If I wasn't with a client, I would have marched over and dumped my coffee on him."

Chills skitter down my spine just hearing his name. Andrea is the only person who knows the whole ugly truth about my ex. She's never once judged me for it, but she expressed concern throughout our relationship. When it ended, she cheered, then cried with me when she found out the truth. She's been a fierce champion for me since. "No. I haven't heard from anyone there."

Andrea's sigh is heavy through the speaker, "I really think you should sue. I know we've talked about it before, but it isn't right, Lily. They deserve to pay."

I've been good about leaving the past in the past. I've even been good about letting go of the anger and the humiliation. "I can't admit it in front of a court, to be shamed and humiliated again. I just want to move on with my life."

"Okay, I hear you loud and clear. Promise me you will think about it some more. I'm glad you have the help you wanted with the book and I can't wait to read your next chapters. I'll check in next week again, okay?"

I let my shoulders sink with the drop of that conversation. "Sounds good, thanks Andrea. Talk soon." With that one call, my motivation is gone. There's still a few hours of sunlight, so I trudge upstairs and change into shorts and a tank top and throw on my running shoes. With an angry playlist in my ears, I head down my driveway and out toward the main road.

Physical release is my go-to for pent up nerves and feelings I don't know what to do with. I guess I should say, sex would be my go-to, but since that's not an option and my toy is on the charger, a run is a great alternative. Setting the tracker on my watch, I get lost in the music. I stay on the main road my little lane is off of and follow it until my lungs are burning and my legs shake, then turn around to do it all again as I head back home.

The fresh mountain air sweeps past me, rays of the setting sun reaching between the trees. Sweat is dripping down my back, despite the dense woods keeping the temperature comfortable. When I finally make it back to Alder Ave, the sun has sunk behind the trees. My body is beyond exhausted, but my mind is clear.

Avoiding looking at the new cracking tiles, I shower quickly, then heat up leftover spaghetti. My bed is calling my name, and my shaky legs barely get me up the stairs to it. Lying in bed, I try not to let my mind wander back to Tyler. Instead, I think of Shadow and if she would be a good painting buddy, or if that's a disaster waiting to happen. I think I'll risk it and bring her over anyway. With thoughts of the loveable black dog and her handsome owner, I drift off to sleep.

The bright morning rays stream through my windows, the no curtain idea bringing a smile to my face. There truly isn't a better way to wake. I am dreading the day I can't enjoy my mornings on the deck, but at least I have a wall of windows to bring some of the outside in. My legs ache from the run yesterday, but I don't let it slow me down.

It's dog-mom day, and I get to spend it with my new favorite furry companion.

Wearing an oversized tee with bike shorts, I make a quick omelet and cup of coffee. When that first hit of caffeine buzzes through my veins, I walk over to Thoren's to get Shadow.

Wandering through the woods like him sounds like a recipe for disaster, so I stick to the road like a city girl. Walking up his gravel driveway takes longer with his house sitting further back than mine. When it finally comes into view, I am stunned by the masculine beauty of it. The cabin is at least twice the size of mine, and is painted black from the roof to the front porch floor. Mahogany wood shutters surround the windows matching the stunning front door. Despite the darkness, it is inviting and raw. The back deck is the length of the house and corresponds with the rest of the color scheme. He has an outdoor table and chairs on one side by a grill and two rockers set on the other side.

Shadow barks and bursts through the back door as I open it. She jumps around me, her butt wiggling as she bounces. I give her a tight squeeze and lots of rubs before stepping inside to grab her leash. I may not need it, but I am dying to peek inside the house.

The back door opens to his kitchen and dining room, and it is surprisingly bright inside. The cabinets are a pretty oak with a white quartz counter and subway tile backsplash. Wide plank flooring spreads throughout the space, giving it a cozy and modern feel, every detail more beautiful than the last. More than that, it is clean. Like, ridiculously clean, not a dish in the sink or clutter on the counters.

My heart beats faster, the OCD side of me thrilled at the sight before me. I expected it to be a little cold, maybe broodier to match the outside, but I kind of want to move in, and I definitely want to keep snooping. Shadow circles between my legs, ready to go, so instead of invading Thoren's space, I grab the leash and close the door behind us.

"Ready to go paint?" I ask the overeager pup as we head back to my place. Just as I thought, Shadow doesn't need the leash. She wanders, sniffing here and there but comes right back to my side when called. As my cabin comes into view she darts ahead and sits patiently by the front door. I let out a small chuckle, already so in love with her.

When I let us in, she scopes out every corner, smelling everything in sight. I let her explore while I set up my paint trays, rollers, and brushes. She eventually makes herself at home on the old couch I need to replace as I start painting the walls. The day passes by quickly as I put two layers of paint on the living room walls between lots of outside breaks to play and eat some shared snacks. Who knew an apple with peanut butter would also be her favorite snack?

My phone rings from somewhere inside, so I rush in from the deck to grab it. I swipe the green button, waiting for Thoren's voice to fill the speaker. "Hey Lily, are you home?"

"Yeah, sorry, do you need me to bring Shadow back over now?" I ask, a little bummed to lose my companion.

"No, not at all. I'm glad she's there with you," his voice sounds far away, like he's talking through a car speaker. "I'm actually hoping to drop something off to you. Can I stop by on my way home in about fifteen minutes?"

"Oh, yeah, I'll be here."

"Sounds good, see you in a bit then."

I mumble a "See ya," before hanging up. *What would he have to drop off to me?*

The crunch of gravel draws my attention so I follow Shadow to the front of the house. Jake's black truck and trailer are parked next to my car, but Thoren hops out.

"Did you steal Jake's truck?" I ask, pointing behind him.

His cheeks heat, turning the cutest shade of pink. "No, this one is mine but the trailer is his. We have the same truck, and before you ask, I had mine first and he copied me." He crouches down, giving his dog the attention she demands. "How'd you know I know Jake?"

The heat travels up my chest and into my cheeks. "Michele told me you guys were friends. She was my realtor, and is the one who gave me Jake's contact information. We may have gotten wine drunk while she told me about all of your guys' high school days."

He groans as he stands back up. "That can never be a good thing." He scratches his hands at the back of his neck. "So I did something, and I don't want you to be upset. I just wanted to help."

"Okaaaay?"

He shifts on his feet then walks back to the trailer. As I follow along I notice long wood planks tied to it. Spinning toward me, he says, "I know you said the deck was next on your list of projects, so I wanted to drop these off for you. I have tools you can borrow for it, too. I'm not sure what all you have or need. I can help with all of it or just the first board or two until you get confident. I know you wanted to do it yourself, and I know you can. I just thought, I'm here and I've done it before…" He rocks back on his heels.

I open my mouth, then close it, at a complete loss of what to say. After one conversation, he listened and took action. Not only that, but he acted without steamrolling me and my desires. I've never had someone do something this nice before, and I will happily take his help. I'll still get that same sense of accomplishment by doing it with him.

"Thank you." I clear the emotion in my throat, "I would love your help. And I'll pay you for the wood and your time."

"Absolutely not. This is my thanks for helping take care of Shadow. I'll unload all this and then run home to change out of my uniform and grab my tools. Are you okay starting on this tonight?"

My eyes rove over his work boots beneath dark green pants that hug tight to his legs, then over his green button up shirt that's taut over his chest. Sleeves rolled to perfection showing off his tattooed forearms that flex with his movements. Forearm porn… it's a real thing. I don't think he needs to change. His unruly hair is mussed to perfection on top, making his rugged look that much hotter.

"I'll help you unload your wood. *The* wood, I meant the wood, not your wood." Holy mother of god, I did not just say that.

His chuckle is deep, wrapping me in warmth. "Come on then," he says, undoing the straps and handing me a few planks at a time. We work in tandem, getting everything laid out in the backyard, before he hops back in his truck with Shadow in tow, promising to be right back.

While he's gone, I head inside to wash up and pull out a second steak for dinner. In the bathroom, I splash some water on my face and try to scrub the paint off my hands and arms. My brush gets caught in the tangles of my hair so I throw it back up in a claw clip. I won't bother changing since I'm covered in paint anyway. By the time I get myself semi presentable again, I hear him pull back up out front.

"Ready to work," he says, holding up a tool box in one hand and a drill in the other as I step out the front door. I try to focus on the tools, I really do, but his stained dark jeans and black tee stretched tight over broad shoulders is stealing the show. Something about a man willing to get his hands dirty and that knows how to fix things just does it for me.

"Let's get to it then," I lick my lips, trying to bring moisture back to my dry mouth. "Thanks again, for helping me with this." His footfalls weigh heavy as he follows me around to the back.

"Happy to. I redid my deck just last year. Not to brag, but I'm practically a professional now," he winks, handing me a crow bar and protective glasses. "First things first, we need to move the couch and remove all the old rotting boards."

Together we get to work, and I balk at how easily some of the boards crumble when pried up. I'm prying up my fifth board when I glance over and see Thoren isn't wearing safety glasses like me. "Hey, where's your glasses?"

"You have them," he says, not bothering to look up. "I only have one pair and I'd rather protect your eyes." He continues pulling up boards like he didn't just blow me away again. *Friends,* I remind myself. I cannot get involved with anyone again. This man seems to be a walking green flag, and I seem to be great at ignoring the red ones, so I might as well ignore the green too. "I took a wild guess on the amount of boards you'd need, but counting it out now, I'll have enough to replace the bad ones and some extra. Do you want to do it all and I can get the rest of the boards later this week?"

"No, you don't have to do that. We can just replace the really bad ones and next summer I can replace the rest. Since I'll practically be a pro by then," I giggle. "We can just put the extras in the little shed." I pull up the last rotting board, noticing that by the time I removed seven, he removed double that.

"That's a good plan. Can you start measuring out lengths and I'll start making cuts so we can get these new boards screwed in?"

I handed the safety glasses to him. I may not know much when it comes to home projects, but I know he needs them with a saw. He shows me how to measure each length, marking it on the wood. Surprisingly, he lets me do it alone, even when I measure incorrectly more than once.

"You're doing great," he assures me, grabbing another one of the spare pieces, when I measure wrong again. "Are you sure this is your first time doing this?"

This man. This dang man. "Thanks, Thoren," I squeak out, knowing full well I am doing a terrible job. "Would you like to stay for dinner? I'm making steak and roasted potatoes."

He looks up from where he's kneeling, sweat dripping down his forehead, his hazel eyes locking on mine. One side of his mouth raises in a small smile, "I would love that, thanks Lily."

He finishes cutting the last board, showing me how to use the drill. I may have to remove a few of the screws in the beginning, but by the end I have the hang of it and do half of them on my own.

The sun is starting to set now as we stand and admire our work. After a good scrubbing of the older planks, the whole deck will look good as new. I know for a fact I could never have done this on my own, even with YouTube. Thoren nudges my shoulder with his, "Look at what you accomplished today. I hope you feel a sense of pride. You did so well." Something about those words in his rough voice have shivers skating down my spine.

"Thank you," I wipe my hands on my shirt, unable to tear the smile from my face. I do feel proud. "I'm going to wash up and start dinner. Would you like to come in?"

"Yeah, Lily, I would love to."

thoren

Lily leads me into her house, and I can feel the change in it immediately. It has a warmth it never had when Gary lived here. Gary was a little rough around the edges, and it showed in the way he let this place fall apart. The smell of paint mixes with the outside air as I take in the open windows and walls lined with painter's tape.

"I like the color choice," I point at the deep green walls. It creates a seamless transition between living room and outdoors, sunlight warming the wooden floor, and the gentle sounds of nature a backdrop to the room's comfort.

"Thanks, Michele helped me pick it out. Shadow kept me company while I painted today." I don't have to see her face to hear the smile there. She washes her hands at the kitchen sink before pulling ingredients from the fridge.

"I'm sure she slept the day away. Probably right in the middle of your couch," I joke, seeing little black hairs on the middle cushion. "Do you mind if I wash up, then I can help?"

"Of course, bathroom is right there." She points to the only door beside the small closet at the front. I take my time scrubbing my hands and arms and splash water on my face and hair. I am still sweaty and covered in sawdust, but somewhat less of a mess for her.

I flinch when something crashes next to me, almost pulling the towel off the wall. I debate ignoring it, but the thought of her slipping on spilled body wash stops me. Pulling back the shower curtain, I find a piece of a tile shattered in the tub. Peering over the shower walls, multiple cracked and missing tiles stand out. The shower head is slowly dripping water, and there's mold forming on the wall behind the missing pieces.

"Hey Lily," I say, stepping into the kitchen. "I don't mean to be nosy, but a tile fell off your shower wall when I was in the bathroom."

She stills, her back to me, as she faces the sink. "Sorry if it scared you. They've been doing that. It's on the list to fix." There's a slight tremor in her voice.

Trying to ease her embarrassment, I cross my arms as I lean against the counter near her. "It happens with these old places. I had to gut my bathrooms, too. Can I help you with it?"

"Oh no, that's not necessary. You already helped with the deck. I'll get it sorted out soon." Her smile doesn't reach her eyes, but I drop the subject for now. I don't want to push her too far. I enjoy spending time with her, she's sweet and funny, beautiful and determined. She has this softness about her, a quiet reservation that makes me want to take care of her. To protect her from the harsh world we live in.

"Okay, then put me to work here."

She passes over a cutting board and knife. "You can dice up the potatoes while I throw together a salad." We work well together, aware of each other's movements in the small kitchen space. I try to focus on my task, and not the fact that she looks like she's naked under that oversized shirt until it lifts up, showing off the tiny shorts below. My arm brushes hers as I reach around her, and I swear I feel heat travel up and settle in my chest.

She pulls back slightly from me with a light smile. "I'll season those and throw them in the oven then start the steaks. Would you like a beer or something?"

"Whatever you are having is great," I say, taking a seat at her small table. I like that the space down here is open so I can watch her work, no matter where I go. I glance around the cabin again and notice there aren't many personal effects. No framed photos on the wall, no kitschy knick knacks. I want to know more about her, where she came from, and where she wants to go. "What does your family think of you moving out here?"

She hands me a glass of red wine before moving back to the kitchen. "It's just my parents and I. They moved to Florida a few years ago, so my moving here doesn't affect them much." Her voice raises a few octaves as her eyes shift around the kitchen.

"You really went as far from them as possible then, huh?" I joke to lighten the tension now around us. "They must be really proud of you, though, pursuing your passions."

She tries to hide her grimace, but I see it all the same. "Not really. They had big ideas for my life. You know, getting the right degree, climbing the corporate ladder, marrying a wealthy man and having the 2.5 kids." She flips the steaks, searing the other side. "I tried to follow their path, I got the degree they wanted for me even though creative writing was my favorite class. I worked at a large financial firm in Phoenix. I just wasn't happy. It's not what I wanted for my life. Not by a long shot."

Her words hit me hard. I have the most supportive parents in the world that didn't care what Riv and I did, as long as we were happy. Jen didn't feel the same though, she wanted the exact life Lily's parents wanted for her. Funny how they traded places like that.

"I'm sorry they feel that way. I'm glad that you decided to live your life for you though. I'll be proud enough of you for both of them. Life is more than money and status. There's a whole world filled with love and laughter, passion, and beauty. It's a shame more people don't make the effort to see it."

She laughs but it lacks humor. "Thanks, Thoren. My mom especially will never see it that way. She's from a strict Asian family, where success and status are demanded. I think it's hard for her to break from that view."

I have been curious what her nationality was. Her flawless olive skin and thick dark hair pairs perfectly with slightly pouty lips and dainty features. It's her stunning blue eyes that really stand out and contrast with her darker features, rounding out her striking beauty.

"Can I ask where you got your blue eyes? They captivated me the moment you walked in the shop last week, and I've been drowning in them ever since." I ask, hoping my words don't freak her out.

I watch the pink in her cheeks turn a deep purple as she pulls the steaks from the pan and plates them. "My dad's European, specifically from the Netherlands. Blonde hair, blue eyes, very fair skin. My eyes seem to be the only physical attribute I got from him."

I get up to bring the salad bowl and utensils to the table while she checks on the potatoes. "Then he at least got that part right. You are beautiful, Lily."

She gives me a shy smile, but quickly turns back to her task and plates the potatoes for us before bringing the plates over and sitting across from me. "So you know about my family now. Tell me about yours."

I swallow my sip of wine and start cutting into the steak. "My parents are incredible. My mom really struggled to get pregnant, so she was thirty-four when she had River. They never expected to be able to have another, so when I came along two years later, they were pleasantly surprised. They've treated us like life's greatest gifts ever since." I groan as the flavors of the steak melt on my tongue when I take my first bite. I love a woman who can cook. "River's been playing baseball professionally for five years now. He loves it, and although he's only a few hours drive away, he's so busy that we don't get to see him as much as I would like. We're still close though. We make an effort to chat weekly and stay caught up on each other's lives. He said he's happy to help answer any questions that I can't."

"Oh, that reminds me," she puts her fork down, retrieving a paper from her fridge. "I wrote out a list of all the questions. If you want to bring it home in case there are any you need to ask him. I have my own copy so don't worry if you lose it." She sets it to the side of the table, face down. It's a small gesture, but a big impact. She wants to be in this moment with me. "Michele said there's some great local beer at the grocery store. If you tell me your favorite I can bring you a six pack this weekend and we can go through them?"

"Anything local is great."

"Okay, does Saturday evening work for you?"

I know that I told her I would help her learn about baseball, and that's why she is coming over. That doesn't stop my pulse from racing at the thought of her wanting to see me again. I would love to spend an evening with Lily. It would be even better if she wanted to stay the night.

She's skittish and there's a haunted look in her eyes that I hate seeing. There's nothing I want more than to uncover her layers and see the real her. This polished version intrigues me, and I'm beyond attracted to her, but it's the hidden version I really want to see. She's been drawing me in since the moment I met her, a tether I can't shake, not that I want to. Just the thought of her wanting to come to my home lights up parts of me that have been pushed to the side.

"Sounds perfect," I say around bites of dinner. "Speaking of perfection, this steak is incredible. The entire meal is, but I am a sucker for a juicy steak. Do you like cooking?"

"My mom ensured I knew how to cook, you know, because the way to a man's heart is through his stomach," she chuckles nervously. "Luckily, I really love it. It's hard cooking for one, but cooking helps me relax from the day and focus on the task at hand."

I don't think she has a boyfriend, but I have been dying to ask anyway. "Have you been cooking for one for long?"

She stares at me, unblinking for a moment, before throwing her head back in laughter. "Was that your way of asking if I'm single? Jesus, Thoren, that was bad." She picks up her wine glass, chuckling to herself as she takes a sip. "Yes, I've been only cooking for myself for a while." Her features drop, a look of hurt crossing her face. "Even in my last relationship, I mostly ate alone. What about you? Do you like cooking, and are you cooking for only one?"

"Very single. The only time I cook for others is when Jake shows up demanding dinner. I do enjoy cooking, but it's not the same when you're alone. There's something special about cooking with someone. For someone. I miss that."

She's contemplative as she takes a sip of her wine. Her quiet voice finally breaks through, "I've never had someone cook for me."

I want to ask more, because at our age, any decent boyfriend has cooked a meal for his girlfriend. Has she only dated wealthy men that only go out to eat, or have private chefs? She mentioned that's the type of man her parents want for her. If that's what she's looking for, she won't find that in this town, and certainly not in me. I am a decent cook and it's fulfilling watching people enjoy something I have made.

"Well that's a damn shame, and getting rectified Saturday evening. My salmon recipe is unmatched and just happens to pair well with beer and baseball." We continue our dinner, and I help her clean up and wash the dishes when we are done. It feels natural spending time with her, like we've been doing this for years and didn't just meet last week.

"I should probably head home and feed Shadow. Thanks again for spending time with her today, and for making me that incredible dinner." I have the urge to wrap her in my arms, bury my head in her neck, and place a soft kiss there. I could just lean in, place a gentle kiss on her cheek. But I don't. She's warm, and kind, and although I have seen the lingering looks she's given me, I've also noticed she's kept a distance between us.

"Of course, I'm excited to see her again Thursday. Thank you for helping with the deck, that was such a huge task and you made it so easy." She shuffles on her feet.

"You're welcome. Have a good night, Lily." I walk out her door, and down her driveway, the dim glow of the moon lighting my way.

"Goodnight, Thoren," she says from the doorway. It isn't until I'm rounding the small bend in her driveway that I see her front door shut in my rearview.

Thursday

LILY:

picture of Shadow in the woods

LILY:

We are going on an adventure before I sit down
to write.

THOREN:

She is the best adventure buddy.

LILY:

picture of Shadow on her back passed out

LILY:

And the best writing buddy.

THOREN:

At least her snores aren't disrupting you.

Friday

THOREN:

Shadow went right back to sleep after breakfast, you wore her out yesterday.

LILY:

Can I still get her today? I'm only writing and cleaning a bit.

THOREN:

Of course. You are always welcome at my home, Lily.

LILY:

Thank you. Looking forward to dinner tomorrow.

THOREN:

I've been looking forward to it since Tuesday.

Saturday

I might have messed up. On Thursday, Lily brought Shadow back right when I told her I get home, and I was able to see her gorgeous face. Friday, though, Shadow was already back home waiting for me. Did I freak Lily out by sounding too eager? Too desperate? I don't want to appear desperate, but this woman already has my full attention. I might be out of my depth here, but I know who can help.

Bros & Hoe Group Chat

THOREN ⚒:

> How do I cook a girl dinner but not be desperate about wanting her?

JAKE 🪜:

Throw away the flowers, man.

Fuck. Am I that predictable? I glance at the bouquet I picked up this morning sitting on the island and cringe.

RIVER ✏:

Don't throw them away. Put them on your counter or somewhere that looks like decor for you, not a gift for her.

Okay, I can work with that. I hate to waste perfectly good flowers.

THOREN ⚒:

> What else? I'm making my cedar plank salmon.
> Nice button up shirt.

RIVER ✏:

Nope again. Clean tee and jeans. Clean house. No lit candles. Just a nice dinner and conversation.

JAKE 🪜:

If it wasn't said it's a date, don't make it one. You're friends hanging out. You wouldn't do that shit for me.

THOREN ⚒:

> Okay, thanks. Gotta go.

JAKE 🪜:

He's gonna blow it.

RIVER ✒:

Guaranteed.

JAKE 🪜:

It was nice knowing ya, Lily.

THOREN 🔨:

middle finger picture with flowers in the background

RIVER ✒:

You fucking called it Jake.

Their little faith in me hurts a little, but they aren't wrong. I'm a relationship guy, and I want to make others happy. I know what I want and I go for it and will not apologize for it. So I'll put the candles away, but the flowers are staying on the table.

I change into a clean pair of jeans and a red tee, before giving the counters one more wipe down and ensuring the wine is in the fridge. I know she's bringing beer, but what if she doesn't like it? Shadow knows something is happening, so she's been dragging her favorite little purple dragon all over the house, her tail never stopping.

By five, I have the house clean and the food ready to grill. Shadow runs for the front door a moment before the doorbell rings. I smooth my shirt as I approach the front door, nudging Shadow aside to open it. Lily's smile greets me, bright as ever. She has on a little red jumper that clings to her like a second skin, her hair is in a high ponytail and there's the smallest bit of makeup on her face. My heart pounds in my chest as she holds up a 12-pack of beer.

"I bought a variety pack," she states proudly. "The kid at the store said it has all the local favorites in it. He didn't look twenty-one, so I didn't ask how he knew." Her eyes gradually peruse down my body, feeling like a heated touch at every inch they drop and rise again. "Hey look, we're matching."

My wide smile mirrors hers. "That sounds perfect," I say, taking it from her and stepping to the side so she can come in. Shadow's nose stays glued to the tote she is carrying as she walks through the house. It's the same tote I gave her two weeks ago which makes me smile. "I know you've been inside to pick up Shadow, but if you haven't snooped yet, this is my home."

She peers into the living room before heading to the kitchen, setting her tote down. "I take offense to that. I have self-control and only peeked at your kitchen. Which is perfection, by the way."

"Would you like a quick tour?"

Her eyes light up. "If you don't mind. I know you said you did it all yourself and I'm dying to see what else you did if this is what your kitchen looks like."

My chest puffs up, the pride seeping through my pores. Before I turn to lead her down the hall, I catch Shadow with her nose in the tote at Lily's feet. "Shadow, knock it off. I'm sorry, I don't know why she's doing that."

"Oh," Lily laughs, reaching in there. "I almost forgot. I found a recipe for homemade dog treats and made some today." She pulls out a small container with biscuits in misshapen hearts. "Is it okay if I give her one? The main ingredient is peanut butter, and it said it's healthy for dogs."

"You made her dog treats?" I look at Shadow, sitting patiently at her feet, tail wagging with a longing look aimed at the container.

"Yeah, is that okay? You can say no. I printed out the recipe in case you wanted to see the ingredient list but I researched first to make sure it was safe." The hopeful look on her face is too cute, and I don't doubt she did extensive research. It's the fact that she did this selfless thing and included Shadow in our night that adds a pressure to my chest.

"That's amazing, I'm sure she will love them."

Lily bounces on her toes as she opens the container and holds one out to Shadow. We watch as my dog devours it, licking her chops and the floor in case of crumbs, before looking back up for another.

"Maybe for dessert," Lily boops her nose, "We don't want to spoil your dinner. Now I have to get a tour of this gorgeous house."

My throat is dry, and I have to fight the urge to take her in my arms again. Some people see dogs as pets, but Shadow is my best friend. She was by my side the day Jen left, and has been my rock every day since. Seeing her being cherished by Lily means more to me than I can comprehend. "Let's start down here. You've seen the kitchen, dining and living room, and down this hall I have an office, and half bath." I show her the small bathroom I painted a deep moody blue with gold fixtures. We move to my office, which is nothing more than a desk, two half empty bookshelves and an old chair shoved in the corner. Tote bins packed with search and rescue items fill the other half of the room.

"Upstairs, I have three bedrooms and two full baths," I explain as we make our way up. "This is the primary. You can check out the bathroom if you'd like, I did all the tiling and pipes myself." She casually walks in my room that has slate gray walls. Jake made the walnut bed frame as a move-in present, and it's covered with a light blue comforter. My dresser and nightstands are white and plain. As she heads to the bathroom, my heart rate kicks up. I want her to like it so she will let me help with hers.

"Oh my god," she whispers as she walks further in.

I went a little moodier with the colors in here. In the corner is a freestanding tub directly below a large skylight. The shower is large and has white marble tiles with thick black and gray veining. Those same tiles cover the floor and match the marble counter on the double vanity. There is white wainscotting on the bottom of the walls and the same deep blue on top from the bathroom downstairs.

Lily turns her wide eyes to me. "You did all of this yourself?"

"I did."

"It's incredible. The large tiles are beautiful, and cohesive, and I am dreaming of sitting in that tub with the lights off at night to watch the stars."

My mind starts conjuring up images of her soaking in my bath, her long hair draped over the edge, nipples sitting right below the water line. My cock twitches and hardens in my jeans. Turning around, I head back toward the room so I can discreetly adjust myself. "You can come kick me out and use it anytime you want. I know you don't have a big tub at your place."

Her laugh is light as she follows me back to the hall toward the guest room. "I might just take you up on that."

Across the hall from the primary is the guest room. I open the door and flip on the light so she can see. It has sage green walls, a simple white bed and dresser, and a pink comforter. She looks at it in question before turning to me. "My mom helped decorate this room. The only people who have stayed in it are Jake and my brother, so the pink is staying, just for them. Actually, my mom helped with the living room too. If you see the pink throw in there, that was her."

"That's really sweet," she says wistfully.

We walk back to the hall and I point to the third guest room. "That's just an empty spare room, and this is the other bath up here." I open the bathroom and hope she doesn't ask to see that room. It's a smaller room, painted a pale blue. I have hopes of turning it into a nursery, but until that happens, I like to keep it closed off.

Lily peeks in the last bathroom. It's a little plain with white marble counters and oak cabinets. There are white subway tiles in the tub and shower combo, and black slate tiles on the floor. The walls are gray, and the shower curtain is the only real pop of color with a forest green. "Your house is wonderful, Thoren. You did such an incredible job and should be really proud of yourself."

I lead Lily back downstairs, Shadow weaving between us. "Thank you. It was a labor of love, but I'm thrilled with how everything turned out."

thoren

I step into the kitchen, pulling the wine and beer she brought from the fridge. "What can I get you to drink before I start the grill?"

"That wine looks amazing, thanks. Can I help with anything for dinner?"

"Nope, it's all prepped and ready." I hand her a glass of wine before slipping the bottle back into the fridge. "Do you mind carrying my beer out to the deck?" I ask, nodding to the bottle as I grab the platters of food from the fridge. "If you want, you can ask me some of your questions while I cook?"

She grabs her bag, my beer, and her wine, holding the back door open for me as we both slip out onto the deck. I have the string lights on, even with the sun still glimmering through the trees. The table is set with plates, silverware, and the vase of flowers.

Lily sets everything down to lean over and smell the flowers. Her jumper rides higher up the backs of her thighs, giving me the slightest glimpse of her ass beneath. I almost fumble the tray before getting it set up on the side of the grill, distracted by that tantalizing bit of skin. When I turn back around, she's sitting in a chair and pulling out a notebook.

"Those flowers smell amazing. My ex used to send me flowers at work sometimes. I forgot how much I love the smell of them."

Now I feel like a jackass that I didn't just tell her I got them for her. *This isn't a date.* "You can take those home with you, if you want."

"And take the joy of seeing and smelling them away from you? Absolutely not," she says, so matter of fact. It's sweet that she thinks I have flowers sitting around and doesn't even bat an eye at it. Like it's totally normal that a single man buys himself flowers.

"What questions do you have for me?" I ask, lighting the grill.

"I was hoping you could start with just explaining the basics of baseball to me. I know they try to hit the ball and then run the bases, and I know what a home run is, and that there are innings with tops and bottoms. If I'm honest, I don't really get the tops and bottoms parts. Or how their game cluster things work."

I chuckle, filing this away to tell Riv tomorrow. He will get an absolute kick out of her summary of the game. I multitask, grilling and explaining the ins and outs of baseball. I explain the rules, the games, the teams in the league, biggest rivals, really everything I can think of. Lily listens intently, writing down notes for things she finds important or relevant, and asks clarifying questions when needed. By the time the salmon, potatoes, and veggies are done, she has three pages of notes written down.

I'm bringing everything over to the table when she stands, grabbing my empty beer bottle. "Can I get you another?"

"I have to feed Shadow, so I can grab another. Can I get you more wine?" Instead of allowing me, she grabs her glass in her other hand and follows me inside. I fill Shadow's bowls with food and water while Lily gets us more drinks, then we sneak back outside before Shadow notices us leaving.

"Cheers," Lily says, holding up her wine glass. "To making new friends and not having to eat every meal alone. Thank you for this tonight. All your help, really."

That *friend* word wipes the genuine smile from my face, but I plaster a small fake one anyway. Tipping the neck of my bottle to her, I clink it lightly against the glass. "I'll cheers to that. I'm truly happy to help."

We both take a sip, our eyes never leaving each other. Lily is the first to dig into her salmon while I watch the way her lips wrap lightly around the fork with her first bite. I grip my bottle tight as a small moan slips from her mouth.

"This might be the best fish I've ever had," she groans out, already scooping up another bite. Her whole body melts as she savors her next bite. "I'm going to need you to make this for me again. Once will not be enough."

I agree with the sentiment. Watching her fawn over my cooking is something I will want to see again and again. "We can make dinners together a weekly tradition, but you'll have to be willing to try out some of my other recipes."

I finally take my first bite, still watching her eat. Her eyes close every time her fork meets her lips, her hum of satisfaction sending blood rushing south.

"We can trade houses every other week. Don't tempt me with an offer you can't hold up to. You know I don't love cooking for one," she says, her shy smile is soft and mirrored by mine.

Dinner with her every week sounds amazing. I want to know her. What makes her laugh, what makes her smile, what makes her blush; and then I want to be the one to make her do all three. I want to know what she turns to when she's upset, what she wants out of life, and who her hero is. And this right here is the exact reason Jake and River think I'm going to blow this. I don't do anything half-assed, when I'm in, I am ALL in. It's been two weeks and I can already tell she is the complete opposite of Jen. Everything I was missing from her, is wrapped beautifully in Lily.

"Before we jump into the questions about River's life, tell me something about you."

She sets down her fork, and takes a sip of her wine, deep in thought. "My favorite color is purple. Specifically, the shades in a lilac bush. My neighbor growing up was obsessed with the smell of lilacs, and every year tried to plant a lilac bush. Most of them died because they aren't meant for the harsh temperatures. But for the few weeks she kept them alive, their color and their scent was my favorite thing."

"My parents have two large lilac bushes outside of the kitchen window. My mom loves to open the window when they are in bloom. The whole house will smell like them for weeks on end."

"When it comes time for me to tackle landscaping, I want to plant a few around my deck. I've got a black thumb though, I might have to ask your mom how to keep them alive," she laughs to herself, oblivious to the smile on my face. *She wants to talk to my mom.* I clear my throat, dislodging the urge to beg her to meet my family tomorrow.

"I think she would love that. Alright, what do you want to know about River's life?"

She pulls out her notebook and pen again, looking over the list of questions. "Did he always know he was going to play baseball professionally?"

"Yeah," I think back to our high school days. He was gifted then already. Not to say he didn't work his ass off for it, because he did. River was just naturally talented from a young age. He had deadly accuracy with throwing and catching, and had a much bigger build than me back then. "He was scouted in high school, and recruited straight to the Rainiers. They kept him on the farm team while he was in college to really hone his skills and help him bulk up. He has been on the MLB team ever since."

"Wow, your parents must be really proud to have successful and athletic kids."

I choke on my sip of beer and cough it up on the deck. She did not just put River and I in the same category, but I like that she noticed one part. "You think I'm athletic?"

Her cheeks flush a deep crimson, as she flusters her words. "Well, you know, you uhhh, you had no shirt on the other morning." She gestures at my body across the table from her, "And you are clearly big, so I assume since you do rescues, and uhhh, you know."

A deep laugh rumbles through my chest. "I am big, thank you for noticing. I run too, great stamina." I wink at her, watching the flush travel all the way down her chest. "What's your next question?"

She writes down my previous answer, then reads the next. "Has his fame impacted his relationships?"

"Most of them, maybe even all of them. Starting in high school, as soon as the scouts started coming around, girls started flocking to him like seagulls on fries at the beach. Even friends started treating him like a meal ticket. Since then, he has had one relationship that seemed genuine, but she couldn't handle the travel schedule. Between people wanting him for his status and money, and those unable to handle the grueling schedule and chaos that inevitably follows him, he's struggled. He started seeing a new woman recently. I haven't met her yet but he said she seems like a good egg."

His life is something I would never want for myself. I enjoy an easy schedule, a lot of time at home and in the woods, and genuine connections. I've never been one to put an emphasis on material things. Not that River is big on material things either, he's great with his money, and humble about his success. Regardless, there is an expectation in the professional sports world, and the women that chase those men seem to have big expectations, too.

We have lived very different lives since we moved out of our parents' house, but I'm grateful we are still as close as we are. He's my hero in a lot of ways, and I truly want the best for him. Getting to make a trip to Seattle to watch him play isn't so bad either. I'm beyond proud of him.

Lily seems oblivious to the fact I've been lost in my thoughts. She seems to be contemplating that life as well. Her quiet voice breaks the silence as she writes down my answer. "I think not being seen and liked for who you are down to your soul is one of life's greatest tragedies."

She looks up when she's done, her eyes muted and rimmed in sadness. It makes me question if anyone has taken the time to really see her for all that she is. "Okay," she clears her throat, breaking the moment. "Here's an easy one. What are the relationships between the teammates and staff like?"

I bark out a laugh, "That is far from easy. There have been seasons where he raves how the whole team is in sync and everyone gels, and seasons where one new trade can throw off the whole dynamic and create divides where there weren't before. His coaching staff has stayed pretty consistent and there is a level of mutual respect between most of them. From what he has said though, the Rainiers management seems pretty selective on who they hire and trade. A scandal can make them turn down a player, no matter their ability or stats."

"So like most jobs then, one bad apple can sour the whole bunch. Last one for now, what does game day look like? How early does he get there, do they really all shower together after and go to the bars with each other, or is that a fable other romance books have sold me?"

That gives me an idea, and I know Riv will pull out all the

stops for it if I ask. "Would you like to go to a game and see for yourself? I'm sure he can sneak you onto the field and behind the scenes a little and show you the game day routine in person."

The minute the words leave my mouth, I regret them. What if this is what she was hoping for with this questioning? What if she just wants a chance to meet him, and a chance at trying to catch his eye? I know some of the guys on his team; if Riv takes her around them they will flirt mercilessly and try to take her home.

Lily immediately puts all those fears to bed when she simply asks, "Would you go with me?"

I swallow the lump in my throat and smile at her. "Yeah, if you want me to."

Her smile is immediate and lights her whole face, "I would love to then. This can be so good for my book, and I've never been to Seattle. Can we go to Pike Place Market? Oooh, and see the Space Needle? I need to order a jersey. Are they called jerseys in baseball, too?"

"I'll call River this week and see when is a good time for us to come. We can see whatever you would like while we are there," I chuckle at her enthusiasm. I'm not a big city guy, but I can admit that Seattle is eclectic and fun to visit and explore. I got my fill of it in college, but I would be thrilled to show her around. The view from the top of the Space Needle on a clear day is incredible, and I would love to watch Lily experience it.

"Do you think he would be okay if I brought my notebook with? I promise not to bombard him with questions but I like to write things down and may have a few things to ask. I'm a little neurotic about lists and writing things down," she says, swirling her wine in the glass.

"He already told me he's happy to answer whatever I can't. Bring a whole binder if you need, he would love it."

She smiles at me, and I want to capture this moment. The last of the fading sun is reflecting in her eyes, brightening the usually moody blue and highlighting the brown tones in her hair. Her clear skin looks soft to the touch, my fingers itching to reach forward and stroke down her cheek.

Shadow's bark at the back door draws our attention, breaking my moment of revery. "I guess she's done with dinner too," Lily jokes, standing as she starts collecting the dishes. I collect the ones she can't carry, and we head inside to put them in the kitchen. Without asking, she starts clearing the plates and putting them in the dishwasher, so I grab containers for the leftovers.

When everything is put away, I curl my fingers under the countertop, taking in Lily. "Do you want to stay for a bit? We can watch a movie or just enjoy the evening air on the porch."

"A movie sounds good. Can I ask a personal question?"

"Sure," I guide her to the living room with a light touch at the small of her back.The heat of her skin under the thin fabric seeps into my fingers.

"Do you get lonely, too? Overwhelmed by the quiet at times?"

I contemplate it before deciding on honesty. "Yes, I do. I was in a relationship for a long time, and while we only lived together for a short time, I still get lonely living alone now. Shadow helps, it's never too quiet with her around, and it's someone to talk to even if she doesn't talk back." Shadow jumps on the couch in between us as we sit, letting out a huff. "Well, not always at least. Are you lonely in the cabin?"

"More than I would like to admit. I'm used to being alone, but I always had a job to go to during the day. I saw people at the office, talked with co-workers at lunch. Sometimes I went out with them for drinks after. I guess I didn't realize when I moved here just how much time I would be spending alone. It's an adjustment, that's for sure."

I notice she doesn't call anyone friends, just co-workers. I think her life has been lonelier for longer than she is admitting, it's just more apparent now.

"I guess we need to get you out more then," I try to make light of the heavy weight now surrounding us. "Shadow is also available for company anytime you would like."

I give my best girl a scratch behind the ear, then grab the remote off the coffee table. I want to tell her that she doesn't have to be lonely. That I will happily spend every free moment with her. But Jake and River are in the back of my mind, reminding me not to blow this and jump in too fast. "What type of shows do you normally watch?" I ask, pulling up Netflix.

"I like rom-coms, action, and comedy. Lately, I have been watching this show to prepare me for winter here," she says while absent-mindedly petting Shadow.

"What show is that?"

She turns to me, that flush creeping up her cheeks again. "Umm, it's called Alone."

My head tips back with a loud laugh, my shoulders shaking with the intensity of it. I laugh so hard I snort, then try to calm myself and look over to see her looking utterly embarrassed.

"I'm sorry, I am not laughing at you. It's just… our winters aren't like that in the show. The snow isn't even that bad some years." I can see her shutting down and I instantly feel like an asshole. There are little things that she gets embarrassed from and scared of easily, and I can't help but wonder who in her past caused her to be that way. "I'm really sorry, I didn't mean to embarrass you. I have learned some great survival techniques from that show. What season are you on?"

"We don't have to watch it," her quiet voice bleeds across the couch to me.

Fuck, I messed up laughing at that. I love the show, I even thought about applying to be on it in the future. The winters here in the mountains can be bad, but they are nothing like being stranded alone in the woods with a few select items for months at a time. I get that she doesn't know what to expect from a winter here though, and it is better to have some knowledge rather than going in blind.

I click on the title, hovering over the seasons, "You better tell me or we are starting over at season one."

"Fine, season two, episode four."

I click onto it and hit play, then reach over and put my hand on hers, giving it a light squeeze. "I love this show, I'm sorry I laughed. Winter in a new climate can be intimidating, but I'll help you make it through. I promise."

The edges of her lips tilt up as she turns back to the TV, leaving her hand under mine. Surprisingly, Shadow doesn't even nudge our hands apart. She's usually greedy and wants hands only on her, but since ours are resting on her, I guess it's good enough. The first episode bleeds into the second, which turns into the third. I stop the show before the fourth episode starts, glancing over to see Lily fast asleep. I'm not sure when it happened, but she's leaning against an equally dead to the world Shadow, her feet tucked up under her.

I stealthily slip from my spot on the couch and take a photo of them together. Even in her sleep, her beauty is astounding. I want to pick her up and deposit her in my bed, but I don't think that will go over well. Kneeling in front of her, I gently shake her leg to wake her.

"Hey, you fell asleep," I whisper, this time not stopping myself from reaching out and tucking her hair behind her ear. Her sleepy eyes blink at me before they warm and crinkle at the edges.

"Sorry," she yawns as I sit back so she can unfold herself from the couch. "Thank you for everything tonight. Dinner was so good. You set the bar high for when someone cooks for me again."

I don't want anyone else cooking for her. I like that I am the only one to make her a meal, even if it's fucked up that none of her exes ever did. Instead of sharing that fact, I help her to her feet and lead her to the kitchen to grab her things.

"I'll leave those here for Shadow." She points to the container of treats, then turns to the furry pup sitting at her feet. "Only if you're being a good girl."

"Let me drive you home," I say, grabbing my keys as we head to the door.

"It's a five minute walk from your front door to mine." She rolls her eyes, like it's no big deal, but I don't care. It's late and dark, and she's tired so I'm not taking no for an answer. I leave Shadow in the house and follow her out, opening my passenger door for her. "Thank you. You really don't have to."

"I want to," I reply simply, closing the door behind her and rounding the front to get in. It takes less than a minute to get to her house but I don't care. I take care of what's mine, and whether she knows it or not, Lily feels like mine.

"Have a good night, Thoren."

"Goodnight Lily." I watch her climb out and shut my door, not pulling away until she is locked safely inside her cabin.

lily

Armed with all my notes from Saturday, I delved into working on my book on Sunday and Monday. Painting the house took a back seat, but I was able to knock out another eight chapters. Andrea is going to be thrilled with the work and the timeline. For the first time since I started working with her, I am ahead of schedule for my deadline. It's probably a mix of no longer having a full time job, and the inspiration I am finding here, but I love that it brings no stress. I just need to fact check my previous writing with everything I learned from Thoren, and then again once we go to River's game and I get to check out the facilities.

I've never been to a professional sports game of any kind before. While Phoenix had an NBA, NFL, and MLB team, I never had the chance to go see one. My parents were not big on sports, and when my company had tickets, they were always snatched by the men right away. I'm not sure if I'm more excited to see the actual game or to just see what it is like to attend a game and see what all the hype is about.

I tried watching the Rainiers games on my tablet a few times, but there is a lot of downtime. The internet assured me that attending a game is a whole experience and not as boring as watching it on TV. I think it will help that I will have Thoren to keep me company and explain anything I still don't understand.

I plan to do something nice for both him and his brother when we go. It's beyond kind of them to do this for me and I want to make sure they know I appreciate it. I get the feeling that Thoren is overlooked for his brother a lot, and I hate that for him. You can be proud of his brother without diminishing his accomplishments and the good man that he is.

And he truly is a good man. He was so patient with me on Saturday, explaining the same thing over and over until I fully understood it, and then driving me home even though I could have easily walked. There are not enough Thorens in the world anymore, and I am glad to have found one in a neighbor and friend. It doesn't help that he is mouthwateringly hot, and *good god,* when his rough fingers stroked my cheek when he woke me up... my body lit up like a Christmas tree.

Focusing on my writing the last two days has kept me from freaking out about that fact. Now that it's Tuesday and I need a break from all the writing, my brain keeps wandering back to Thoren. My body never responded to Tyler that way, and we were together for two years. I just thought that the 'butterflies in stomach, tingles down to your toes, fireworks behind your eyes' type feelings were romanticized in books and movies, but weren't realistic. I thought maybe they happened with once in a lifetime loves, not everyday love. A ping from my phone drags me from my introspection.

THOREN:

What are you up to today?

LILY:

Just enjoying my coffee at the moment. Might paint another room, or do some online shopping for new bathroom tile ideas. Your bathrooms inspired me.

THOREN:

Sounds productive. Want to get outside with Shadow and I instead?

LILY:

Yes! What are we doing?

THOREN:

Perfect. Be ready in an hour. Dress for hiking.

Exactly one hour later, I have my hiking backpack filled and ready to make Thoren proud. I dressed in my hiking boots, bike shorts, and a sports bra with a loose top thrown over it. It's eighty-six degrees already, and it's only the end of June. Michele told me August has peak temperatures around here, so we are in for a hot summer. I guess it's a good way to ease myself into the difference in weather from Phoenix.

The front hall mirror reflects my image as I twist my long hair into a high ponytail, disturbed by a truck door slamming outside, setting off the flutter of butterflies low in my stomach. Grabbing my backpack, I step outside to find Thoren rounding the front of his truck toward me. His brown hair is messy on top, his beard a little thicker. Today, his hazel eyes look dark under thick eyebrows. He has on hiking boots like me, cream cargo pants with dirt smudges on them, and an olive green tee that hugs tight to his chest. The rugged outdoorsman is a mighty fine look on him.

"Have you guys been hiking already this morning?" Shadow leans her head out the passenger window to whine at me.

"Kind of," he rubs the back of his neck, before walking around the truck to open my door. "Shadow, back. I ran a SAR training session this morning. We worked on a repel rescue," he explains as he shuts my door once I'm in and then hops in himself. "Sorry if I'm dirty and sweaty. Just thought it was pointless to shower just to go back in the woods again."

"I don't mind. It completes your whole mountain man look."

"Mountain man look?" His laugh is deep, filling the truck cab. "Didn't realize I had a look. Is it a good one?"

"Oh yes," I agree before thinking it through. "I mean, rugged mountain men are hot. The whole 'I could fight a bear' vibes really do it, you know?"

His lips tick up in a sexy smirk as he thinks it through. "I want to clarify that I could not fight a bear."

"Well don't ruin it for me. So, where are we headed anyway?" He's driving further into the woods, away from downtown. A wave of heat rushes in through the open window, the air thick with the fragrance of pine and the heavy, sun-baked scent of the earth as the trees crowd closer to the road. I have explored a few short hikes to break in my new boots, but haven't been on a big adventure yet.

"There's a spot up here that not a lot of people use. It has a few different trails, but one leads to a waterfall with a small swimming hole. It's peaceful and it's Shadow's favorite place to swim." The dog in question pokes her head between our seats at the sound of her name, nuzzling her head into Thoren's shoulder as he reaches up to scratch her chin. Her wet pink tongue pokes out, licking a stripe up the side of his face.

We drive another ten minutes up the road, where he turns off into a small gravel parking lot. While there is only one other car parked here, the area looks like it could fit at least ten. There are no signs off the road alerting you to the fact that this is a hiking spot. According to Thoren, there are many spots like this all over these woods with hidden hiking trails.

Shadow unceremoniously climbs over the center console to jump out behind Thoren. "You know I have to get my bag from the back seat. You can wait five seconds to be let out from there. We do this every time," he scolds her playfully. He grabs his large backpack, then looks over, watching me strap mine on. "You don't have to bring yours. I packed enough for both of us, plus some snacks for when we get up there."

My heart sinks in my chest. I was really proud of myself for having brought it, fully stocked, to show him I followed his list. He must see something in my expression as I take it off and slide it back in the truck because he is standing in front of me in an instant. His knuckle notches under my chin and tips my head up to look at him.

His golden gaze locks on mine, letting me see everything he's feeling. "I'm proud of you for being prepared and bringing it, and I would love to hear what all you put in it. You can bring it if you would like, it's just kind of a steep hike. I thought it would be easier for you to not have to carry it, and I packed mine with both of us in mind."

He stays like that, holding my chin between his thumb and finger, letting me see the truth in his statement. Slowly, I nod, bringing a smirk to his lips. He takes a step back so I can shut the truck door, leaving my backpack inside.

"Good girl," his low voice growls. He turns on his heels toward the trail head, completely unaffected. I glance down at Shadow, still sitting next to me, tongue hanging out of her mouth as her tail sweeps over the gravel. Her eyes are firmly planted on a retreating Thoren as a drop of her drool slips off her pink tongue.

Same, girl, same.

The trail head starts wide and easy, a mix of dirt and gravel, with small sporadic inclines. Aside from the trail, the ground is covered in moss, ferns, brush, chittering squirrels, and whistling birds. The trees are thick with a mix of different varieties. The smell of hearty earth and pine, mixed with crisp wind through the branches assaults my senses. My feet stop of their own accord for me to deeply inhale, filling my lungs with the fresh, clean mountain air.

"The Douglas firs are very fragrant today. On the right day, you can pick out the different scents, specifically the Juniper trees and the Douglas fir," Thoren says over his shoulder to me. My gaze is constantly drawn to him, watching him reach out to touch some of the trees that we pass. Other times, he slows to grab my hand when roots stick out onto the pathway. His shoulders are relaxed, his stride even, and a wide smile graces his face. He truly comes alive out here.

"What other types of trees are in these woods?" I find myself asking, just so I can watch his eyes light with excitement.

"So many, depending where exactly we are. Different varieties of hemlock, spruces, pines, firs, and cedars. They all grow in abundance out here. Just wait until you hike these trails in the fall. The changing colors, paths filled with crunchy leaves, and the crisp air. It's the most magical time of year."

It does sound magical, and I can almost picture it. Reds, oranges, and yellows overtaking the field of greens currently around us. Cool air that sends shivers down your spine, the vibrant chatter of forest life overshadowed by crinkles of crisp leaves. I can see myself on this hike at that time, hopefully with these two companions still by my side. Shadow runs ahead of us, taking a path to the left where the trail splits.

"Is she going the right way?"

"Yeah, she knows this hike by heart. First left, then right, then two more lefts and we will be there. With so many paths, this is one of the easier trails to get lost on, but absolutely worth it."

"I trust you to get me there."

We walk together in silence, the trail getting steeper with a rougher terrain. Thoren grabs my hand more often, his long legs easily stepping over large rocks and steps where my short ones struggle. At some point, he stops letting go, keeping my hand nestled in his for the rest of the hike. The part that surprises me is that I let him, his calloused fingers strong and warm, wrapped around mine.

My parents weren't big on physical touch growing up. I don't have memories of snuggling with them or frequent hugs. It was so rare that I could probably count on one hand the amount of times I was hugged in a year. There were never displays of physical affection with my ex either. In fact, I can't think of a single time he held my hand. Was something broken in me that I was so desperate for Thoren to keep his hold on me? Even Michele's hugs that were surprising in the beginning are a source of comfort for me now. I gripped his hand a little tighter, keeping the intimate connection between us.

An hour into the hike, the steady stream of rushing water becomes audible above the sounds around us. It can't come any sooner, with sweat dripping down my back and my legs fatigued. The thought of a break and dipping my toes in the water spurs me on to finish the last little bit. The trees are getting sparse ahead, opening up to a hidden gem.

"Welcome to our secret spot," Thoren says, giving my hand a small squeeze before dropping it to take off his backpack. My head is on a swivel taking it all in. Directly ahead is a large rock wall about twenty feet tall with rivulets of water trailing down the protruding rocks before careening into a round swimming hole. The beach is more rock than sand, but there is a grassy section off to the side where Thoren is setting out a blanket.

Shadow is already splashing around in the water, tongue out and tail a blur, looking like the world's happiest dog. It's truly breathtaking and beyond peaceful. The sound of the water trailing over the rocks isn't as loud as a typical gushing waterfall, and it immediately sets my soul at ease. Shadow grabs a stick from the edge of the water, dragging it to where Thoren is seated on his blanket.

He takes it from her, tossing it into the water for her to retrieve. "You coming, or are you going to stand there all day?" He chuckles, holding his hand out for me. I leisurely make my way over to take it as he pulls me down beside him. "What do you think?"

"I'm speechless. That hike was hell on my legs, but absolutely worth it for this ending."

He reaches into his backpack, pulling out a tub with sandwiches and some cut up fruit. "I'm glad you agree. Are you hungry? I have turkey and cheese or ham with cheese." He holds them both out to me. I take the turkey from him, unwrapping it and taking a bite.

"Holy crap, this is good," I say in the most unladylike fashion, mouth full of food.

He chuckles, taking a large bite of his own sandwich. "My mom makes this incredible aioli that I added to them."

I love that he talks about his family so much, and that I can see the love he has for them. The last man I dated actively avoided talking about his family, and I didn't find myself talking about my parents often. Who wants to bring up parents that are disappointed in you?

"I really need to meet your mom now." The blush on his cheeks spikes my heart rate, but he doesn't say anything.

We finish our sandwiches and pick at the fruit while he throws the stick every time Shadow brings it back. He asks about what items I put in my backpack while I proudly tell him that I got everything on his personal list. He tells me about his other favorite hikes in the area, and how often he is able to go. When the tray of fruit is empty, he puts it away, then leans down to unlace his boots. His nimble fingers work with ease, bringing unbidden images of what else they could do with ease. My weekly date with my vibrator may need to be moved up.

"Wanna get in?" he nods toward the water, pulling his socks off.

I glance toward the crystal blue water, Shadow swimming in the middle of it with the stick in tow. It looks inviting, and I am covered in drying sweat. I nod, undoing my boots as well. By the time I have my boots and socks off, Thoren is standing and pulling his shirt over his head. I try not to watch, but his hands lower to unbutton his pants and I am rooted to the spot. He slips them down his hips, exposing his thick thighs, dark hair trailing down his muscled legs. My gaze slips back up to the bulge in his boxers, my lips parting on a gasp. It's a *large* bulge.

He looks up, catching me staring and winks, before heading for the water. His black boxers hug his skin, and I have a hard time swallowing past the lump in my throat. I'm certainly not stripping down to my undies, so I slip my tee off and meander over in my shorts and sports bra.

I don't have a whole lot going on in either department. I'm petite and toned, but my boobs are small handfuls at best, and my booty is perky but also on the smaller side. The way that Thoren's eyes are trailing over every inch of my exposed skin makes me feel like Jessica Rabbit, with curves for days and everything a man wants.

As my toes touch the edge of the water, the cooling sensation flows through me. The rocks are slippery underfoot, but manageable, so I continue further in the water, cautious of my steps. I feel Thoren's stare as I continue until the chilly water laps around my thighs.

He is standing further in, only his pecs and above exposed. His eyes are hooded and dark, still tracking my every movement. They stall on my hard nipples poking through the sports bra before finally reaching my face.

"Are you coming?"

"Nah, I don't have a change of clothes." I'm enjoying the refreshing water swirling around my legs. I want to tell him that this place is magical. I feel small, and inconsequential in this big forest, and something about that feels freeing. Like my problems aren't so big, and I don't have to stew over Andrea's words about Tyler, or that being this close to him half naked makes my body come alive. "You know my favorite color, but I never asked yours."

"Blue," he answers immediately. "Blue like the sky on a hot summer day. Like the crystal waters we are standing in. Like the sapphire blue of yo- Shadow, NO!"

I follow his line of sight, right as Shadow stands directly over my discarded shirt and shakes. A startled laugh leaves my lips, as Shadow sits on the now soaked shirt. Her head cocks to the side as she stares at us, confused.

"I'm so sorry," Thoren wades through the water behind me. "I have a spare shirt in my bag. I grabbed an extra shirt and shorts in case we decided to get in. I'll wash your shirt too, it's going to smell like wet dog." He seems distressed over a little water and dirt on my old tee.

I touch his arm, letting him see the sincerity in my eyes. "It's okay, it's just a shirt. And she's a dog. It's not a big deal."

He looks down at me, the heat radiating off his body. His gaze searches my face, but I'm not sure what he's looking for. Prickles of awareness touch my skin as his warm breath coasts over my face, and cold water droplets slip from his hair onto my over-heated skin. I let my hand drop, trailing down his arm as it goes. Shadow's sharp bark breaks the moment, and he steps back, breaking eye contact.

"I guess we should pack up and go before it gets too late. The hike back always takes longer."

He pulls a rolled up tee from his backpack and hands it to me before packing up everything and shoving it back in. He pulls on fresh shorts and his same green shirt, and we head back out the way we came. If the trails to get here were confusing the first time, they seem even worse now. I would have been lost in an instant without Thoren leading the way. He seems lost in thought and distant since our moment in the water. I think he was going to tell me his favorite color was blue like my eyes, and a part of me wanted to hear it, even if I shouldn't.

The walk back remains quiet, both of us focusing on the nature around us. His hand stays wrapped around mine again though, and I really like that. He feels present in this moment with me, aware of my footfalls and breathing. He slows when I get a little short winded, his thumb coasting over my knuckles when roots overtake the path.

Before I know it, we are back at the truck. Thoren opens the passenger door for me before he puts Shadow and his backpack in the back seat. Shadow's wet and dirty head pops over the console, giving us sad puppy eyes, as he starts the truck.

"I'm guessing she's used to sitting in the passenger seat," I joke, giving her a chin scratch.

"Yeah, you kind of stole her domain. I try to keep her in the back, but she just jumps over the seat right away. I don't mind having a passenger princess though," he smirks. He rolls the back window down, pulling Shadow's attention toward it. With the front windows shut and the back open, the wind billows his large shirt I'm wearing. My mouth waters as the scent of his cologne wafts up. It's a mix of the woods, sage, and amber, reminding me of a warm hug on an autumn day.

I try to subtly lift it to my nose, taking a deep inhale. "Thank you for taking me with you today. I needed an excuse to get out of the house. Your secret location is safe with me, but I may go there again. It brought on a peace like I've never felt before."

A smile touches his lips when he turns to me. "I feel that

there, too. There's no service that deep in the woods to distract me, and something about that little open space surrounded by nothing but thick woods makes me feel like I'm in my own little world."

He turns onto our lane, and pulls up in front of my cabin, leaving the truck running. Leaning his head back against the headrest, he rolls it to look at me again. "Shadow will be alone most of Thursday, if you would like to spend time with her again."

"I would love that. Thanks again for today, Thoren," I open the door and grab my backpack from by my feet as I hop out.

He nods, a faraway look crossing his features. "Have a good night, Lily."

I shut the door, and head into the cabin. I fight a smile when I notice his truck doesn't pull away until my front door is shut.

thoren

Thursday morning, Jake and I are tasked with driving through local campgrounds and boat launch sites for safety and standard checks. He snags the keys off the hook for one of the ranger's trucks before I can, stomping outside. He glances over as he turns to reverse from the spot, "Spill it."

"Spill what?" I feign innocence.

"You returned my trailer when you knew I'd be gone last week for starters. Then you never filled River and I in on how Saturday went, and now you've been pensive all morning. I'm guessing it all has to do with Lily, so spill it."

"I don't know where to start."

"Start with borrowing the trailer last week. How'd it go with the deck?"

"So well that she cooked me dinner as a thanks. She helped the entire time, never getting discouraged. So different from what I'm used to, ya know?" A small grin pops out, just thinking about spending that evening with her.

"Not to be a dick, but the bar isn't exactly high to be better than Jen." He gives me a pointed look as he turns into the campgrounds and slows our pace to a crawl. "How did Saturday night go? You fucking blew it, didn't you?"

"No, it went really well, actually. I didn't make it a date, and I didn't give her the flowers. We had a nice meal together, and I answered all her baseball questions for her book. I told her I would take her to Seattle to see River play."

His head whips to me again, shaking subtly. "Why would you do that, man?"

I take my time looking out the window, making sure there aren't piles of trash laying around or any destroyed property. "It's not like that with her. She didn't ask to go, didn't even ask to meet him. I offered it up."

"I just don't want to see you taken advantage of. You have plenty to offer on your own. Hell, don't tell Riv, but I think you have more to offer someone. Make sure she's in it for you. So, are you guys dating now?"

The sudden sting in my eyes is surprising. River is worth millions, plays professional baseball, and is genuinely a good guy. I know that isn't everything in a relationship, but it makes a difference. Jen made sure to drive that point home frequently, comparing my brother and I anytime we fought. She made me feel like my love, devotion, and care for her would never be enough. I took care of her financially as well, but that still wasn't enough. Having my best friend validate my worth doesn't make up for all that, but it fills me with a warmth all the same.

"Nah, we clicked, and there is a definite connection there. She seems like she's not interested in a relationship right now. I'm not really sure, but I don't mind being her friend for now. I enjoy spending time with her, in any regard."

He hums in answer, thinking it through. "Jen never deserved you, and I don't want you holding onto something that might not be there for her. You deserve someone who fights for you," his quiet voice is deep and filled with emotion.

"Hell, I knew you were a big fucking softie. Thanks man, but we are still just getting to know each other. All I know right now is I like her, and I want to spend more time with her." I grip his shoulder. "You're my best friend, and I appreciate you looking out for me."

He keeps his eyes trained out the window, bobbing his head in acknowledgement as we patrol the rest of the area.

"Are you going to tell me the rest of it?" he asks, "Why you're being a surly dick?"

"I'm not being a dick. I just…I don't know. I took her hiking Tuesday afternoon. We went to the little waterfall Shadow loves, and it was going so well. Conversation was flowing, I held her hand, she took a dip in the water with me," I note how he angles a brow at me. "No, she didn't strip down, but she watched my every move as I stripped to my skivvies."

He chuckles and shakes his head at me again. "Okay, so what was the problem?"

"We had this moment, in the water. Shadow shook all over her shirt, getting it soaked and dirty. You know Jen would have lost her shit at something like that. But Lily just touched my arm saying it was okay and laughed it off. I just stood there like a stunned jackass because all I could think was 'I could really fall for this woman'. More than I already have, like truly fall in love with her without even trying." I rub at the tightness in my chest. It's too soon to be feeling like this. Too soon after Jen, too soon with Lily. Despite my head's reservations, my heart is wide open and ready for her.

I thought I was ready to be with someone again, but what if I'm not? I gave my all to Jen, and she ripped my heart to shreds before tossing me the pieces. It's not that I'm not over her, because I am. It's more that my heart is just learning to heal. I can't risk someone pulling apart all the tape and glue I have been slapping on there.

"You're afraid of getting hurt," Jake guesses accurately.

"Yeah. I don't know much about her past. What if I'm nothing like she normally goes for? What if she is still in love with her ex and she's just hoping to be chased? What if she discovers that small town life doesn't suit her after all?"

He's quiet for another moment, looking at all the campsites we pass. It's fairly clean, but that is typical for weekday campers, it's the weekend only people who tend to make more of a ruckus and mess. "What if it all works out?"

That scares me as equally as if it doesn't. It's hard to focus on the possibility of it working out when the other side of that coin is getting my heart broken again.

"So what about you? Are you still getting orders left, right, and center?"

Jake rubs a hand down his face before answering. "Yeah, it's kind of been crazy. I'm getting so many that I feel like I have to tell the showroom to put a sign on my work saying three to six months wait. I think it's almost time for me to lose this job and build full-time."

"Then do it. Don't stick around on my account. We'll still see each other, I'll just come annoy the hell out of you at the shop." He laughs, punching me in the shoulder. "I mean it. That's been your goal all along. If the opportunity is there, then take it."

"What if a year or two down the road the orders stop coming in, and it's no longer a full time gig? I don't want to tuck tail and beg for this job back."

I throw his earlier words back at him, "Yeah, but what if they don't and you succeed?"

With all the locations on our list checked off, we decide to stop for lunch in town. Just as we are sitting down with our loaded sausages, my phone rings. The office number lights up my screen, so I answer immediately.

"Hello?"

"Hey Thoren, where are you at right now?" Niles, one of the other rangers, asks.

"Just sat down with Jake for lunch in town. What's up?"

"We might have a missing hiker. Someone called saying their friend went for an early morning hike, saying they would be back within two hours. That was five hours ago. Can you head back to the office to map out where she was and decide if your team needs to go out right away or not?" he asks, sounding concerned.

"We'll head back to the office now, okay? Just write down everything you know and I'll get on it. Thanks Niles." I hang up and nod to Jake who is already getting up and grabbing a to-go container.

"Search and rescue?" He unlocks the truck and we hop in. Jake was the first one I told when this position was handed over to me. While I have been consistently volunteering with the team, Jake only does it here and there when he can. His support was overwhelming though, and really meant a lot. It's intimidating taking on something that literally puts lives in your hand, but he has had my back the whole time, encouraging me.

"Possible missing hiker. I'll know more once we get in, but they only went out this morning."

"You worried?"

"Yeah. I never wanted this job. I want to run our department, not the SAR team. It's a lot of pressure that I still don't feel ready for," I answer honestly.

"You'll be okay, you've got a good team behind you. Plus, it's only until they find a permanent replacement."

"Thanks, man." I grab my lunch as he pulls back into the office, and head in search of Niles. He's posted up outside the conference room waiting for me, with papers spread all over the table. He's new to the job, and even newer to the search and rescue team. So new, in fact, he hasn't even been to one of the training sessions yet, hence his nerves.

"I've got the map laid out, with the location her car is at, as well as the approximate location her friend said she normally hikes to. The protocol is six hours right, then we go looking? Is it six hours from when she left, or six from when we are notified?"

I clap my hand on his shoulder attempting to calm him. "Take a breath, it's always best to go into this with a clear head and a plan. After six hours of her being missing, we will start the search. I'm going to grab the list of who should be available today and then we can start planning out buddy searches and who goes where, okay?"

He trembles beneath my hand, but nods, taking a deep breath, then heads into the conference room. My next stop is my office to grab my laptop and SAR binder. Stacking my lunch on top, I make my way back to the conference room to join Niles to form a plan.

By the time we hit the six hour mark, I have nine volunteers on their way to the trailhead along with Niles and I, and four more able to take a shift or join us within four hours if we still haven't found the hiker. Parking the truck next to the missing hiker's SUV, I pull the cooler from the back seat and add it to the bins in the bed.

The cooler is filled with water, gatorades, and some protein bars. The bins in the bed are filled with some of our gear. There's a sked, used for transporting injured persons, ready on the edge with one bin filled with a few spare backpacks filled with first aid kits, flashlights, knives, and other basic supplies. Another bin has walkie-talkies for all of us, one has ropes and harnesses. We aren't really sure what type of rescue we will be looking at yet, so I brought a few basics for any scenario.

A few of my seasoned volunteers have their own backpacks,

but the rest dig in to grab one from my truck. We all clip our walkie talkies in place, walking through our game plan and who will be buddies. I put Niles with me since he is new, and I know I have a lot of knowledge I can divulge as we search. As everyone grabs the last of their things, ready to hit the trail, Sherry pulls up.

"Hey everyone," she sings out, waving like this is a fun get together. "So sorry I am late, I had to go home and get changed."

It's then I take in her outfit, from her miniscule shorts to her boobs spilling over the top of her tank top, a pound of makeup on her face. She wasn't on the list of volunteers available today, so I had no idea she was coming.

"You know this could be an all-night rescue, right?" Kyle asks, staring at her outfit with disgust. "You're going to get cold. We talked in the meeting how comfortable, but covering, clothes are best to help us with the elements. That tramping through bushes might be necessary." He's always been a straight shooter, and today I extra appreciate that about him.

"Don't you worry, I have leggings and a sweater in the car, and these are my comfortable clothes," she winks at me. "So who am I paired up with? Thoren, honey, are you free?"

"Nope," I respond quickly, clapping Niles on the back. "Doing some training with Niles along the way, so it's best you join a random group since everyone is already paired." I look around the group as everyone looks anywhere but at Sherry. I'll let them figure that out. "Alright everyone, you know the drill. We all have our zones, but never stray too far so everything gets searched. Hiker's name is Kelsey, she's thirty-six and knows these woods well according to her friend. Chances are high we are carrying her out so be ready for that. Anyone that needs a break, radio the group so we know where everyone is. Back up crews are ready if this ends up being a long night, but as long as you can stay for is greatly appreciated. Let's go."

I lead the group down the start of the trail, Niles hot on my heels. Before we get too far and I lose service, I send a quick text to Lily asking if she wouldn't mind feeding Shadow dinner and letting her out to potty this evening if she doesn't hear from me by six since I'm out on a SAR case. Her response is immediate, a photo of her and Shadow sitting on her porch, with a message saying good luck and that they will be having a 'girls night'.

A smile breaks out on my face, both from her response and the photo. I hold my phone closer, admiring her stunning face with the biggest grin, blue eyes shining in the sunlight. When I volunteered with the SAR team previously, I always had to drop Shadow off with my parents or hope Jake was free to check on her. I take one last look at the photo before pocketing my phone and focus on getting Kelsey out of here safe and sound.

CHAPTER TEN

LILY:

I hope you don't mind if someone crashes our girl dinner tonight.

MICHELE:

Absolutely not, who is joining?

LILY:

Shadow, Thoren's on a SAR case so I'm keeping her with me.

MICHELE:

Ooooh girl, we have catching up to do. I need the tea.

I finished putting a second layer of paint in the living room yesterday and peeled the tape off this morning. The kitchen is next, and I have it all taped off, but I decided not to start until tomorrow since I have Michele coming over for dinner tonight. I've been marinating chicken all day, and made a fresh loaf of bread for the side. I even made a small platter of fruits and vegetables for us to snack on. My parents often hosted dinner parties when I was a kid, but they always felt stuffy. It ingrained a desire in me to be an accommodating, but relaxed, host. Serving others is such a joy for me, so I may be going a little overboard, but I can't help it. I've never hosted like this before, but it turns out, I really love it.

Shadow has been my sidekick again, and I have fallen in love with her. I've never looked at dog breeds, but when I took a break from writing earlier I looked up information about her. It turns out labs are known for being loyal, affectionate, and intelligent, which isn't the least bit surprising. All of those attributes fit her well. I also learned you can make healthy treats for them besides the peanut butter biscuits I previously made. I now have a lick bowl in the freezer for her filled with blueberries, strawberries, and bananas.

Mostly, I've been trying to keep my mind busy. Since my conversation with Andrea about Tyler, she has texted a few times begging me to put more thought into it. It has been weighing heavily on me, and I could use an outside female perspective. I don't dare call my mom and let her know because I already know how she'll react. Michele has been kind and open, and I respect her opinion. I hope she's ready for me to unload on her tonight and that it won't scare her off.

Beeps from Michele's SUV alert me to her arrival as I remove everything from the oven. Shadow lets out some happy woofs when she knocks on the door and I holler for her to come in. She gives the pup some love before coming in, holding up two wine bottles.

"I brought the goods!" she laughs, setting them on the table. She looks put together again, in sleek trousers and a pretty blouse. It's a polished but comfy look, and she pulls it off effortlessly. "It smells incredible in here, Lily. And look at the paint, it suits the space so well."

Heat rises up my cheeks at the compliments. "Thank you. Do you want to open one of the bottles and I'll get out plates?"

Michele opens the bottle of Pinot Grigio and pours each of us a glass, while I move the food to my table and set out plates and utensils.

"Cheers," she says as we clink our glasses together. "Now, I know you said you had things you wanted to talk about, but first, I need to know all about you and Thoren."

I smirk and swallow my mouthful of food. "There is no 'me and Thoren'. He's been a great neighbor and friend, and I've been helping out with Shadow. Really, even that doesn't feel like I'm helping him, more like it's keeping me from loneliness."

"Have you seen that man?" she wiggles her eyebrows, taking a sip of the crisp wine. "You could have the dog and the owner, two for one special."

My laugh is loud and free. "Yes, I have eyes. He's clearly god's gift to women, wrapped in a rugged and filthy hot package. Have you seen him use power tools? I swear my panties incinerated on sight."

Her brows narrow in speculation. "He really is just a great friend. He bought all new boards for my deck last Tuesday and helped me replace the rotting ones. It was really sweet, but I feel awful that he wouldn't let me pay him for his help or the wood."

Michele smiles down at her plate, cutting up her chicken. "Don't feel bad, that's just the type of man he is. He's always been selfless, always more concerned with the happiness of others. I really like you, Lily, and I don't think you ever would but... don't take advantage of that fact about him. Too many people already have."

I smile around my wine glass, taking a small sip. I should feel like an outsider, that she's protecting her old friend over her new, but I don't. I appreciate the fact that she cares enough about others to look out for them. It only endears me to both of them more. "I promise, I would never."

"Good. So the deck is the only time you've spent together?"

I poke at the vegetables on my plate, a small smile gracing my lips. "He also cooked me dinner Saturday, but that was so he could explain baseball to me. And we went hiking this past Tuesday."

Her sharp eyes take me in, reading whatever is on my face. "I just ask that I be your first call when your 'just a friend' becomes something more."

We finish up our meal, talking about what properties she's showing currently and how my book is coming along. When she brings the dishes to the sink, I start packing up a little of everything into a container before putting the rest away.

"Is that for me?" she glances knowingly at the container.

"Oh, it can be. I was going to put this one in Thoren's fridge later so if he makes it home tonight he doesn't have to worry about cooking. Do you want me to make one for you, too? There's plenty of leftovers."

"Nope," she pops the p, "I kind of figured that's what you were doing, but wanted to check. Nice to see someone take care of him for a change." With that, she grabs the open wine bottle and her glass and meanders out to the back deck.

Trailing behind her with my glass and the frozen treat I made for Shadow, I set it on a towel on the deck so she has something to do, before running back in to grab the plate of snacks I made for us. Michele is emptying the rest of the bottle into our glasses, feet tucked up under her on the couch when I return. With the living room lights shining through the large windows, the outside light isn't necessary. Under the slight cover of darkness, I feel a sense of invisibility and comfort.

"So, what did you need to talk to me about?"

Drawing in the warm night air, I ponder how to start. "I have a situation that I am not sure how to move forward with, and I would love your opinion. This story isn't going to paint me in a great light, so if you don't want to be friends after this, I'll understand. I just need help figuring out the right thing to do."

Michele turns fully toward me, not saying a word, just encouraging me to continue when I'm ready. Tyler's face flashes behind my eyes, his bright green eyes, the subtle grays starting to touch his hair. The soft feel of his hands on me, the flower deliveries on my desk. All of the good things that we had, until we didn't. The happiness I felt, until he crushed me.

My integrity.

My career.

My heart.

"I worked at a financial firm back in Phoenix. My parents wanted me to have a degree and a career that took me further in life. I double majored in Business and Financial Planning, just like they wanted. The summer between junior and senior year, I interned at this incredible firm. When the summer ended, they offered an extended internship that would end in a job offer when I graduated, so of course, I took it." Gulping down half my wine sends heat down into my belly. Reveling in the feel of the cool condensation soaking my fingers, I steady my voice to continue.

"My first official day there after graduation, I met Tyler. He was one of the Controllers, and had a hand in orientation for new hires. Even though I worked under one of the account managers, one that worked under another Controller in the company, he helped set me up. There was a spark that first week, as he checked in on me everyday. But he was older, and had a wedding ring, so I kept it professional. For the next three years we saw each other here and there. In meetings, work events, in the break room. We were always friendly, but over time he started to get flirty, toeing the line of professional." I twirl the wine glass between my fingers, growing uncomfortable. Michele's stare hasn't left me from where she still sits quietly, waiting for me to continue. Her face is passively blank, her posture relaxed in comparison to mine.

"Finally, one day he walked past my desk as he was leaving. He mentioned some people from his department were meeting for a drink and invited me along. I didn't have many friends, so I went. As the night carried on, he moved closer to me, until our legs were touching. He told me that he and his wife had been having problems for years, and just decided they were going to get a divorce. He told me how beautiful and smart and funny I was. How he had seen my worth from day one. I was dumb and naive, and I ate it up. I let him come home with me that evening." My voice starts to wobble, a single tear slipping free. I shouldn't let myself be affected by this. But I loved him. For years, I loved him and he played me for a fool.

Michele reaches over, giving my knee a reassuring squeeze. Her eyes are kind, and full of empathy, so I continue. "We started seeing each other after that, in secret. He told me I would be up for a promotion soon, and he didn't want people thinking it was because we were together so we had to keep it to ourselves. Tyler was sweet, you know? Sending me surprise flowers, taking me to nice restaurants, he even took me on a weekend trip away. We never went to his house though, and it was rare that he would stay the night. He told me his wife was looking for a new place and was staying in the guest room, and that's why I couldn't go there. I believed him. Sometimes I would cook dinner for us, and he wouldn't show. He always had a good excuse, but things slowly got worse. He would leave right after we had sex, and was critical of things I did or said. I would bring it up, and he would apologize and paint a pretty picture of our future; about us getting a house together, once my promotion went through. I thought we were going to build a life together."

I saw the way he changed around me, losing some of his posh attitude, and taking on narcissistic behaviors. The way he would gaslight me when I brought up ignored calls and texts or missed plans. Over time, his behavior changed from a tender gentleman to a manipulating and controlling man, but I didn't see it so clearly at the time.

"Oh, Lily," Michele's voice is soft as she takes my hand. "Keep going."

"We had a party at a nice hotel downtown to celebrate fifty years of business. Cocktail attire, catered food, dancing, open bar. We were supposed to go together. I waited for him to pick me up. I waited for almost two hours, and he never answered his phone or showed, so I went on my own. When I walked in, he was already there, his wife draped on his arm. Turns out, they were never getting a divorce, never even separated. I was just the other woman." The tears are flowing freely now, but Michele's tight grip gives me the strength to keep going.

"I didn't make a big scene, I didn't even confront him. But when his wife went to the restroom, I followed her in and told her everything. I told her how sorry I was but that he told me they were getting divorced and that I had been seeing him for the last two years. *Two. Freaking. Years.* She slapped me across my face so hard that I was bruised for a week, then stormed out, not saying a word to me. I slipped out of the hotel and cried the whole way home. When I got into work the next Monday morning, I was ushered into HR and fired. They said my performance wasn't up to their standards, when all of my reviews had been stellar. I called you three weeks after that. Sold my condo, bought this place, and made a deal with my editor for a book series so I could afford it all."

"What the fuck," she whispers. She shifts on the couch, her face is beet red, and eyes downturned.

"Here's where I need the advice. My publisher, Andrea, is the only other person who knows what happened. She thinks that I should sue for wrongful termination. I am so torn. I'm the one that was in the wrong. I saw the red flags and ignored them. I should have never gotten involved with a coworker, let alone one that wasn't verified divorced. I am so ashamed, and I don't ever want to face him or anyone else there. No one stood up for me. No one reached out to me. I was all alone." I set my shoulders, letting the anger of it all wash through me again. "But what if I do nothing, and he does it again? Management knew I shouldn't have been let go, but went with it anyway. There was a high turnover rate with women in the company, but I never put much thought into it. How many others have been taken advantage of or used, then fired when they realized or spoke up? I think I should sue, I'm just not sure I'm strong enough to stand up and speak up."

I know my voice is weak, my resolve already crumbling again. I can't stand up against a company of 'good old boys'. They will eat me alive in a courtroom, paint me as the scorned lover causing problems at work. My shame will be front and center for everyone to see. I hate cheating, absolutely despise it. Yet, there I was, the other woman for two damn years.

I finally get the nerve to turn to Michele, and the only clear emotion on her face is anger. I get it, I'm angry at myself for being so foolish, too. "Lily, I have a lot to say, but the first and most important is that this was not your fault. You were lied to and manipulated and that is on no one but him. Fuck that guy. As a woman, I can tell you for a fact that I have seen red flags after the fact and wanted to smack myself, but when I was in it, I didn't see them. You wanted to be loved, there's nothing wrong with that. He took advantage of your love. Can I ask how old he is?"

"Thirty-nine," I whisper.

"Old enough to know better and to know exactly what he was doing." Her words are harsh but true, and the cruelty there isn't aimed at me. She takes a large gulp of her wine, finishing it off before continuing. "I think that, as women, we often know what we want and what we deserve, yet we accept way below that. Not because we have to, or even because it's easy, but because it's expected. It's expected that we take what's offered, even if it's scraps, and then we're told to say thank you for it. We don't make waves and make noise, especially in a corporate setting because it's expected that we respect the men around us, even when we don't get that same respect back. And I'm sorry, but fuck that. Fuck the expectations. Fuck the scraps. Fuck the tiny dick prick that lied and cheated and abused his power, then tossed you aside like trash. You're more than that, Lily. So much damn more. You should be angry. You should be furious. You should rain down hell on every bastard there and walk away with your head held high. I think it's time they expect the blowback for their actions. That they be sued and fired and held accountable for being shit human beings. That's what I think." She wipes at the tears streaming down her face, while I stare at her open mouthed in awe. "Sorry, I cry when I'm angry," she mumbles.

"I think I love you," I squeeze her hand this time, but she pulls me into a tight embrace instead.

"I'm so sorry that happened, but I think you need to fight it. He deserves to pay," she says in my ear.

"And if you don't have the strength to do it on your own, then lean on us," Thoren's deep voice cuts through the night air. He looks like an avenging god, eyes dark and filled with fire, his fists clenched tight at his sides. I was so distracted with Michele we didn't see Shadow leave the porch or hear Thoren walk up.

"How much did you hear?" my voice trembles.

"Enough," he steps up to the porch and kneels in front of me. "I'm with Chele on this. Fuck that guy, and make him pay." He places one finger under my chin to bring my eyes to his. "Let us help. You are not in the wrong here, he was. Please believe that, and let us support you through your next steps."

His handsome face is blurry through my watery eyes, but before I can wipe them, his thumb is there doing it for me. The sweet action causes more tears to fall. These two beautiful souls who I hardly know, just heard my greatest shame. Here they are anyway, supporting me, comforting me, getting angry with me.

Thoren moves then, standing me up and taking my seat before pulling me into his lap. I try not to, but I lean in taking in his woodsy and clean scent while choking on my sobs. "I'm so sorry," I rasp out around them, but he just pulls me in tighter to his chest.

"You have nothing to be sorry for," Michele adds. "Thoren is right, and we are going to be here holding your hand through whatever your next steps are. We will support whatever your choice is, but I think we both hope it is to take their ass to the cleaners and get fuckface fired."

A month ago, I was asking how my life was turning out the way it was. What I had done so utterly wrong for it to be taking the turn that it was. I felt defeated, worthless, and utterly alone. One month down the road, and I am living in a dreamy town, pursuing my passion, all while being surrounded by new friends. I don't want to go back to where I was, but to be able to fully move forward, I need to face the past head on.

Thoren's hand runs up and down my back, his touch both soothing and searing. His other hand is wrapped in my hair, holding my head against him. His chest rumbles with his quiet whispers telling me that it will be okay, and that he has me now. I let his heat and strength soak into me, taking everything he is offering.

I never expected support from anyone except Andrea in this situation. In my mind, Michele would give me her opinion, but my confession would cause our friendship to drop off. Lasting friendships are not something I am familiar with. I'm not sure if it's my quiet nature, my straight and narrow pathways my parents set out for me, my lack of self worth, or even a mix of it all.

Having two people here that are making a conscious effort to have my back is shaking me to my core.

With my drying tears, I set my shoulders back, sitting up from where Thoren has me wrapped up in his strong arms. "Thank you. You're right, I'm going to get a lawyer and see what I can do." I stand, because as good as it feels to be in his arms, I am not in a place to be with someone again.

"We will help with getting a lawyer, if you want?" Michele's eyes cut to Thoren quickly before facing me. "We can find you the best, and we will stay involved as much or as little as you want."

"We have you, Lily," Thoren adds. "Whatever you need, we are here for you."

"I have some dinner for you, are you hungry?" I turn to Thoren, brushing away the last of the tears and changing the subject. I need to do something with my hands, or something to distract myself from the shame still washing through me. I appreciate their help, and I'll take it. I just need a moment to take a breath, and let it sink in that I really am going to do this.

"She was going to leave some dinner in your fridge," Michele cuts in before he can answer with a devious smirk on her face. "Isn't that sweet?"

Thoren's gaze locks on mine, a glimmer of something shining there, I'm just not sure what. "It's very sweet, but my appetite is gone right now. I really appreciate it though, and would love to take it home for later if that's okay?"

"Of course," I manage, sitting back down on the other side of him again. "How'd the SAR case go? Was everyone okay?"

"Yeah," he sits back against the couch, his arm stretching out behind me. "A hiker twisted her ankle pretty badly and couldn't walk back. Unfortunately, she's a trail runner and she was almost four miles in so it took us quite a while to find her and then get her carried back out. She's okay though, and the team did great."

"I'm glad she's okay," I watch Shadow meander over to Thoren and whine at his feet.

Thoren strokes my shoulder, "I better get her home. Thank you so much for taking care of her, Lily."

"Let me get your food before you go." The small couch empties as we all stand, vacating my sturdy deck.

"I better go too. Thank you for dinner, and we will talk more about what we can do to help this weekend, okay? I'll walk him out," Michele says, as they bring in the wine and platter from the porch, setting them on the counter. I inhale Michele's floral scent when she wraps me in a hug. I pass Thoren his food, unsure of the appropriate action with him.

"Have a good night, Lily," Thoren makes sure our fingers touch as he takes the food, sending goose bumps up my arm. Michele winks at me from behind him, heading to the front door.

"Goodnight," my voice sounds breathy as they head out the front, closing my door behind them.

I feel thoroughly lost, yet renewed all at once.

CHAPTER ELEVEN

thoren

I shut Lily's front door behind me, turning to find Michele leaning against her car with her arms crossed and a smile on her face. Shadow runs back and forth between us as I make my way over to her and lean against my truck that's parked next to her.

"What's that look for?"

"You'd be good for each other," she says simply. "I'm just not sure she's ready to be with someone."

"Her story tonight made that glaringly obvious," I mutter. "I'm going to fucking kill that guy."

I kick at the gravel beneath my boot. I had to leave her house before I started breaking things and scaring her. I'm furious, the anger coursing hot through my veins. Tyler deserves to pay, and I will ensure that he does. The tiny dicked fucker used her and lied to her for two damn years. Cheating is the one thing I will not tolerate, and by the disgust and shame written all over Lily's face, I would bet she feels the same. Yet, he put her in that position without her knowledge. I'm not mad at her, but I am mad. She probably needs someone to hold her and be by her side after that admission, but I can't be that person tonight. I need to go for a run. Or hit something. Preferably both.

"Put your hammer down, Thor. She's going to need you around after we crush this guy, so we need to help her do it legally. Might be the one time to use your brother."

A part of me hates that she's even bringing him up, but she's right. River has connections and sway that I will never have, and even though I try to never take advantage of his place in life, I will for Lily. Not that he will see it that way. He's always trying to use his money and connections to do more for our family, even though we continually refuse.

"Yeah, I was already thinking that. She's so pure, Chele. She watches my dog and makes me dinner, and she still hardly knows me. How could someone make her feel like less than she is?"

"The world is full of assholes. You and I both know that. She's special, that's for sure. Go home, eat that amazing dinner she made, and call me this weekend," she says, climbing into her car.

"Michele," I call, before she shuts her door. "I'll wait for her, you know? To be ready." Her smile is bright as she shuts her door before backing out and driving away. I open my passenger door and set the container on the seat before calling Shadow up to sit there, too. I shut the door, taking a moment to stare at the small cabin, marveling at how quickly this woman is worming her way into my heart. Then I hop in the truck and head for home where I can plan Tyler's demise.

Shadow is waiting dutifully by the door for me on Friday afternoon when I get off of work. Today was a shit day. I couldn't focus on anything but the anger still flowing through me. I know better than to let anger fester, so I change into shorts and head straight to the garage gym before I have dinner with my parents tonight.

Shadow sits on her mat in the corner, chewing on her bone, her eyes never straying far from me. She knows me the best, and she's seen me push myself too hard in here when I am upset. She was by my side when I was almost crushed, pushing my chest press, and when I almost passed out after maxing out my deadlift. I had a lot of anger to work out when Jen left; anger at her, at myself, at the world in general.

I know Shadow can feel that same tense energy radiating off me now. I am furious at the world again. Cheaters piss me off, and when I heard those words tumble out of Lily's mouth, it churned my stomach. I could feel the deep shame surrounding her, trying to drag her under. That whole situation is not her fault. He was the one in a position of power, the one manipulating and taking what should have never been his. He broke Lily, the woman who exudes light, kindness, and passion. The type of woman he could never deserve.

I finish my last set of squats, sweat dripping down my face and chest. My body still feels wound too tight, but my parents will be waiting on me, so I take a quick shower, load up Shadow, and head for their house. They live on the other side of town, which I am really starting to hate. I worry about them, not that they have given me a reason to. They're getting up there in age and have a lot of land they still care for. My dad was a police officer who retired five years ago, and my mom was a school counselor at the high school until I graduated. She retired then too, and now they have a large garden that they use to fill the local food bank and farmer's market.

Shadow knows exactly where we are as we pull into their long driveway. Her nose is pressed to the window, tail whipping me, ready to sprint out the moment I stop. She hops right over my lap and out of the truck the minute my door is open. The little shit sits right on their front mat and barks, knowing full well my mom will open the door with a treat in hand. The first time I brought her here, my mom showed me the treat container she bought and put on the entry table for her 'new baby'.

Sure enough, as my boots thud up the steps, my mom opens the door to a patiently waiting Shadow. Her wild black tail swishing back and forth is the only thing giving away her excitement as the rest of her sits still as a stone. My mom places the treat carefully on her nose and gives her ear a scratch before giving her the okay to take it. Shadow flips it off her nose, catching it midair and runs inside with it.

I shake my head, as my mom wraps me in a hug. "I still don't understand how you do that. I try at home sometimes, but she never waits for permission to eat it."

"It's a grandma thing," she shrugs, leading me into the kitchen. "Wash up and you can chop the veggies while you tell me about the SAR case this week."

"How do you always know everything?" I huff, washing my hands at the sink.

"That would be a mom thing. Be lucky I'm not asking you about the girl yet," she winks, moving to remove a dish from the oven to place it on the island. I swear, I never see my mom in town, yet she is always up to date on all the latest gossip. "Go get grandpa," she tells Shadow, opening the back door that leads to their garden.

I tell her about the rescue while we finish preparing dinner together. In my mom's true fashion, she gushes about how proud she is of me for leading a successful team. It would feel good, but it was an easy rescue, all things considered. I found where communication between the team was lacking, and what we need to focus on with our next training. The fact that we got Kelsey out of there and she's going to be fine is really the most important though.

My dad finally stomps his way into the house, dropping a kiss to my moms head on his way to the sink. They have a love most people dream about. It's not to say they haven't faced hardships, because they have, they've just loved each other harder through each one.

"Hey son," he claps my shoulder, leaving a dirt handprint behind. "Did I miss the inquisition about the girl?"

I roll my eyes lovingly, dispersing the plates and dishes on the table. "Nope, mom saved that conversation just for you."

We all take our seats, Shadow directly under my mom like always. "We just want to see you happy. That's all we've ever wanted for you and River, and I happen to think you have good love karma coming your way after everything with Jen."

I mumble around a bite of potatoes, "Is good love karma even a thing?"

"Probably," my dad answers. "River said her name is Lily?"

Of course it came from River. My mom has been pestering him about settling down and making her a real grandma for years. It's no surprise he pawned that attention off onto me.

"Yep, Lily bought Gary's old cabin. She's beautiful, kind, gentle, and loves Shadow. She isn't in a place to date right now, though. The last guy did a real number on her, and she's getting a lawyer involved. I was going to call Riv tonight to get the name of a good one."

Both my parents go still, shoulders stiffening as they sit up. "Anything I can help with?" my dad asks. "I can get a restraining order started tonight, just let me make a call."

"No, nothing like that dad. Plus, he's in Arizona, where she's from. Thanks though."

"Does she have the support she needs?" I give a warm smile to my mom, ever the counselor and silent protector.

"She has me, and Michele has taken her under her wing, too. Her parents are in Florida, and don't seem that involved with her."

"I always liked that girl," mom says about Michele, sneaking some food down to Shadow. The loud smacking of lips always gives her away. "You can bring Lily here for dinner. We can keep our mouths shut, but sometimes, it's good to just know people are around."

"Thanks, mom. I was actually going to ask if I can bring her next time anyway. I think she'd like to see your garden, and she writes those romance books you like."

"Oh lord, not another one," my dad grumbles. "Do you know how often I have to hear about what's happening in her books?"

I can't help but chuckle. I've heard my mom's ramblings many times over whatever she is currently reading. She gets fully immersed and invested in every book. My dad can gripe about it all he wants, but I know he likes to listen to her recaps. I wonder if Lily is the same. I'll have to ask her more about what her book is about, besides just baseball.

My mom waves her hand in my dad's direction, dismissing him. "We would love to have her here. Now, tell me more about what's going on. Can we help in any way?"

"She dated an older coworker who lied to her, took advantage of her, and then got her fired. It's a lot more in depth than that, but that's the gist. She's going to sue for wrongful termination though," I say, picking at my plate of food. "I would like to do a lot more than that."

Both my parents nod at the sentiment. If there is one thing that my whole family shares, it is the fierce protectiveness we feel for those we care about. My parents saw a lot of people get mistreated and neglected through their careers. They always used the walnut analogy with River and I growing up. How, in this world, it is important to have a hard exterior in order to allow others' words and actions bounce off of us, especially while standing up for others who may be missing a hard shell of their own.

With that hard shell, we needed to have a soft inside. An inside filled with empathy, compassion and love. A soft place to feel the way we felt, and to care for others and ourselves. River always preferred the tough shell, but I tried to be the perfect walnut that my parents were. It's why I feel so strongly about Lily's situation. I want to be the protective barrier for her to keep her from any more hurt, but also have waiting arms for her to seek comfort in.

"It's settled then," my mom breaks me out of my thoughts. "She will come with you next time. Now that we have covered your love life, has River told you anything about Vanessa? The only information we have gotten from him is her name."

Chuckling, I put my hands up in surrender at her meddling. "I'll ask for all the juicy details when we talk next, I promise."

"Good. Your mom bought Shadow three new bandanas last week. She needs an actual grandbaby, and soon," dad grumbles playfully.

"Oh!" My mom drops her fork, leaving the room and coming back with a bag of goodies. "I forgot about those. They were buy two, get one free. I had to get three of them, David. I also got some new treats but wanted to check with you first to make sure they were okay to give."

My mom pulls out a bandana with flowers printed on it, before passing me the bag to check the treats. She carefully ties it on Shadow's neck, then slips her another bite of food. Watching both my parents gushing over my dog and continuing to rib each other over the appropriate spoiling level of a dog, I am hit with a conflicting wave of grief and joy. I am so lucky to have parents who are so involved in my life and care so deeply, but it guts me that there are people like Lily who have no siblings and absent parents. I want her to feel the love and chaos that family brings. She deserves it.

We spent the rest of dinner talking about their garden, and what was growing well this year. The weather has been kind to them and it seems to be flourishing, much to their enjoyment. When our plates were empty and stomachs full, I helped my mom clean up while my dad threw on the sports channel to watch the highlights with my dog.

"Can I steal a few clippings from your lilac bush before I leave? They're Lily's favorite, and I told her about yours."

Mom stops putting the plates away, grabbing the scissors and handing them to me with a smirk. She places her hand over her heart, a twinkle shining in her eyes. "You've always been my softie. Never change that heart of yours, baby."

It's getting close to the end of season for the lilacs to bloom so I scour through the bush finding the best and most fragrant flowers. By the time I get inside with a handful, my mom is waiting with a small vase already filled with water for me. I say goodbye to my parents, promising to get the inside scoop on River's girlfriend and to bring Lily by as soon as I can. The heavy set of my shoulders feels lighter when I hop in the truck and head home.

When I pull down Alder Ave, I put my truck in park behind the trees at the end of Lily's driveway and walk the flowers to her door. Leaving them on her front mat, I knock on the door and run to the woods, hiding behind some trees. Staying put, I watch her open her door in a pajama set, a fuzzy sweater wrapped tight around her. She looks around before spotting the vase of flowers. The smile that takes over her face is enough to light me up for a week. Lily stays on the porch for a minute breathing in the flowers before she giggles to herself and steps back inside.

Shadow is impatiently waiting for me in the truck when I trudge back, and we head home for the night.

I change into lounge shorts, grab a beer from the fridge and splay out on the couch. Grabbing my phone, I tap River's name and wait for him to answer.

After the fourth ring, his loud voice answers, "If it isn't the god of thunder!"

"Har-har, dickbag. You know my hammer brings the thunder." I quip back.

"Gross, don't talk about your dick. How are things? You haven't called since your date last weekend."

We usually talk weekly, but it has been a minute. I hate asking my brother for things, and now I am about to ask him for two favors. "Things are going. I do want to catch up, but I also called for a reason."

"What's up?" His voice takes on a serious tone. We like to joke, River more than me, but he can change his tune quickly when necessary.

"Well, first, I want to bring Lily out for a game. I was hoping you could show her around the dugout and locker room or whatever to help her with her book?"

"Done, pick a day and let me know. I'll get good seats and take you guys to dinner after so she can see what it's like being in public with me and ask anything she wants. What's the next one because you sound too upset to be asking about a game."

"I need a lawyer. And not just any, I need the best. A woman if possible." I didn't ask Lily about this yet, but I think she would feel more comfortable being honest in detail with a woman. Someone who will be understanding and not run the risk of another man making her feel small. She didn't ask us to find her a lawyer, but this is one thing I can easily do to take off her plate.

"What trouble are you in? I don't have a game tomorrow, I

can be on the road in twenty," his voice is stern and there's a rustling in the background as he moves around his apartment.

"Not me, I'm fine, you can calm down. It's for Lily."

He's quiet for a moment on the other end before he breathes out, "Explain."

So I do. I tell him everything that I overheard her say and what happened to my knowledge. How upset she was, how angry I was, and that she agreed to get lawyers involved. I even told him I tried to Google the guy, but I don't know his last name, and I don't know which of the two major financial firms in Phoenix he works at.

River remains pretty silent through it all, grunting or hissing out a 'fuck' here or there. By the time I finish, he sounds as pissed off as I am about the whole situation.

"Kinsley DeWitt is your girl. I haven't worked with her, but one of the team docs has. Said she helped her through a defamation and harassment suit in a previous workplace. DeWitt is known for being a shark in the courtroom, but the doc said she was understanding and a girl's girl."

"Sounds like you know a lot about that situation," I needle him, poking for information.

"It's not like that, she's a good friend. She's the one who introduced me to Vanessa. Let me get in touch with DeWitt and have her reach out to you guys. I've got the fees covered."

I roll my eyes even knowing he can't see. "I don't need you to do that, I'm taking care of them."

He grunts in response. Besides Michele, River is the only one who knows I've been buying land and property since I turned twenty. First, it started as an idea to have a nice plot of land to retire on, then it turned into wanting to preserve the land and stop some commercial real estate. Now I buy a few properties here and there because it's a good investment and I can be a fair landlord to those that need it.

"So, now with that part done, I had dinner with mom and dad tonight," I move the conversation along.

"Fuck. I'm not getting married, I'm not having babies yet, and Vanessa is a very nice lady that I have been official with for about three months. That's all you get," he grumbles.

His summary makes me chuckle. Our parents will never change. We stay on the phone for another twenty minutes talking about life, work, and women. Between my conversation with my parents and the call with Riv, I feel a lot better about everything. I just need to let Lily know I might have found her a lawyer and convince her that she's doing it pro bono. When we end the call, my phone dings with a text.

LILY:

Thank you.

THOREN:

For…?

LILY:

The flowers. My whole cabin smells heavenly already.

My smile breaks free, and I get the urge to go over and smell it for myself. I haven't talked to her since yesterday evening besides a text to thank her for the incredible dinner. I just needed to clear my head and have a plan before I see her again.

THOREN:

That sounds nice. Someone must have been thinking of you. You busy tomorrow morning, say around 9:30?

LILY:

Nope, free as a bird.

THOREN:

I'm leading a group hike, Fremont Falls. Want to come?

The three dots pop up then disappear again. I wait only for her to leave me on read. I let Shadow out one more time, then brush my teeth and climb in bed. Right as I turn out my bedside lamp, my phone pings again.

LILY:

Michele and I will be there. Looking forward to it.

CHAPTER TWELVE

lily

Saturday morning I woke before my alarm, nervous energy thrumming through me. Not that a hike was something to be nervous about, but besides a thank you for dinner text and the surprise lilac delivery last night, I haven't talked to Thoren since Thursday. Michele sent me a text Friday, reminding me how brave and strong I am, and that she was thinking up the perfect revenge plan. Neither of those texts settled my nerves about seeing them though. What if they looked at me differently? Would there be pity or disgust in their eyes?

When I asked Michele if she wanted to go on the group hike with me last night, she jumped on board and said she would be at my house at nine to pick me up. That left three hours for me to sit in my feelings on the back porch and overanalyze everything.

I spent the first hour looking up corporate lawyers, but the majority looked like smarmy jerks and were out of my price range. I wasn't broke by any means. I had a full-ride scholarship for college, and I lived well within my means in Phoenix, saving a good chunk of my paychecks. On top of that, I sold my condo for almost double what I paid for this cabin and I was doing okay.

However, fighting a large corporate firm that could easily drag things out would drain all that saved money in an instant.

For the hour after that I wrote out a pros and cons list for getting a cheap versus expensive lawyer in the hopes of winning the case. I also wrote out all the things I was hoping to gain out of winning the case, since I absolutely did not want my job back. The last bit I wrote out was everything I could think of that would help my lawyer; my supervisors, instances where Tyler lied, and my performance reviews.

Once all of that was written out I felt marginally better, so I made a smoothie, took a quick shower, and got ready. I put on my favorite workout set, mauve leggings with a matching tank top, and laced my sneakers up. With my water bottle filled, I was ready to go by the time Michele parked out front. Thoren sent a text this morning letting me know I could leave my trusty hiking backpack at home since it was an easy trail. These events the Park Rangers did often had varying age ranges and activity levels.

Michele honked her horn with impatience as I locked up. "Hello, lovely lady," I slid into the passenger seat. "Thanks for going with me."

"I'm so glad you asked. I love an excuse to get out of the house, and I don't have a showing until this afternoon." She pulled out of my driveway before diving right into all her thoughts. It's one thing I really love about her; the ability to be so vulnerable and open with everyone. "So I haven't found you a lawyer yet, but I can guarantee that Thoren has. I did however, look up creative ways to torture people from afar. Do you happen to have his address? I think we start small with a glitter bomb, then slowly escalate from there. Maybe make a dating account for him and put his phone number on it. If you know enough about him we might even be able to get his water and power shut off."

I double over in laughter, trying to drag in breaths between hysterics. The grin on Michele is proud as punch. "You are diabolical and I love it. I think I'll just stick to the legal routes though. I did some searching for a lawyer this morning and I'm sure I'll find a good fit soon."

"Don't knock my ideas, two of those will punish his twit of a wife too, and I think that's fair game."

Green blurs past the window I'm fixated on as I try to hide my smile because she's not wrong. That just isn't who I am, even if sometimes I wish that it was. Tyler and his wife, Angela, deserve a bit of hell, although I do still feel bad for Angela. Would I have hit the woman who told me she was sleeping with my husband for two years… no. I could understand the desire to though, and maybe she was just as stunned and that's why she walked out.

Before long, we are turning into the parking lot with a small playground off to one side, a pavilion in the middle, and trails on the other. There's a group of about fifteen standing near the trail-head, which must be where we want to go.

"Shit," Michele mutters, getting out of the car. She's wearing running shorts with a pink tank top that molds to her porcelain skin. Her ample cleavage is covered but certainly not hidden, making her hourglass figure look even more like a goddess.

"What?" I whisper conspiratorially, rounding the front of her car.

"Sherry's here." She looks toward a leggy blonde in the tiniest set of shorts and a sports bra. She's practically attached to Thoren's side as he talks animatedly to the group in front of him. When she sees my confusion, she continues. "We went to school with her. She was the self-appointed 'it girl' and was every bit as fake then as she is now. She will also claw your eyes out to get to Thoren."

Glancing over to them again, it's clear Thoren is not giving her any attention. Despite her eyes being glued to him, he hasn't looked to her even once. Thoren's gaze drifts to our approaching forms, and his smile widens.

"You made it!" his voice rings out. He sends a wink our way. "You ladies look lovely. We are going to wait about five more minutes for any stragglers then we will be on our way."

Thoren squeezes past the group, walking over to us, Sherry hot on his heels. He looks delectable in shorts that hug his thighs, and a tee that is equally snug around bulging biceps. The forest that is inked there stands out in the sunlight. I don't miss the way he takes me in, tingles lighting up every inch of my skin that his heavy gaze touches. My cheeks are already turning pink and it has nothing to do with the blazing sun. Before he can say anything more, Sherry plants herself at his side again.

"Michele," her voice drips with fake cheer. "It's been a while. I don't think I've seen you in spin class at all this year. You know they have other classes, right? Ones that might be better suited for you."

My mouth drops open with the audacity of this chick. Michele may not have the same petite frame as us, but she is stunning with curves in all the right places. Curves I would kill to have, and her personality far outshines Malibu Barbie here.

"Yeah, having a thriving career, nights with friends, and being a home and business owner really keeps me busy. To each their own, right?" Michele quips back, not letting the snide remark phase her.

Thoren looks just as angry and taken aback as me, but recovers quickly, throwing his arm around Michele. "Plus, I've known you since we were kids and I think you are aging like a fine wine." He places a kiss on her head and she rolls her eyes, swatting him in the chest.

Sherry's lips purse, but she flips her hair over her shoulder and reaches for Thoren's arm. "I think it's time to go, don't want to fall behind."

He reluctantly follows after her, calling out to the group that we are about to leave for the hike. Before he gets to the front of the group though, he looks back at us with a sympathetic smile.

"Told you," Michele says under her breath as we move to the middle of the group and follow Thoren. "Don't worry, that man only has eyes for you."

For the next thirty minutes we all follow the easy path through the woods that leads to a small set of rapids in the river. Listening to Thoren point out different trees and plant life, while also telling about the history of Cedar Ridge, was more entertaining than I imagined. His love for what he does radiates into his every word, drawing you in.

It's rare these days to find someone who truly enjoys what they do for a living. I never felt that way working in finance. It was a good job, and a good company, or so I thought, and I got to use my skills, but that's it. It wasn't my passion, it wasn't even something that interested me. It was just a job that my parents were proud of that paid the bills. Writing is where my true happiness comes from. When a story comes together, when my fingers fly over the keyboard putting my thoughts into words, I know the smile on my face rivals Thoren's.

When we reach the rapids, he informs the group that we are going to hang out here for thirty minutes before making the trek back. A group of older ladies find a bench to sit on and chat, while a few couples meander near the river to take photos. That leaves Sherry, Michele, Thoren, and I. Michele subtly tugs at my arm to lead us to Thoren when Sherry sidles up to him once again. Her hand lands on his arm where it stays despite his flinch and grimace.

"Mike said he would be reaching out about a business deal this week. I peeked at his documents, there were a lot of zeros attached to his offer," she practically purrs.

Michele and Thoren bristle as we step up. I notice the gaze

they flick toward each other, but before I can ask what that's about, Thoren removes Sherry's hand and steps to my side.

"Sorry, I need to talk to Lily about something personal."

He guides me away from them, as Michele turns an icy glare on Sherry. "We need to talk about how private business negotiations are meant to be exactly that. Private."

Thoren's hand finds its way to my lower back as he leads me to a corner of the clearing near the river. He takes a seat on a large rock and pats the spot next to him for me. I want to tell him that his touch heats my blood and makes me feel wanted in a way I haven't been in my past, but I bite my tongue.

"I really do have something to talk to you about, but I would have lied either way. That woman is an absolute trainwreck and my walking nightmare. Her voice sounds like nails on a chalkboard and she can't think about anyone but herself."

His knees subtly spread bringing his leg to rest against mine, as he takes in the scene before us. I wait for him to keep going while soaking in the heat from his body. He left quickly after he heard me bare my soul on Thursday looking upset. A heavy sigh leaves his chest before he finally breaks the silence.

"First things first, I need to be honest about something. I saw my parents yesterday and talked to my brother. I kept your confidence with my parents, but they asked about you and are demanding you come to dinner soon. I didn't keep your confidence with my brother though," he looks at me with an apology written in his eyes.

I feel shame start to wash over me again. Not only is that one more person who I have to look in the eye, but I am humiliated because he is also doing me a huge favor. I want to be mad at Thoren, but I can't be. It's not like this will be a secret once I get a lawyer involved.

"I was so mad about it still, and I asked him for a lawyer recommendation. He wanted to know what the issue was and I told him most of it. I shouldn't have betrayed your trust like that and I'm sorry." He takes my hand, rubbing his thumb over my knuckles.

"He did put me in touch with a lawyer who I think would be amazing to you and for your case, and for that, I'm not sorry. I talked to her this morning and she's perfect. I told her that you are kind and nervous and need a lawyer against a previous employer who was a dick. She's also going to take you on pro bono, if you would like to go with her."

"What?" I squeak out.

That was information overload. He already talked to her? And she's not going to charge me? I have so many thoughts running through my head, I don't know where to start. He just solved my lawyer problem in one call, and again, acts like it's an everyday thing. Everything he has done for me has been monumental and he plays it off like it's nothing. I'm sure my face is conveying everything that I am feeling, but Thoren just knocks his knee against mine.

"I'll let you think on this, and we can talk when we get back. I have her information for you if you want it, and I really hope you do. She represented someone River knows who said she was understanding, patient, and kind while still being a terrifying badass in court. Just think about it, okay?"

He eases off the rock, leaving me alone with my thoughts. My mind is reeling with everything. I'm not upset that he told his brother, more surprised that between them, they found a lawyer so quickly. On top of that, a female lawyer who sounds exactly like what I was looking for. People tend to talk a lot, without the action to back it up. Thoren takes action without the flair, showing his heart with no ego involved. It might be the most attractive quality about him so far, and that is saying something.

I want to talk to the lawyer and see if we're a good fit. I make a note to get her information to call her on Monday and maybe schedule a meeting. I have a feeling the fact she would take me pro bono has something to do with River, and I need to find a way to thank him for that. That's when something Thoren said comes back to me. He talked to his parents about me, and they want to meet me. This friendship is starting to feel like more, but that thought doesn't scare me nearly as much as I expect it to.

Michele appears out of nowhere, her hand outstretched to help me off the rock. "Come on, we are heading back. I need all the dirty details on what he said to you because you sat here looking lost for fifteen minutes while he moped around."

I take her hand, clamoring down. We are at the back of the group, but I like the privacy for this conversation. "He found me a female lawyer who is going to take me on for free. And he said his parents invited me to dinner," I whisper, even though I doubt the old ladies cackling in front of us can hear.

"Good, I figured he would get that taken care of for you. David and Evelyn are the best around, you'll love them. Does this mean you guys are more than friends now?" she wiggles her eyebrows suggestively.

"I don't know what it means, but I can't deny there is something there. My head might not be ready, but my heart doesn't seem to have received the same memo."

The panic I expect to take over at admitting that out loud doesn't come. Getting over Tyler happened faster than I would have expected. I'm not sure if it was due to the circumstances, that I never truly loved him, or if my heart was always waiting for the other shoe to drop with him. It might have been a mix of all those things. Had I ever really been in love with him? He was my longest relationship by far, and after about a year we started saying 'I love you' to each other. I never felt an overwhelming sense of happiness with him though. The butterflies in your stomach, searing touches, and the sensation of not wanting to be apart were never there.

I clear my throat, asking something that I'm not sure I want the answer to. "Is there a past with Thoren and Sherry? She seemed to know something secret about him, and I can't get hurt again."

Michele laughs so loud half the group turns to look at us, including a glowering Sherry from right behind Thoren. "Absolutely not. He wasn't interested back in the day and he certainly isn't now. Her dad's company wants something from Thoren that he's not willing to give. Sherry works for her dad and just sees Thoren as a meal ticket if it were to go through."

That's cryptic. I want to ask how she knows all this, but if her or Thoren wanted me to know, they would tell me. At least now I don't have to picture Sherry's perfectly manicured nails scratching down Thoren's back the way mine want to. We finally crest the woods to the park where everyone disperses into their cars.

"Lily," Thoren calls out, jogging after us, as we make our way to Michele's car. "Would you like to go to lunch with me? We can talk more about what I said back there, and River just texted with some possible dates for us to go to a game that we can look over?"

Behind him, Sherry stands at her car with her arms crossed, a death glare pointed in my direction. I glance behind me where Michele is smiling from ear to ear. She unlocks her car, slipping my purse out and into my hands with a nod.

"Go ahead, I have a showing soon anyway. We'll talk more this week," she promises.

I turn back to a waiting Thoren as he grabs my purse, slinging it over his shoulder. "Are you in the mood for anything in particular or do I have free reign here?" His hand slips into mine as he leads me to his truck. We walk right past a huffing Sherry, but he pays her no mind.

"You're the local expert, surprise me. I haven't had the chance to explore the local restaurants much yet."

He pulls open the passenger door for me, ushering me in. Once I'm seated, he leans in and buckles my seatbelt for me, then places my purse on my lap. Those butterflies I just mentioned never having felt were taking flight in droves. When he hops in on his side and buckles up, he flashes me a heart stopping grin.

"I know just the place."

thoren

Lily's vanilla scent hit me when I buckled her into the truck, and now I am salivating over it. She smells warm, like freshly made muffins on an autumn day. She looks so pretty today, but then again, I always think she does.

"Thanks for coming today, and I'm sorry about Sherry. We grew up together and she's one of the volunteers on my SAR team. She's unique."

"She is certainly something," Lily mumbles under her breath.

Unique isn't the word I want to use, but I don't want to call her a bitch even if she was one today. Seeing her car pull up this morning sent a full body shiver through me in the worst way. I was Pavlov's dog and everytime she came near it put a grimace on my face and my balls shriveled up. There was a moment where I sensed a look of jealousy on Lily's face when Sherry put her hands on me and I hated it. I need to set the record straight because even if my blood heats at the thought of her being jealous over me, I don't play games like that.

"Just to clarify, there is nothing, has never been anything, nor ever will be anything between her and I," I tell her as I pull into a parking spot in town.

A blush travels up her cheeks as she unbuckles, changing the subject. "Michele told me that. Where are we going for lunch?" Dainty hands reach to open the truck door.

My hand snaps out to squeeze her knee before I can stop it. "Wait." I hop out and jog around to her side, opening the door for her. I love the way those pink cheeks are now a rosy red as I hold my hand out and help her down.

"Thank you."

"When you ride with me, you never open your own door, understand?" She sucks in a breath when I cup her face, but I don't move until she nods. "Good girl," I clasp her small hand in mine. "I thought we could go to a staple around here. Cedar Ridge has a Bavarian history, and what comes with that is beer and brats. Is that okay?"

Her face lights up as we walk into the outdoor seating area of Munchen Garten. "I've been wanting to eat here! You have to tell me what to get on my brat like a real local."

"Do you trust me?" I seat her at a small picnic table.

"Yes." Her confident reply makes me preen.

"Okay, I'll be right back."

I wait in line at the ordering window, ready to blow her mind with the best beer and brat combination she will ever have. Today is turning out to be amazing. I got DeWitt on the phone this morning and she was everything River promised. Understanding and kind, but with a bit of an edge to her. She agreed to tell Lily that she would be working pro bono and send me the bill, so that was a huge bonus. Then I got to do one of my favorite parts of my job, and now here I am having lunch with Lily.

When the line clears, I place our order and wait for them at the next window. I ordered us pork brats with apple cider sauerkraut and a crisp pilsner on the side. By far the best things on the menu in my opinion, and all of it is made locally.

With food and beer in hand, I walk straight to our table. Lily's eyes widen when I place hers in front of her and she sees the size of the sausage. She digs right in, taking a monstrous bite without testing if she might like it first.

My dick stirs watching her wrap her pink lips around it, and all the blood rushes south when that's followed by her shoulders sinking into a low moan. *Fuck.* Watching sauerkraut drip onto her chin should not be turning me on like this. Reaching for my beer, I drink down a few gulps, trying to think of anything but the show in front of me.

"This is amazing," she says after swallowing her bite. "Thank you, Thoren. This might be the best sausage I have ever had in my mouth."

Beer flies from my mouth as I sputter, trying to remember how to breathe. I grab a napkin from the table, wiping my face and the mess I made, coughing up the rest of the beer. The tips of my ears feel hot as I face Lily who looks beyond proud of herself for that comment. I raise an eyebrow at her, but she just shrugs it off.

"You were quiet over there, not even touching your food yet. I thought I would perk you up," she giggles.

"It perked something up."

She changes the subject quickly. I like that she's getting bolder with her words, but that bravery never seems to last long. "I thought about the lawyer. Thank you for finding one for me. I would like to talk with her, and maybe meet with her. Is she local?"

"She's in Seattle. River sent me his home game schedule for the month, maybe we can kill two birds with one stone. Go to his game and you can meet with Kinsley DeWitt?" I slide my phone from my pocket and open our text thread. "I'm sending you her phone number and the home schedule. When you call her, see if there are any of those dates where she could meet with you, and we can go from there."

I was hoping that it would work out this way. I want to be there for her through all of this. This isn't something she should have to go through alone, and I want to protect Lily. She needs a safe harbor, someone to hold her and give her strength when things get tough. I don't want her to have to see the lawyer alone, and this way I can be there if she needs me.

"Thank you, for all of this. The lawyer, helping me with my book, going to Seattle with me, being my friend. It all means so much to me," she says, placing her hand on mine.

I turn my hand over to lace our fingers together. She keeps using the friend word, but as I let my thumb glide over the sensitive skin inside her wrist, I watch the goosebumps travel up her arm. There's a connection between us and I know she feels it just as much as I do.

We finish our lunch, sipping our beer and watching people shop. I collect our trash when we finish, throwing it away as we walk back onto the street. I'm not ready to give up my time with Lily yet, so I put my hand on her lower back and steer her to the store next door.

"Want to do a little window shopping? Explore some of the best shops in town?"

"Yes! I've been dying to go to the hat shop, and I looked up the pet store that I really need to go to."

"Lucky for you, both are down the road. Hat shop first?" I ask, holding the door to it open for her. It's a ridiculous store, but it's beloved by locals and tourists alike. It has every hat you can think of, from local baseball caps to ones with rubber chickens and spinning umbrellas. Lily goes through every section of the store trying on the ones she finds delightful. She turns to me every time asking how ridiculous or crazy she looks, but all I can focus on is the light in her eyes and the ease of her laughter. Plus she's cute as fuck in every single one of them.

"Please, oh please, put this on," she begs, holding out a purple fuzzy cowboy hat that is at least three feet tall and three feet wide. It's so big she can't lift it up to my head, but I oblige and slip the thing on. It's not even fully seated on my head before she's doubled over in laughter, tears leaking from the corners of her eyes. "You have to let me get a picture," she wheezes out between bursts of more laughter.

I plop a hat with fake dreads coming out of it on her head, and tell her she can only have a photo if she's in it with me. My hat is so big we can't fit it in a selfie, so we ask another shopper to get one of us. I gently place my hand on Lily's hip and pull her into me for the photo. She's stiff at first, but as soon as her back touches my chest, she melts into me.

"You better send me that picture," she says as we put our hats back on the shelves and head to the next store. I peek at the photos they took and send the one of us both smiling at the camera to her. "Ooh, can we stop at Cedar and Sage? I bought a candle from there when I first moved here and it's almost burnt out."

I follow her into the small boutique as she heads straight for a table of local items in the back, including candles. I have to admit, it smells nice in here, so I ask Lily to pick one out for me. I keep my home clean, but Shadow likes to roll outside, so a candle can't hurt to fix the dog smell.

Lily picks out some candles, refusing to let me pay since I bought us lunch. The girl behind the counter has red rimmed eyes, and looks like she hasn't slept in days. I try not to stare and make her feel worse, but Lily shocks me by asking her about it.

"It's Amber, right?" The woman nods, continuing to ring her up. "I had to come back and get some more of these candles that you sold me last month. You were so kind to me that day, and helped me get some little gifts for my realtor. Can I, umm… can I repay that kindness by giving you a hug?"

Amber looks up at Lily, her eyes glassy. She stares at her open mouthed for a moment, but instead of replying, she walks out from behind the counter. Lily immediately wraps her in a hug, rubbing her back as the woman's shoulders shake slightly. I glance around, but we are the only ones in the store, so I take a few steps back to give them a moment.

They stay in the embrace for a few minutes, talking to each other in hushed voices. When they finally separate, they both wipe their eyes, then go to their respective sides of the counter like nothing happened. Lily thanks her, pays, and we walk out. We walk down the sidewalk in silence and I can feel a heavy weight on her shoulders. Before we get to the pet store, I lightly grab her waist and move her against the storefront behind her. My body is hovering over hers, giving her the space to express her feelings without prying eyes.

"Are you okay?"

Her bottom lip trembles, but her voice remains strong. "Her mother had a stroke this week, and the recovery is not looking good. She seems so heartbroken. I don't do well when others are suffering."

Her empathy to a total stranger is astounding, and ridiculously attractive. I can't imagine if my mom had a stroke right now. I make a mental note to ask my mom to stop by there this week and see if there's something she can do. She loves setting up meal trains, and last year, I found out she has been visiting people in the hospital with long term stays that don't get visitors. Apparently she's been doing it for years, she just didn't want to make a fuss about it.

Lily reminds me of my mom in that way, and that thought secures her grip on my heart a little more. I wrap her in my arms, soaking in her vanilla scent again. "That is horrible, but I think what you did today made a big difference. What did you say to her?"

"I told her that I recently discovered how comforting a hug

can be, and while I can't do much, I can give her that. It took you and Michele constantly giving me physical reassurance for me to realize how touch starved I have been in my life. Your small acts of hugs and a hand squeeze startled me at first, but have turned into a sense of solace for me."

That confession brings an ache back to my chest. I was raised in such a loving household that I don't even register touch half the time. I want to be the place where she heals, the place where she gets everything that has been missing from her life. I take the bag of candles from her when we separate and grab her hand to lead her to the pet shop. "What do you need from here?"

"I wanted to get one of those purple dragons for my place. I really love having Shadow over, but I feel bad that she doesn't have toys."

She grabs a basket on our way in, and within fifteen minutes, it's filled with toys, treats, and a water bowl. We are in the aisle with kitschy things when Lily squeals with delight.

"Can I get this? Oh, please, let me get this. I know she's not really my dog, but I feel like I have some parental rights here. I mean, we do share joint custody sometimes."

I turn to see the set with a coffee mug that says 'World's Best Dog Mom' and a bandana that says "I Woof My Mom". I have to admit, it's cute and Shadow has grown to love bandanas at the rate my mom buys them for her.

"I think we need to ask your lawyer to draw up something official. You know, stating that you have rights to a minimum of one Shadow filled day a week," I joke, adding it to her basket. "Shadow will love it."

The light is back in her eyes as we walk to the register. I slide my card to the cashier before Lily can, drawing a scowl from her. I don't care, I like taking care of her. Plus these things are for my dog. *Our dog.* We spend another hour strolling through town, popping into shops here and there, just enjoying each other's company.

Eventually, we make our way back to my truck where I buckle her in again. Jake might be onto something with his kink, because knowing Lily is tied down and safe in my truck gets my blood pumping.

"I had fun today. I enjoyed watching you work. Your love for your job is palpable, and I learned a lot. Thank you for inviting me and showing me around town."

I feel hyper aware of her presence beside me. The soft slope of her nose, the tiny almost imperceptible kiss of freckles there. The way her eyes look a lighter shade of blue when she is happy and like the dark depths of the ocean when she's upset. The fact that she likes what I do, even if it isn't a fancy job that will never make me wealthy, makes me inherently happy. I like everything about this woman, and I would happily spend my days in her presence no matter what we are doing.

"I'm glad you could come. Are you upset with me? For telling River?"

"I'm not. I was in the moment, but then I thought about it and that's not fair. If this lawsuit goes to court, it won't be a secret anymore. Plus, he helped you find a lawyer so I can't be upset at that. I don't see it as you betraying my trust, like you said. I never told you that you couldn't say anything. I am more embarrassed and ashamed than anything when it comes to telling others."

"You shouldn't be. He was rightfully pissed for your sake, just like I was. We both hope you and DeWitt take the bastard down. He's really excited to meet you though, and I promise he won't bring up anything but baseball."

When I drive up to her house, she waits for me to open her door which makes my dick stir again. I've picked up on a possible praise kink with her, so I decide to test it again. I walk her to the door, and as she unlocks it, I gently tug her waist to turn her toward me.

"You are brave, facing the demons in your past, and I am so proud of you. Lily, you are such a genuine soul and I love every moment I get to spend with you. Let me know when you call DeWitt and the date you guys decide on for the game and meeting, okay?"

Her breathing turns slow and shallow, her eyelids heavy over stormy blue eyes. Her perfect lips part on a soft exhale, "Okay."

A small smile plays on my lips at her reaction. I was absolutely right. Tucking her hair behind her ear, I place a gentle kiss on her forehead, "Have a good night, Lily."

My boots crunch on the gravel back to my truck where I wait until she is locked in her cabin before backing up and heading home. The short drive fills me with satisfaction that she is so close. Shadow greets me at the door, her tail wagging a mile a minute.

"Hey my girl, how was your day? Sorry I was gone so long, I was with Lily. Yeah, your other favorite human," I talk to her as I give her a full body rub down. Should I be embarrassed that I talk to my dog like she's my kid? Maybe, but I'm not.

Shadow was kind of my savior when Jen and I broke up. She was just a little squirt, and she only met Jen a few times, but she kept me busy and distracted after so I couldn't wallow. Lily is the first woman Shadow has spent time with besides my mom, and they both got attached quickly. I worry that one day Lily might leave our lives and Shadow will feel the loss as deeply as I will.

I push that thought from my mind, instead focusing on the fact that today she let me hold her. She let me wrap her up in my arms, and hold her hand, securing that nothing has ever felt so right. Her small body fit well against mine. She has to feel the strings pulling us together, that everything feels like it's falling into place when we are near.

Seeing her be so genuine and selfless, so utterly and unapologetically herself today was the highlight of my week. She let herself feel all her emotions out in the open which just made her more endearing. On top of that, she has had a rough week and still felt more for a stranger than for herself, taking the time to make her feel better.

That is something in all my years of knowing Jen that I never once saw her do. Her feelings and what was happening in her life were always at the center, just the way she liked it. I didn't realize how much I disliked that about her until I watched Lily today. Jake and River tried to tell me how self-centered she was, constantly asking me what the last thing she did for me or to support me was. I never listened because I liked taking care of her. I didn't think I needed someone to take care of me back.

Seeing Lily care for a stranger, my dog, and even me is changing that perception. Maybe it was just Jen's care that I didn't desire, or maybe it was that I knew she wasn't capable of putting others before herself. But now, I crave Lily's attention and time. I want her to put her focus on me, with quiet mornings drinking coffee together and making meals together. I know what that feels like with her now, and I'm not willing to let it go.

lily

I soak up the warm sun on my small balcony, watching the wind blow through the trees. I let my thoughts wander to yesterday, focusing on Amber, Sherry, and my potential lawyer. In between all of that, I let myself be consumed by thoughts of Thoren.

Every time I think about how much my life has changed recently, I can't help but consider calling my parents. I want them to know what is going on in my life. More importantly, I want them to be proud of me and to be actually interested in what I'm doing. The last text I sent to them said I was moving to Washington, asking if there was a good time for me to call. My mom responded by asking what job I had gotten here and when I replied I was pursuing writing full time, I never heard back from them.

My phone sat heavy in my hand, my thumb hovering over my dad's contact icon. I debated taking the plunge and just calling, but decided against it. If they wanted to be in my life, they would make the effort. Instead, I click on Andrea's name. I know it's Sunday, but she's always working and willing to take my call.

"I'm important again," her cheery voice comes through the line.

"Oh, hush, we just talked two weeks ago."

"Too long, if you ask me. Good timing though, I was just going over cover artist options for your book and was going to send them to you. Swap me to video and we can go through these together."

See, always working. I transfer to video as her smiling face overtakes the screen. She's always polished, a full face of makeup, with a silk blouse and slicked back pony. I, however, have a nest of hair piled on my head, not an ounce of makeup on, and a coffee stain on my shirt.

"Okay before we get into the cover options, how's the book coming? Did you meet with the baseball player yet? Oooh, light-bulb! Can we use him as a cover model? Oh my god, I looked him up, women would go feral over him in his tight baseball pants with no shirt," she rambles like this is already a done deal.

"Absolutely not. Nope. Not happening. He is already doing so much for me and I will not ask that of him. I'm a little over a third of the way complete. I'm meeting with River soon. He found a lawyer to go against Tyler that I'm calling tomorrow. The hope is to meet both of them on the same visit to Seattle. Plus, I was thinking of going illustrated for this cover."

The thought crossed my mind for half a second to ask River to model for the cover, but I don't want to take advantage of people, and the more River continues to do for me, the less I want to use that. That mindset only got deeper engrained when Tyler used me, and now I was hypersensitive to everything I asked of others. My mom harped it into me from a young age that you never use anyone's status or overstay your welcome. She ensured I knew I was to make my own success to be able to offer others, specifi-cally a man. I believe her exact words when she decided on my majors for me in college were, *As a woman, you should be seen and not heard, and your successes should speak for themselves.* She didn't seem to see the misogyny and contradicting nature of her thinking though. *It's how women should be raised, Lily. To honor their father and mother in preparation of honoring their husband.*

I honored Tyler, and look where that landed me. I can stand on my own two feet with my career, yet that still isn't enough for her. It's not a career she can proudly wave in front of her friends and our family, so no matter how successful I become, it will always be an embarrassment to her. It's the same thing Tyler told me when I finally admitted to him that I was an author on the side. *You write porn Lily, that's not an accomplishment.*

Andrea lets out a long whistle, "There's a lot to unpack there. First, I am so damn happy you are taking action against him and that company. That's a hard step and you're doing it. I hope you burn that place to the ground. Back to the book cover, though… illustrated and not a sexy man… can you at least sneak a picture of him for me when you meet him?" she jokes, but I hear the seriousness behind it. "How are you feeling about the book so far? I have been beyond thrilled with the chapters and was going to send back a few notes this week."

"I'm not commenting on the creepy photo taking. I am really happy with where the book is going. I think this might be my best book yet, and with River and Thoren's help, I think it has the potential to be a bestseller." I want to be humble, but the words have been flying from my fingertips lately. Having an inside look into the professional baseball world will draw my readers in even more. "Now, let's look at those cover artists."

We discuss the different style options, prices, and availability, ultimately deciding on a newer illustrator with incredible skills. I explained what I was picturing, and Andrea was fully on board with it. With that conversation behind me, I researched everything I could find about Kinsley DeWitt. From what I found, Thoren was right. She is a beast in the courtroom and has a history of defending women in the workplace. I still can't believe that he found her and she's willing to take me on pro bono, but I know better than to look a gift horse in the mouth.

When the sun sinks behind the trees, the rays of light creating hues of orange and pink, I realize I've spent the entire day on my balcony. Tomorrow I will get back on the productivity train and go for a walk, paint, and call the lawyer. I should probably do a quick whole house clean too, and make a grocery list. The notebook that lives on my little side table is in my hand in no time as I write out my to-do list for tomorrow. My phone pings in my lap, but I ignore it until my list is complete.

THOREN:

You still being a slug?

He texted me this morning asking if I was enjoying a porch coffee. It was the first morning in a while I hadn't, but my bed was just too comfortable to leave, so I told him I was hibernating for the day.

LILY:

Haven't moved in 4 hours.

THOREN:

How did I know? When you do finally move, check your front porch.

That got me to leave my post. Did he come to my house and I didn't even notice? I fling open the balcony door and skip down the steps to my front door, where a plastic bag awaits me. I glance around as I grab it. Thoren is nowhere to be found, but I'm starting to like that he leaves gifts on my porch. Inside, I put the bag on my counter, pulling out warm containers. There's a water bottle filled with pale pink liquid, a container with a roasted sweet potato, and one that holds grilled chicken strips with what looks like a mango salsa topping. My phone pings again beside me.

THOREN:

I discovered I don't own to-go cups that won't spill. The water bottle has a rose and chamomile tea in it. My mom's favorite.

I don't even know what to say. He knew I was having a reset day, so he made me dinner. I have never felt so seen or cared for in my life. My parents never took rest days. They said it was lazy and set a bad precedent. When I allowed myself one, I was met with disappointment. Yet here Thoren was, bringing me food with zero judgement.

LILY:

Thank you, it all looks and smells amazing. How'd you sneak it over?

THOREN:

There was no sneaking, Shadow and I just dropped it off on our way out for a run. Enjoy your night, Lily.

Crap. I really didn't think I was ready for another relationship, but Thoren is no ordinary man. He came out of nowhere, throwing around green flags like they were beads at Mardi Gras. I didn't listen to the red flags from Tyler, and I learned the hard way from that mistake. Tyler taught me not to take a man's words at face value, yet here I am, trusting Thoren. He also spoke with words and actions, which is something my dad always talked highly about when I was a kid, telling me *The words of another means nothing without the actions to prove it. Watch the way a man treats you and those who can do nothing for him, meisje, and you will know if his words hold weight.* Thoren's words held their weight. Hell, half the time he didn't even use words, just actions. His actions tell me he's a good man, who in just a month's time cares deeply for me already.

Those feelings were mutual. I want to have a closed off heart, one that is surrounded by impenetrable walls to keep me safe. The tattered organ in my chest seems to beat easily around him though. His soft smiles, the way he always finds a way to touch me in the most reassuring of ways, his subtle dominance in keeping me protected. He stokes a fire inside of me just by being himself. Maybe I need to let myself feel what my body and heart are clearly craving from him.

I carry the food and tea to my small table and dig in. The man can cook, and I'm starting to think there's not much he can't do. He has the body of a Greek god, he can renovate a house, fix my deck, cook amazing meals, and he's selfless and loves his family. I never stood a chance against him.

I send off a thank you for the incredible dinner and retreat upstairs. I may have done nothing today, but I'm mentally exhausted at just the thought of the phone call with the lawyer tomorrow. My hope is she will be okay with a brief explanation so I can tell the full story to her in person when we meet. I don't want to recount it all on the phone and again when we are together.

Since moving here, I have allowed myself time to reflect and rest when my body and mind call for it. I never realized how much one day of reprieve could have such a major impact on my stress level and outlook. I don't think I can ever go back to a rigid corporate schedule with no 'me time' after this.

After an early bedtime, I rose with the sun this morning. With coffee and notepad in hand, I reclaim my usual morning routine on the back porch to start on my grocery list. I only have milk written when a rustling in the woods and Shadow's telltale woof interrupt me. She comes barreling onto the deck and straight to my feet, waiting for pets.

Her furry face, floppy ears, and tongue hanging out make my entire morning, but it gets even better when Thoren steps up onto the deck with his morning mug of coffee. Much to my disappointment, he has a shirt on this time, but his work uniform of dark green utility pants and a green shirt sitting tight over his broad chest is just as drool worthy.

"Morning," he says nonchalantly as he takes a seat next to me. "Did you sleep well?"

I grin into my coffee as I bring it to my lips. "Good morning, neighbor. I did, did you?"

"I slept wonderfully." He leans back on the outdoor sofa, stretching his free arm out behind me. He smells good, his crisp woodsy scent blending with the morning dew around us.

"So is this our thing now? You two hooligans showing up to drink our coffee together?"

He takes a long sip, not dropping eye contact. "Do you want it to be?"

I think for a moment, tapping my finger on my chin. It certainly starts my day off right, seeing both of their smiling faces. Plus if he's going to be in this uniform for me to drool over… yeah, I could get used to mornings like this.

"I wouldn't mind it. What happens if I'm not up?" It's not even seven, and there are days I may not drag my butt out of bed on time to do this with him before he leaves for work.

"Shadow seems to know. She didn't run to you yesterday and you said you weren't out here. Today, however, she raced over here the moment I opened my back door."

I peek down at my favorite girl, rolling around on the deck and chewing on a leaf she found. My chest squeezes at the sight.

She seems to be as in tune with me as Thoren is. Having her here today would make things easier knowing she's by my side.

"Can she stay with me today?"

His boot slides out to nudge her lightly, "You good with that, Shadow?"

Shadow lets out a small bark, then moves to sit in front of the back door. We both chuckle, taking that as a yes. All three of us enjoy the quiet of the morning while Thoren's hand behind me plays lightly with a strand of hair, sending chills throughout my body. The slightest touches from him send heat to my core, and the smug look on his face tells me he is well aware of it.

"I have to head to work," he finally says. "You ladies have a good day. And call DeWitt, I promise you'll be glad you did. You've got this." He squeezes my shoulder before getting up and giving Shadow some head scratches. I watch him walking back through the woods to his house again. Like I said, I never stood a chance.

Shadow and I head inside when my coffee is empty and I trade out her bandana that has pine cones on it out for the new one I bought her. I show her the little basket in the living room corner that I put all her new toys in. While she takes her time dragging out every toy and examining them, I finish taping off the rest of the house and paint the first layer.

It goes fairly quickly since the cabin is such a small space, and before I know it, it's lunch time. I make a sandwich for myself, giving Shadow some lunch meat and a piece of cheese. After we have eaten and cleaned up, I slide out my phone with shaky hands. It's now or never. I sit on the couch with Shadow next to me for moral support and make the call to Kinsley DeWitt.

I spent thirty minutes on the phone with her, delighted to find Thoren was correct. She is exactly the person I need in my corner for this, and she was so kind. I told her the condensed basics of the scenario with Tyler and she got to work. We decided on meeting Wednesday afternoon of next week where she would have a list of all our options moving forward. She said I could email the details if it was easier on me, or go over it all in depth next Wednesday. I decided on emailing, and that alone took the burden of saying what happened out loud again.

I couldn't believe how easy it was talking to her. She reminded me of Michele in the way her feminine rage came out over him lying and me losing my job because of it. Getting to work with her is the best case scenario.

With that problem behind me, I finished writing out my grocery list and planned out a dinner to make for Thoren and I this evening. Shadow whined at the door as I put my shoes on, so I let her pile into Marge with me for the drive into town. I made sure to leave the windows down and park in a shady spot while I flew through the grocery store faster than ever before.

Once we got back home, I put the groceries away, enjoying the breeze wafting through all the open windows due to the paint drying. The day is too nice not to take advantage of, so Shadow and I ran back to Thoren's for her leash and harness. It felt really good after my lazy day yesterday, so when we got back home, I decided to do a pilates workout on the back deck. My stressful day was turning out to be anything but. With another hour before I needed to start dinner, I painted a second layer on my walls. The cabin was looking less and less dingy and more like my own every day.

Needing to wash the sweat and paint from my skin, I hopped in the shower, trying to ignore the fact another tile was falling off. I kept the bathroom door open since I painted the bathroom walls today, too, and I didn't know if the steam would ruin anything. Shadow scared the crap out of me twice by sticking her snout through the curtain to check on me, but I liked her company anyway.

With a fresh set of running shorts and a tank top on, I meander into the kitchen to start on dinner. I sent Thoren a text asking if he could pick Shadow up on his way home. That way, he can decide if he would like to stay for dinner, and if not, he can take some home. I decided on homemade pizza, one of my comfort foods. I top one with pepperoni and the other with sausage and peppers.

By the time Thoren is knocking on my door, I have one on the cooling rack and one in the oven. I surprisingly beat Shadow to the door, but she's busy playing with her new purple dragon. I open the door wide, inviting him in.

"Hey Lily, how was your- oh my god, what is that incredible smell?"

A small chuckle escapes me, "I made pizza. Would you like some? You can eat here or take it home if you don't want to stay."

His imposing body steps into my space, forcing my body against the wall. I crane my neck to look up into his hazel eyes. One of his hands settles on my hip, the other on the wall above my head, sending heat to my core.

"I want to stay," he says with a gruff tone that rocks straight through my body to my suddenly wet panties.

"Okay," my voice comes out barely more than a whisper.

I try to blink out of my lustful haze and move past him, trying not to rub on him like a cat in heat. In close proximity, the heady amber scent is stronger than the juniper. Thankfully, my oven timer pulls me back to focus and I step around him to remove the second pizza.

"The walls look nice. Can't even smell the paint over the pizza," he comments while washing his hands in the kitchen sink.

"Thank you, I did them today. They should be almost dry, but still be careful of where you touch."

I cut the pizzas into the best slices that I can manage and pull out two plates, pointing to the fridge where I have beer, water, and wine. It's not lost on me how domestic this is, how easily we float around each other in the kitchen again. "How was work today?"

He scrubs a hand down his face, breathing in a heavy sigh. "Long. Jake gave his notice, so I'll help cover shifts until we find a replacement. Did you have time to call the lawyer today?"

I can't keep the relief out of my voice. "I did, and you were right. She's incredible. She said she can meet next Wednesday afternoon. River has a home game on Thursday. Is that something you can make work?"

His face lights up as his shoulders relax. I know he thought I was going to chicken out on calling the lawyer. I feel bad that he has even more responsibility on his shoulders at work now and I'm asking him to take time off with little notice. He doesn't seem to feel nearly as bad though.

"That's perfect, I'll call Riv tonight and let him know. I already gave my boss a heads up that I might need a few days off soon. I haven't taken a vacation day in a long time, plus I have SAR training again this weekend, so I am due for some days off."

We take a few bites of our pizza while Shadow begs beneath us. Another green flag to add to Thoren's ever growing list is that he can sit in the silence with me. Tyler always had something to say, which inevitably led to talking badly of others or complaining about things constantly. I know Thoren had a long day; it's written all over his tired face. Still, he's sitting here enjoying dinner with me and not one negative thing has left his mouth.

When our plates are about empty, my brain goes into planning mode. "Will you be staying with River when we go? If not, I can get you a hotel room with me. It's the least I can do. We can take Marge and I'll pay for gas and all our food. Is there anywhere out there that you would like to go that we might have time for?"

His shoulders shake as he looks at his plate, shaking his head. "You can't stop, can you?"

"Stop what?"

"Planning. Being prepared for anything and everything." His

eyes catch mine when he looks up. "When was the last time you had the chance to sit back and enjoy something?"

I think about it for a moment, "When you took me hiking."

His grin is downright devious. He pulls out his phone and starts typing out some notes before putting it back down on the table. "Okay, then it's settled. I am planning everything. You pack your bag and be ready for me Wednesday morning at nine. Oh, and who the hell is Marge?"

thoren

The day is finally here, and I am beyond ready for it. I dropped Shadow off with my parents, packed my bag, and planned everything for the next two days with Lily. The last ten days sucked, filled with working overtime, a search and rescue case on Thursday, and training on Sunday. Lily was a godsend through it all. She spent most of her days with Shadow in tow, left pre-made meals in my fridge for my late nights, and still was up early to spend a few quiet minutes on her deck with me each morning before work.

We have gotten ourselves into a routine without even realizing it, and I hope it doesn't stop. Next week, Jake's replacement is set to start, so hopefully my schedule will calm down and I will have more free time to spend with her. That is a thought for later, though, because I am about to pick up my girl. I stopped in town on my way back from my parents' place to pick up a coffee and muffin for Lily. I also had a small gift waiting in the passenger seat from my brother.

She must be just as ready for this day as me because she is waiting on her porch with her bag before I can even get the truck in park. I jump out to open the back door, taking her bag and adding it next to mine on the back seat. Moving to the passenger door, I open it and hold out my hand to help her in. Her fingers wrap around mine as she steps into the truck when she sees the bag on the seat.

"What's this?" she asks, moving it to her lap as I lean over, buckling her in. Her warm vanilla scent is subtle today, warming me from the inside out as my thumbs brush over her thighs.

"A gift from my brother for tomorrow. There's also a coffee for you, pick either one, and a bag of muffins behind you," I add before closing her door and climbing into the driver's seat.

She picks up both coffees, reading the labels for a white chocolate latte and a caramel latte. I think she's going to choose the white chocolate because last week she talked about finding that flavor creamer in the store. If not, though, I got caramel because I know I've seen that flavor in her fridge.

Like I figured, she puts down the caramel and hums as she takes a sip of the white chocolate. "Thank you, this is delicious. Can I open the present now?"

"Sure," I respond, reaching back to move the little brown bag with muffins to the center console in case she wants one later. "He asked if you had one, then sent this the next day."

She carefully removes the tissue paper from the bag, setting it next to her. In true River fashion, he sent it already wrapped in a nice bag with a card and everything. Lily pulls out a Rainiers jersey with my brother's number and last name on the back. It's an authentic one, and he added a sweatshirt with the team logo as well. I guessed her size for him, so I hope they fit.

"These are so cool! You both have done so much for me. I'll never be able to repay you for all this. It's too much," her voice slowly tapers off.

I reach over, giving her knee a squeeze. "Kindness doesn't have to be repaid. We are doing these things because we want to and because we can. Now drink your coffee and put on some music. We have three hours to kill."

I'm not going to give her time to argue. If I want to take care of her, then I'm going to, and I am man enough to let my brother spoil her, too. She grabs the cord and attaches her phone, scrolling through her playlist. Her music choice is a mix of pop and indie that she keeps at a low volume so we can easily talk over it. She didn't drive this way when she came up from Phoenix, so she points out all the new and exciting things she likes.

"I have a few options when we get there," I tell her as we draw closer to Seattle's city center. "Your meeting isn't until two, so we have two hours to spare. We can get an early check in at the hotel to drop off bags, grab a light snack and relax until then. Or we can go grab lunch by the water. I don't know how you handle nerves, so you're in charge of what's best for you here."

"Lunch on the water, please." A soft smile plays on her lips. "I'm a nervous eater, and I want to see as much of the city as we can."

I was hoping she would choose that option. There's a spot my brother told me about that he claims has the best fish and chips in Seattle. The downtown traffic isn't too bad for a weekday afternoon, and surprisingly, neither is parking. Duke's is a smaller place, with benches out front on a pier that the host seats us at. From here, we can see the Space Needle, Mt. Rainier, and watch the ferry traveling back and forth to the islands. I have to admit that although I'm not a big city guy, Seattle is beautiful. Our server brings our food out, checking to see if we need anything else before leaving us to enjoy our lunch.

"The mountain's out today," Lily says with the widest smile on her face as she plops a fry in her mouth.

I snort around my bite of fish. "Did you hear someone say that?"

"Nope," she says proudly, popping the p. "I looked up Seattle slang last night when I couldn't sleep. Apparently, that's what the locals say whenever it's clear enough to see the mountain. I guess it's a rare occurrence."

God, she is so adorable. "It is. How are you feeling? Did the nerves keep you up all night?"

I struggled to sleep last night, too, half nerves, half excitement. This little getaway with her gives us time alone, time to really get to know each other better. I was also nervous that I would fuck up somehow. That maybe things wouldn't go well with the lawyer, or that she will think I'm being presumptuous with only one hotel room.

"Yeah. I sent her everything I could think of Monday night after we talked. Every detail of our relationship, my performance review paperwork, email correspondence, all of it. The legal talk went over my head, but she said there was a process to all this and the first step was to send it somewhere for an investigation. I got an email from her yesterday afternoon saying they got back to her and we would review it and our options today. I just want justice."

"He'll pay, I promise."

We finish up our meal and head back to the truck. Lily offered to drive in her car, Marge, but I didn't want her to have any added stress. We have about fifteen minutes until the meeting and the anxiety is pouring off of her.

"What's my truck's name?" I ask, trying to distract her.

"Huh?" she mumbles, squeezing her fingers and looking out the window.

"My truck. Your Jeep's name is Marge, what should I name my truck? I've never named a car before. He needs something manly."

Her laugh is light, "Cars only have girl names. It's an unspoken rule." She thinks it over, clearly putting thought into her decision. "Freya."

"Freya?"

She finally turns those sapphire blues on me again. "Yes. She's a Norse goddess known for love, beauty, and material things. Since you have the whole Thor, built like a god thing going for you, I think it fits."

"That's not the first time you've alluded to my body like that. Like what you see, Lily?"

She turns even further toward me, slowly perusing every inch of me from head to toe and back. "I do," she says without an ounce of embarrassment. My dick jumps, happy with her assessment.

I don't have time to respond, as I pull into the parking garage for the lawyer's office. With Freya in park, I turn her off, feeling the nervous energy radiating from Lily. "Would you like me to stay here, or come in with you?"

"Please come with me," she says, chewing on her bottom lip.

I hop out and round the truck, opening her door to help her step out. My hand reaches for her and she takes it with no hesitation. With fingers intertwined, we walk into the office and get ushered into a small meeting room by the receptionist. We barely have time to sit before the door opens again and a tall brunette in a power suit steps in.

"Hello Ms. Wilks, I'm Kinsley DeWitt. You can call me Kinsley or Dewitt, I respond to both. Who do you have with you today?"

"This is Thoren, and you can just call me Lily, please," she squeezes my hand tighter under the table. "Can he stay?"

"Absolutely. You are in control here." She takes a seat across the table from us, laying out a folder as she opens her laptop. "First things first, I'm sorry you're even in this scenario. That being said, I think we have options here. I called your former place of employment Monday when we got off the phone, and they basically laughed in my face when I brought up mediation. I immediately filed with the EEOC, the next step, after that and heard back from them yesterday. They said they found no fault, but you have the option to sue, if you so choose."

My fingers are losing feeling with how tight Lily is squeezing them. I reach over and pull her chair closer to mine to give her knee a squeeze before grabbing her hand again. "What does it mean that they found no fault? Does she still have a chance to win in court?"

"Yes, I think we have a good case, and I haven't even done more research or subpoenaed anything yet. The government hardly ever finds fault in these cases, but it's a step we had to take. I will reach out to the company one more time offering mediation, and if they refuse again, then we will bring a lawsuit against them. We are hoping for mediation. It tends to be less ugly, but even that can get rough. Are you sure you want to move forward, Lily?"

"Yes," her voice shakes, but her shoulders straighten. I am so proud of her.

"Good. Let's nail these bastards," Kinsley smiles as she opens a folder in front of her.

We leave the office two hours later, both of us feeling an odd mix of exhausted and relieved. Kinsley has a plan in place for moving forward that Lily is comfortable with. She will try for mediation one more time, which she doesn't have high hopes for, and then will serve them with a lawsuit. This is going to cost me a good chunk of change, but is absolutely worth every penny.

I take us straight to the hotel, seeing the weariness start to creep over Lily. It's a nice hotel with a great view of the Space Needle from the window of the room I booked. Before I take her in there, though, I need to walk her through the options.

I unbuckle both of us, turning in my seat to face her. "Before I ask how you're doing, I want to go over tonight. My brother offered to let us stay with him, but I also booked a hotel room here. The choice is yours and I am up for whatever you choose.

Us both with him, us both here, me with him and you here, the options are endless. Before you make that choice though, know that my brother has a routine before home games, and that routine usually involves… very audible sex." I wince and rub the back of my neck. How do I tell her that the few times I have stayed at River's before a game, he and his girlfriend have fucked on every surface they could find in the apartment? I'm sure he would keep it in his room with Lily there but still, not the mood I was going for on this trip.

Her cheeks are just as red as mine feel. "I think the hotel sounds lovely."

I let out a slow breath, "I only booked one room. It has two beds, but I can get a second if you're more comfortable with that. I just didn't want to book two in case you wanted to stay with River."

"That's okay. One room is fine, it's silly to pay for two. Will you at least let me pay for dinner tonight?"

That went over better than I expected. I'm not trying to get her alone in a room with me, even if that sounds like heaven. I really didn't want to pay for two unused rooms if she wanted to stay with River. I should have known she wouldn't, though; she doesn't like to overstep, even if it's offered. Not that I'm complaining. Thoughts of her climbing into a bed right next to me, where I can be with her all night, are swimming through my head.

I climb out of the truck and open her door before grabbing our bags. "I'm afraid dinner is on River. He's taking us somewhere special tonight."

She leads us into the lobby after I refuse to let her carry the bags. "I don't want to ruin his routine or take up any more of his time," she says, a little unsure.

"This dinner is as much him showing off to his new girlfriend as it is for us all to have a quiet evening together. He will be able to talk you through baseball and show you around tomorrow, but tonight, he just wants to catch up and get to know you." I don't like that she's always so nervous and unsure of everything. I don't know if it was tiny dick Tyler that made her this way, or the way she was raised, but I intend to help her find her self confidence and worth again.

After checking us in, we take the elevator up to the twenty-eighth floor. Lily leads us to our room, unlocking it while holding the door open for me. Together, we walk into the room and take in the wall of windows and glass front balcony. Brilliant oranges and fiery reds dance on the Puget Sound's surface as the sun descends, igniting a warmth that mirrors the joy in my soul.

"This is incredible," comes Lily's soft voice. She slowly turns and looks at the luxury room, two queen beds, a brown leather couch, and the large en suite with a double shower head and jacuzzi tub. "This is too much, Thoren."

I set the bags by the closet, stepping into her space. I need her to really hear and understand me. "You deserve nice things, Lily. This is not too much. It's not nearly enough."

I let my words linger in the air, feeling her chest rising and falling in front of me. Slowly, I step back and bend down to unzip my bag. "Now, did you pack a nice outfit like I said? Our dinner reservations are in an hour."

She breaks out of her stunned silence, grabbing her bag as well. "Where are we going for dinner?"

I turn and point to the large structure out our window like it's no big deal. Her giggle is cute, as she pulls things from her bag.

"I figured somewhere out there, but where?"

I lightly grab her shoulders, turning her toward the Space Needle and point again. "There's a restaurant at the top. We're eating there."

"What?" she shrieks in excitement. "I thought it was just a lookout on the top."

"Nope. It has a restaurant as well. It rotates very slowly, one rotation an hour, so you get 360-degree views while we are up there. Food is pretty amazing, too. I'm going to take a super fast rinse, if that's okay? Then the bathroom is all yours." I grab my new clothes and toiletry bag, laying them out.

"Go ahead," she says, still rifling through her bag.

I take the fastest shower I can, knowing women take time to get ready and we have to leave in forty minutes. My scruff is cleaned up, so I comb my hair to lay nicely. I pull on my dark gray slacks and white button up and head back to the room so Lily can take over. She has a dress laid out on her bed, a pair of heels sitting on the floor below it. She's not in the room though, she's leaning on the railing on the balcony, her hips pushed back toward me, and my mouth dries. Her long hair is cascading down her back, and I can see the smile on her face. She's radiant, and dirty thoughts cross my mind at how badly I want to truss up her natural beauty. To bend her further over that railing and eat her from behind while she enjoys the world at her feet.

Fuck. Now I'm hard and these pants hide nothing with how fitted they are. I do my best to hold my dirty clothes in front of me and make my way to the open balcony door.

"The bathroom is open for you." She straightens and turns at the sound of my voice. Her eyes widen as they trail down my body, the lust in them showing. My chest puffs out, knowing she likes what she sees.

"Thank you." She grabs her dress and toiletry bag and takes over the bathroom.

I hear the shower turn on and debate taking care of my problem, but I don't know how long she'll be in there. Instead, I think of every unsexy thought I have ever had until my body has calmed down. Thankfully I didn't because Lily is in and out of the shower in two minutes. I feel bad that she's rushed. Jen used to take almost two hours to paint her face and get ready, but this was the only reservation time available. Surprisingly, I hear the bathroom door open with ten minutes to spare.

Lily steps out, and my soul leaves my body. She has on a long navy blue dress that hugs her every curve. It is simple, a halter style, but when she turns to grab her heels, I see her entire back is exposed. She slips on her heels, grabs her clutch from the bed, then stands and faces me. Loose curls frame the bottom of her long hair, dark liner rimming her blue eyes, and the lightest pink sheen graces her lips. As my eyes trail down, I see the slit on the side of the dress, exposing her lean leg and I have to bite back a groan.

"Can you spin for me?" I ask, before I can stop myself.

Her smirk is wicked when she replies, "Only if you spin for me, too." She holds her hands out to her sides, then does a slow twirl so I can take in how dangerously low the back of the dress goes, and how it hugs her perfect ass. When she gets all the way around, she twirls her finger for me to do the same. I laugh, but comply, copying her slow spin.

By the time I turn around, she's staring in a lust filled gaze aimed straight at my dick. "I can't tell if I like this or the work pants better."

"I hope the work pants because you'll see them a lot more. Lily, you look breathtaking. Literally, I am struggling to get a full breath in."

She giggles and slaps my chest with her clutch. "Oh, hush. Let's go. I am dying to go to dinner."

While we wait for the elevator, my phone pings in my pocket. I slip it out to see an email from Kinsley with the latest bill attached and two sentences: *I really like her Thoren, don't screw this up. Tell your brother I said hi.*

Yeah, Kinsley, I really like her, too.

CHAPTER SIXTEEN

I think I've died and gone to heaven. The whole way to dinner, my nerves were lit with excitement that only doubled as we rode the elevator up to the restaurant. The minute those elevator doors opened, Thoren's warm hand settled on the exposed skin on my lower back as he led us to the hostess. Between the heat of his rough hand, and the dining room completely surrounded by windows overlooking the city, I was dying.

"Reservation under James," Thoren says to the hostess, still not dropping his hand from my back. If he leaves it there much longer, I'm afraid my dress will catch fire with the way my blood is heating.

"Right this way. The rest of your party is already here."

The server leads us to a table by the window where River and a beautiful woman sit. They are a good looking couple, and I have to admit, River is hot. He has the same hazel eyes as his brother, but with a clean-shaven face and longer, straighter hair. River's smile stretches wide when he sees us, standing to greet his brother. Thoren is a big guy, but River stands a few inches over him, and is more bulk and less defined in his frame.

They wrap each other in a tight embrace. "It's good to see you. Looking more like Thor every day, eh?" River jokes, squeezing Thoren's shoulder.

"He wishes he looked this good," Thoren quips back. His hand snakes around my waist again. "River, this is Lily. Lily, my brother, River."

River wraps me in a tight hug before stepping back. "It's so nice to meet you, Lily." He looks back to the girl who is still sitting, watching us. "This is Vanessa, my girlfriend."

Thoren pulls out the chair closest to the window for me to take, and I reach my hand across the table to shake hers. "It's nice to meet you." She shakes it with a soft, "likewise."

The sun is just setting outside, and the views are beyond what I could have imagined. You can see the mountains, the Puget Sound, and the islands, along with every tall building and the unique hilly landscape of the area.

I'm so busy staring, I don't realize the conversation has been flowing around me. Thoren's arm wraps around my chair as he leans in, his lips brushing against my ear, sending shivers down my spine. "What would you like to drink?"

I turn sheepishly, his face mere inches from mine. His minty breath skates over me. "Sorry, it's just so pretty. A glass of wine would be great."

River keeps his eyes fixed on us from across the table. "Do you like red? I can get a bottle for the table." At my nod, he orders a bottle from the waiter, who hurries off to get it for us. "If you want to know how it is dating me, take a look over your shoulder," he adds, nodding behind me. There is a table not too far from us where the patrons are not so subtly taking photos of us, or more realistically, River.

"Does that happen everywhere?"

"Not always. Rainiers fans always recognize me, but not everyone is a baseball fan, so I can get away with flying under the radar sometimes. It happens, though. Sometimes they are subtle, sometimes kind, and sometimes, not so much."

"Someone ran up to him last week and all but knocked me over to throw herself on him while we were at Alki Beach. Times like those are a little rough," Vanessa adds in, not looking thrilled about the situation. I can't say I blame her. Heck, I didn't like Sherry fawning over Thoren, and he isn't even mine. That thought sits heavy in my chest, and the realization hits. Do I want him to be mine?

I think I am getting around to that idea. He has been slowly immersing himself in my life, offering friendship and support. His subtle touches and hand holds haven't gone unnoticed, and I am starting to crave his hands on me. If this was his plan all along, it's working.

The server brings the bottle of wine and four glasses, pouring them for us before taking our orders.

"How many books have you written, Lily?" River asks, leaning forward with his hands folded on the table.

"I have four currently published. I am hoping to turn this one into a series, following a few of the different players. I can't thank you enough for allowing me to get a behind the scenes look. Research only goes so far, you know?"

"It's no problem, but make sure you stay by Thoren's side tomorrow. Some of the boys can be a little rowdy." Thoren's hand that was resting on my chair reaches forward, his fingers drawing small circles on my shoulder. I like his subtle claim on me, his quiet reassurance that he has me.

"How long have you guys been together?" I ask River.

"Three months," Vanessa answers. She seems nice, but is a little standoffish with her responses. "It's going really well, though." She leans into him, putting a hand on his chest. It's a claiming move, but in a way that is wholly unnecessary.

I let the comment drop, and River picks up the conversation.

He and Thoren catch up with how the search and rescue team is doing, how their parents are, and how River is feeling about his season. Vanessa and I listen and add in our two cents when it's welcomed. It is heartwarming to see the bond between Thoren and his brother. I have picked up on the fact that he feels he lives in River's shadow, but he doesn't let it show when he's with him. They both seem proud of the other and just happy to get to spend time together.

"Tell me more about yourself," River says as the waiter delivers our desserts.

"Not much to tell. I grew up in Phoenix, I'm an only child, and now I live in Cedar Ridge. You kind of know the history there," I feel my face getting hot. "Thank you for connecting us with Kinsley, by the way. But now I'm fixing up my cabin and pursuing my passion for writing."

Thoren's hand wraps around the back of my neck, giving it a reassuring squeeze before going back to stroking my shoulder. River's eyes darken, a scowl taking over his face. "You're welcome. If you need anything else, please call me." He takes a bite of his cheesecake before continuing. "How's the renovations coming? I hope you're putting my brother to work. I've heard Thor knows how to swing his hammer."

I choke on a laugh as Thoren chokes on his bite of chocolate cake.

"Dick," he mutters.

River's laugh is loud and hearty, head thrown back at his own joke. "What? I meant because you renovated your place recently, too." He smirks, winking at me.

The sun is set by the time we are finished, the city lights flashing below us, and I am dead on my feet. It's been a long day, and although everything was really wonderful, it's also been over-whelming. As we pile into the elevator to head back down, Thoren puts a hand on my hip pulling my back to his chest, letting me lean against him. My breaths mimic his as his heat soaks into my exposed skin. It's a comfort I didn't know I needed after today. We say our goodbyes at the bottom, setting a time to meet at the stadium tomorrow so we can get a small tour before the game.

By the time we get back to the hotel, I am beyond ready to crash. He lets me take over the bathroom first, where I go through my nightly routine. I remove all my makeup, brush my teeth, and put on my silky tank and shorts pajama set. I didn't know when I packed these that he would see me in them, but I'm glad he is. There is something changing with us, and I'd be lying if I said I'm not eager to explore it.

Thoren is already lying on his bed when I step out, dressed only in shorts, with one hand behind his head while he reads something on his phone. Tattoos swirl over his chest, leading to abs above the perfect Adonis belt. It's visible with the low set of his shorts, a light smattering of hair trailing down just below his navel. He glances up, dropping his phone as he does a double take. A chill runs down my spine as his intense gaze lingers on me, causing my nipples to tighten and ache under the scorching heat.

"Your turn," I breathe out, breaking his stare. His muscles flex as he sits up, the tension in the room building. The attraction between us is palpable, and if I wasn't so exhausted from not sleeping much the night before, I would climb this man like a tree. I watch him retreat to the bathroom, every movement flexing the muscles in his back. When the bathroom door closes, I take my first real breath since walking in here. I quickly retreat to my bed, tucking myself in so I don't do something rash.

A few moments later, he slips from the bathroom, and I try to keep my eyes anywhere but on him. When the rustle of his sheets settles, I finally turn to face him. He's lying in his bed, the blanket tucked under his arm, facing me as well. Thoren reaches forward, turning out the light.

"Goodnight, Lily," his soft voice breaks through the dark.

I want to say goodnight and let sleep drag me under, but I also don't want this night with him to end. Thoren has wormed his way into my life and into my heart. From a young age I was accustomed to being alone. Before Tyler, I found it hard to date and nothing ever turned into a relationship. There was this sense that my life was destined to be spent alone. After Tyler, that thought became overwhelming, like I really was meant to be alone and bad things happened when I wasn't. I'm starting to see that's not the truth at all. I just hadn't found the right person. Thoren feels like the right person, and I want to call this man my own.

"Was it nice to see your brother?" I ask instead.

His chuckle is low and smooth. "Yeah, it was. We only see each other a couple times a year, so it's always nice to get to spend time with him."

"Hmmm."

"How are you feeling after everything today?"

I take a deep breath, mulling it over. I was hoping for things to be settled outside of court, so hearing that likely won't be the case was rough. It feels nice to have a plan in place, though. Meeting River and Vanessa surprisingly brought on a lot of nerves for me, too. I realized I wanted River to like me. That his opinion matters simply because he is Thoren's brother. "Overwhelmed. Good. Scared. Overwhelmed some more. It was all a lot."

It's his turn to hum in response. "Hey, Lily?"

"Yeah?"

"Can I hold you?" his soft voice asks.

"Like right now?"

"Like all night, baby. You've had a long day, and I just want you to feel secure. Let me take care of you?" Now that my eyes have adjusted to the dark, I watch as he lifts the covers and scoots back.

There it goes. Thoren just took down the last barrier I had around my heart. Without hesitating, I slide out of my bed and crawl into his. He drapes the blanket over me, pulling me into his body. His strong arms wrap around me, securing me just like he promised. Warm hands gently rub up and down my back as his legs tangle in between mine. My body doesn't know how to respond; my heart feels like it's going to beat out of my chest while my muscles completely succumb to him.

"I can feel your pulse racing," he whispers into my hair. "Relax, I've got you now."

"You called me baby," I whisper back. That little sentiment didn't escape my notice, and I like how it felt.

"I did."

My chin lifts as his lowers, our faces hovering inches from each other. I watch every flutter of his lashes, the slight uptick in his lip as he takes me in. His chest breathes deep against mine, rubbing my sensitive nipples against him every time. When the look in his eyes changes to something headier, I close that small gap between us and press my lips to his.

It's soft. Sweet. His lips part slightly, deepening the kiss, his short beard scratching deliciously against my skin. I lick along the seam of his lips, begging for entrance. I need more of him like I need my next breath. He parts our lips further, taking control of the kiss as one hand glides into the base of my hair, gripping it tight.

A soft whimper escapes me as his tongue strokes against mine. His minty breath mixes with mine as his tongue languidly explores my mouth. All too soon, he pulls back, panting for breath. His forehead leans against mine until our breathing is back to normal, his warm breath tickling my face. Ever so slowly he shakes his head, dropping a lingering kiss to my forehead.

"Go to sleep, Lily. We have a busy day tomorrow."

I should be upset that he pulled away, but I'm too exhausted to fight it. I wiggle in closer to him, wrapping my arms around his strong back. His erection nestles heavily between us and I fight the urge to reach down and stroke him; to feel the weight of his soft skin as it hardens under my hand.

His hands move down to my back again, this time kneading into my muscles. His woodsy, amber scent envelops me, his soft lips brushing tender kisses onto my forehead and in my hair. I realize as I'm falling asleep that I was wrong earlier. This is what heaven must feel like.

I'm warm, wrapped tight in heavy blankets that cocoon me in place. There's a bone deep comfort that I feel in this bed, and I know it's not the mattress I have at home. My brain catches up to my body, remembering that I'm at a hotel in Seattle with Thoren.

Thoren.

Thoren that I kissed last night. Thoren that is currently wrapped around me, not just the blankets. His chest is to my back now, his skin warming mine in all the places my pajamas don't cover. Blinking against the bright morning light, I see one of his hands stretched out from underneath my pillow. There's a tingle between my thighs seeing evidence of his hard work written all over the rough calluses. They lead up to forearms wrapped in corded muscle, and I get the urge to run my fingers through the hair on them.

His other arm flexes around my waist, pulling me further into him. His erection digs into my ass as he buries his head in my neck and inhales.

"Good morning, how'd you sleep?" His sleepy voice is raspy, adding to the growing heat in my core.

"Like a rock. How'd you sleep?"

"Best sleep I've had all year. I want nothing more than to stay in this spot all day, but I have morning activities planned before we need to head to the stadium. Want to order us room service while I go shower? Get anything your heart desires," he says, slipping out of the bed already.

I feel the loss of him immediately. I've never been great at flirting or expressing what I want sexually. With Thoren, though, I don't want to be this quiet, timid woman. I want to do things that make him call me a good girl again, and feel his lips on mine. No time like the present to take those steps, right?

"Are you going to take care of that in the shower?" I ask, letting my eyes trail down to his hard cock straining to break free from the confines of his shorts.

He chokes, trying to cover it with a cough. "Yes," he says as a blush rises on his cheeks.

"Will you say my name when you come?"

Waking up in his arms solidified the fact that I want this man. Body and soul, Thoren is the best man I have ever known and I want this small ownership of him. This small claiming, that for one moment, with his hand wrapped around his hard cock, saying my name, he will be mine.

"Fuuuuck, baby." Both of his hands run through his curly hair, pulling at the ends. "You don't know what you're saying."

"No?" I ask coyly.

He is on me in an instant, his broad chest hovering over me, hands on either side of my head. There's a wild look in his eyes, and I revel in it. Sweet and submissive, if not dismissive, is all I have ever known. This feral, demanding side of Thoren is a mystery to me, and it's one I want to explore.

"You don't think I've been saying your name every day since you walked into the shop? That your blue eyes don't meet me in my dreams every night? That I don't wake up aching for you, my cock wrapped in my hand wishing it was yours? That it's your hand, your soft mouth, your pretty pussy that I know is dripping for me? I'll say your name, like I always do. Just know that one day very soon, I am going to make you mine. And when that day comes, it's my name you'll be screaming."

Just as quickly, he pushes off and heads straight to the bathroom. I lay in stunned silence, fanning my face that has to be beet red. My panties are soaked, and all I want to do is follow him into that shower. Something he said stops me, though. He said he was going to make me his first, and after that little show, I will happily wait for that moment.

Pulling myself together, I try not to focus on the fact that Thoren is less than ten feet away, stroking himself to thoughts of me. Instead, I busy myself with ordering a mix of healthy and sweet breakfast foods for us through room service. With the food ordered, I have two options; stand at the bathroom door and drool over the man behind it, or enjoy the views from the balcony far from the object of my desires.

I decide on option two, reveling in the city's noise below to distract my thoughts. The soft whir of the balcony doors sliding open alerts me to Thoren's presence, but I didn't need the noise. I felt his heated gaze the moment it landed on me. His hands grip the railing on either side of my elbows, where I'm leaning over the railing. The scent of a warm forest day radiates from him, enveloping me like a hug.

His hot breath tickles my ear as he whispers, "When I saw you standing here yesterday, just like this, all I could think about was how good you'd look bent further over with my face buried between your thighs. Watching the world below you like the queen you are." He stands up, giving my ass a sharp smack. "Go get in the shower before I do just that."

I turn to face him, taking in his black tee, fitted tight around his shoulders, and jeans that hug his thick thighs. "What if I want that?"

"When I finally get my mouth on you, I won't want to come up for air. Our breakfast is already getting cold, and you need to get ready for the day. Please, baby, I'm hanging on by a thread here," he pleads.

"Okay," I relent, walking past him toward the bathroom. At this point, I might need to do some stroking of my own in the shower. I know I'm pushing both our boundaries and limits, but I never knew it could be this fun. It's thrilling to see what he might say or do next. "Only because you begged so sweetly." His groan is deep as I slip into the bathroom, laughing as I shut the door. I am giving him one week to make his move before I incinerate.

After I finished getting ready in jeans, some comfy sneakers, and a blue tank top, we ate breakfast together. The food was a little cold, but still delicious. Thoren told me about his plans for us to explore downtown for a bit, checking out the widely known Pike Place Market and going to ride the ferris wheel by the water before we would have to make our way to the stadium.

It was everything I wanted out of the trip, and the fact that he listened and delivered was not lost on me. With our breakfast finished and our teeth brushed, we packed up the last of our things to head out. I grabbed the jersey River had bought for me and threw it on over my tank as we walked out the door.

Thoren looked down at me when we got to the elevators, doing a double take at the jersey.

"What?" I ask. "Does it not look okay?"

His eyes softened as he picked up my hand, brushing his lips over my knuckles. "It looks amazing. I like seeing my last name on you."

With that, he dropped my hand to grab the bags, stepping into the elevator. Thoren can say what he wants, but if that statement isn't him making me his, I don't know what is.

CHAPTER SEVENTEEN

lily

The morning flew by as we explored downtown. I loved getting to see all the unique things Seattle had to offer, but the hustle and bustle of the city solidified my decision to move to the mountains. There's no serenity in all the chaos, like there is alone in the woods. Thoren's hand never left mine as we looked through the little shops at Pike Place and walked on the pier below. We even got to see the iconic gum wall, which I was more grossed out with than anything.

River told us to meet him at noon, and we parked at the stadium right on time. The Rainier's stadium is newer and open at the top. I've never been to a professional sports game, so to get to see behind the scenes for my first one is wild. He meets us at the entrance and ushers us in. We walk the halls as he tells me about his typical game day routine which varies depending on the start time of the game, but seems generally consistent. He eats the same general foods, stretches the same way, and plays the same playlist. I didn't bring my binder, but I have my notepad out, writing down every tidbit of information that I can.

"This is our locker room. I told the guys you were coming and to behave, but I'm going to peek in and make sure everyone is decent," River says, opening a door letting loud chatter filter out into the hall.

Thoren has given me space so far, mostly to give me room to write while we walked, but is pressed up against me now. "Marking your territory?" I joke.

"Claiming what's mine," he quips back, placing his hand on my hip. Goosebumps erupt down my arms as his hand splays wide over my hip bone. I turn to look up at him, a smile on my face. He leans down, placing a soft kiss on my lips when River pops back through the door. Thoren doesn't rush to pull away, lingering just a touch before nodding at his brother and giving my hip a squeeze.

We follow River into the locker room, which is a lot cleaner and nicer smelling than I expected. There are half-dressed men everywhere, but they all at least have their baseball pants on. I try not to let my looks linger, but I think I might enjoy watching baseball if these are the pants they wear. I glance to my side at Thoren's tree trunk legs and ass that is molded to his jeans and now all I want is to see him in baseball pants.

"We each have our own locker space," River points, walking us around the open room. Wooden shelves line the room, each filled with jerseys, bags, and photos. In the center, there's a couch and some chairs spread out, filled with guys relaxing before the game. "There's a room here for PT and for us to get worked on. We have some bikes over here to get our bodies moving, some mats and tools for stretching here," he continues, pointing as we move along.

"Damnnn, she looks good in a jersey. Want my last name instead, sweetheart?" someone calls from behind us.

"She'd look even better in just the jersey," another guy calls out, high-fiving the first.

"Hey River, you letting your brother take the hot ones now? Does he share?" comes from the other side of the room.

Thoren's jaw ticks, and I don't miss the smirk on River's face. I have a feeling he told them to heckle me to mess with his brother. After some of his comments last night, hinting at us being a cute couple, and asking when Thoren was going to lock me down, this seems like something he'd do. He gives me a wink before he elbows Thoren's side. "Sorry bud, they asked if Lily was single and I didn't want to lie."

Before Thoren can respond, a player moves in front of me, holding out his hand. "Nice to meet you, Lily. I'm Case, number nine. Watch me out there, and I might just hit a home run for you. Stick around after the game and I'll give you my real number," he winks.

I shake his hand, smiling kindly, "Nice to meet you. I have plans after the game, thanks though." I lean further into Thoren's side, his hand on my lower back flexing. I'm all for a little harmless taunting, but Thoren's anxiety is palpable. Part of me wants him to claim me as his right here and now, but the other part of me loves that he's allowing me to make my own choices.

"Case," Thoren nods to the man still in front of us. "Wanna get your boys in check? They will talk to her with respect or they won't be talking at all."

Case's laugh is loud, catching the attention of those around us. "Yes sir," he mock salutes. "It's your brother's fault."

"Hey, hey now, all I said was that Lily is single and to be respectful," River turns to the rest of the room, speaking loudly. "Which we will need to cover the parameters of being respectful again."

There are groans around the room and I hear more than one muttered, "sorry, dad." I try to hide my chuckle at how River commands the group. Seeing Thoren in protective mode is hot, and watching his brother be a menace is fun. I want to push myself to be more bold, but now I want Thoren to be the bold one. I want to poke him until he brings out the side that straddled me this morning, telling me how often he strokes his cock to thoughts of me.

River leads us out of a side door into another hall and points us to the exit that leads to the stadium seats. He pulls out his phone and takes a quick selfie with the three of us before slipping it back into his pocket. He hands Thoren two tickets with our seat numbers and pulls him in for a bro hug. I don't miss a whispered exchange between them, but it's not loud enough to hear.

River pulls me into a hug next, squeezing me tight. "Sorry about the guys. It's just too fun riling him up. Take care of him, Lily. He's a good man," he whispers in my ear.

"I will," I mutter before stepping out of his embrace. "Thank you for everything, River. Better make some big plays today or I might make my next book about hockey again."

He groans, "Get out of here, trouble. You two have fun." With that, he disappears back into the locker room, leaving Thoren and I alone in the hall.

I turn to Thoren, trying to plaster an innocent look on my face. "Do you think Case will really give me his number?"

THOREN

What did she just say? There's no way I heard her right. Not after last night or this morning. This sweet, shy woman did not just ask that. I was going to wait until we got home, with a nice home cooked meal and candles, to ask her to be my girlfriend. Was it cheesy, and maybe a little elementary? Probably, but Lily deserves to have all the stops pulled out for her.

There's no way in hell I'm waiting now though. I stalk her like she's my prey, crowding her until her back is flush with the wall. "Lily, if I didn't make myself clear enough before, I'm sorry. Let me make it very clear now. You are beautiful, kind, selfless, funny, strong, and I could go on forever. I like everything about you, and I've become a man obsessed. I had a whole speech planned to tell you every little thing about you that has captivated me, but you are pushing my buttons," I put one hand under her chin, drawing her face even closer to mine, the other hand landing on the wall above her head to hold me up.

"I will be patient if you still aren't ready, but I want you to be mine. I want to care for you, cherish you, and support you. I will be everything you need, but I will not stand around and let another man have my girl. If you keep pushing me, I will bend you over my knee and spank that perfect ass raw. Am I clear enough now?"

Lily's chin slowly lowers as she nods, her chest heaving against mine. "Good," I continue. "Will you be my girlfriend, Lily?"

She barely gets out a whispered "yes" before my mouth crashes down on hers. I part her lips with mine, licking her sweet taste from her lips before sliding my tongue in. My hand moves to stroke her jaw as her soft lips follow my lead. The kiss with her last night felt unlike any kiss I've had before, but this one? This one is even better because this stunning woman in front of me agreed to be mine.

There's a commotion somewhere behind us that I try to ignore until the whistles and cheers start. A mix of catcalls, "get some," and a very familiar sounding "that's my brother!" has me pulling back from Lily. Children, the whole lot of them. Her cheeks are flushed, her pupils blown, and her lips swollen from the kiss. I don't want anyone else seeing her like this, so keeping my body poised in front of hers, I turn to see the locker room door open with half of the team trying to look out of it at us.

Lily's light giggle pulls my attention back to her, and I can't help but shake my head at my brother's antics. "I'm sorry," I whisper to her, but she just shrugs and leans into my chest.

"Alright, show's over," I hear my brother say, and with the

closing of a door, silence sweeps the hallway again. I wrap my arms around Lily's small frame, letting our breaths even out and will my throbbing dick to stand down.

When it's half on board, I reach down, making a quick adjustment before taking her hand. "Shall we go get some snacks before we find our seats?"

Unsurprisingly, River got us some of the best seats in the house. Our seats are directly behind home plate, allowing us a perfect view of the game. I know for some, baseball can be a slow game, but Lily stays engaged the whole time. She asks questions about each throw, and cheers every time one of the Rainiers takes a base. For a little payback, she even heckled River every time he was up at bat.

My favorite part though, was when Case did indeed hit a home run, he pointed at Lily and winked as he tagged in at home plate. She smiled at him, then turned to me and gave me a soft kiss. Her claiming of me, in front of my brother's entire team, settled something in me. She truly wanted me, and not a stepping stone to more.

Around the end of the ninth inning, my phone pings.

Bros and Hoe Group Chat

RIVER ✎:

selfie of River Thoren and Lily

RIVER ✎:

You're missing out Jake.

JAKE ▤:

Where was my invite, dickbags?

THOREN ⚒:

... I wanted alone time with Lily.

RIVER ✎:

picture of Thoren kissing Lily in the hallway

RIVER ✐:

"alone time"

JAKE 🪜:

Damn. I guess you didn't screw it up.

THOREN 🔨:

middle finger emoji that picture gets my dick hard

JAKE 🪜:

...mine too.

RIVER ✐:

GAG I'm out. Happy for you bro, glad you could make it and drive home safe. Jake, stop by next time you go to your showroom, bud. I miss you.

JAKE 🪜:

Will do.

Those two are absolute hooligans, but damn, I love them. I save the photo of Lily and me in the hallway because I wasn't lying; it's fucking hot. By the time I get my phone back in my pocket, the game is over. Hand in hand, Lily and I shuffle our way out with the rest of the fans and head to Freya for the drive home.

"I still can't believe my truck has a girl's name."

"Hey, don't hurt her feelings. She's a warrior and deserves respect," she chastises me. I open her door, helping her in, and buckling her seatbelt.

"Maybe her name should be Lily then." Her cheeks heat, and I love that I have that effect on her. "Are you hungry for dinner, or do you want to head straight home?"

"I had so many snacks there. I'm good with going home. A long shower after sweating in the sun all day sounds amazing."

I do just that, taking us home after our perfect little getaway. A long shower is calling my name, too, but after I drop Lily off, I have to get Shadow from my parents and I know my mom will bombard me with questions. No doubt River has already told her that Lily and I are together now. I still am a little shocked that Lily is willing to take a chance on me, but I won't waste it. Tyler treated her like a doormat, and I intend to treat her like the queen that she is.

Lily's phone dings, and she slips it from her purse, checking the message. In my peripherals, I watch her face light up, only to quickly shut down again. Her cheeks turn red and her hands tremble as she turns away from me.

"What is it?"

"It's nothing," her subdued voice says with a slight tremor.

"Baby, please don't lie to me. What's going on?"

She slowly turns back to me, silent tears tracking down her face. "It was my mom. She hasn't talked to me in months, and she only reached out to criticize me."

I flex my hands on the steering wheel, gripping tight as my anxiety bleeds into anger. "What did she say?"

"I guess the cameras at the game caught the interaction with Case and then me kissing you. Her friend called her to ask about it. She said I'm embarrassing her, and asked that if I'm going to continue making these choices, that I at least do it in private." Her lower lip trembles as she squeezes her fingers together. "I don't even know what choices I'm making that she's talking about. Living my life? Having a relationship? What am I doing that's so wrong?"

I reach over, grabbing her hand into mine, pressing a light kiss to her knuckles. "Nothing, baby. You are doing absolutely nothing wrong. You are not responsible for her feelings or how she chooses to respond to things. I'm so sorry that she is making you feel this way."

I have a lot of things that I want to say, but none of them would be productive right now. She doesn't need me to tell her that Tyler mom is being selfish. That her mom has her own life to live, and that

Lily gets to be her own person and choose her own path. She's a successful and published author, for God's sake, and she owns her own home at twenty-six. She should feel nothing but pride for those facts alone. Add in the fact that she is selfless, caring, and brave, and it puts Lily leagues above everyone else. I let our joined hands fall and rest in her lap, trying to give her my support and not my anger.

Heavy silence fills the rest of the drive, broken only by Lily's quiet sniffles echoing through the car. My hand moves back and forth between holding hers to rubbing her leg. I want nothing more than to pull over and wrap her in my arms, but she needs the reprieve of a shower and to crawl into bed, so I stay the course. When we finally pull up in front of her house, I help her out and grab her bag while she unlocks her door. Setting her things inside the front door, I pull her into me. I hold her tight as her shoulders shake in silent sobs, trying to bleed my strength into her.

She settles, drying her eyes to look at me. "Thank you for the amazing trip. I'm sorry it ended like this."

Cupping her jaw, I rub my thumb over her tear-stained cheeks. "Don't be sorry. I'm going to pick up Shadow and get her home, then I'm coming back to check on you. I'd like to tuck you in and hold you until you fall asleep, if that's okay?"

Her chin trembles again, and my heart breaks for her. "Okay. See you soon." With a gentle kiss on her forehead, I leave for my parents' house. My mind is a mess, just wanting to be with her. How her mother can speak to her like that blows my mind. As I pull up to my parents, I put my truck in park and pull out my phone. I want to see the video her mom is freaking out over in case I'm missing something.

I don't even have to search. River already sent it to me but with a heart emoji followed by a gagging emoji. It's a brief clip where the camera pans out from Case as he rounds home plate and turns to point and wink at Lily. She turns red immediately, but smiles sweetly at him before leaning over and placing a swift kiss on my lips. That's it; that's the whole video that her mom is upset over.

Barking steals my attention as my mom opens the front door and Shadow bursts out, running straight for my truck. Hopping out, I kneel down and give her my love before following her toward the house.

My mom is waiting with a glowing smile, a knowing glint in her eyes. "How was your trip, honey?"

Settling in the kitchen, I tell her and my dad about the trip, leaving out a few details. They ask about River and Vanessa, and how Lily is doing with everything. I break and divulge to them about the text from her mom today and how much it hurt her. The more I talk, the quieter my mom gets, until I catch a tear dripping down her cheek. My dad silently reaches over, rubbing her back. I love my mom even more at this moment, for feeling so deeply for a woman she has never even met.

We move on to discuss how Shadow behaved when my phone rings on the counter. Lily's name flashes on my screen, drawing my attention. I utter an apology to my parents before answering the call.

"Hey ba- Lily, what's wrong?" Her soft cries are all I can hear through the phone.

"I wanted," sniffle, "to unpack first... I uh, I like order, but then," more incoherent sobs echo. "My shower, half the tiles fell," she gets out between her sobs. "I can't shower and I know it's stupid, but I just really needed a cry in the shower. But half the wall is broken in the tub."

"Lily, baby, take a breath for me." I don't continue until I hear her suck in a deep breath. "Good girl. You're going to drive over to my house, okay? There is a spare key taped under the third railing on the front porch. Go draw yourself a hot bath, there are bubbles under the sink. I'm heading back home right now. I'll be there as soon as I can."

"Okay," her voice sounds dejected. "Thank you."

I hang up, gathering my things to leave. My mom, the saint that she is, hands me a bag and a glass container. "The bag is Shadow's things, and the container has dinner with enough for you both. Go take care of your girl, we'll talk soon."

With a hug to both mom and dad, I rush out the door with Shadow and race home. The house is quiet when we enter, but Shadow runs straight upstairs. I'm halfway up them when I hear Lily's soft laugh drifting down.

I drop my bags in my bedroom and knock on the partly open bathroom door. "You doing okay?" I call in.

"Might as well come in and make it a party," Lily laughs. When I pop my head in, I see Shadow poking around the edge of the tub, trying to find the best place to climb in.

"Out," I motion to her and she whines, but listens, jumping on my bed. I shut the door behind her, kneeling at the edge of the tub by Lily's head. She looks beautiful with her hair in a bun on her head, resting on the edge, red-rimmed eyes and all. The bubbles she has in the tub are popping, giving me the barest glimpses of her naked body. All my blood travels to my dick the longer I look, so I turn back to her face.

"What do you need right now?" I ask, stroking my thumb down her cheek.

"For you to join me."

thoren

"Are you sure?" I want her to say yes and no in equal measures. Every inch of me wants to crawl in that tub behind her, but being naked with her body pressed to mine will be my undoing.

"Please?"

I can't deny her anything. I never will. Standing, I pull my shirt over my head, feeling her heated gaze like a touch. Next, I undo my jeans, slipping them down with my boxers. My cock springs free, hard and ready for her. There's no getting around it, so I keep undressing, pulling my socks off and adding them to the pile.

"Sit forward, baby," I urge, watching her tongue trace along her lower lip in the way I want to. She complies, giving enough space for me to slide in behind her. My legs wrap around her small waist, as she leans back onto my chest once I'm settled. My cock is nestled into her back, every movement making me see stars. I haven't been with anyone since Jen; I don't know how I am going to make it through this bath.

I let my fingers trail over her shoulder and down her arms. "How are you doing?"

"Better," comes her breathy reply. "Being with you helps."

I grab the washcloth she has set out on the edge of the tub and let it follow the path of my fingers. She wiggles a little, causing me to hiss as her ass rubs against me. I continue the trail back up her shoulders, this time dipping over her collarbone and down her chest. The washcloth trails over the tops of her breasts as a gasp slips from her parted mouth. Neither of us move, not wanting to ruin this moment. Slowly, I let the cloth drop and run my thumbs over her tight nipples. Her body shivers, so I do it again, this time rubbing them between my thumb and finger. The moan that leaves her soft lips lights a fire in me.

"Tell me to stop," I beg, letting one hand trail down her stomach.

"Please don't."

When my fingers get to the apex of her thighs, the smooth bare skin there has me biting back a groan of my own. I continue down, letting my middle finger circle her clit once, twice, three times, before pinching it and her nipple at the same time.

"Thoren," she cries. "More, please, baby."

Hearing her call me baby is everything I didn't know I needed. My middle finger lowers, teasing her entrance before slipping it in. I stroke her a few times before adding another finger as she grows wetter. I keep up my ministrations, playing with her nipple while stroking her pussy, letting the heel of my palm rub her clit. Lily arches her back, pushing her perky breast further into my hand while rocking her hips.

When her head falls to the side, I trail kisses up her neck, stopping at a spot just below her ear. I can feel her winding tighter, floating on the edge of orgasm. I keep my rhythm, not daring to change anything until her breath hitches.

"Come for me, princess," I growl, sucking on the sweet spot below her ear. Lily explodes around me, crying out my name as her orgasm crests. Her pussy squeezes my fingers, warmth emanating from her. I slow my strokes until she's a boneless heap on top of me. My mouth trails lightly over her shoulder and neck again, dropping gentle kisses.

"Time for bed, baby."

She lets out an adorable whine, "But I want more. I want all of you."

I lean her forward, slipping out of the tub. With a towel wrapped around my waist, I help her out and take my time drying her off. Her eyes stay glued to my painfully hard cock the entire time. When I'm satisfied that she's dry, I place the towel on my counter and put her on top of it.

"Stay here, I'll be right back," I demand, with a kiss on her nose. I clearly can't keep my hands or mouth to myself when it comes to her. And now that I've seen her come apart in my hands, I have no desire to fight that. In the guest bathroom, I find one of the spare toothbrushes I keep in stock for Jake and River if needed. On my way back, I grab a tee and some boxers from my dresser, placing them and the toothbrush on the counter next to her.

"These are for you. Are you hungry?"

"No," she yawns. "Just tired."

"Okay baby. I'm going to feed Shadow and take her out real quick. I want you snuggled in my bed by the time I get back up here."

She hops off the counter, wrapping her arms tight around me. "Thank you," she mumbles into my chest.

Kissing the top of her head, I give her one squeeze before leaving her there. I threw on some boxers to take Shadow out, dropping my mom's food in the fridge on my way. I'm going to suffer from a serious case of blue balls, but it's definitely worth it for my girl. Shadow finished her business, so I locked up the house, turning out the lights as I went.

Lily is waiting where I told her to, wrapped in my blankets, her silky hair fanning out over my pillows. Sneaking into the bathroom, I brushed my teeth and got ready for bed. By the time I walked out, Shadow was laying at Lily's feet, both of them asleep. Moving quietly, I crawled into bed next to her, wrapping my arms around her and pulling her into my chest.

She lets out a contented sigh as her body melts into mine. This is everything that I had in mind when I was renovating. Coming home from work to find my woman soaking in the tub, going to bed with her body held against mine, Shadow at our feet. I hold her tight all night, reveling in this feeling.

The early morning light pokes through the curtains, waking me like it always does. My body's internal clock never lets me sleep past six, even on days I don't work. Lily's snuggled into my side, her head resting on my chest. The streams of the rising sun bring out the chocolate tones in her hair as I run my fingers through it. Her warm vanilla scent is mixed with mine, creating an intoxicating smell.

No matter how badly I want to keep her here in my bed every night, I know she needs to be able to make her own choices. She needs the freedom and ability to stand on her own, but that doesn't mean I can't help. With a soft kiss to her lips, I slip out of bed. Throwing on some clothes, I take Shadow downstairs with me. We go through our morning routine where she eats and potties while I make coffee. While she's out doing her business, I scrawl out a note for Lily, letting her know there's fresh coffee in the pot and that I will be back soon, slipping back upstairs to put it on my pillow.

I snag Lily's keys from her purse, and put Shadow back in the house. The sleepy pup is going to jump back in my spot on the bed and go back to sleep like she always does after time spent at my parents. I don't want my truck to wake Lily up, so I trudge in my work boots and sweats over to her house, needing to see how bad the damage in her shower is.

Unfortunately, when I get into her house, I find she wasn't exaggerating at all. A shattered wall of tiles lies across the floor and in the tub. It seems to get worse from there with mold climbing the insulation and wall and cracks riddling the exposed copper piping. Her entire bathroom needs to be re-piped, potentially her entire house. The walls also need to be ripped out for mold remediation to see how far it expands.

Lily's water will need to be shut off for the whole renovation, and this is her only bathroom, so even if she had water, she will have no toilet or shower. A mix of emotions washes through me at the thought of what this means. For her, it means a lot of money and time getting this done. For me, it means that I can ask her to temporarily move in with me and have her in my bed every night until this is done.

I take some pictures of all the damage, then head back to my place. I'll need to talk to her before I dive into this project. She may not want me to do it, or to even help. She may not want to stay with me while this is getting fixed. Yes, she agreed to be my girlfriend, but Lily is independent and has been on her own for so long. Moving in with me after one day of dating may drive her away.

That's the last thing I want to happen, so I make a plan. I'm going to offer her the guest bedroom, with no pressure to move our relationship along. It will be easier for her to spend time with Shadow that way, too, and I can cook us dinner at night. I'm working full time, have responsibilities with the Search and Rescue team, and if she agrees, will work on her renovations. So in reality, we won't even see each other that much; it will just be a place for her to stay. That's exactly what I'm going to tell her when I offer it, knowing full well I will be by her side every chance I get.

When I walk in my front door, Lily's soft voice reaches me right as the smell of bacon does. "Just one piece, sweet girl. I don't want your daddy to be mad at me and I can't have you getting sick, okay?"

I kick off my boots and walk into the kitchen to see her back turned to me, stirring eggs on the stove. My shirt swallows her small body, hanging halfway down her thighs, exposing her lean, toned legs. She's stunning with her hair pulled back in a bun, her hips swaying just slightly with each movement.

"You spoiling our dog again?" I ask, leaning against the side of the island, arms crossed over my chest.

"Crap!" she shouts, dropping the spatula and jumping around to face me. "You can't sneak up on someone like that, Thoren. Death by spatula was a real possibility."

My lip twitches with a smile, "Sorry baby, I won't do it again. How are you doing?"

"I'm okay. Have a seat, breakfast is almost ready. Where'd you run off to?"

I take a seat on a stool at the island, dropping her keys on the counter. "Your place. Want the good news or the bad news first?"

Her shoulders slump as she turns off the stove and fills two plates with bacon, eggs, and toast. "Bad, I guess."

I want to shelter her feelings, but Lily needs to know the levity of the situation and I respect her enough to be honest. "Your entire bathroom needs to be gutted. The pipes are old and cracking, and there's mold behind the tiles. I don't know how far back it goes. Everything needs to be ripped out and replaced. While the pipes are being replaced, your water will need to be shut off and you won't have use of your bathroom for a majority of the renovations."

She puts one plate in front of me as she slides onto the stool beside me. "And what's the good news?"

"You can stay here. The guest room is open for you, the house will be quiet for you to write, and you'll never be alone with Shadow here. And I can do the renovations if you don't want to hire someone. It may take a little longer, but you can be more involved and help whenever you want."

I glance over to watch her pushing eggs around her plate with the fork. This has to feel like life is piling it on her, but I don't know what else I can do to help. Her glassy blue eyes meet mine, vulnerability shining through them. "Okay."

"Okay?" I ask, needing clarification.

"I will stay here, if you're sure it's okay. But I will be the one cooking dinner and paying for groceries, and I will also pay you for the renovations." Her slender throat swallows. "Thank you. I know I'm saying it so much, but I really don't know how else to express how grateful I am for you."

"You can eat your breakfast and pack your things. I have a meeting this afternoon, but the guest room is clean and ready for you. Pack whatever you need and I can help you move it all when I come back. How does that sound?"

"Good," she says, taking her first bite. I love how submissive Lily is, while still holding onto her independence. I expected more of a fight from her, but the fact that she trusts me and listens… it does something to me.

"To be clear, I want you in my space, in my bed, and in my arms. If you are more comfortable in the guest room, though, I understand." That pretty flush travels up her cheeks again, making me want to trace the path with my tongue. We eat our breakfast, then go our separate ways so I can do the dishes while she takes a shower before heading to her place to pack.

As soon as she leaves, I hop in the shower, loving that she used my soap, yet it still somehow smells like her in here. My dick has been at half mast all morning, seeing her walk around the house in my shirt. God, just the thought of her naked in here has my dick turning to stone. Wrapping my hand around myself, I make long slow strokes, spreading the pre-cum down to the base. With thoughts of her dusky nipples and her tight pussy squeezing my fingers, I shoot my cum in hot ropes along the shower wall.

I'm still unsatisfied, left wanting more of her. All of her. Something about our short time together tells me I will always feel this way. I change quickly, not wanting to be late to the meeting and piss off Michele. She's amazing, but she also scares me a little. I read over the proposal she sent, and although I don't want to accept the offer, I am taking the meeting out of respect.

Mike's ostentatious SUV is already parked outside Michele's office when I arrive. It only gets worse from there when Sherry pops out the front door as I hop out of my truck. She's dressed in a skin hugging red dress that barely covers her ass and stiletto heels as she waves with a saccharine smile.

"Hey sweetie, we are all set up and waiting for you," she coos. I try to hide the revulsion on my face at her voice, her outfit, her in general.

"Sherry, please don't refer to me as anything other than Thoren or Mr. James," I say through gritted teeth.

"Oh, come on, we're closer than that."

I give a wide berth walking around her and into Michele's office. "We aren't. I don't appreciate it and neither will my girlfriend."

Michele smiles wide when she sees me, saving me from the tension Sherry now has radiating from her. "Now that everyone's here, let's all have a seat so we can go over everything." She moves closer to me, squeezing my arm, and whispers, "We are talking after this."

I nod in confirmation because I need her help with some

things, and I'm sure she has an opinion about all of this. Once we sit, Mike starts off talking about the three different parcels of land that he is interested in buying from me. I told him when he first reached out that in order for me to even consider it, I wanted to know exactly what he had planned for the land. As he speaks, Sherry hands over mock-ups of what would go on each. For one, he has a luxury condo with amenities planned out, another is a high end gated community, and for the third, he has a large plaza that he plans to fill with a spa, restaurant, and boutique stores.

The thing is, while Cedar Ridge is small, we are a tourist destination in the fall and winter. Thirty minutes away is a large ski resort that has been gaining in popularity over the last few years. His plans aren't off base, and I'm sure they could do well to bring in more revenue and tourists to the area. The problem is, the town does fine on its own and he would destroy acres of forest. I bought the land not only as an investment, but also to preserve the land.

"As you can see," Mike drones on, "I already have retailers lined up for all the spaces so they won't sit vacant. My offer is way above market value for the land, Michele can attest to that. This should be a no-brainer, kid."

Sherry leans over, making her fake tits all but spill from her dress, as she hands me another paper. Her hand lingers until I look up, and she winks at me, biting her lip. "This could more than set you up for life, *Thoren*," she accentuates my name. "You could settle down, start a family, and not have any worries. Jen always said that's what you wanted."

Michele bristles next to me, but I try to ignore her come on, focusing on the numbers on the paper. The paper lists each plot of land, and for each one, the offer exceeds seven figures. Just one of the offers alone is over five times what I paid for all three pieces of land.

"When do you need an answer by?"

"One month, then I start making offers on other land. I have other options, but as a favor to Sherry, I'm bringing these to you first." Mike says, giving his daughter an annoyed look.

"Okay, I will have an answer for you by then. Thank you for taking the time to get this all together for me." I stand, shaking his hand, as he and Sherry pack up to leave.

Before they go, Sherry corners me, putting her hand on my chest. "Think about this logically, Thoren. That money is life changing. Your wife would never have to work," she purrs as her hand trails down my stomach. I can't step back fast enough, her stifling perfume is overpowering and her hands are the last ones I want on me. With that, she and her father walk out, finally leaving Michele and me to breathe in peace.

"What the fuck was all that?" I ask, plopping back on Michele's couch as she hands me a water bottle, sitting across from me.

"From what I gathered from town talk and their bickering before you got here, Mike is paying Sherry a fair salary, but she is completely cut off otherwise. Something about a six-figure shopping spree in Seattle," she snickers. "All those zeros in your offer have her money hungry ass salivating."

"Ugh," I groan, rubbing my hands down my face. As if I don't have enough going on already. "Before we dive into all that, I need your help with something. Lily's bathroom needs a complete gut, so she's going to be staying with me while I fix it. I want to give her a writing space, but I don't know where to start or what to put in it."

Michele has a knowing smirk on her face, and I flip her off playfully. "She texted me this morning to say you guys were official. We agreed I would be the first to know."

"Well, Riv was kind of there, so he beat you to it. And I told my parents last night. She's slacking on her friend duties," I joke. "But honestly, she had a rough night, so go easy on her."

If Lily hasn't confided in Michele yet, I don't want to break that level of trust again and tell her. When she's ready, she'll share what's going on with her parents.

"How'd it go with the lawyer? And how'd you get her to do it pro bono?" she asks, raising an eyebrow like she already knows the truth.

"I'm paying for it. I wanted Lily to have the best, and Kinsley is that. I know she is living off of a small income and can't take on an expense like that. You can't fault me for that."

"I can fault you for lying to her. Can you afford an expense like that?"

I rub at the back of my neck, then take a sip of water to stall. I have money, but the lawyer is going to cost more than I anticipated and we aren't even far into things yet. There's the option to break into my savings, and I will for her, but it's still a big expense.

"I'm managing it." Michele stares at me, shaking her head. We've known each other long enough that I know she thinks I'm being an idiot. But it's the right thing to do and we both know it.

"You know selling even just one of those slots of land would take care of that problem. Where's your head at with all that?"

"I don't know, Chele. It's a lot of fucking money." I drop my hands to my knees and hang my head. "Sherry was right about one thing; I'd be stupid not to take the deal. I just always thought that land would be used for something better. I don't know what, but I figured I would hold on to it until I knew."

So many possibilities existed, but I never thought it would be developed for commercial use or attract more versions of Sherry to our town. That is the last thing I want or need. Maybe this isn't meant to be about me, though. I can talk to the city council and see what they think about it all.

Michele stands up, patting my shoulder as she walks by. "You have time to think about it. I have a showing to get to, so lock up when you leave. I'll text you with some ideas for Lily's office." With that, she grabs her purse, leaving me to wallow.

CHAPTER NINETEEN

Lily

I used to live in a perpetual Groundhog Day, going to the same job, seeing the same people, doing the same things. I rarely deviated from my routine, only occasionally seeing Tyler, and even then, most of our time together was tiny moments at my place. Since the day I got fired, I feel like no two days have been the same. I was finally settling into a new normal here, getting a sort of routine going. Until my bathroom crumbled, and crushed all sense of normalcy with it.

I moved in with Thoren a week ago, and things have been busy ever since. He spent Saturday and Sunday tearing apart my bathroom and wouldn't let me help because of the mold. He came back home every evening absolutely wrecked and went straight to bed after dinner. This week hasn't been much better either.

Monday after work, he started working on replacing the pipes, and has been doing that every evening since. He let me help, but I think I was in the way more than anything, so I used that time to make us dinner and pack a lunch for him instead. It's been nice, doing mundane chores for him like cooking, cleaning, doing his laundry, no matter how much he insists I don't need to.

He's been so busy trying to do all that for me that even though

I've been sleeping in his bed every night, nothing more has happened between us. I don't want to complain, but I haven't even laid a hand on his magnificent dick yet, and I am desperate to.

I told him this morning before he left for work that he couldn't work at my place at all this weekend because he deserved a break. Selfishly, I just want more time with him. I haven't heard any more from my parents, and Kinsley called on Wednesday to let me know they denied mediation again. Today at 4:30, right before everyone leaves for the weekend, they will be served with the lawsuit paperwork.

My nerves have been all over the place, and writing certainly hasn't been happening, so I took Shadow on a walk to calm myself down. We did some exploring through the woods, and it was going great until my furry little bestie decided to roll.

In something dead.

That had not been dead long.

She smells horrible, and has bits of an animal I don't care to identify sticking to her fur. "What were you thinking, crazy girl? You're going to need a bath now," I scold her.

We make our way back to Thoren's, where I hose her off outside to the best of my ability before texting Thoren.

LILY:

If I were doggy soap, where would I be?

THOREN:

Under the sink in the guest bath. What did the troublemaker do?

LILY:

Rolled in something foul.

THOREN:

It's a nice day, leave her outside and I'll give her a bath when I get home. She doesn't love them. Also, don't make dinner tonight. I have a surprise for you.

There's no way I'm leaving the bath for him. It's my fault she smells, and he doesn't need anything else to do after this week. I'll Google ways to keep dogs happy during bath time. Is he planning to take me out for dinner? I hope not, because all I want is to jump his bones, and that will be hard at a restaurant.

LILY:

Is the surprise sausages? Because I'm drooling at the thought of tasting yours.

THOREN:

Behave.

Why did that one word send heat flooding through my body?

LILY:

Or what?

THOREN:

Baby, you're going to find out soon enough.

Shadow zips past me, doing her zoomies in the yard, pulling my thoughts from all the things Thoren is hopefully going to do to me tonight. I'm not inexperienced; I slept with a guy in high school and Tyler tried to have sex with me every time he came over. Saying my sex life was good, though, would be a lie. It was lackluster at best. I only ever got off when I was on top and controlling things. Tyler's tastes were very vanilla, which was fine, but I wanted something… more.

Thoren's demanding and dominating touch, his gravelly hard voice when he commands me, his light hold on my neck when we kiss, and don't even get me started on his praise. Those are things that set my body on fire, that make my panties wet and my pussy ache.

Shadow zooms past me again, almost taking me out as she runs in circles. "Let's go get that bath, wild girl."

As it turns out, giving dogs a bath is easy, thanks to a quick trick. Peanut butter spread on the side of the tub was all it took. Shadow is happily standing still while I scrub her down as long as I keep the peanut butter coming. A sense of pride isn't something I feel often, but it's happening here pretty frequently. I've never been around animals much, and here I am, nailing my first dog bath.

"Your daddy is going to give you so many snuggles tonight when he smells you," I tell Shadow as I rinse out her doggy shampoo.

"As if she doesn't get enough snuggles as is," a deep voice rumbles behind me, scaring the ever loving life out of me.

Shadow's tail thumps against the tub as I turn around to see Jake leaning against the door, arms crossed over his chest.

"Where did you come from?" I squeak. "You scared the crap out of me."

He lets out a low chuckle, still staring at me. "Sorry, I knocked, but you didn't answer."

"So you just let yourself in? Is that a normal thing for you guys?"

"Honestly? Yeah. You're sleeping in my room, ya know?" His stare bores into me, his mouth lifting into a smirk. "If you're even sleeping in there."

I sputter a cough and turn back to rinsing Shadow, trying to hide my red cheeks. I haven't slept in there once. Why would I when I can spend the night in a loving embrace, surrounded by Thoren's comforting scent?

"Well, it's good to see you again. What are you doing here?"

"I wanted to talk to you, and Thoren wanted me to check out your bathroom. He thought I could make a cool vanity for in there," he says, still just watching me.

"The first part sounds ominous, but the second part sounds amazing. Thanks, Jake."

"I'll be downstairs when you're done here and we can talk," he replies, finally leaving me to finish up with Shadow.

That was weird. Thoren and Michele have great things to say about Jake, and he seems like a nice guy, if not a little scary. The tone in his voice made me feel like I was getting called to the principal's office. I rack my brain on what he could want to talk to me about, but come up empty.

With a fresh smelling puppy, I dry Shadow off the best that I can, then let her loose in the house. I scrub the bathtub clean before making my way downstairs to find Jake. He is sitting in the living room watching the sports channel, so I take a seat across from him on the couch.

"It was nice of you to give Shadow a bath," he says, still staring at the TV and scratching her ears where she's sitting by his feet.

"Well, she rolled in something nasty on our walk, so it's the least I could do. Plus, I love her."

He mutes the TV and turns to look at me. "This talk is not happening. Do you understand?"

I feel my hackles rise, but nod in agreement.

"Did you know Thoren got Shadow before Jen left him?" he asks, but he's not really looking for me to answer. "She begged him for a dog. She begged him for a lot of things she didn't deserve, but he also really wanted a dog. So he looked around, and waited for the right time, and finally found a litter of black lab puppies. He picked out Shadow and brought her home. When she got home and saw the puppy, she lost her shit, and not in a good way. Jen wanted a small lapdog, something to carry around in a purse, even though Lord knows she wouldn't be the one taking care of it."

He shakes his head, frustration written on his features. "She left him two weeks later, and it was the best thing to happen to him. He took it hard for a while. They had been together for years. Shadow got him through those hard times, and she's been his support ever since. Seeing you care for her... it's healing something in him you didn't break."

I nod in understanding because Thoren was also healing parts of me that were broken before him. I haven't really asked too much about Jen, and maybe that was a mistake. I've never really done the relationship thing except with Tyler and clearly that was only a real relationship to me and not him. I don't know what the protocol is for asking about exes. All I know is that Thoren is the best and deserves the best, and I am going to do everything I can to be that for him.

"Lily, he's one of the best people I know. He cares deeply, and will do anything for those in his circle. Jen took advantage of that and I can't watch that happen to him again. He doesn't ask for much out of life, just someone to love him for who he is and to have a big family. Thoren won't talk to you about any of this, but he has a huge fear that you're just here temporarily. She left him to find a bigger and better life, and that's not something he will ever want. This is his home, where his family is, and where he wants to raise his kids. If this small town getaway even has the possibility of being a temporary thing for you, please let him go. The way he talks about you... you're different and he won't survive losing you."

I sit in stunned silence as this burly man pleads with me to protect his friend. I want to be offended; I want to dive into my thoughts about what he said about me being different, but mostly, I want to hug him for looking out for the man who looks out for everyone else. At this moment, I decide that I really like Jake despite his grumpy appearance.

"I'm not going anywhere. I've never felt more alive, free, or like I'm where I'm meant to be than right here in Cedar Ridge. This place has become my home, and somehow, despite all the crap going on in my life, Thoren is starting to feel like home, too. You're a good friend, Jake, and he's beyond lucky to have you in his life."

Jake stares at me again, looking for any lies in my statement, but he won't find them. I have been living here for almost two months now. I can't imagine going anywhere else. This town and these people have infiltrated my life and shown me what it is like to truly live. To find your place, and people who care for you like one of their own, and I will never give that up.

Jake's phone dings from the couch next to him, where he glances at it, then stands. "Want to go show me your bathroom now? We can talk about some options for your vanity?"

"Sure, that sounds good."

I follow him out, leaving Shadow in the house since she's still damp and I don't want her getting muddy. As we walk over, he asks about the trip to Seattle and how River is doing. I didn't realize the three of them, Thoren, River and him, were so close, but I guess they all talk frequently. When we get to my place, he steps aside to make a quick call, letting me know he will meet me inside. I wait in the cabin, cleaning up some tools that are lying around.

Jake isn't outside long, but he takes forever talking about the vanity. He measures and re-measures at least four times, talking about all the different wood options, finishes, and countertops that he can do. Thoren and I haven't picked out tiles or flooring or even a color scheme. I finally convince Jake that the wood and finish is up to his discretion and a neutral counter would be great.

He's acting weird and asks to see my deck to check over

Thoren's work when my phone rings. I rush to answer it to get out of this awkward moment.

"Hello?"

"Hey, baby," Thoren's smooth voice comes over the line. "What are you doing?"

"Uhh, showing Jake the bathroom at my place. I guess you guys talked about him building a vanity?" I try not to sound annoyed that they decided that since it was actually really sweet. I was a little annoyed at this whole scenario because I was anxious for the special thing he has planned for tonight.

"Oh, yeah, that's great. I got off work a little early and am home if you guys want to head back."

"Okay," my excitement stirs. "I'll see you in a few."

Jake must have heard the conversation, because he is already waiting at my front door. As our feet crunch on the gravel in Thoren's driveway, I see his truck parked right next to Jake's and can't help but laugh.

"I think I need to hear the story on the matching trucks," I say, walking in the front door.

"That's not the only thing we have matching," Jake mutters under his breath. Before I can ask what that means, Michele's head pops around the corner.

"Lily!" she squeals, wrapping me in a tight hug. "It's been too long, we need a girls' outing ASAP."

"What are you doing here? I've missed you, too."

"Back off my woman," Thoren growls, playfully shoving Michele out of the way. His big arms swallow me as he drops his lips to my neck. "Hey, baby."

At some point, that term of endearment won't affect me, but today isn't that day. I melt into his embrace, taking a deep inhale of his rugged scent. My arms stay locked around him, needing to convey how much he means to me. I don't want him to have fears about us, no matter how new things are.

He pulls back slightly, cupping my face. "What's going on, Lily?"

"I just really missed you today."

His soft lips meet mine in a sweet kiss. "I missed you, too. Now, I have something to show you. Our friends helped me pull this off," he says with a wink. I look around, but both Michele and Jake are gone. "Follow me, princess."

He leads me upstairs, stopping in front of the last bedroom that I haven't been in yet. "Since you're stuck here for another few weeks at least, I wanted you to have a space to write. I know your book is going to be amazing, and I wanted a space for you to feel that. Go ahead," he motions to the door.

I push it open to see a desk and chair set up, with my laptop already on it. There's a vase of beautiful purple lilacs on the desk next to a small lamp. In the corner is a small shelf with some pens, notebooks, sticky notes, and two framed photos. On closer inspection, one is a quote that says 'Make Today Amazing' and the other is a photo of Thoren and me from the hat store. It's not the one he sent me though, in this one I'm smiling at the camera, but Thoren is smiling down at me, completely enraptured. The tears are silently falling as I look at what he did in the forty-five minutes Jake and I were at my house.

"I know it's not much, but it's what Michele and I could come up with and do with a short time frame." His smile is shy as he leans against the desk.

"This is amazing. Thank you. No one has ever done something like this for me."

Thoren is on me in an instant, pressing my small body against the wall behind me. His kiss is searing, his hands threading through my hair. "You," kiss, "deserve," kiss, "the world," he says, peppering kisses over every tear. When his lips meet mine again, they have a salty tang, but I welcome it as I arch further into his body.

One thigh presses between mine, and I can't help but grind myself over it. Our groans are instantaneous, as his kiss turns even more feverish. One hand moves to slide up my shirt until his fingers are brushing over my peaked nipple. Our tongues clash as I grind against him again.

He pulls back suddenly, the loss of his body against mine jarring. "I want nothing more than to make you choke on my cock until those tears are streaming again. You left me hard and aching for you all day with your teasing earlier. Our friends are on the deck waiting for us, but know that it's coming, Lily. They won't be here forever." He drops a kiss to my head, adjusting himself in his jeans as he turns toward that door like he didn't just soak my panties with his words.

I follow him downstairs in a lustful haze, wondering how this sweet and caring man can have the filthiest mouth. Furthermore, how everything that comes out of it scares me and turns me on in equal measure. Is something wrong with me that I want him to shove his dick so far down my throat that I can't breathe? That I hated sucking off Tyler, but I am on the verge of orgasming at the thought of Thoren coming down my throat?

Shadow is at our feet the minute we step onto the back deck. Jake and Michele are sitting at the table, pizza boxes and plates set out in front of them. I try to wipe the lust from my face, but I must fail because Michele gives me a knowing smirk before sauntering over.

"We'll grab drinks, what would everyone like?"

Thoren and Jake both say beer, so I follow her back into the kitchen, where she turns on me when the door shuts. "Tell me everything right now. Did you guys fuck upstairs? I had more hope for his stamina for you," she tsks, grabbing beers from the fridge.

"No!" I whisper-yell at her. "We haven't even had sex yet. He promised a dirty punishment for making him hard, though.

Michele, he has such a dirty mind. I don't know if I can keep up. I've only ever been very vanilla. I've never even watched porn."

She turns around, gaping at me. "What?! Oh, you sweet, sweet girl. He's so head over heels for you, he'll be gentle. Just talk to him about it. I mean, I hope he still fucks you into next week, but he'll take it easy if you tell him you're scared."

I bite my lip, debating how much to say. I've never had a girlfriend to talk about these types of things with. I know whatever comes out of my mouth will never be judged by Michele. "What if… what if I don't want him to take it easy, but I'm not good at rough? I don't know what I'm doing half the time. He threatened to choke me on his cock, and I almost came on the spot."

"Fucking hell," Michele fans herself. "I always knew he was a freak in the sheets. Just take it one step at a time. Communication is key. Come up with a safe word and let that man go to town."

A safe word? I hadn't thought of that. I write about dirty talking men that have sex like gods, but I kind of thought it was all fiction. I am dying to find out if I've had it wrong all along; that maybe my book boyfriends are modeled after men like Thoren.

With arms full of beer bottles, Michele nods toward the back door. "Let's go. Now I'm thinking about your boyfriend's dick and it's weird. I need a pizza distraction."

I laugh at this crazy woman who is my new best friend and follow her back outside, knowing no amount of pizza can distract me from thinking about Thoren's dick.

thoren

"I think you found her," Jake says, the minute the door shuts.

"Found her?"

"Your one. In one day, I watched her put more effort into taking care of you and making you happy than Jen did in years. That girl in there is all in, and I can see that you love her already." He points at me when I open my mouth, cutting me off before I can protest. "Don't deny it. You fall fast, it's just who you are, and I see why you fell for her. She's good for you."

Focusing on the setting sun, I let that sink in. When Jen left, everyone close to me was supportive, but let me know they felt it was a blessing. I loved Jen, but the more I look back, the more I realize I loved the idea of her the most. It was best for both of us that she left to find her something more. Do I love Lily though?

Just the thought of seeing her puts a smile on my face. I'm aware of her movements, thoughts, and emotions, as much as she is of mine. I am happily giving up my time, money, and energy to make sure she is protected and cared for. Making her smile is constantly the highlight of my day, and I hate every moment we are apart. When I look at it that way, and think of how she is selfless with me, constantly thinking of my needs, and how her eyes fill with joy when she sees me… yeah, I definitely love that girl.

I pull out the chair next to me when the girls come back outside, making sure I get my girl by my side. Michele passes out beers and we all dig into the pizza.

"How often do you guys do things like this?" Lily asks around bites.

"Not often enough," Jake replies. "We used to get together for dinner in town a few times a year at least, but life's just gotten busy and we kind of stopped. It's been about a year, at least."

Shit, has it really been a year? I need to make this a priority again, especially with Lily part of the crew now. Michele wasn't part of our friend group in high school, but we were friendly enough. She dated River's friend Ethan for a while, and they were inseparable.

"When was the last time you talked to Ethan, Chele?" I ask.

Her bright eyes dim as she swallows her bite. "It's been a few years. Last I heard, he was in Colorado following in his dad's footsteps."

"Who is Ethan?" Lily's sweet voice asks.

"A kid we all grew up with. He and Chele dated in high school for a while before his family moved. His dad was a fire chief and got a job offer out of state." I lean over to Lily, whispering in her ear, "Michele's first, and to my knowledge, only love."

She looks at her friend with a sad smile before scooting a little closer to my side. Her small fingers make teasing strokes up and down my jean-clad thighs and I can't help but think she really wants the punishment I threatened her with.

"How's woodworking full time?" Michele asks Jake, clearly uncomfortable with that topic.

"It's busy. I got an offer from a showroom in Spokane to put my furniture there as well. They know the waitlist may be months, but they still seem interested anyway. I'm driving over next week to check it out and see if it's the right fit," he shrugs.

"That's incredible, Jake. Quit being so damn humble, you're killing it and you should be proud. It's everything you've wanted and have been working toward for years," I kick his foot under the table across from me to make sure he's paying attention.

"Thanks, Hammer," he kicks me back.

"You're welcome, Ladder."

Lily and Michele look between us like we're crazy and I realize if we explain this, they will think we are. Jake rolls his eyes but smirks, so I know he's going to spill the beans. We were on a roll there for five years, keeping it hidden.

"So I get the hammer," Michele points to me, then turns to Jake wide-eyed. "Please tell me there's a double meaning with the ladder."

When he winks at her, she almost falls over in her chair, cackling. "Oh my god, yes! This is amazing. Can I see it? Wait, no, I don't want to. Actually, yes I do. You have to show me, it's Friendship 101."

"I'm so lost," my sweet naive Lily says next to me.

"Thor over here," Michele says, pointing back at me, "has been calling his dick his 'hammer' since he moved back from college. Jacob's ladder, you know the joke, works with this idiot over here, but I just discovered he has the piercing, too!"

"What piercing?" Lily asks again.

"The dick piercing! You know, barbells like rungs on a ladder through his dick. How many do you have? You know what, I'll just count when you show me," Michele says, practically giddy. I'm cracking up just as much as she is at the horror equally matched on both Lily and Jake's faces.

"You're not seeing it," Jake declares adamantly.

"Oh, yes, I am, or I'll start telling all the girls in town that you're a big softie and your penis is small."

His eyes narrow and I have to spare him, so I blurt out the last secret. "That's not even the best part of it all."

"What's the best part?" Lily asks, her voice full of trepidation.

I stand up, turning to face my ass toward the girls, and begrudgingly, Jake does the same. In tandem, we pull down a side of our pants to reveal our matching ass tattoos. Mine, a small hammer, and Jake's, a small ladder. We lost a bet with River right out of college and, well, that was our punishment.

The girls' laughs are loud and instantaneous, both dying over our tattoos. I should be embarrassed, but I'm not, and I saved Jake from having to whip out his dick. I would have had to punch him if Lily saw it, and I'm fairly certain he would then proceed to kick my ass.

Easy conversation and laughter filled the rest of our dinner. Jen rarely joined our friend dinners when we did them, and when she did, they never had this much happiness. I'm so grateful to be surrounded by friends that support me and my girl. When Lily finishes her last piece of pizza, I pull her onto my lap, hating not having my hands on her.

I've been half hard since our kiss upstairs, with her breathy moans, and the way she rubbed herself against me. My cock thickens again thinking about it, and I know she can feel it because she adjusts herself, subtly rubbing her ass over my growing length. My fingers grip her hips tight, trying to hold her in place before I embarrass myself.

Thankfully, Jake looks over and knows exactly what I'm thinking, so he starts packing up the table and offers to drive Michele back home. She drove with me up here for the surprise, and while I am grateful, I'm even more grateful I don't have to take her back. With a quick adjustment while standing behind Lily, I follow our friends to the front door to say goodbye.

As Michele and Lily say goodbye, Jake gives me a bro hug, muttering, "She's worthy of your hammer."

I bark out a laugh and whisper back, "Michele's still gonna want to see your dick."

He shoves my shoulder hard and turns to give Lily a half hug before storming out to the sounds of my laughter. After locking the front door, I turn to Lily. The little minx already has her shirt off, discarded on the floor next to her, with her eyes glued to my cock.

Leaning against the door, I raise an eyebrow in challenge. "Finish what you started, Lily. Show me what's mine."

I've seen her naked already, hell I've had my fingers in her tight little cunt, but that was all for her. That night, she needed someone to relax her and care for her, so that's what I did. After she's been teasing me all day, this first time is for me. I watch with rapt attention as she slowly peels her shorts down her legs, kicking them off at the bottom. She's standing before me like a goddess in a matching pale pink bra and panty set. Both are lacy and see-through, causing my mouth to water at the sight.

Lily has subtle curves, with lean legs I want to bury my face between, and the most perfect small handful of tits. Her olive skin is glowing in the dim light of the entryway, her blue eyes shining with excitement and nerves. Her dainty fingers reach back, unclasping her bra that she lets slide down her shoulders and fall to the floor. With her hard nipples on display, she reaches for her panties.

"Stop," I growl out. "Turn around first."

Like a good girl, she listens without hesitation. Her hips hinge as she drags her panties down her legs, her round ass on full display for me. By the time she gets them down to her feet, I can see just how wet she is for me. I bite back a groan as she stands back up and waits for further instructions. I love how obedient she is, and I can't wait any longer to see just how compliant she will be.

I grip her at her waist and throw her over my shoulder, taking the stairs two at a time to get to my room. Her squeals of delight warm my chest as I plop her down at the foot of my bed. I kick the door closed behind me to make sure Shadow stays out, then grab a pillow from the bed and place it on the ground.

"Get on your knees for me, princess."

She drops down wide-eyed, her pupils blown. My fingers stroke down her cheek as my thumb runs over her bottom lip. "Such a good fucking girl. Take my cock out."

A shiver runs through her body as she gets to work, her shaky hands undoing my jeans. I think it's from anticipation, but something in me needs to check in case it's not. I want her lust, excitement, screams, and tears, but her fear is not something I'm after.

My large hands cover hers, stopping them. She looks up at me through her dark lashes with a questioning look. "I like to be in charge here, but you have all the power. You say stop, and we stop. Do you understand?"

"I don't want you to stop. I'm out of my depth here, but I want it. I want to be your good girl, Thoren. Choke me with your cock, and make me say thank you."

Fuuuuucking hell. She's a secret sex vixen, and she doesn't even know it. I want to ruin her.

I move my hands off of hers and nod for her to continue. She shimmies my pants down with more determination than a minute ago. As soon as my boxers follow, my cock springs out like the heavy hammer that it is.

Lily is looking at it like it's her next meal making pre-cum leak from the tip, showing her exactly what's in store. Her warm hand reaches out, holding it in place as she licks the slit clean. Before I can process the sensation, she opens wide and swallows half of me down. Her hot mouth moves up and down my shaft as her hand strokes me in even strides.

My head falls back as her tongue swirls around my tip, causing more pre-cum to leak out. She hums her approval, the vibrations radiating through me and I almost lose it. I promised to fuck her face, and that's exactly what I'm going to do.

"Put your hand on my thighs, baby. I'm going to fuck your mouth now, and if it's too much, you tap there and I'll stop, okay?"

She moves her hands, nodding excitedly. One of my hands moves to the back of her head to grip her hair at the roots. I give it a little pull until her blue eyes look up and meet mine.

"Eyes on me, princess," I grit out, as I thrust into her mouth. Her wet tongue adds the perfect pressure and I know I'm not going to last long. I set a punishing pace, rutting into her perfect hot mouth. My cock hits the back of her throat, causing tears to stream down her cheeks, but my girl takes it, her eyes never leaving mine.

"You're doing so well, my perfect girl. Are you going to let me cum down your throat?" She nods slightly again as my balls draw up, and white hot heat barrels down my spine. "Swallow me down, princess, don't spill a drop," I groan as the first spurt of cum shoots from me. I swear the room spins around me as my cum spills down her throat. She works to swallow it all down, but a little leaks down her chin. To my utter surprise, she uses my cock to wipe it up, then licks it clean.

With that one move, I am done, completely gone for this girl. I pick her up and kiss her deep, tasting myself in her mouth. "So fucking perfect," I whisper against her lips before wrapping her legs around me and crawling onto the bed with her. "Now say thank you."

"Thank you, sir. Now get naked and fuck me."

"Did my girl just swear?" I ask, pulling my shirt from my body and discarding my socks. "Oh, baby, I am going to ruin you in all the best ways. Say it again."

"Please fuck me, Thoren."

I want to spend the next hour between her legs, drawing

orgasm after orgasm from her until she's a crying, shaking mess. I want to worship her pussy the way she just worshiped my cock, but I'll never deny this girl anything. If she wants me to fuck her, I'm going to fuck her with everything I have.

"Condom?"

"I'm clean, and on birth control," is her breathy reply. "I've never gone without, but I want to feel you. I need to feel you."

My chest rumbles with another groan. I'm trying to ruin this girl, but she's the one doing the ruining. There's no doubt I'm so stupidly in love with her, and she has no idea. Grabbing my cock that is hard again and begging to be inside of her, I rub the head through her slick entrance. I coat myself in every bit of her dripping essence, then grind against her, making sure I hit her clit.

My hips rock over her again and again until she's mewling under me, dripping down her thighs and begging for my cock. I grip her knees, spreading them wide, and slowly push into her. As soon as my head is in, our moans mingle.

Inch by inch, I grind into her tight, wet heat. "You feel so good, squeezing my cock as if you were made for it."

When I'm fully seated inside of her, I give her a minute to adjust to my size. I've gone bare before, but I swear it never felt like this. With the slight bunch of Lily's brows smoothed out, I move, grinding into her. Angling my hips to rub her clit with every stroke, while keeping her legs spread for me.

"You are so beautiful, Lily, every inch of you on display for me." I lean forward, taking her mouth in a passionate kiss, as I continue to work my cock in her. Dainty hands wrap around my back, her nails digging in and scratching down my back. That edge of pain spurs me on as I drag my mouth from hers, moving down her throat. I nip and kiss my way down, stopping to lick along her collarbone.

Her breathing is faster now, as she whines out a needy, "More, baby, please." I lick my way down to her nipple before drawing it into my mouth. She arches her back, pushing it further into my mouth for me to suck and lick. I pick up my pace, fucking her harder. Her pussy flutters around me, telling me she's close. My orgasm has been on the edge, ready to explode the minute she does.

I put my lips to her ear, commanding, "Come for me, princess. Milk my cock," before leaning back down and biting her nipple hard.

She shatters around me as she screams out my name, her nails biting into the skin on my back. Her orgasm sets off my own, as her pussy squeezes the life out of my dick, milking every last drop of cum from it. My body gives out, the strength of the orgasm draining my last bit of energy. I collapse onto her, then roll to the side with Lily still tight in my arms.

We lie in contented silence, coming down from the earth shattering, soul-destroying sex. I look down at her blissed out face, hair a tangled mess around her head, truly marked as mine, and a feeling of peace washes over me. This is what I have been waiting for all my life. This feeling of mutual destruction, so we can build ourselves back together, weaving our hearts together as one.

Dropping a light kiss to her head, I gently slip out of her and head to the bathroom to get a warm, wet rag. She's barely awake, wrapped in a ball in the middle of my bed when I step from the bathroom. Exactly where I intend to keep her. I carefully spread her legs, cleaning her up, before covering her back up and tucking her in.

"My beautiful Lily," I kiss her soft, swollen lips. "I'm going to let Shadow out and lock up. Sleep, baby, and I'll be back to cuddle you soon."

I throw on some boxers before heading downstairs to do just that. I clean up the rest of the dinner dishes, let Shadow out, and pick up Lily's clothes to put in the hamper. At the top of the stairs, I see the new office door open, drawing me to it. I have had this door closed and room empty for so long, it's weird seeing it with furniture. It's a great space for her to write, but my heart skips a beat at the thought of one day walking in here to see her putting our baby to sleep.

That day will happen. I can feel it in my bones. Jake may be right, that I love fast and hard, but it's different with Lily. I don't believe in fate, but I believe in listening to the world around you. Loving Lily feels like it gives me the steady strength of the trees in the forest, the warmth of the early morning sun rays hitting my face, and the rush of stepping into the river water on a spring day.

With that thought, I make my way back to the bedroom, crawling into bed next to my future. She latches onto me instantly, letting out a sigh when my arms wrap around her. Sleep drags me under easily, where I dream of the perfect summer day with my girl.

lily

"Good morning, baby," Thoren steps into the room, handing me a cup of hot coffee.

I sit up to take a sip, noting that it's made exactly how I like. "I preferred how you woke me up this weekend, but this is a good second."

"Nothing would make me happier than to have you for breakfast every day, but I'd never leave and I have to work."

I feel a rush of arousal at just the thought of that. Saturday and Sunday, he woke me up with his face between my legs, and the man can eat. He did things that have never been done to me, and didn't stop until he had wrung every ounce of pleasure from my body. I truly don't know how his jaw doesn't hurt, but there are no complaints from me. I read once that women's cum can turn a man's beard white, and if that's the case... well, there's no hope for him.

"Sorry I slept in and missed our coffee on the deck tradition."

"It's okay, it's raining out anyways. I just wanted to say bye, and let you know I'm taking Shadow to work with me today," he says with a kiss. "Have a good day, baby."

He leaves me to it, so I drag myself from the cozy bed to throw on some sweats. I love writing in the rain. Something about the comfort and sound of it really gets my creativity flowing. With my coffee in hand, I meander down the hall to my new office. I don't know what this room was before, but it's the perfect cozy office. With the calming pitter patter of rain, I dive into my chapters.

My stomach growls, breaking the spell my writing had on me. I intended to only write for an hour before grabbing breakfast, but looking at the time now, it's almost past lunch. With three chapters done, I'm not even slightly upset. With phone in hand, I head downstairs to make a sandwich and take something out for dinner.

It's too quiet in the house without Shadow, so I pull up some music on my phone, but a text notification stops me in my tracks. It's from a number I know very well, despite having deleted his contact. Tyler's text reads, 'Drop the lawsuit, Lily' and nothing more.

I see red; anger radiating through my body. The audacity of him to lie to me, and treat me like he did and now finally, the first thing he says to me after getting me fired is to drop the lawsuit. There is no way in hell that's happening. I immediately pull up Kinsley's number and call her office, knowing she will tell me what to do with this.

Her receptionist puts me on hold while she gets her, then Kinsley's kind voice answers, "Hey Lily, what's going on?"

"Tyler texted me telling me to drop the lawsuit."

Her voice is hard when she responds, "Send me that. Screenshot, and send it to me, but absolutely do not respond. Anything at all from him, text, emails, calls, whatever it is, record it and send it to me."

"Okay. Is this going to keep happening?"

"I don't know, but if he's already sent one, he is probably

stupid enough to send more. My team has the subpoena submitted to get their phone and email records. I'm going to add yours to the list, too," she says, her voice softening again. "If he's texting you, that means he's scared and he damn well should be. We're going to nail him and that entire company, Lily, don't worry."

"Okay."

"As messed up as it is, it works in our favor that he's reaching out. If he makes a threat, we can press criminal charges against him on top of everything. Let me know if he does again, but for now, I'll keep working on gathering everything I need and you write that book."

"Okay." I'm aware I sound like a broken record, but I'm not sure what else to say. We end the phone call as I slump down onto a stool at the island.

I was looking forward to a new week with a fresh start. I need to get a lot done on my book, and being a stressed out mess won't help. Tyler's been out of my life for over four months now, yet I still feel like he has a hold on me in ways that he doesn't deserve. It's not fair to Thoren for me to be sulking around, worrying about my parents' opinions or if Tyler will reach out again.

He has been working so hard on making sure I am emotionally, mentally, and physically cared for. I need to get myself together for both of us. Between his actual job and working at my house last week, he easily put in seventy hours. If there is anyone that deserves to be taken care of, it's him, so that's exactly what I'm going to do.

With a plan in place, I grab a small snack, my appetite long gone, and head back upstairs to write some more. I get one more chapter written by the time Thoren should get off work, so I drag myself back downstairs to get dinner started.

"Honey, I'm home," Thoren calls through the front door, mixed with Shadow's excited woofs as she barrels straight for me.

I don't think I'll ever tire of her excitement when she sees me. "What smells so good?"

"I'm making teriyaki wings and sticky rice for dinner," I smile over my shoulder at him as he leans in for a kiss before moving to the sink to wash his hands.

"And what is all this?"

"I thought homemade apple pie sounded delicious."

"What did I do to deserve this?" he asks, wrapping his arms around me from behind. He mentioned in Seattle that apple pie is his favorite dessert and it breaks his heart that people mostly eat it once a year.

"Go relax while I finish this and get it in the oven, and then we can talk."

"Miss Wilks, are you calling me to the principal's office? I do hope you'll punish me," he smacks my ass, walking away. "I'm going to take a quick shower and change. Give you some time to make sure my punishment matches my crime."

The ease with which he approaches life blows me away. If someone told me we were going to have a talk, I would have an internal panic attack thinking of every worst-case scenario possible. I love that about him, that he balances me out in that way. There are a lot of things that I love about him, and that scares the crap out of me.

With the pie in the oven and dinner done, I clean up the kitchen and set the food out on the table for us. Thoren steps into the dining room and I try not to stare, but I'm failing. Gray sweats and no shirt should be illegal on him, with the corded muscles of his arms wrapped in tattoos. His sculpted chest is still damp, his hair a little wild, giving him a freshly fucked look. It reminds me of the first day he popped out of the woods into my backyard. To think that was only two months ago. Look at us now.

"Close that pretty mouth before I fill it," his deep voice rumbles, pulling me from my wayward thoughts.

My cheeks heat, but I take a seat and start dishing out our plates. My hands shake as I set his in front of him, and he latches onto my wrist before I can pull away. "What's going on, baby?"

I feel so stupid. It isn't like he's in trouble, or this is even a big thing to talk about. I just don't do well being assertive and holding my ground, and I'm expecting some pushback from him on this.

"I'm setting a limit for you."

"A limit?"

"Yeah. You're doing too much; working too hard. I would like to hire someone to finish my bathroom. You're doing such a great job, and I'm so appreciative, but I can't let you do it anymore. You've hit your limit on things you can do for me."

His chuckle is a little sinister as he grips my wrist tighter, forcing my eyes to meet his. "There is no limit on what I can and will do for you, Lily. If you want me to work on it less, I will. If you want me to take a week off work and get it all done, I will. If you want to hire someone because you don't like my work, that's fine, too. But not letting me do this because you think I'm doing too much for you is not something I accept."

Well crap, that's not where I expected this to go. I don't even know which option to choose, but I know I can't let him burn his candle at both ends for me. "Two days," I blurt, "You can work on it two days a week, maximum. I can find another rental, or maybe stay with Michele for a bit since it's going to push the timeline back."

"Abso-fucking-lutely not. My home is your home until the bathroom is done. You're lucky I didn't end up having to re-pipe the kitchen, too, because I would love nothing more than to have you here with me for months. I'll stick to two days if that's what you want. Is this all you wanted to talk to me about?"

It's on the tip of my tongue to tell him that Tyler reached out, but the oven timer saves me. I slip away to pull the pie out, setting it on the trivets to cool. I should tell him about the text; he's been with me every step of the way through this. He just worries about me so much already, and I can't keep adding to that. If he reaches out again, then I'll tell him about it.

We finish up eating as I tell him about how my writing is coming along and he tells me about his day at work. I refuse to let him clean up dinner, so he sets up a movie for us to watch, and gets the pie and ice cream ready.

"I picked Bad Teacher, since I didn't get my punishment I was hoping for," he smirks before taking a bite of his pie.

The moan that leaves him is unholy, making me desperate to hear him do it again. I watch as he savors every bite he takes, licking the fork clean each time. Heat sears through my body, traveling south at the thought of that tongue licking me the same way. It gives me the courage to do something crazy.

Putting my bowl on the coffee table, I sink to my knees on the floor in front of him and pull down his sweats. He lifts his hips, helping me get them down, his hazel eyes boring into me with a question written in them. His cock is quickly growing under my gaze, and I lick my lips before licking him from his balls to the tip. The low moan rumbles from his chest again and I smile at the thought of bringing it out of him.

He brings another bite of pie to his lips, casually eating while I suck his cock. An idea forms in my head, so I turn to my bowl and slip a bite of ice cream into my mouth before wrapping my lips around his thick purple head. His stomach muscles tense as the cold sensation hits him, but I slide my lips down as far as I can, cooling and warming him as I go. The ice cream melts in my mouth as I suck and lick every drop off.

"You look so pretty with your lips wrapped around me," he says, taking another bite of his dessert.

His praise spurs me on, sucking him down until I'm gagging on his cock. This isn't something I've really done before, making noises and being sloppy while giving head, but it's clear Thoren loves it. His fingers are tight around his bowl and his knuckles are turning white. I know he wants to thrust into me, but he's holding back.

I take some time to give his bulbous head extra attention, swirling my tongue around it, getting rewarded when pre-cum leaks from the tip. Never did I think I would crave the taste of a man, but I want his cum. I want to earn every drop while watching him lose all control because of me.

Moaning as I lick the glistening cum from his slit, I pull off of him with a loud pop. "You're my favorite flavor."

My lips trail down his dick, taking one ball into my mouth, then the other, sucking and swirling my tongue around him. I bob back down on him, sucking him with fervor, hollowing out my cheeks as I suck him like my life depends on it. I love the silky feel of him, the feel of bringing this man to his knees. His bowl is discarded on the couch next to him as one hand flies to my hair, the other gripping my throat, unable to stop himself.

"Fuuuu- I'm gonna cum," he grits out as the first shot of him hits the back of my throat. I don't dare stop, continuing to work to earn my reward. Hot ropes of cum fill my mouth while his hand grips tighter to feel me swallow it down as fast as I can. When his hands finally loosen, and he sags into the couch, I give his tip a kiss, then tuck him back into his sweats.

Grabbing my bowl off the coffee table, I take a seat next to him and continue to eat, trying to focus on the movie he put on. His head rolls to the side, staring at me with a dazed expression.

"I'm going to marry you one day, Lily Wilks."

I huff out a laugh, and continue eating while his words float around me, warming me from the inside out. I don't think he means it, but it heals another piece of me. Tyler used to tell me marriage wasn't in the cards for him again, but I just assumed his mind would change eventually since he still promised a future together. I should have listened.

Thoren lets me finish eating, but the moment I set my empty bowl down, he launches himself on me, pulling me down the couch under him. His hard body crowds over me as he drops his hips, thrusting his hardening cock over my wet center. I've never gotten wet from giving head to anyone else, but Thoren's thick veiny shaft fills me with need when it glides over my tongue.

His lips hover over mine as he pulls my hands over my head and holds them together. "Don't move these," his husky voice skates over my chilled skin as he lowers himself down my body. He places soft kisses on my belly where he lifted my shirt as he works my pants down, finding me bare and dripping for him. "So fucking needy and weeping for me. Let me take care of you, baby." He trails a finger lazily through my slick pussy, circling my entrance before sliding it in. My head falls back on a low moan as he glides his tongue over my clit. He adds a second finger, stroking and licking in tandem, taking his time to make me feel good.

I feel his hot mouth suction around me, driving me closer to that edge. My hands want so badly to run through his hair and pull him tighter to me. Thoren works me right to the brink, my body lit like a Christmas tree before he sits up and hastily removes his sweats. His hands wrap around mine again as he leans over me, his lips taking mine in a passionate kiss as he pierces me in one quick thrust.

I cry out, feeling so full of him. His thick cock stretches me wide, the slight burn a welcome feeling. Our tongues tangle, the slight tang of my arousal hot on his lips. Calloused hands grip my wrists tight as he rolls his hips, fucking me into the couch. Seeing his wild eyes trained on me while he holds me captive below him strokes the fire in me. My legs wrap around him of their own accord, digging my heels into his ass to drive him deeper.

"You're taking me so well, baby," he grunts against my lips, hitting my clit with every glide of his hips. "Your pussy was made for me. Made to be stretched by my cock. Fuck, Lily, you are so perfect."

His words send a flutter of butterflies through my belly, heightening every emotion and the feel of him inside me. My orgasm hits me full force, barrelling through me as my senses fail and all I can feel is tingling down to my toes and the hard thrust of his cock.

"So beautiful when you come for me." His lips press to mine as his rhythm stutters and he stills, his dick pulsing as he spills into me. Our kiss turns lazy and tender as we calm down. With careful movements, he pulls from me and rushes to the bathroom for tissues to clean me up. I beat him back to the couch as he puts our dishes away, cuddling back into the cushions.

He grabs my socked feet when he sits, putting them in his lap to rub for the rest of the movie. It almost feels like we are trying to one up each other in the things that we do, but I know better. We are doing it because we want to, because we get joy out of caring for each other. It's the purest expression of our feelings for each other, and I am quickly realizing it is rare. These feelings that we have, the way we treat each other, the ease with which every moment flows together; they are the things fairytales are made of.

I retreat to the bedroom when the movie is over to shower while Thoren lets out Shadow and locks up. This feels much better than the rushed exhaustion of last week, and I'm glad I put my foot down on how much he can help with my renovation. Right as I'm slipping out of the shower, he slips in with a passing kiss.

Strong arms wrap around me when he climbs into bed behind me after his shower. "I forgot to tell you, my parents want us over for dinner Friday night. Is that okay?"

"Mhmm. I'm looking forward to meeting them."

"They're going to love you, baby."

God, I hope he's right. I already have one set of lackluster parents around, but knowing Thoren and River, I know they were raised by incredible people. Maybe it's time I try to reach out to my parents again, though the thought makes me shiver. I get pulled in closer with the movement, and settle into my favorite place, drifting off to sleep.

CHAPTER TWENTY-TWO

LILY:

Can we stop in town on the way? I would like to get your mom flowers.

THOREN:

Absolutely baby.

LILY:

Should I wear a dress? I should wear a dress.

THOREN:

They won't care what you wear.

THOREN:

Scratch that. Wear a dress and no panties.

LILY:

I can't do that!

THOREN:

Do it princess, and I'll reward you.

This week has flown by with both Thoren and I working overtime. It's been wet and cold out, which was perfect for Thoren's team to simulate risky training situations. He was out most of Wednesday evening, coming back soaked to the bone and exhausted. His week left him physically tired, while I'm mentally drained. I was a little behind on my book, but with my new cozy office space and Shadow's company, I wrote another fifteen chapters this week. I am almost done with the first draft now, finally back on schedule. Mostly, I needed a distraction from everything going on around me and writing gave me that escape.

The more I use writing to escape, the easier it is to see this is what drew me to it in the first place. I've been hiding inside my shell since I was a child, and this is my one creative outlet. Writing gives me the escape from the confines that I have given myself, allowing me to be myself and express my thoughts and emotions in a way that was still hidden from the world. As a teen, it was the one thing my mom couldn't criticize me for. She never knew I was writing then, so I could let all the emotions she made me suppress bleed onto the pages. I guess in a way, I have her to thank for this budding career and love for pouring myself into written word.

Andrea has been blowing up my phone with questions about the lawsuit and the book, and I have been terrible at answering. No time like the present to divulge it all to her since I just sent off my newest set of chapters.

As always, she's polished and working when I video call. "You've been avoiding me Lily," she chides in a kind voice.

"Not avoiding, just busy working. I sent over fifteen chapters today."

Okay, I might be avoiding, but I haven't told Michele or Thoren about Tyler's texts and if someone is going to break me, it's Andrea. She's been my publisher since the beginning and was there through every stage of my relationship with him. She never liked him, and while she was furious about the whole situation, his deceit wasn't a shock to her; she was just glad I was free of him.

"You did? I can't wait to dive in. I'm obsessed with your characters. Are you done with the book, then?"

"Not quite. I need the ending and it hasn't quite come to me yet." It turns out, happy ever afters are hard to write about after yours gets crushed. With Thoren around though, I think it will come to me. I've never written over ten chapters a week before this, and it's obviously due to him.

"It will come when you're ready. How're things with the lawsuit?"

I chew on my bottom lip, debating telling her everything or just skimming over the basics. "They denied mediation, so we are going to trial. Tyler texted me."

"Shut up! He did not! What did he say?"

"He told me to drop the lawsuit."

Andrea's face turns a mottled shade of red as she grinds her teeth. "I fucking hate that guy. Do not let him intimidate you, Lily. He deserves everything he has coming to him and more." A pensive look crosses her features. "You write these incredible, badass women who take what they want and know their worth. I know that same woman is inside you, she just needs the guidance to see the light of day. Stay the course, Lily, and don't let him break you down again."

A silent tear tracks down my cheek that I don't bother brushing away. "Thank you."

"You're welcome. Now, go be the beautiful badass that I know you are and keep me in the loop. I need to go read your book while picturing River."

"Get out of here with that. I appreciate you, and I promise I will keep you informed."

We say our goodbyes in time for me to get ready for the evening with Thoren's parents. I needed the distraction before hopping into the shower to do my 'everything' shower. By the time I am out and drying my hair, Thoren is home and taking my spot in the shower.

I'm a nervous wreck waiting for him to get out so we can go. He asked me to pull out clothes for him, so I'm rifling through his clothing, trying to find a nice outfit. I went with a knee length dress and boots for me and a nice flannel and dark jeans for him. His lumberjack look gets me hot every time.

I'm pulling on my second boot when he steps through the bathroom door, completely nude, drying his hair with the towel. Water droplets trail down his abs to the small smattering of hair at the bottom.

"Lily, baby, stop looking at me like that unless you want to meet my parents with my cum dripping down your thighs."

He looks down at me with a wicked smirk before discarding the towel and pulling on his boxers. How he gets more mouth watering every day, I will never know. Leaving him to finish getting dressed on his own, I bring Shadow downstairs to put on a fresh bandana. With the three of us ready to go, we load up into Freya. Thoren pulls a beautiful bouquet of wildflowers from the back seat, setting them on my lap when he buckles me in.

"I will tell her they are from you," he winks at my frustrated sigh.

"I was supposed to get them for her."

"You also weren't supposed to wear panties. Did you listen?" My cheeks heat as his eyes bore into my lap like he knows I didn't.

"Show me, Lily."

Slowly, I slide my dress up my thighs to reveal a red cotton thong. Thoren tsks, shaking his head as he navigates us through town. "Take them off, princess."

"What?" I squeak.

"Take. Them. Off."

Reluctantly, I listen, lifting my hips to slide them off. Thoren delicately plucks them from my fingers, before tucking them into his pocket. "Good girl."

I'm not sure if I'm upset or turned on, but I think it's a good bit of both. That seems to be a common occurrence around this man. I shimmy my dress back down with a mock glare, and the smug jerk just winks at me.

"Do your parents know I'm staying with you? And about Tyler? Oh god, did River tell them about our make out in the hall?"

His chuckle stops when he sees the genuine panic on my face. "They know about you staying, and they know you are having issues with an ex, but that's it. They're good people, baby, you don't need to worry. There's not a judgemental thought between them." He squeezes my thigh as he pulls up to their house.

He lets Shadow out of the back, before coming over to open my door. Thoren pulls me down and into his arms while I take some steadying breaths. "They already love you, Lily. They will see the beautiful, strong, and kind-hearted woman that I see every day." He swipes the flowers from the seat and gives them to me in time for us to see the front door open.

He grabs my hand, leading me to the porch where Shadow is waiting patiently for a treat. Thoren's mom has a clear routine with her, which is both adorable and impressive. She looks up, giving us the biggest smile when Shadow finally gets the treat and tears through the house.

"Lily," she opens her arms wide, embracing me fully. "It's so good to finally meet you. I feel like we've been waiting forever. Come on in." She ushers me in the house with her.

"Hi mom, good to see you, too," Thoren grumbles behind us.

"These are for you, Mrs. James," I say, handing her the flowers. "Thank you for having us over."

"Please, call me Evelyn. Thoren, honey, can you put these in water for me? Then tell your dad to come inside? He's in the garden again."

Thoren looks at me with a questioning look and I nod, letting him know I'm okay on my own. He heads to the kitchen while Evelyn leads me to the living room. "I'm sorry to steal you away right away," she says, taking a seat on the oversized couch, patting the spot next to her. "I just wanted to talk to you without the boys around. I've been looking forward to meeting you; both my sons have done nothing but sing your praises."

"That's really nice of them. They are good men. Thoren has done so much for me; they actually both have."

"They're the best boys. Though I'm afraid River gets most of the praise."

River only met me for dinner and the walkthrough of the stadium, but I'm not surprised he squealed to his mom about me. He seems genuine, and his love for his little brother shows. He seemed beyond thrilled for Thoren and me to be together.

"I picked up on that. He was wonderful to me, and I'm sure he deserves it. It surprises me that people overlook Thoren so easily, though. Men like him are hard to find, with his loyalty, heart, and giving soul. I thought men like him were only real in fairytales."

Evelyn's eyes shine as she watches me talk about her son, and I suddenly feel like I'm over sharing. I've never met a boyfriend's parents or family, so I move to a safer topic. "He talks so highly of you, always bragging about your food, garden, and things you did while he was growing up."

"That's always nice to hear. Thoren mentioned your parents weren't really in the picture?"

The blood drains from my face as my muscles lock up.

"Umm, yeah, they had different plans for my life, so we don't talk much."

"I'm really sorry about that. It's hard to grow up with that, and it's hard to continue to feel that loneliness and disconnect as an adult. I know I'm not your mom, and while I have hopes, I can't know where things are going with you and Thoren. Regardless, I am here, and I am available anytime. I've read your books, and you are so incredibly talented. You should be beyond proud of yourself and what you're doing."

"Thank you," I swallow around the lump in my throat.

"No, thank you. You have brought hope and happiness back into Thoren's life. He's lucky to have found you. That video of you two at the game warmed my heart, seeing him getting chosen like that. We all worry about him, even River. The world puts him in River's shadow despite us doing everything we can to keep their accomplishments separate. You, sweet girl, impacted our entire family in ways you will never know with that small action."

Her hand pats mine lovingly, "You are so strong, and I know that there is a lot you are facing right now. I see your selflessness, your grit, and your heart. River saw it the minute he met you, and David and I have seen it in the way you take care of our boy. You're not alone, Lily. We are all here to help you through these next parts of life, and to cheer you on along the way."

Evelyn's face blurs as the tears threaten to spill over. What must it have been like to grow up with a mom like this? And what have I done to deserve to have these people in my life now? I blink back the tears, discreetly wiping the few that break free.

Hearing her say she is proud of me makes me realize the only time I heard those words come from my mom's mouth was when I graduated top of my class. She has never sat with me to just talk, or to see who I am outside of my career and education. Although those were things I wanted from her, I think I realized a long time ago I would never get them. Making peace with knowing you are a disappointment to your parents is hard, but I thought I got there. Evelyn's kind words sending me into a tailspin of emotions says I'm not there yet.

"Thank you, Evelyn. For raising such good men, and for saying that. It means more than you'll ever know."

"You ladies ready for dinner?" Thoren's voice rings through the house.

Evelyn stands, giving me a soft smile. "Come to the kitchen when you're ready." She disappears down the hall, giving me a moment to collect myself. When the time comes, I hope I can be half the woman and mother that she is.

thoren

"Hey mom, where's Lily?"

"Living room, honey. You go get her, and we will have everything ready in the dining room." She pats me on the shoulder as she grabs food from the oven.

I find Lily sitting on the couch, staring blankly at the wall. When she turns to me, her eyes are glassy, but her smile is bright. Taking a seat, I pull her onto my lap. "What's going on, baby?"

"I love your mom," she breathes into my neck.

"Well, of course you do, she's the best. Are you okay?"

"Yeah," she leans back, giving me a soft kiss. I stand, setting her on her feet, and lead her to the dining room. My mom and dad are setting out the rest of the food while Shadow runs around hoping to get scraps that are dropped. I don't miss the soft smile my mom gives Lily as she takes her seat. Dad comes over to officially greet Lily before sitting next to mom across from us.

"This all looks delicious. Thank you so much for having me over," Lily says as I dish us both up.

"It's family dinner, of course you're invited," my dad replies around bites of food, completely oblivious to the fact that Lily has gone still beside me. I give her knee a reassuring squeeze and a wink. I know she prefers actions to words, so my parents accepting her into the fold like I told her they would is exactly what she needed.

"River told us the book you're writing is about him. How in depth into his personal life did you delve? I love your books, but I don't think I can read about my son's sexual preferences," my mom casually throws out.

"Oh Evelyn, what have you done? What if she bases some of the *scenes* off of her personal life? Now we are going to read about both our sons!"

I glance at the poor girl next to me, her face as red as mine. I don't even know what to say, or how to take any of this. Lily could use the backup, but fuck, I haven't read her books so I didn't even think to ask where her sex scene ideas come from. My cock stirs at the thought of her writing out her sexual fantasies, and now I want to know the answer, too. I know she didn't ask River about his sex life, but that doesn't mean she didn't write about ours.

Just when I think I need to jump in and save her, Lily's soft voice answers, "You read my books, too, David?"

My dad's cheeks turn pink as my mom cackles beside him. "I made him read your first book when Thoren first told us about you. He picked up the next ones all on his own."

"I haven't even read any yet! I can't believe you're reading smut, Dad."

"It's spicy romance, thank you. I raised you better than that. How haven't you read her books yet?" Dad shakes his head at me, disappointment evident in his eyes. "I'm sorry Lily, we tried our best with him."

"My question was never answered," mom adds.

Lily takes another bite, buying herself some time. "There is nothing in this book influenced by River's actual relationships."

She leaves it at that, and I think everyone sees her desire to change the subject.

I don't miss that she doesn't mention us, and now I'm dying to read this next book. My hand slips higher up her thigh, drawing circles under the skirt. The resulting shiver up her spine draws a smile to my face as I slowly slide my fingers higher. When they hit the heat of her center, I'm reminded her panties are currently tucked in my pocket.

My blood rushes south as I let my fingers trail through her wet lips just lightly. The slight hitch in her breath has me dying to do more, but all I can focus on is getting a taste of her.

"Is Shadow by your feet?" I ask my parents. When they both look down, I pull my fingers to my mouth and lick them clean, never removing my eyes from Lily. Her pupils are blown wide, and goddamn, I want to taste her sweetness. I love eating pussy, or more specifically, eating her pussy. The way her nails dig into my hair, the breathy little moans she makes, and the delicious juices she coats my beard with are my own version of heaven.

"Yeah, she's being good like always." Mom's voice breaks me out of my trance.

"How's the bathroom coming along?" my dad asks.

"The pipes are finally all replaced. Next is wiring and drywall, then installing the tub, tiles, toilet, and vanity. Jake is making her one right now. Flooring, painting, and lighting all need to be done, too. Lily said I was doing too much, so it's slow going."

"I'm free this week. Why didn't you ask me to help?"

"You're free every week; it's called retirement. Please take him," mom quips.

I didn't even think of that. My dad helped me a lot with my renovations. He's always been handy and fixes everything himself. The fact that he is volunteering to help do this for Lily means a lot to me, but doesn't surprise me one bit. It's just who he is.

"I can't ask you to do that, David. But thank you so much for offering."

"You didn't ask, sweetheart. Plus, I need something to do while Evelyn is visiting the new friend you made her."

"What?" Lily asks.

"I've been visiting Jana a few times a week," mom says quietly. She gives me a pointed look and I realize that's the lady I told her about a month ago. "Your friend Amber's mom, honey. The one that owns the boutique in town."

"You've been visiting her mom?" Lily's voice is watery. "Thank you. I have been meaning to go back in and check on her. How's she doing?"

"Good days and bad days. She's worried about Amber. I get the sense she's all alone with Jana in the rehab facility."

Lily nods along, like she understands that completely, and I sense that she does. I can tell from the look on her face she's going to go back to that store this week. There's the saying that you marry your parents, and I always thought it was a little weird. I understand the sentiment that you tend to end up with someone of similar attributes or characteristics because it's what you know or are used to. Being with Jen, who was nothing like my parents, the saying felt weird. I get it seeing the similarities between Lily and my mom now. I would be lucky to have a wife that is as considerate and tenderhearted as my mom, and Lily is exactly that.

The rest of the dinner conversation stays neutral, talking about our weeks and plenty of stories about my childhood. Hearing Lily's laughter ring throughout my parents' house is worth every ounce of embarrassment that I felt.

"I made cookies for dessert," my mom says. "Do you want to hang out in the living room while I clean up and I'll meet you in there with the cookies? I can make coffee, too."

"I want to show Lily my old room first, then we will be back down." I take her hand, leading her up the stairs. My room isn't totally the same. My parents have made it a little more 'guest room' friendly, but it has all my photos on the wall, and my yearbooks that she might get a kick out of. Mostly, I just want a moment alone with her.

I am so gone for this girl, and it hit me hard this evening. Seeing her interact with my parents, having her here feeling like a part of my family, a part of my future, is giving me all sorts of feelings. The minute I shut the bedroom door, she is pushed up against it. My hand at her throat, holding her in place, stealing the breath from her lungs with my kiss. My lips mold to hers, my other hand gliding up her inner thigh. She gasps when I push two fingers in, allowing me to shove my tongue in her mouth the way I'm about to with her pussy.

I drop to my knees and use the hand that was around her throat to push up her dress. "Look at you glistening for me, baby. You're soaking my fingers," I groan out before latching my mouth to her clit. My chest rumbles with satisfaction at the taste of her. "Stay quiet, princess. I finished my dinner like a good boy, and now I'm going to make you flood my mouth with my favorite dessert."

Lily clenches around my fingers as her head falls back to the door with a light thud. I nip at her clit, making her eyes shoot back down to me, right where I want them. She lifts one leg, throwing it over my shoulder, as her hands spear through my hair, holding my head in place. I love when she gets comfortable and takes what she wants.

My fingers set a ruthless pace, stroking the front wall of her delectable pussy as I alternate between flicks of my tongue and nips on her clit. My cock is painfully hard, and seeing her ride my face is enough to drive me to the brink of orgasm with her. Our chests are rising and falling in sync, her deep blue eyes conveying emotion and vulnerability, sending hot tingles bearing down my spine. Her pussy tightens and spasms around my fingers, and her soft voice pleads my name like a prayer.

Fuuuuuck.

I stroke her through her orgasm as my own barrels through me, making a mess in my pants. When her body slumps against mine, I pull my fingers out and lick them clean. Gently, I lick long, languid strokes up her thighs, all the way back to her sweet pussy. Satisfied I licked up every drop, I pull her dress back down and stand. Her eyes trail down to the wet spot on my jeans.

"Did you..?"

"Come in my pants from just the sight and taste of you coming? Yeah, baby, I did, and I'm not ashamed. You're so damn sexy, and I would live between your thighs if I could." I kiss her deep, making her taste herself on my lips. "I've got to clean up. I'll meet you downstairs."

"I didn't even get to see your room," she huffs with the cutest little pout.

I grab my senior yearbook off the shelf and hand it to her. "Take this with, and we can look through it together." Then I slip into the upstairs bathroom to clean myself. Thank god she picked out dark jeans and a large flannel, or this could have been a lot worse. With semi-wet boxers, I make my way down to the laughter of my family.

"He and Jake were inseparable, but the oddest pair," my dad says as I round the corner into the room.

"What's that supposed to mean?" My dad deadpans toward me like the answer is obvious.

"You were a scrawny, shy thing, and Jake was a little hellion, getting into fights and beefy by eighth grade. Love you both, but it was always funny to see." I grab a cookie from the coffee table and scoot in next to Lily, who is flipping through the photos.

"Jokes on you, now I'm the beefy one."

My parent's laughter startles me as Lily lightly pats my arm.

"You're very handsome and strong, but Jake the giant is way beefier than you. Also, can we not use the term beefy, it's weird. Stacked? Ripped? Muscley?"

"Hunky!" my mom adds through her laughter.

"You all are menaces. I'm telling the group chat you said that, mom." I say, pulling out my phone. Instead of my phone though, I pull out Lily's. We both put ours in the cup holder of the truck when we got in, and I must have grabbed hers by accident. When I hit the home button, it lights up with a text from an unknown number. I can see the first part of the text causing my skin to heat instantly. My fists clench of their own accord, and I can feel my blood pressure rise.

Lily must feel me stiffen beside her because she looks over, then drops her face to the lit up screen. The way her face pales and her gaze turns apologetic tells me this text isn't a surprise. My vision tunnels with the realization that she has been getting threats and I haven't been keeping her safe. I take a steadying breath to not make a scene in front of my parents, but I need to get us out of here.

I deposit the phone back into my pocket, and close the yearbook Lily is holding. "Thank you so much for dinner, mom, it was amazing as always. It's been a long week, so I think we're going to head out."

My mom's eyes rove between us at the sudden change in conversation. Whatever she sees has her not saying what's on her mind, as she nods and stands. "I expect you back here soon. Lily, you're welcome anytime, even without this big guy."

We all exchange hugs, and as my mom walks Lily to the door with Shadow, my dad holds me back. We've had countless talks over the years about how to treat women, love, relationships, and how he knew that my mother was the one. He's a firm believer that you can fall in love multiple times, but you only have one true love. "Is she the one?"

"I've only known her for two months, dad."

"Time doesn't matter."

"Yes. She's the one."

He wraps me in a hug, slapping my back. "I knew it. Love that girl hard, son."

"I will, dad. I'll see you this week when you come help with the bathroom." I let him go, plant a kiss on my mom's head, and follow my girls out the door. Anger and love are swirling around in my gut with equal fervor. I'm beyond pissed about the text on Lily's phone, but I'm also in awe of the fact that in all the time I spent with Jen, my dad never once asked me if she was the one.

I open Lily's door and help her in before getting Shadow and myself in Freya. We wave to my parents, who are still standing on the porch, wrapped in each other's arms. The drive is deadly silent and I can't take it anymore.

"How long?" I grit out, wrapping my hands tighter around the wheel.

"He texted me Monday. This is the only text since." Her voice is hoarse, like she's holding back tears, and I instantly feel like an asshole. I may be mad that he is threatening her, but she's the one getting threatened on top of all the other shit she is dealing with. My hand finds hers, threading our fingers together.

We ride the rest of the way in silence again, while I revel in this new information. I have so many questions, and I want to know if she's talked to Kinsley about this. Nothing would make me happier than beating this guy's ass. I bet River would happily track him down and do the beating for me on his next game series in Phoenix.

Lily seems defeated when we get home, so I head straight upstairs to draw her a bubble bath. I add salts and lavender bubbles, then head downstairs to find her. She's cuddling with Shadow on the couch, absentmindedly stroking her fur while staring at the wall. I kneel in front of her, grabbing her chin to get those beautiful blues on me.

"I would like to read his texts, then carry you upstairs and put you into the bath I drew for you while we talk about this. Is that okay?"

She nods at me, so I pull her phone back out and hand it to her. With a swipe of her thumb, she pulls up the texts as I take a seat next to her. The first one is a simple 'drop the lawsuit' text, but this second one is threatening.

UNKNOWN NUMBER:

Drop the fucking lawsuit, Lily. You're making a mistake coming after the company, and you're going to lose. We are going to bury you, is that really what you want? Stop wasting your money and my time.

The balls on this guy. I don't know what she ever saw in him. I put her phone down to scoop her up, carrying her upstairs to the bathroom. I undress her as all the questions flow through my mind.

"Why didn't you tell me?" I ask, pulling her dress over her head.

"It was just one text at first, and I told Kinsley about it. I thought that would be it, and didn't want to pull you further into my problems."

I undo her bra and help her step into the tub, watching her sink down. Grabbing one of her clips from a drawer under the sink, I pile her hair into a ball and clip it in place. Parking myself on the rug outside the tub, I rest my arms on my knees and look at her. "When will you see that you're not a problem to me, baby, but a choice? I chose to stand by your side through this, and I will continue to do so. What did Kinsley say?"

She skims her fingers through the water before looking at me. "She said to screenshot and send it to her, but she also subpoenaed my phone records so she can see that way, too. I guess him texting me can help in the case, and I'm not supposed to respond."

"Will you tell me if he contacts you again?"

"Yes. I'm sorry I didn't. I never meant to hurt you." I lean forward to grab her hand and rub my lips lightly over her knuckles.

"You didn't hurt me. I can't say I'm happy that you didn't tell me, but I can understand it. My only worry is you. I'm beyond upset that he is threatening you, and I need to run out this anger. Stay here and relax. I'll be back in a bit, okay?" I lean forward, placing a tender kiss on her lips before leaving her to it. Pulling on shorts and a sweater, I grab my running shoes.

I need to call Kinsley and see if there is anything I can do to keep him from her. Would it be too extreme to get her a new number and phone? I can leave the old one open for him to keep digging himself a hole, while keeping her from having to see the threats. I grab my small head lamp from the back seat of my truck and throw it on before hitting the road.

My parents were right, that I was the scrawny, tender kid for most of my life. It was a small town, so I knew mostly everyone, but I wasn't close with many. People were always trying to change me; comparing me to others and I resented it. *Why don't you try to play sports like your brother? Why don't you work out more, I'm not into the skinny type. If you did this one thing, maybe more people would like you.* Jake was the first one to really see me for who I am until Jen came along. Even then, I think Jen saw parts of me and intended to mold those parts how she saw fit. I allowed myself to bend to her will and let her shape me how she wanted.

Jake and my family are the only people who have never tried to change anything about me. They have always loved me for who I am, not who I could be. I am finally confident in the man that I've become and what I have to offer. Lily sees me and I see her. Her family treated her the same way, forcing her onto the paths they wanted for her. People have never loved her for who she is, but who they thought they could make her become.

She didn't deserve that then, and she doesn't deserve it now. I want to show her that she is perfect exactly how she is and that after this mess is over, we can build a life together. No one deserves to have a family that makes them feel like they are less than. Her trust issues are justified, especially when you add in a man who lied, cheated on, and manipulated her for years.

I'm no longer the scrawny kid and will fight for what I want - a future with Lily. Tyler has taken enough from her and I won't let him take any more. I'll fight tooth and nail to make her see that I am here for her, that together we can have it all, and that once we bury this prick and the entire company, our future will be waiting with open arms.

I'm not sure how long I run for, but my legs are shaking and the house is quiet when I get back. Not wanting to wake up Lily, I shower in the guest bath before crawling into bed with her. Lying there, with the girl of my dreams tucked into my arms, I come to a horrible revelation. I was upset that she didn't tell me about one text, when I've been lying to her about paying for her lawyer. I know I need to come clean, but she can't afford to keep Kinsley on her own, and I don't think she will accept my financial help. If she hardly lets me help do little things like work on her bathroom, how will she take knowing I'm spending tens of thousands of dollars on lawyer fees?

It's a horrible catch twenty-two and I have no idea what to do. I try to sink into the feeling of her next to me, safe and protected, but it doesn't work. At the first light of the morning sun, I crawl out of bed and do the only other thing that ever seems to clear my head.

I've become accustomed to waking up wrapped in Thoren's arms, and it's a feeling I crave. I know he came to bed last night and was here at some point, but as I slide my hand over the sheets behind me, it's fur that I find. Shadow's tail thumps with the realization that I'm awake, and her cold nose pokes over my shoulder, nudging my cheek.

"Morning little lady," I coo to her, as she moves her entire body weight to plop down on me. "Okay, not so little lady," I wheeze out.

Her wet tongue licks every exposed inch of skin until I give up with a groan and roll her off me. She normally gets up with Thoren, but he must have left the bed before she was ready. I take care of my bladder and do a quick teeth brushing before I throw on one of his sweaters and head in search of coffee and my man.

Last night was a whirlwind of emotions and events, and having the time to think things over in the bath was unexpectedly nice. Evelyn is wonderful, and her maternal side shocked me. Despite having just met me, she was willing to be in my corner, and that's something I never had until moving here. The love she has for her sons was expanded to include me without thought.

How different my life might have turned out if I had parents like her and David who encouraged me to pursue my passions from day one. I would probably be further in my author journey, and I doubt I would have accepted attention from someone like Tyler. It's no secret that people who weren't raised in loving households seek out attention, often accepting less than they deserve. I know now that's what I did, trying to please my parents by dating someone they would have approved of, as well as someone who showed even an ounce of interest in me.

If that were the case, though, I wouldn't have moved here and met this ragtag crew of people. I can say with absolute certainty that I would be missing out without them in my life, even grumpy Jake. The love and acceptance I have found with them is something I have been seeking for years. The fact that his parents read my books and joke about what is in them means more to me than they will ever know.

When Thoren took me upstairs after dinner at his parent's house, what he did to me... well, that was the last thing I expected to happen. The way he makes me feel so alive and cherished when doing depraved things is altering my brain chemistry. His grunts of pleasure as he came in his pants from getting me off were so hot, it sent shock waves of ecstasy through my body while I came down from my orgasm. I was riding such a spine tingling high when I shakily made my way back downstairs. I'm pretty sure his parents knew what happened upstairs, but they smiled sweetly and played naive. It was such a good night until that text came through.

I didn't expect to hear from Tyler again, but his text sent me into a tailspin. He was demanding in his career and sometimes with me, but never threatening. His obvious threat scared me. It's the reason I was cautious to fight in the first place. I feel bad that Thoren found out that way, but I'm glad he knows. He took care of me and ensured I was okay despite his anger.

There's a half full pot of coffee, so I make myself a cup before stepping onto the deck in search of Thoren. My eyes turn at the sound of wood cracking, catching on his broad figure chopping wood. This might be my favorite look on him yet. Sweat drenches his white shirt, clinging to his muscular chest, while dirty work pants hug his legs, and suspenders stretch taut over his shoulders. He is exuding raw power as every muscle flexes and tenses with each swing of his axe.

I stand there a little too long, drooling over every inch of him, when I lock onto his face. He looks exhausted, with red eyes and a tortured expression. There's a growing pile of cut wood next to him that must have taken a few hours at least. I track back inside to discard my coffee mug and grab him a cold water bottle.

Shadow slips outside with me this time, running straight to her dad. When he puts down his axe and glances up, our eyes connect and the vulnerability in his almost takes me out at the knees.

"Did you sleep at all last night?" I hand over the water, watching him guzzle the whole thing.

"No."

"Is it because you're mad at me?"

His head hangs as he sucks in a deep breath. "No, I'm not mad at you. I'm angry over him threatening you. I'm angry that he even put you in this position and got you fired. I'm sad that you didn't want to come to me with the first text, and I'm angry with how I'm handling all of this."

I can understand all that, although I don't think he's handling it wrong. He's not taking his anger out on me, but I don't think pushing himself past the brink of exhaustion is necessarily healthy either. "Take it out on me."

"What?" his head whips up.

"You're exhausted, and clearly this isn't working if you're

still this upset. So take it out on me. I brought this pain into your life, let me be an outlet for it."

"Baby, you don't know what you're asking."

"I do. I'm not made of glass. Your hammer won't break me, Thor."

He wars with himself until the look in his eyes changes to something darker. His hands reach up, slowly pulling down one suspender and then the other as they hang at his sides. In one swift move, he pulls his shirt over his head and drapes it over the stump where he was splitting the logs.

"Bend over, hands on the stump."

My pussy clenches at the authority in his voice. He has shown this feral, domineering side in bits, but I know he's holding back. I don't want him to, I want pain at his hands because I know it will be laced in pleasure. He doesn't want to hurt me, but he wants to own me and I am ready for him to take it all. I stride over to the stump, doing exactly as he said.

His heavy footsteps fall behind me before his fingers grip the edge of my panties and pull until they tear. He tosses the pieces onto the stump next to me, the careless act sending a shiver down my spine. Rough hands firmly grip my ass, sliding up and over my back, taking his shirt I am wearing with it.

"If this is too much, you tell me to stop and I stop. Understand?"

"Yes, sir."

A growl rips from his throat. "I will make you scream that pretty throat raw, and if you're a good girl, I'll soothe it with my cum."

My pussy drips in anticipation, coupled with an edge of fear running through me. I've never done anything like this. Thoren is expanding my sexual horizon every time we are together and I have yet to experience something that hasn't blown my mind. His hands rub down my back, landing back on my ass before disappearing.

Without warning, he smacks my ass hard, causing my whole body to lurch forward with the force of it. I whimper at the sting as he gently caresses it.

"Do you need it harder, princess? I said I want you to scream for me," he grits out. The pain is there, but it's not unbearable. He needs this, and I can take it for him. I like the thought of wearing his mark on me. I lean back, sticking my ass out further, and settle my feet better into the damp ground.

His sharp inhale is the only warning I have before he spanks me again, on the other cheek this time. The pain is enough to rip a cry from my lips.

"Three more."

He rains the slaps down one after the other, as I scream out with each bite of his palm. His calloused hands rub gently, peppering kisses over each cheek, praising me until the sting from his slaps is gone.

"You're dripping for me. Did you like that, Lily?" he asks, unzipping his pants with one hand while stroking his fingers through my wet lips with the other.

"Yes," I hiss, as he reaches forward to stroke my clit.

"My good fucking girl."

His hand disappears again, only to be replaced by the head of his hard cock as he strokes me, coating himself in me. He notches at the entrance, and with one hard thrust, he is fully seated inside me. I cry out at the sweet mix of pain and pleasure.

He takes me hard and fast, not waiting for me to adjust to his size, his hands gripping tight on my hips. At this angle, he can get deeper than he has been before. The stretch of his thick cock hits that special spot deliciously. His hips piston into me, drawing a mix of moans and cries from me.

"You look so pretty impaled on my cock. You take me so

well, this hungry pussy squeezing me so tight," his deep voice pants out.

He leans forward to grip my hair at the nape, pulling me up flush against him. That hand settles around my neck while the other dips down my stomach, finding my swollen clit. His fingers circle it furiously as he continues to pound into me.

"Please, Thor," I beg for him to make me come.

"Come on my cock, baby. I need to feel you."

With a pinch to my clit, I shatter. Blinding colors cloud my vision as the strongest orgasm I have ever had tears through my body. I scream out his name as he calls mine like a prayer, painting my insides with his cum. My body slumps against his, but he holds me in place effortlessly. Stroking his hands down my stomach, telling me how well I did and how proud he is of me.

When both of us have caught our breaths, he pulls out of me and scoops me in his arms. He carries me clumsily into the house, and then I notice his pants bunched around his thighs because he never fully removed them. Kicking off his boots, he lets the pants and boxers slide down his legs before taking the stairs two at a time. I hiss when he sets my bare ass on the cold counter to turn on the shower. He strips off his socks, then comes to pull his shirt off over my head. Large hands bracket me on the counter as he buries his face in my neck.

"I wasn't too rough, was I?"

"No. It was the perfect amount of pain and pleasure. Feel free to do that again next time you're upset."

"Yeah?" His hot breath tickles my neck, "You liked that, dirty girl?"

"Mhmmm."

He picks me up, carrying me straight into the warm spray of the shower. His gentle hands travel over my body, rubbing out my tight muscles as he washes me. Thoren takes his time scrubbing the shampoo into my hair before tilting my head back to rinse it out and doing it again with the conditioner. When he is satisfied that I am clean and relaxed, I take over doing the same for him.

By the time we step out of the shower, we are exhausted, so we crawl into bed naked together. I attach myself to his front while he holds me to him like he plans to never let go. My fingers trail lightly up and down his side while he rubs up and down my back.

"Are you still angry?"

"No, baby. Can I ask you something?"

"Anything," I speak softly into his chest. I mean it, I want no secrets or hidden truths left between us. Anything that he wants to know, I want to tell him.

"Can you tell me about your relationship with Tyler? We haven't really had an in-depth 'this is our past' talk."

My hands stall before slowly resuming. "I didn't date in high school. It was a mix of things; my strict parents, my desire to please them through good grades and extracurriculars, and I think my race played into it, too. Phoenix has a very small Asian population, and I know I'm not everyone's cup of tea. I wasn't a popular girl, and I had no problems keeping to myself. College was more of the same. I was a little timid and lived with my parents for the first two years. I had a one-night stand that took my virginity, which was a huge mistake. Then I started interning at the financial firm, and I met Tyler.

"He was older, and he paid attention to me. It was innocent, at first, but it eventually developed into something more. He was my first boyfriend, and I thought things were going well. It started with all the sweet things: flower deliveries, him showing up with dinner, telling me how beautiful I was, that kind of stuff."

Thoren's hands are still stroking up and down my back as I choke out the next part. "That didn't last long, though. He still had his moments, but he wasn't great with communication. He wouldn't call or text as much. Sometimes he would stand me up when he was supposed to come over. Red flags started popping up, but I finally had someone that cared about me… that said he cared about me. I saw what I wanted to see. I wanted someone to love me and be proud of me, and he said all the right things. It took a while to see that those words were never backed up by actions. I stayed longer than I ever should have, and finding out he was still married was the best and worst thing to happen to me."

Thoren is quiet, his hands never leaving my body. To my surprise, he doesn't ask for more, or scold me for not leaving sooner. "Jen and I knew each other since we were kids, small town and all. She wasn't interested in me, no girls were, but she was friendly. When I moved to Seattle for college, I started working out and filling out. Jake moved with me, and River was there, and between us three, I learned how to talk to women. I lost my virginity and had hook-ups. And yes, my dick got nicknamed the hammer."

"Appropriately so," I giggle. "That thing is the size of my forearm."

He tickles my side, making me squirm. "When I moved back home, I looked like a completely different guy, and Jen latched onto me pretty quickly. She never left for college and loved talking about Seattle and city life. She wanted to take trips there all the time, asking to go see River's games. She was a little materialistic about the things she liked, but I didn't mind. I had the money to spend on her, so I did because it made her happy. There were some red flags; my family and friends were always cordial with her, but I could tell that was the extent of it. She never asked about my job or wanted to go hiking with me. When I bought this place, she made her distaste for it known. Still, I loved her. I planned for the future I wanted, that I thought she wanted, too. One day, she packed up and told me this small town wasn't enough for her anymore."

I hear what he doesn't say. That he wasn't enough for her anymore. Whether or not she said it, that's what he felt. Looking up into his hazel eyes, I see the vulnerability and sadness there. Not for the loss of her, but for the future he wanted and the hurt he felt.

"You are enough, Thoren." Reaching up, I wipe under his glassy eyes before scratching through his messy beard. "You have a kind heart and a soft soul. You fiercely protect those around you; you're funny and witty. You're an incredible friend, a caring son, a loving brother, and a partner beyond comparison. You. Are. Enough."

One tear slips free from his dark lashes, bringing out the green flecks in his eyes. How can this man not see himself exactly how I do? Every single day, I am floored by him and what he does. I am going to make it my mission to get him to see just how worthy he is to have someone stay and fight for him.

"What does that future look like now?"

After clearing his throat, he looks up to the ceiling before answering, "The same, but different. I still want a wife and kids, a house filled with love and laughter, creating memories with each other to last a lifetime. I want that future here in this town, close to my parents, in this home that I built. When I saw that future before, I longed for it so deeply. It wasn't until you entered my life that I realized I wanted those things in general, not with Jen. Now, when I see my future, I picture your belly swollen with our baby, rocking in a chair in your office that was meant to be a nursery. It's you holding the hand of our little girl with silky black hair and Shadow at your side. My future is you, Lily."

The lump in my throat is thick as the tears sting my eyes. "I've felt lost for so long. Like I've just been wandering through life looking for my purpose. Since the day I moved to Cedar Ridge, that purpose has slowly come into view. Every day, I feel like I am wandering closer to a future that I've always dreamed of. One where I can pursue my passion, feel alive, and be surrounded by people who truly see me and love me all the same. It's clear now that I have been wandering to find you."

Thoren pulls me on top of him, tangling his hands through my hair. His lips press against mine, hot and searing, pouring every ounce of the love that I know we both feel into it. Tyler gave me empty declarations of love, but Thoren gives me declarations of the future he plans to give, and shows me his love through every touch and every action. It's overwhelming and frightening, but I think I'm ready for it. This man smoothed over the cracks I tried to mend on my own with every wordless gesture.

Our lips stay locked together, our passionate kisses turning into lazy and soft kisses as we enjoy being wrapped in each other's embrace. We stay that way until we both fall asleep and spend the rest of the weekend showing each other just how much we mean to one another.

CHAPTER TWENTY-FIVE

MICHELE:

I need a girls night.

LILY:

Yes! Can I invite someone new I met in town?

MICHELE:

Of course. Queso and margs on Thursday?

LILY:

Sounds perfect, I'll be there, hopefully with Amber in tow.

It's been almost two weeks since Tyler sent the threatening text. When Thoren came home from work last Monday, he had a new phone for me under his plan. He told me I didn't have to use it, but he didn't want me to have to worry if or when Tyler would reach out to me next. It still surprises me the lengths he goes through to show how much he cares for me. I took advantage of it, sending my old phone to Kinsley so she could monitor the texts from Tyler. I didn't have all that many people to update with my new phone number, so it made the switch simple.

257

I feel like I have done nothing but write or hike the last two weeks, or hike to places where I could write. Whenever writer's block hit, I slipped on my hiking boots and backpack with a notebook and pens. Finding remote locations with no internet or cell service to distract me was the cure, and I was able to finish up the first draft of the book. I sent it to Andrea yesterday before running into town to hunt down Amber. Unsurprisingly, she was working at her boutique again, and I begged her to come out to dinner with Michele and me tonight. After some light bribery, she agreed, and I can't wait to get us all together.

Now that my book is done and awaiting review and read-throughs, I have nothing to do today. As I sit on the couch debating whether to take Shadow on a hike or deep clean the house, someone knocks at the door. Shadow beats me there, her tail swishing excitedly. Pulling it open, I'm surprised to see David standing on the other side.

"Hey Lily," his kind eyes and warm smile greet me. "Are you busy right now?" he asks, leaning down to pet Shadow, who is begging for attention.

"Nope, I am free as a bird."

"Wonderful! I came to check on the progress in your bathroom and saw that drywall is the next step. Thoren has all the tools and supplies there, but it's more of a two-man job. I was wondering if you would be up for helping me out?"

I haven't talked to Thoren's dad since dinner at their house, and the chance to spend some time with him sounds fun. "Of course. Let me get some shoes on. Thank you so much for helping me with it. Did Thoren tell you I helped with the piping? He wouldn't let me touch the wiring though," I tie my sneakers before following him out.

"Smart man. Not that you couldn't do it, but you should have seen how many times he shocked himself while working on his house before he learned to always triple check that the power was cut," he laughs to himself as we walk over to my cabin.

"I've never hung drywall, and I'm still a little timid around power tools. You might have to walk me through this a bit."

"The only tool we should need is a drill. One will need to hold the drywall in place while the other drills it in. You can do either job, but the ceiling will be a little tricky. I think it's phenomenal that you are so involved and learning to do these things."

He says it all so earnestly, like he isn't being more supportive and encouraging than my parents have ever been. My dad always put in a little more effort than my mom when it came to talking to me instead of at me, but he still never believed in me. They had all these expectations of me, and then had this equal mix of shock and indifference when I met those expectations. It was like they didn't think I could do it, but also weren't impressed that I didn't exceed what they laid out for me.

I can see where Thoren gets his encouraging and supportive ways from. David patiently talks me through each step and is kind when I miss a few times and screw a hole in the drywall into the nothingness behind it instead of a beam. I know those will need to be fixed later, yet he doesn't suggest that I should do the holding instead of the drilling.

David has a great sense of humor and keeps me laughing through the entire process. We finished the small room in two hours, which I'm sure he and Thoren could have done in twenty minutes. His gentle demeanor puts me at ease.

"Can I make you lunch? If Evelyn isn't waiting for you to get home."

"I would really like that. She's probably still at the hospital, so she won't even notice." He waves it off as we head back to Thoren's house.

"Is it just Amber's mom that she goes to see? I still can't believe Thoren asked her to do that."

"She's been visiting with people stuck in the hospital and rehab facility for years. Evelyn has atherosclerosis, and five years ago it caused her to have a minor heart attack. She was okay, but she had to spend a few days in the hospital. When she got home, all she could talk about was how lonely she felt, even with all the nurses and doctors around. Thoren and I visited her daily, but I was still working and River was in the middle of a season. Since then, she's volunteered to spend time with people who don't have family or who have long-term stays there. Her favorite is when they have babies in the NICU that need snuggling. She seems to have really hit it off with Jana though."

I point him to a stool at the island when we get to Thoren's as I pull items from the fridge. "She's the type of woman I strive to be. How's her health now?"

David looks down at his hands, squeezing his fingers. "It's okay. It's a heart disease that never goes away. She's at a higher risk for heart attacks, strokes, and blood clots, but her team of doctors monitors her closely." He lifts his head, meeting my gaze. "She's my other half, my best friend, and the one person in this world who can brighten my day without a word. Who can fill my cup simply by sitting in silence with me. She's given me every good thing in my life. I'm scared every day that I could lose her."

Emotion sits hot in my throat at his words. Losing someone you love is terrifying, but so is never experiencing that love. They say you can't miss what you never had, however that's not true either. Being alone while knowing there is love out there changing people's worlds every day can hurt just as bad.

"You're lucky to have each other."

"We are, but we aren't the only lucky ones." He smiles softly at me, a knowing look in his eyes. The emotions feel too heavy, and I'm not ready to think that all through yet.

"Thank you for helping today. I know Thoren will be grateful, too. He's not thrilled that I limited the days he can work on it," I say, placing plates in front of each of us, taking a bite of my sandwich.

"You're good for him. When he is in on something or someone, he's all in, and it often leads to him forgetting about himself. He would happily burn himself down to make sure the ones he loves are warm. Evelyn and I have watched it happen time and time again, so thank you for not letting it."

I nod while chewing my food. I saw that happening, and it makes me upset that he's been this way his whole life and people let him. That his parents have had to watch him get taken advantage of and that he just allows it to happen. His kind heart should be treasured, not exploited.

"He means a lot to me. I will happily put his needs before my own because it's exactly what he deserves."

David gives me a knowing smile, but drops the subject. We talk about tile and flooring options while we finish eating, and then meander outside to throw the ball for Shadow for a bit. I don't know if it's normal to hang out with your boyfriend's family, but I hope it is. A part of me hopes and prays for a future that they are in, because David and Evelyn would make the best grandparents. They are the type of family I dreamed of as I kid, and what I want for my own future children.

Giving Shadow one last ear scratch, David heads toward the front door. He stops when he gets there, patting my shoulder tenderly. "One thing, Lily. He'll give you everything, every piece of himself, and all he will ask for in return is you. Keep taking care of him, and just be you."

His words stay with me the rest of the day. I told Thoren that he was enough and meant it. Am I enough for him? He has given no reason to believe that I'm not, but I can't help feeling like there is an imbalance. What have I given him except more things to do and worry about? I clean the house with my mom's words weighing me down. *What do you have to entice a man if you don't have a thriving career? You should do it all, like I did. You can have kids and a high-powered career, it's not like it's hard. Lily, you don't want to be just an added problem for a man.*

Her words hurt then, and they hurt now. I was on my way to a high-powered career and I was empty inside. I had an empty relationship with a crappy partner, and spent so much time alone that I started to write out my hopes and dreams, then turned them into novels. My passion flourished through writing, but working in finance drained my soul. Moving here, I finally felt the tightness in my chest ease as I lived my life the way I envisioned it. What if she is right, though? Is it enough to have a small career that brings you joy if it means you have nothing to offer a man? Is being a good wife and a present and loving mother when the time comes going to be enough?

I contemplate it all as I make a pasta dish that will reheat nicely. Thoren has a SAR meeting after work, and I don't want him to worry about cooking. Plus, I like to take care of him. I can't offer much financially, but I can clean his house, cook his meals, and be his sounding board when he needs it.

Putting the heavy thoughts behind, I get ready for a night out with the girls. It's been too long since Michele and I went out and adding Amber to the gang makes me happy. They say pain recognizes pain, and I see something in her that calls to me. Hopefully she will feel comfortable enough to open up to us, and if not, at least she will know she has people around.

I slip on a simple purple wrap dress with sandals and throw my hair in a ponytail. There isn't much humidity up here in the mountains, but these August nights stay warm. Michele is seated at a table when I arrive, sporting a flowy summer dress as well. She envelops me in a quick hug, holding up a pitcher of orange liquid when she sits.

"Peach this time," she says, pouring a full glass for me.

"I can always count on you. How have you been?"

"Really good, actually. I went on a date this weekend, and I think I might see him again."

"Hey Lily," a timid voice startles me.

I turn to find Amber in a pair of boyfriend jeans and a bright pink crop top. A long bob haircut frames her face with an adorable mess of curls, her make-up trendy with winged eyeliner.

"Jesus, how do you have an ass in those jeans?" Michele gawks.

Amber's cheeks turn the color of her top as she takes the open seat at the round table. I smack Michele's arm, but she has no shame. "I, uh, well it's part genetics, part my obsession with the gym. I'm Amber, by the way."

"Sorry, that's Michele. Who has a delectable butt herself, by the way. I'm so glad you could make it," I cut in, filling her glass. "I hope you like peach margaritas."

Amber gives me a grateful nod, her shoulders easing as she sets down her purse. "I live for margaritas. What were you guys talking about?"

Michele's smile brightens as she winks at me. "I love her already. I went on a date for the first time in... a while this weekend."

Something in the way she says it makes me want to ask for details, but I won't in front of Amber yet. Has she dated since Ethan? Surely she has gone on dates since high school, although Thoren did say that was her only love.

"What does he look like? Where did you go? Spill it."

"He's a short king, but the muscles on him are pristine. You can't laugh at his name because it doesn't fit him at all," she eyes us both before continuing. "Oliver took me to the little Italian place down the road, but he's going to cook for me this weekend."

I can't hold it back, the laugh bubbling out of me. "Oliver? Chele, that's so cute. But I need a height reference because I am totally picturing Lord Farquaad." Amber almost spits out her drink as she joins in on the laughter.

"He's like 5 '6 and built like Thoren," she gives me a pointed look.

"Go girl, get you some," Amber clinks her glass with Michele's. "I'm assuming Thoren is the man you came into the shop with? Not that I was really looking, but…"

"But that man is hotter than sin," Michele finishes for her. They both nod, and I beam with pride.

"He is, and I believe in museum rules, so look all you want."

Our waiter comes over to bring us chips and takes our orders. We decided on a trio of appetizers to share and another pitcher of margaritas. I might have to leave my car and Uber home, but it's worth it.

"How's the book coming along?" Amber asks, around a sip of her drink.

"First draft is finished. I need to start on the next book while this one is in the first round of edits, but I feel like I should spend my time doing things for Thoren instead."

"What do you mean?" Michele questions. "He brags to me all the time about all the things you do for him. He said the only time he cooks anymore is when you cook together or breakfast on the weekends. That man is obsessed with you already, you don't need to do anything else."

I swirl my chip through the queso, embarrassed I even brought it up. My mom's words just won't stop replaying in my head, and it's taking a toll on me.

"Relationships should be 50/50. He found a lawyer for me, is housing me, fixing my bathroom, and is my safe space when all this crap boils over; which it does constantly. That's on top of all the little things that he does to care for me." I bite my chip to give myself a moment.

"He makes my coffee just the way I like it every morning.

There have been fresh purple flowers on his dresser and the dining room table, constantly, since I moved in. He draws me a bath every time he sees that I'm overwhelmed. He alternates between rubbing my feet and scratching my back every night that we watch movies. I got my period last week, and he came home with a heat pack because he didn't have one and a bag of chocolates. I didn't even tell him I got my period, he must have just seen the tampon box. What do I have to offer that man?"

Amber and Michele are wearing matching looks of empathy. Amber places her hand on mine, giving it a light squeeze. "Good relationships aren't 50/50, Lily. Each person brings something different to the table, and neither person is going to be at their best all the time. I hardly know you, and I can see that you are selfless, kind, and have so much to offer. Just because you give in different ways doesn't devalue you."

"Get your shit ass parents out of your head," Michele points her chip at me. "I know that's what this is. You clean his house, fold his laundry, pack him lunches, and make him dinner. You take the time to do his favorite activities with him, take care of his dog who is his best friend, and make an effort to get to know his family. You brought peace and happiness back into his life. You, my dear, are everything he has ever wanted."

I know they are right, but it's hard to rewire what I have been told my whole life. Thoren and I both give each other everything that we have. He is everything that Tyler wasn't and he shows me every day how cherished and appreciated I am. He turned the room he was saving for a nursery into an office for me, for god's sake. I need to get over my own issues and think of something else.

"How's your mom doing, Amber?"

"She's doing okay. She's not actually my mom, she's my great-aunt. Jana's been raising me since I was eleven, and she's the only family I have left."

"Well, shit," Michele says. "What happened to her?"

"She had a stroke and has been in a rehab facility since. Total recovery isn't a possibility, and she's mostly bed bound now, but her mind is still sharp. It's been rough. I only have one part-time worker at the store besides myself, so finding the time to run it and go visit her and deal with everything has sucked."

"Jesus, Amber, you just let me whine about my boyfriend being too good of a man, and you're going through all that. Do you have anyone else to help?" All of my problems feel a lot smaller, and I want to wrap her in a hug. I don't have to start my next book right away, I can easily help out at the shop if she needs it.

"Nah, I've kind of always been an outsider here. It's my own doing. I was angry at the world when I moved here, and in this small town, all the kids already knew each other. When they tried to be nice, I essentially told them to fuck off, and no one has really given me a chance since. I'll figure it out. I always do."

Michele is out of her chair in an instant, pulling Amber out of hers and wrapping her in a hug. "Get in here," she motions to me as we all stand in the middle of the restaurant in an awkward group hug. "You have us now. I don't listen when people tell me to fuck off, so I'll still show up if you do."

Amber subtly wipes at her eyes when we break apart and take our seats again. As I look at her, I see myself right after I got fired. I felt completely alone in the world, trying to figure out how to move forward. These people in this town have become my family, and I want her to have that, too.

"I'm stopping by next week," I say, full of determination. "If you need help with any finances, I'm your girl. If not, you're going to teach me how to work at the store. You don't have to pay me, but I will work at least one day a week so you get some time off. No arguments."

Her eyes turn watery as she grabs my hand again. I may not

have money rolling in from a prestigious career, but I can do this. I can be a friend, and give my love and my time freely to those who need it. I want friends that are real and true. That laugh and cry with you, and show up at the drop of a hat because you need it. Knowing I have those types of friends feels like I am one step further from the daughter my parents want, and one step closer to the woman I want to be.

thoren

Bros and Hoe Group Chat

RIVER ✐:

I feel out of the loop.

JAKE 🪜:

That's because you are.

RIVER ✐:

Dickhead. Have we fucked up the tiny dick prick yet?

THOREN 🔨:

No, they should have a court date set soon.

RIVER ✐:

Cool, let me know and I'll be there.

THOREN 🔨:

It will be in Phoenix.

RIVER ✐:

...and?

JAKE:

Count me in too.

THOREN:

I love you guys.

RIVER:

Gross. GTG, Vanessa wants my bat.

THOREN:

Stop trying to name your dick. You can never top Hammer.

JAKE:

I need a girlfriend.

"It would be cheaper to just get whatever flower is in season, you know?" Mrs. King asks as she wraps up the bouquet.

"Yeah, but purple is her favorite color."

"You buy her new flowers every week. I think she'll love them no matter what."

"I'm still sticking with purple. Can you add this bunch, too?" I pluck a pretty wildflower mix from the fridge next to me.

Michele has been my savior these last few weeks. The least I can do is buy some flowers for her office. I know I could use a lawyer, but Michele knows contracts, and she knows what I want. She's been combing through all the paperwork with me for the sale of some of my land. I decided to sell just one of my plots to Mike. The lawyer fees are pretty astounding, and the profit from the sale will pay off my mortgage and give me a nice little nest egg.

I pay for the flowers, and head to Marge, shaking my head at the fact that I am calling her car that name. She took my truck to pick up the tiles we ordered, and Jake is going to meet her at the house later to help her unload them. My friends and family have quickly accepted her into the fold and are just as captivated by her. My mom told me earlier this week that she and dad are keeping Lily no matter what, so I better not mess up. I'm not even mad at it because I hope they do.

Opening the passenger seat, I carefully set the flowers down when I hear the worst sound.

"Thoren, dear, is that you?" Sherry's annoying voice says from too close behind me.

Standing up, I grip the door tightly, willing myself not to slam it shut as I turn to face her. "Hey Sherry."

She runs a hand through her long blond hair, trying to subtly pull down her shirt on the way. Surprise; it's as subtle as a hammer to the head. "I'm so glad I ran into you. I heard you were signing the papers today. You made the right choice. We should go get drinks after to celebrate."

"No thanks," I step away from her and walk toward the driver's side door. "I have plans with my girlfriend." In the car, I don't even bother waving.

The drive to Michele's office is quick, and I see the notary is already here and waiting. Grabbing the wildflowers, I make my way into the office and slip them on her desk. Her eyes go wide, then soft as she takes them in before looking away. "The notary arrived right before you. All you need to do is sign," she says, leading me to the couch where the lady is waiting.

"Thank you for doing this all for me. Is everything finalized and ready to go?"

"Yeah, they signed off on the new additions. They sent them back within three hours, so I don't know if they fully read through the changes. But it is in there and signed by Mike that you will get 1.5 million dollars for the land, and if he does anything with the land but build the agreed upon condos, you can negate the deal and keep half the amount."

"Michele, you are a damn genius." I kiss the top of her head before we sit down. The only way I was comfortable enough to sell was with the guarantee that he wouldn't build something stupid on the land. Mike makes smart business decisions; it's how he has made such a successful company. If he were to change his mind and build a resort, or the luxury homes he talked about previously, I fear it will fall flat and in a few years we will have abandoned buildings where there once was a beautiful forest. I think the condos have the potential to do well and bring in revenue for the town, so that's all I will allow to be built there.

"Thanks, but no more compliments until you tell Lily. About this and the lawyer."

I politely ignore her as I sign all the papers and get them stamped before sending the notary on her way. It's painful to let the land go for something so superficial. It's a great location, and could be used for better things, or just preserved for the forest it is, but it will be worth it. It feels just as selfish holding onto that land when I have other plots and properties.

"I'm going to tell her about the land tonight." I don't bother mentioning the lawyer because I know how she feels about it and she's not wrong. I know how important trust is to Lily. I just can't risk her refusing the help and not getting the justice and closure that she deserves. She needs a win after everything, and I will make sure that she gets it.

Michele shakes her head walking back to her desk. Her fingers rub at the petals of one flower, but she doesn't pick them up. "Ethan was the last person to get me flowers until today."

"Oh Chele, I didn't know. I'm sorry, I just wanted to show my gratitude for all your help."

"It's fine. It's been twelve years, Thoren. Twelve damn years, and my heart still hurts. Why can't I get over my high school crush?" her voice breaks with the last word.

I pull her into my chest, holding her as she lets the tears flow. "He wasn't just a crush. He was your first love. You either need to find him and fight for him, or you need to try to move on."

"I did. I flew out to see him six years ago. The minute we were together again, it was like no time had passed. He's the other half of my soul, and I told him that. But I won't leave Cedar Ridge; I want a family and to raise my children here. He wanted to chase wildfires across the country and for me to follow." She steps out of my embrace, wiping at her eyes before turning around to mess with the papers on her desk. "I'm trying to move on. I really am."

I knew they had sporadically talked over the years, but I had no idea she went to go see him. I can't imagine the pain she must have felt putting herself out there like that, only for him to crush her so thoroughly. When Lily told me that I was enough last week, it was like she blew air into my lungs, and I was able to take my first full breath in years. Like I had been just wading through the rough waters for the last few years and she pulled me to the surface and into her boat. Everyone deserves to feel like they are enough just the way that they are, especially the incredible woman who can't look at me. "You'll find him one day. And when you do, everything will be right in your world. I gotta go get my girl. You okay here?"

"Yeah, I will file the papers and you should have a check next week," she says, still not turning to face me. I make it all the way to the door before she calls out, "Thanks for the flowers."

Hopping back into Marge, I race toward home. Even with mixed emotions, I just made over a million dollar sale and I'm excited to tell Lily. My truck isn't home when I get there, but she might have left it at her place. Shadow's waiting at the door for me, but when I call out for Lily, no one answers. I throw out the wilting flowers on the dining room table and replace them with the fresh ones before heading next door.

Mine and Jake's trucks are outside, and it seems someone has already brought in all the tiles. The front door is unlocked, so I let myself in, immediately greeted by laughter. A smile forms unbidden at the sound of these two letting their guards down and enjoying each other's company. Jake is a surly guy who doesn't let people in easily, so I love hearing his deep laugh with Lily's carefree one.

"I did not show Michele my dick," Jake swears when they calm down.

"This again?" I ask, rounding the doorway into the bathroom.

"I just want to know the truth," Lily grumbles. "She turned bright red when I asked if she saw the ladder thing and you know she doesn't blush."

"Ugh, fine. She saw my piercings. Happy now?"

"Well, everyone but me has seen them, so no. That doesn't seem fair," Lily counters. Jake's eyes go wide as I tackle her on her spot on the floor.

"You better watch it, baby," I whisper into her ear as I pull her into my lap. "My cock is the only one you see."

"I've just never seen a pierced dick. It's intriguing."

Jake slips his phone from his pocket and types something before turning it toward Lily and I. "This is what the piercing looks like," he says, showing a rubber dick with the Jacobs ladder piercing. His eyes meet mine. "Not a real dick, so you can't get mad at me."

Lily turns in my arms whisper-yelling, "Don't ever do that. It looks so painful."

"Worth it," Jake smirks.

"Don't flirt with my girl, dickhead. What are you guys working on?" I ask, finally taking in the bathroom we are all squished in. Jake's sitting on the edge of the tub we installed last week, and Lily is on the floor with tiles and a baggy by her feet.

"Jake said he had some free time, so we started on the tiles. Or, he started on the tiles. I'm very good at handing over new tiles and spacers when he needs them. Not so great at laying the tiles without spending twenty minutes over-analyzing if they are perfectly in place or not. Now that you're here, I can make you guys dinner if you want?"

"I can whip something up." I know she wanted to be as hands on as possible with this reno, and don't want to take away from that.

"You've hardly seen each other since you don't work together anymore. Have bro time or whatever it is men do. Can I bring you guys beers, too?" she asks, separating herself from me, but not before planting her soft lips on mine.

"Please, if I have to watch that," Jake grumbles playfully. Lily reaches into the bag on the floor and flicks a spacer at his head. We both watch her retreat, and when the front door closes, Jake shakes his head, looking down. "You better marry that girl."

"One day. She's nowhere near ready, and I won't rush her. I have to bite my tongue every day to not tell her how madly in love with her I am." I take over applying putty to the tiles for Jake, handing him one ready to go. "I've been so consumed by her I haven't checked in. How are you?"

"I'm good, overwhelmingly busy, but I needed a break from sanding today. I think I might hire an apprentice. The orders are coming in too fast to keep up with alone."

"That's great, man. I knew you would have a thriving business in no time. How's life, not just work?"

He chuckles, "Oh, you get a girlfriend and suddenly you think I need a life outside of work. You lived to work just a few months ago." I shove his shoulder, knocking him off balance. "I'm kidding, fuck, don't ruin my work. I'm beyond happy for you, it just made me realize I might also be a little jealous. I spend my days alone in the shop and I'm over the bar scene. I want someone to come home to."

I sit stunned at the vulnerability of his confession. Jake never talks about his conquests, but every time I joined him at the bars in town, he had girls flocking to him. Honestly, I thought he would live that playboy lifestyle forever. He was outgoing with a bad boy edge in high school and college. When we moved back, he lost a bit of his outgoing side, but that never kept the women away. I just assumed he liked being alone.

"Finally ready to hang up the one-night stands and settle down?"

He gives me a long stare, an unknown look flickering over his face. "When was the last time you saw me take a woman home? Not just talk to them, but actually take them home with me?"

That gives me pause as I think about the few times he dragged me out with him. I can't remember him ever leaving with a woman, but he often stayed later than me. "I don't know," I admit.

"I go out because I'm lonely, and for a few hours I don't have to feel alone anymore. I'm not out fucking everything with legs. I mean, I get laid, but not as often as everyone seems to believe. Can we change the subject? This is fucking humiliating to talk about," he says, taking the next tile without making eye contact.

I want to tell him I'm sorry that I never considered that. That I played into the narrative that everyone placed on him. Instead, I give his shoulder a squeeze and drop the subject so we can move on. We talk about the new hire that replaced him and who he is considering hiring as an apprentice. By the time Lily shows up with her homemade pizzas and a case of cold beer, the shower tiles are complete, so we all move to the deck to eat and enjoy the summer night.

I offer to let Jake stay the night, but he politely declines and heads home. He lives in an apartment in town that he hates, but it is right next to the shop space he rents out, so he tolerates it. I'll need to make more of an effort to spend time with him and have him over. He has always been there for me, and I hate knowing I have been letting him down.

Back at home, Lily and I crawl into bed with Shadow, sinking into each other's arms. "I missed you today," she whispers, pressing a kiss to my bare chest.

"I missed you too, baby. I uh, I did something big today after work."

"What's that?"

"I should start by saying I have been investing in properties since college. In and around Cedar Ridge, I have five empty plots of land and six homes in town. I rent them out as income proper-ties. River signed on the first few with me, but the rest I own. Today I sold one of the plots of land." I let my fingers glide through her hair.

"Wow, that's incredible. Are you happy about the sale?" her lips tickle as she speaks against my skin.

Her words bring a smile to my face. I know Lily, and yet a small part of me thought she might react in a similar fashion to Sherry, seeing dollar signs. "I think so. It's a large chunk of money and I think the condos the developer wants will be good for the town. It's just not the reason I bought the land, which bothers me a little. I also should tell you, I sold it to Sherry's dad."

She stiffens slightly in my arms. "I really dislike her."

I chuckle lightly, "Yeah baby, me too."

The silence washes over us as we lie together in bed. I want to give this woman the world, and yet she asks nothing of me. I was honest when I told Jake that I am ready for my future with Lily to start now. I know that she is the woman that I want to marry and have a family with. When I saw the amount of money I would have left over from the sale after paying the lawyer and mortgage, all I could think about was the rock I wanted to buy to put on her finger.

Jen wanted to take fancy trips and travel the world, and while I like to travel, I never had the desire to with her. Lily though, never asking me for anything, makes me want to give it all to her. I want to take her to places she has always dreamed of, put my ring on her hand, and give her the wedding of her dreams.

"If you could go anywhere in the world, where would it be?" I whisper into her hair.

"Iceland," she sleepily responds. "To see the northern lights. What about you?"

"Wherever I'm with you."

CHAPTER TWENTY-SEVEN

LILY:

Are you in the office today?

THOREN:

Yeah, I will be all day. I have loads of paperwork
to catch up on. Are you still working at Ambers?

LILY:

It's a slow day so she told me to go home.

LILY:

Can I bring you lunch and eat with you?

THOREN:

Are you the meal?

LILY:

I'm always down to be dessert.

THOREN:

I love watching you go down.

I've been helping Amber for three weeks now, since our girls' night in town. She refuses to let me work an entire day because I refuse to get paid, but it gives her a few hours to see Jana and catch up on rest and errands. We usually spend an hour or two chatting when she comes in to take over and I have loved getting to know her better. Jana wasn't having a good morning and needed rest, so Amber came back earlier than expected and told me to go enjoy some time with my man. I will never complain about that.

I haven't been to Thoren's actual office, but it is just as bland as he described. His office is small, with one window, a desk, a chair in the corner, and a dog bed where Shadow is currently napping, belly up. He's focused on his computer when I rap my knuckles on the open door. His immediate smile warms me down to my toes, as does the heated look he gives me.

Leaning back in his chair, his thumb trails along his bottom lip. "My beautiful girl bringing me lunch? The only thing better than this would be if you lifted up that pretty dress of yours to show me what's underneath."

I put the takeout bag and my purse on his desk, rounding it to his side. Shadow's tail thumps against the wall, but she remains sprawled on her back as I stand in front of Thoren. Slowly, I pull up one side of my dress, inch by inch, leaving it just below my panties, before following suit with the other side. My thighs bracket his as I straddle his lap, scratching my nails through the short hairs on the sides of his head.

"Hi baby," I whisper against his lips.

His control snaps, his hands gripping my hips tight, pulling me flush against him as he slams his lips against mine. His kiss is demanding, his tongue forcing its way in as he plunders my mouth. He guides my hips to rock over his growing erection, drawing a whimper from my lips. Thoren's hands tangle in my hair, angling my head to deepen the kiss when my phone rings from my purse.

It breaks our connection, both of us breathing heavily. Thoren's forehead rests against mine as he tries to catch his breath. "I guess that's a good thing, because I was about to take you on my desk."

My hands trail down his shoulders as I slide off of his lap, reaching to pull my phone out. "I can't believe we just did that in your office. Anyone could have walked in."

"It's a ghost town around here on Fridays. I wouldn't have shared your sexy moans with anyone else." He adjusts himself in his pants before reaching for the bag of food.

My phone stops ringing before I get to it, but Kinsley's name pops up as the missed call. It's been a while since I've heard from her, so I immediately redial and place it on speaker. Thoren has been so integral in this process, and having a second set of ears to hear and go over everything is helpful.

"Hey Lily, how are you?" Kinsley answers.

"I'm doing alright. I have Thoren here with me. What's going on?"

"Well, there's good news and bad news. Good news, we have a court date on November 18th, about two and a half months from now. My team has been combing through texts and emails, as well as paperwork, and we have some pretty damning evidence against them. I never make a guarantee, but I would be shocked if we didn't win this case. I am pushing for the CEO to step down, but I doubt that will happen. We ran some numbers and are aiming for a three million dollar payout, and again, I would be surprised if you don't get close to that."

I slump into the corner chair, trying to take in her words. Shadow's nose bumps my knee, my sweet girl always being there for me. My hand delves into her fur, letting her calmness wash over me as she rests her head on my lap. I'm probably going to win this lawsuit. Knowing I was wronged and validating that are two different things. Thoren's soft eyes are trained on me when I look up, but his hands are white knuckled in his lap, waiting for the bad news.

"Now for the bad news, which I suppose could be good, too, if you choose to look at it that way. In the month that I've had your phone, Tyler has reached out twenty-two times. Fourteen texts and eight phone calls where he left some pretty demeaning and threatening voicemails. I can't tell you what to do, but as your lawyer, I am going to kindly suggest that you get a restraining order against him and that we open a criminal suit against him as well."

Thoren is up and out of his chair before she even finishes speaking, pacing the room as she talks. "Are you worried about him coming here and hurting her?"

"No, I don't think that will happen, but we have enough from these messages to do both those things. In the last voicemail, he mentioned sending something to her, but didn't say what. I would like to protect Lily's peace and keep him from harassing her any further."

There's a part of me that wants to know exactly what he said, but the other part is glad I don't. How I spent two years with such a cruel and callous man, I will never know. Unease is written all over Thoren's face. He's by my side in an instant, grabbing my free hand with his as he strokes a hand down my face.

"It's up to you, baby, but I think we should do it. I can call my dad and my parents can meet you at the police station to file the report. I also think you should consider the lawsuit. If you want him personally to pay, this is the best way."

I can see his anger brimming just below the surface, and I get it. I feel that same anger at the audacity of Tyler to keep trying to mess with my life when I only ever loved him. Yes, I told his wife that he was cheating on her, but if he didn't want her to know, then he shouldn't have done it. From her response, though, I was under the assumption that she already knew, or at least suspected.

Tyler took something from me by making me the other woman. I won't allow him to take my peace now that I have finally found it. For most of my life, I have allowed myself to live as a half authentic version of myself. I saw the box that my parents, professors, coworkers, and men set out for me to fit into, and I molded myself to fit into it for them. The parts of me that didn't fit, I tried to hide away for so long. It wasn't until I started writing my first book that I allowed myself to stop hiding who I really was and step outside that box.

I am not as cutthroat and heartless as my career sometimes demanded me to be. I am not the career focused woman my mom wanted from me, or the soft-spoken and obedient woman Tyler wanted. My desires lie outside of being materialistic and the societal expectations of women. I don't want the fancy house and car with the big career and family on the side. I desire a quiet life in a small town, with a love unlike any other. To be surrounded by friends and family that truly want to support each other through life and to pursue my passion of writing, even if it doesn't make me rich. It is time for me to fight for that woman.

If Michele were here, she would tell me to say screw that guy and do everything in my power to make his life hell for what he put me through. I look up to her in so many ways, but especially for her ability to be unapologetically herself. Channeling my inner Michele, I put my metaphorical foot down.

"I would like to do both. What do my next steps need to look like?"

Thoren's eyes shine with pride, his shoulders slumping with relief over my choice. Although I didn't do it for him, I'm glad he's getting some comfort from it. He has been my stronghold through everything; taking on all my pain, sadness, and anger from the situation and never once complaining about the weight it has put on him. He is my constant, my steady Oak tree standing through the whipping winds and pouring rain. With his hand, warm and reassuring on my thigh as he kneels before me, his eyes filled with a tenderness that makes my heart swell, I know. I am so deeply in love with Thoren James.

"I will send you an email as soon as we get off the phone. It will have everything you need for the police to start a restraining order. If you can send me the name of the officer you speak with, I can make sure he puts a rush on it and we get it signed ASAP. As for the lawsuit, I will get everything together and have it ready so he can be served with that and the restraining order at the same time. I bet I can make sure it happens at work in front of every-one. God, I love poetic justice," she chuckles, and I can't help but agree with her.

Kinsley promises to keep me in the loop with everything before letting me go. Thoren's lifting me from the chair and smashing me into his broad chest before I can put the phone down. I sink into his embrace, soaking in his strength and heady amber scent. He lifts up my dress until his rough hands are on my skin as he wraps me tighter to him, letting his fingers trail along my sides as he squeezes. His chest rumbles with his deep laugh as his touch causes goosebumps to erect over my skin.

"Sorry, just needed to feel you. I'm so damn proud of you, baby."

"I'm scared," I admit against his shirt.

"Yet you did it, anyway. You are so strong, Lily. I will be by your side through every step. You can do it on your own, but anytime your fear tries to break through, just look to your side and I will be there." He unwraps himself from me, smoothing my dress back down as he goes. "I'm going to call my parents. Are you still hungry?"

I nod, scooting the chair closer to his desk. Shadow follows me closely, not moving more than a few inches from my side. I pull out the sandwiches and the little bag with slices of turkey I had added for my best girl. She gently takes them from my fingers before gobbling them whole.

Thoren relays the gist of the phone call with Kinsley to his father before asking him if he will meet me at the police station in an hour.

"You can't come with me?" I ask when he hangs up.

"If you need me there, I will be," he says, unwrapping his lunch. "My parents will be there either way."

"No, it's okay. It should be a quick and easy thing, and it's not like you can do anything."

His eyes hold mine, both of us still feeling rattled. "Thank you for bringing me lunch, and getting Shadow a treat. I'm sorry it got derailed."

"Not your fault, just another day with more of my baggage."

He takes a bite, chewing as he looks down at the desk. When he swallows it, he grabs a water bottle from the bag to wash it down with. "I don't know if you've noticed, but I have strong shoulders, and I can unpack like nobody's business. Your baggage is nothing, sweetheart."

Tears prick at my eyes as Thoren once again chooses me. After a lifetime of feeling like a burden, a second choice, a thought thrown in at the end, Thoren is showing me that I am his first choice. His only choice.

We eat our lunch in companionable silence as I replay my conversation with Kinsley. I still don't know what he would send me unless he has similar thoughts as Michele and glitter bombs or a bag of dicks are what he has in mind. That isn't his style, though. He has to be in control, the one with all the answers, the biggest man in the room. I know he can't stand the idea of someone fighting back against him, showing the small, insecure man he really is.

I toss our trash when we finish, grabbing my discarded purse. I'm ready to get this next part over with. I slip onto Thoren's lap, snuggling into him one last time before I leave. He nuzzles into my neck, pressing his full lips to my sensitive skin there.

"You've got this. My dad will take care of everything, and my mom will hold your hand. I'll see you at home tonight, okay?" His lips move to rub over mine, giving tender kisses.

"Okay. Thank you," I give Shadow some love on my way out, "You be a good girl for daddy, I'll see you later."

Evelyn and David were already waiting for me with open arms when I arrived at the police station. They stayed with me through every step of the process. They sat on either side of me, Evelyn's hand squeezing mine when they read through the text messages that Kinsley emailed me. I'm beyond grateful for their support and for letting me feel like I had parents in my corner.

Filing the restraining order felt like I was finally taking my power back. It felt like Tyler was one step further from me, and that I was one step closer to being rid of him and this whole situation. Even with the heaviness of the day, I felt lighter leaving the precinct.

Since getting home, I have tucked myself away into the office, working on the first round of edits. My developmental editor got it back to me this week, so I have been fixing plot holes, character developments, and other things she pointed out. I know most authors hate this part, but I love adding in little tidbits that I didn't think of the first time around. I am so immersed in the editing cave that I'm startled when Thoren calls out that he is home.

"Upstairs," I call back, finishing my thoughts before closing my laptop. Shadow bursts into the room, tail wagging, tongue out, as she beelines for me. Thoren's handsome face isn't far behind as he leans against the door frame, arms crossed as he watches me.

"Hey baby," his voice is full of grit, and I notice he isn't in his work uniform anymore.

"When did you change?"

"Well, it wasn't great timing with everything that transpired today, but I only worked a half day. I had a delivery and some last minute things I needed to take care of before your surprise tonight," he says, striding over to drop his lips to mine. "Are you up for a small walk?"

He takes my hand, intertwining our fingers as he leads me down the stairs. I slip on some shoes, and as a family, Thoren, Shadow, and I make the short trek to my cabin. The sun hangs low, just behind the Evergreens, leaving beams of light dancing through the branches. Our steps crunch on the gravel as I take in my house. It looks the same from the front, but I know he must be showing me the completed bathroom as a surprise. While it will be nice to have it done and have my place back, I'm going to miss spending every night in Thoren's arms.

He leads me onto the porch, halting our movement before he opens the door. "This was going to be a fun surprise for you today, but it feels heavier now. Before we go in there, I need you to know this has nothing to do with what happened today. I'm not kicking you out or running. I know how important it is to you to have your own things. Your own home that you worked hard for, with projects that you completed." His free hand reaches up, thumb trailing over my bottom lip. "Do you understand?"

"Yes."

"Good." His smile is devastating as he opens the front door and moves out of the way for me to enter first. The first thing I notice is a new couch and rug in the living room. I still had the previous owner's couch with a cover over it, but in front of me is a cream-colored couch with light purple and green throw pillows and blankets on it. The rug on the previously bare floor is a light green with purple lilacs sewn into it. The walls have two new pictures added as well, one of Thoren and me and one of Shadow.

I walk forward on autopilot, moving into the bathroom and turning on the light. Everything is complete, and it's even prettier than I imagined. The vanity Jake made is a beautiful walnut with a white basin in the center. The fixtures are all black, matching the black floor tiles that have white and gray veining throughout. The subway tiles on the shower are white with gray veining. The white paint on the walls ties it all together, aside from the pops of color he added. There's a pretty lavender shower curtain and hand towel, and on the counter is a candle, making the whole place smell like lilacs.

Thoren's right there when I turn around, his face softening as he takes me in. The pads of his thumbs wipe under my eyes, catching the tears I didn't realize were falling. God, this freaking man.

"I love you," I blurt out.

He sucks in a sharp breath as his wide eyes find mine. "Say it again."

"I love you. I love the way you care for me and those around you. I love the way your eyes light up when I walk in a room and never stray from me. I love the way you protect me while still encouraging me to make my own choices. I love the way you see strength where I see failures. You have become my best friend and quietly loved me until I could love myself again. I love you, Thoren."

His lips descend on mine as he kisses me like I am his next breath. When he pulls back, his hazel eyes shine with unshed tears. "I am so in love with you, Lily. From the moment you stepped into my life, I have only seen you. The light that you radiate wherever you go, and the warmth you share with everyone you meet. You have shown me that a love like my parents have is not only possible, but right in front of me. You are my home, Lily, and I love you."

I smile through the tears that are flowing freely down my cheeks. "Will you stay here with me tonight?"

thoren

"I was hoping you'd ask." I scoop her up, carrying her up the stairs to her bedroom. Lily loves me. I've known for a while that she does, evident in the way she looks at me with vulnerability and complete trust. I just didn't think she would admit it to herself or to me so soon.

I drop her on the bed, immediately following her onto it, my body hovering over hers. Her small hands press on my chest, holding me up as her deep blue eyes search mine. "Thank you. Thank you for the bathroom and the furniture. For the little touches that you added for me. I've never had someone care for me the way that you do."

I kiss a lingering tear. "I would do anything for you, my sweet Lily." My lips press to her forehead, "But I can't sleep without you in my arms anymore, baby." I kiss a tear on the other cheek, "If you're here, so am I."

"I don't mind playing Chinese fire drill with our homes. Might need to get a dog bed for Shadow. I don't think she can fit on the couch with all those pillows," she smiles up at me.

"I might have gone a little overboard with online shopping. I kept seeing things I knew you would love and wanted you to have them all. I'm not going to apologize for it. I'll never apologize for doing what I think is right for you."

Her hands slide up, wrapping around the back of my neck where she scratches her nails through my hair, pulling me down to her. Our lips meet in a passionate kiss, her soft lips molding to mine. Her vanilla scent surrounds me as I settle my weight between her legs. I lick the seam of her lips, requesting entrance. Our tongues tangle together, lazy and exploring.

I pull my shirt over my head, discarding it off the side of the bed as Lily sits up, letting me do the same with hers. Her bra follows soon after, thrown behind me as I take her mouth once again. We have spent every night in bed together for weeks, yet our hands are exploring each other like it's the first time.

"Make love to me, Thoren," Lily breathes against me, causing a shiver to run through me. I readjust, discarding my pants and boxers, never taking my eyes off her. She was right when she said my eyes never stray from her. They couldn't even if I tried. Her beauty captivates me, the way her silky hair flows around her slender shoulders, the slight curves of her tits that fit perfectly in my hands. The way her lithe body moves with ease and grace, and her radiant smile that sets heat soaring through my body. Her olive skin looks so pretty under my rough hands, begging for me to mark it with my lips, my teeth, my cum.

I slide my hands under her hips, tugging her jeans and panties off in one swift movement. Grabbing one of her legs, I place a tender kiss on her ankle, kissing and nipping my way up her thigh. Her glistening pussy is dripping when I reach the apex. I blow on her lightly, sending shivers up her spine as her musky vanilla scent hits me. My mouth waters to taste her, but I gently place her leg back on the bed, repeating my path on the other side. She's writhing by the time I make my way back to her wet center. I settle my shoulders between her spread thighs, taking a deep inhale. My cock is painfully hard, aching to be inside of her, but

I'm going to take my time. I'm going to make love to her with my mouth, my fingers, and then my cock. If I have any say in it, we will take a food break after a few rounds, then continue all night.

"Please," Lily begs so sweetly when my tongue glides through her pussy, giving her pleasure without giving her what she wants. I love hearing her beg, so I lick her again from her slick entrance up to her clit. Every pass of my tongue drives her back further into the mattress as she tries to grind her hips into my face. I know she needs more pressure, but I love driving her wild.

"Please, Thoren," she begs again. I love the way she says my name like a caress. My lips suction around her swollen pink clit, sucking hard before finally giving her what she desires. I circle my tongue as her fingers dig into my hair. Moving lower, spearing into her pussy and fucking her with my tongue. I rotate back and forth between the two until she is crying out and begging for release.

When she's right on the edge of coming, I sit up and shove my cock deep in her, setting off her first orgasm of the night. Her head falls back in pleasure as she squeezes around me in the most magnificent sight. As her body relaxes around me, her hands cup my face, pulling me down for another tender kiss.

"I love you," I whisper against her lips, slowly pulling out and pushing back in. My hips roll against her, setting a slow rhythm as we cling to each other. Our bodies slide against one another, covered in a light sheen of sweat.

"I love you, Thoren James," she whispers back. Her ankles wrap around my back, changing the angle and allowing me deeper. My breath hitches at the feel of her stretching fully around me. I push up onto my elbows, bracketing her face as I continue to move inside her, each roll of my hips rubbing her sensitive clit. I show her with my every move and every touch how god damn much she means to me.

"Look at you, so pretty beneath me. You were made for me,

body and soul." I lean down, taking her nipple between my teeth and clamp down on it. She lets out a cry of ecstasy, pushing further into my mouth. I circle it with my tongue before moving back up to her mouth. I'm holding back my release when I feel her body tremble around me.

"Come with me, Lily." Her cry of pleasure sets me off, euphoria shooting through me as I fill her with my cum. Each jet of cum feels like the last, but her pussy continues to squeeze out every last drop. She's still trembling around me when I crash onto her, rolling us to our sides so I don't crush her. Stroking her hair, I tell her how good she did until the final waves of her orgasm cease.

"Can we eat and shower, then do that again?" her hoarse voice breathes against my chest, drawing a chuckle from me.

"That was my exact plan, baby."

Saturday morning, we take our time getting out of bed, dragging ourselves out when Shadow makes it clear she has to potty. I let her out as Lily makes us coffee and meets me out on the deck in sleep pants and a sweater. It's only the first weekend in September, but the mornings are brisk before turning into warm early fall days. She sits on her outdoor sofa and tucks her feet up under her like she always does in the morning, humming as the first sip of coffee hits her tongue.

"So, does this mean I have to move you back into your place?" I ask, taking a sip of my coffee.

"I would like to at least vacate my things from your guest room. I wouldn't mind leaving a few things there. Like you said, I've gotten used to waking up in your arms and I don't really want to change that. I don't mind taking turns staying with each other."

As much as I love the sound of that, I want her in my home. I want it to be our home. I know this cabin is important to her. She has put in so much hard work, and it looks completely different from what it was when she moved in almost four months ago. There is no way that I will rush her out of here, but I don't want her to leave.

"Orrr, you could just move in with me permanently." I test the waters.

She chokes on her sip, sputtering it onto the deck. "I don't know if we are ready for that. I just need some more time to stand on my own two feet. To show my parents and myself that I can. I know I owned my condo alone in Phoenix, but this is different. This is me proving that I can live my life the way I want, where I want, doing what I want without crumbling."

Well shit, when she puts it that way, I feel like an ass for even asking. "We will move you back in today, then. Have you tried talking to your parents lately?"

The light drains from her eyes, and I hate every second of it. "No, I was thinking of calling my dad today. See if he wants to video call and see the house."

I know she wants to make her parents proud, but I'm afraid they are only going to hurt her more. If they don't want to see her place, or gush over all the hard work she's put into it, it will crush her.

"How about we head back to my place? I can make us break-fast while you pack and you can call them when we get you settled back in."

"That sounds perfect," she says, leaning toward me to place a lingering kiss on my lips. "Thank you again for everything. I couldn't have done any of this without you."

We round up Shadow and make the short trek back to my place. Lily starts in the guest room, while I make bacon and eggs. By the time I have food ready, she's got everything together. She didn't have much besides clothes to begin with, and she promised to leave some pajamas here. I wouldn't be upset if she didn't. It's my favorite when she only wears one of my tees to bed.

After breakfast, we load her bags in the car and drive them to her house. We unpack it all and clean up the mess we made in her room last night. The nerves are radiating from Lily as she paces the living room, adjusting the pillows, and wiping invisible dust from the cushions.

"Do you want me to stay or go for this?"

Her response is instant, "Please stay."

I settle onto the couch and pull her down next to me. Threading my fingers through hers, I give her an encouraging nod. Her hand trembles as she pulls up her dad's contact. She sent both of her parents a text when she got her new phone number, which only her dad responded to with a thumbs up. Other than that, she has heard nothing from them since her mother slammed her for our kiss at the ballpark. I'm glad she wants me here, but if I hear them belittle her, it will take everything I have not to take the phone and yell.

The line rings a few times before a masculine voice answers. "Hi dad," Lily says with a shaky voice. "How are you doing?"

I lean closer to her so I can just make out his words. "I'm good, Lily. About to head out to go golfing. What's going on?"

"We just haven't talked in so long, I wanted to reach out. I have a lot of new things going on in my life I thought you might want to know about."

I can hear someone in the background before her dad says, "Your mom would like me to put it on video."

"That's perfect," Lily perks up. "I would love to show you guys my new home." She hits the button to turn the call into a video chat, but keeps me just out of the frame.

As soon as her parents pop onto the screen, her mother scowls and her dad replies, "I don't know if I'll have time for that if I want to make my tee time."

"What time is it there?" Lily's mom cuts in. "Did you just get out of bed?"

I look over at Lily. Her hair is in a slicked back ponytail, not an ounce of makeup on her flawless face, just the way I like it. She's wearing a scoop neck sweater that looks adorable on her. I don't see a single thing wrong with her or her outfit.

"No, mom, I've been up for a few hours. I just wanted to fill you guys in on what's been going on with me lately," she says, dismissing the comment. I give her hand a light squeeze.

"Well?" her mom says, impatiently.

"I'm living in Cedar Ridge as you know, and my next book is set to come out October 25th. My publisher thinks it's my best work yet. I've made wonderful friends here, and I'm dating the most incredible man."

"What does he do?" her dad cuts in this time. "Can he support you while you dabble in this little gig you have going?"

"Tyler had the means to support you. He could have helped you work your way up in the company. I still don't understand why you quit and left him," her mom purses her lips again.

"He was married," Lily blurts out. "He was married, and when I found out, he got me fired. I'm actually suing the company for wrongful termination and bringing criminal charges against him because he's been threatening me."

I expect to see shock on their faces. Maybe empathy, sympathy, or even anger. Instead, I watch as her dad's face morphs into disappointment, and her mom radiates disgust. Before the words even leave their mouths, I know I am going to intervene. Knowing these people treated her poorly, and seeing just how much she downplayed it floors me. How the sweetest, most empathetic woman I know came from these two people, I will never understand.

"How could you allow that to happen?" her dad cuts in.

"That's not how we raised you to take care of your financial troubles," her mom's words follow.

My hands snag the phone from Lily before I fully realize what I am doing. "Allow that to happen?! She trusted the words of a man who promised that he loved and cared for her. It's his fault for lying and betraying that trust. It is your fault for not showing her what real love and care looks like. If you two had raised her in a loving household, supporting her and encouraging her like any decent human being should, she might have seen that he was giving her less than she deserved. Lily has the kindest heart, not a selfish bone in her body, and she is surrounded by people who love her. And not that you cared to ask, but she is financially independent and is doing more than fine. Her life is richer than yours in every sense of the word." My chest is heaving as I stand in her living room and spit out all the things I want to say to them.

My eyes leave the phone to glance at Lily, who is sitting stock still, tears streaming down her cheeks, with the smallest smile aimed at me. Pride and love shine from her glassy eyes. "Your daughter doesn't need your negativity and bullshit in her life. When you are ready to apologize and be decent, encouraging parents, you can reach out to her. Until then, don't contact her." I hang up the phone, tossing it on the couch, and wrap Lily in my arms.

"I am so sorry, baby. I'm sorry for the way they treat you, and for taking over without permission. I will never be sorry for being the bad guy in your story, though, if it means protecting you."

Lily leans up on her toes, pressing her salty lips to mine. "Thank you, Thor. It was kind of hot watching you swing your metaphorical hammer for me."

"Want to watch me swing my real one?" I playfully grind myself into her.

She swats at my chest, "Get out of here with that." Her forced smile doesn't reach her eyes. I know she's putting on a brave face, but that conversation had to hurt. Parents are the people you are supposed to be able to always count on. The ones that love you no matter what, and if it wasn't clear before, they just made it clear they are not those people for her.

"What do you need? A hike to our peaceful place, or a bottle of wine and a tub of ice cream on the couch?"

Her bottom lip quivers, her blue eyes a deep ocean color. "Hike, please."

Lily is quiet the entire hike, and I let her process. Shadow normally tramps through the woods on our hikes, hopping back on the trail every few minutes, but she doesn't leave Lily's side today. When we reach the clearing and her shoulders visibly relax, I know this was exactly what she needed. I pull out my blanket, setting it out with the snacks that I packed and watch as my girls cuddle up together on it.

I throw a stick for Shadow, but she just stares at me like I'm an idiot, scooting closer to Lily's side. At this moment, I am even more grateful for my wild pup and the love she has for her mom. I toe off my socks and shoes, and then remove Lily's as well.

"This place has always been my go to spot when I need clarity. When life feels overwhelming, I find peace here. It may be something in the hike, or it may be something in the isolation, but I have always felt like it's something in the water." I reach my hand out for her, helping her stand. Bending down, I roll up her leggings so they won't get wet.

"There's something about stepping into the cold crisp waters here that feels like healing. Want to give it a try?"

There's a trusting look in her eye as she nods her head and reaches for my hand once more. We get to the water's edge, taking a deep breath before stepping in. The water stays pretty cold year round, but on a mild weather day like today, it freezes our toes instantly.

"The healing doesn't come from the water though; it's the

shock to the system that the cold brings," I continue as Lily breathes through the shivers that rack down her spine. "It forces you to be in the moment, to focus only on your body and the way you feel right now. Focus on that, baby. Be in this moment, feel the contrasting cold of the water and warmth of the sun peaking through the trees. Listen to the birds chirping and Shadow splashing her happy paws through the water. You will be okay. It will all be okay, if only for this moment."

She tilts her face towards the sun, the light highlights the warm brown strands in her hair and the bright blue flecks in her eyes. Her smile widens as she inhales deeply, and a lone tear escapes, tracing a path down her cheek. Lily remains still, her strength and beauty mesmerizing me.

"Better?" I ask, when she turns to look at me.

"I feel free without the weight of their expectations and disappointment. It doesn't matter anymore. Not when I have you and the family I have made here surrounding me with love. You are my peace, this place just accentuates it. I love you." She lunges at me, catching me off guard, but I catch her in my arms and twirl her around. Her laughter is light and free, healing the last of the scars on my heart. My frozen feet fumble over rocks as I bring her to the blanket, gently laying her down. We spend hours there, talking, kissing, and chasing Shadow around. The sadness in her eyes eases as the day goes on. By the time we crawl into her bed that evening, exhausted and happy, it's the best feeling in the world.

lily

After another wild and exhausting week, I'm enjoying a lazy day. It's 3:30 and I am still happily in bed in my pajamas with no intention of moving. Shadow has been curled up next to me all morning while I read and slept and played tug of war with her.

Sunday evening, we went to Thoren's parents for dinner where Evelyn mothered me the whole time. She made sure I felt love and support, and of course, asked if she could get an early copy of the new book. On Monday, I got a photo from Kinsley of a very red faced Tyler getting served at the office, which was everything I didn't know I needed.

Tuesday, I closed the store for Amber because Jana was having an especially bad day. Michele stopped by, and together, we worked on a plan to help Amber through this all. The financial burdens are crushing her on top of the added work and stress from running the boutique solo. Wednesday and Thursday, I holed myself up in the office for over fourteen hours each day, completing my editing and sending it back to Andrea. Knowing that it was submitted and out of my hands from this part on was both terrifying and a huge stress relief.

Hence the mental health day today to relax after the week I've had. I should probably shower before Thoren gets home, but I told him dinner would be of the frozen variety tonight. Movies cuddled together while eating junk food sounds like the perfect end to a long week, and he agreed. This week was just as taxing on him, with a hard SAR case on Tuesday. Someone's child disappeared from their campsite, and it took sixteen hours, the SAR team, local law enforcement, and civilian volunteers to find him. Thankfully, he was okay when they located him.

Shadow jumps up from beside me, giving me her best puppy eyes. "Potty time? I guess I should put my pretty new bathroom to use, huh?"

Her tail thumps against my comforter as I slip from the bed. I follow her down the stairs, letting her out the back door to do her business, before turning on the shower. This thing is downright luxurious now, with dual shower heads and pristine tiles. After letting Shadow back in and giving her a bone, I hop into the warm water.

Showers have always been where I do my best thinking. My book ideas always seem to come to me when I am in the middle of a shower, and life seems less scary behind that curtain. The longer I spend under the spray of the water, the more I feel like I had a great week overall. Were my emotions all over the place? Sure, but it was all good things. Maybe things are finally turning a corner for me.

I can't help but see the abundance of good in my life lately. My book is done, my house is updated and cozy, I have good friends, a relationship with a man I love, and things are moving in the right direction with the lawsuit. Letting go of the past hurt from my parents and Tyler is getting easier every day.

Stepping out of the shower, I feel a renewed sense of energy. I jog upstairs to get dressed before hopping back down the stairs to whip up some snacks and desserts for movie night. Pulling out my blueberries, blackberries, and huckleberries from Evelyn and David's garden, I decide on a berry pie. I find an easy recipe on my laptop and start on the dough.

I'm so ingrained in what I'm doing, it takes me a moment to realize Shadow is growling by the front door. I wipe my hands on my apron when someone knocks and Shadow's growls turn to barks.

"It's okay, honey," I nudge past her, opening the front door. I'm not expecting anyone, but no one drives all the way out here without a purpose. Shadow refuses to leave my side, pushing into my leg, snarling in the entryway. I'm so focused on keeping her settled from the odd display of aggression that it startles me when a familiar voice greets me.

"Hi Lily," Tyler says.

Ice fills my veins as my eyes snap up and I feel the blood drain from my face. He shouldn't be here.

"You can't be here, Tyler. I have a restraining order."

"Oh, come on with that bullshit. What the fuck were you thinking with that? Do you know what it looked like being served with that at work?" he spits out.

Shadow's hackles are up, her growl low and incessant, but she doesn't move from my side. I should have known not to open the door with her reaction. I really shouldn't poke the bear in front of me, but to hell with this arrogant and belittling man. He deserves a taste of his own medicine.

Casually leaning against the door frame, I cross my arms to fake my bravado. "I know exactly what it looked like. My lawyer sent me a photo of the encounter," I smirk. "Say your piece and leave before I call the police."

Anger flashes across his face and a sneer settles on his lips. "You little bitch. This is what you left me for? This piece of shit house in some podunk town? You could have been in my position in ten years, making life-changing money, and I was going to make it happen. You were perfectly happy with what we had before you saw Angela on my arm. You wanted to use me to further your career, Lily, and no court is going to see it any other way. You had it all and your behavior got you fired."

I am stunned by his words, because what the actual hell? He never spoke to me like this, always posing as the proper, well-educated man. The anger in his eyes and absolute vitriol in the way he is speaking are scaring me. His words deserve no justification. I never wanted that. I wanted love, not a step up in life.

Subtly, I try to feel my pockets for my phone when I realize it's still on the kitchen counter. There is no help up here, and it hits that he could do anything and no one would hear me scream. He's never been violent before, but the hate in his eyes holds threats beyond bitter words.

"Okay, you got it out of your system, now you need to leave," I try to take a step back to shut the door. His hand slams out to hold it open, my eyes trailing to it and its smooth soft lines. Hands that I used to let touch and take from every part of my body. Hands that haven't done a single day of hard work in his life. I want to rip everything from those hands, but I need to do it in court, not when he is a real threat to me.

"Move, Tyler," I try to keep my voice steady.

He shoves harder against the door and reaches for my arm. His hand clamps around me in a vice grip, surely leaving a mark. Shadow's sharp bark startles him, but he doesn't let go, gripping tighter instead.

"Drop the goddamn lawsuits, Lily. All of them," he yells, as his eyes harden. "I should have known better than to fuck a desperate little slut like you. No pussy is worth this shit." He accentuates his words by shaking me like a ragdoll with his nails digging deeper into me.

My eyes screw shut as my head smacks against the door frame and I let out a sharp cry of pain. I have no escape from this man with my phone too far away. His hand is suddenly ripped from me, tearing my flesh as it goes.

"What the fuck did you just say to her?" Thoren growls out as Tyler screams.

"Your dog just bit me!"

Thoren smiles down at Shadow with pride, as the pup stays crouched and ready to pounce with eyes locked on Tyler, a snarl back on her lips. There's a small tear in Tyler's slacks where Shadow must have nipped at his leg in warning. I was so focused on Tyler that I didn't even hear Thoren drive up. Looking around, I see his truck parked halfway down the driveway, his door still open. He must have seen the scene and rushed out to get to my side. On shaky legs, I make my way closer to them, trying to calm my anxiety now that Thoren is here.

He's gripping Tyler by his throat, hovering over him. "I don't give a fuck what my dog just did. What did you say to Lily?"

"I just told her to drop the suit," Tyler chokes out as Thoren squeezes tighter.

Thoren's laugh is sinister, the smirk on his face equal parts sexy and terrifying. "Apologize to her, and mean it, because those are the last words you are ever going to say to her."

Tyler sneers in my direction, not saying a thing. Thoren follows his line of sight, drawing his eyes to mine. "Are you okay, baby?"

"I'm okay." I put my arm on his free one to reassure him, but that's when I notice the blood. Thoren's eyes lock on the streaks of red dripping down my arm where Tyler ripped chunks of my flesh out with his nails.

"Motherfucker!" Thoren roars as he cocks his fist and punches Tyler in the gut. He doubles over in pain and Thoren knees him in the face, causing a sickening crunch. Tyler falls to the gravel, howling as he clasps his nose that is pouring blood. He lunges on him again, alternating punches between his gut and face.

Blood sprays from Tyler's face, splattering on his shirt and arms. Tyler grunts, trying to block his face, but his movements quickly go lax, his arms falling to his sides. "Stop, Thoren, stop!" I scream, trying to pull him off. "You're going to kill him. Please stop!"

His hazel eyes are glazed over as he slumps into the gravel. Tyler's body is lifeless beside him, but I don't care enough to check if he's alive. I drop to Thoren's side, wrapping myself around him.

"I'm okay. We're okay," I whisper as his strong, familiar arms wrap tight around me. I slide my hands through his hair, trying to tame the wild strands. "We're okay."

"I'm so sorry I wasn't here. I'm so sorry I didn't protect you."

"It's okay, baby. But we need to call the police and probably get him an ambulance." I look over to where Tyler is starting to groan in pain.

"Jake's on it. I was on the phone with him when I drove up." He lightly lifts my arm, examining the deep gashes with an angry scowl. Shadow nudges her nose between us, licking my face.

"Good girl, protecting your mom." He scratches behind her ears. "I have a lot of questions, starting with why you opened the door for him, but I'll wait until you recount it to the police. Just promise me you're okay."

"I am now, because of you."

"Is she okay?" Jake shouts out the window of his truck, stuck behind Thoren's that is still running and blocking my driveway.

"Yeah, he's not though," Thoren yells back, nodding toward Tyler.

"Who cares? Move your damn truck. The ambulance isn't far behind me."

Giggles rise up in my chest, quickly turning into an unstoppable fit of laughter. It's not funny, none of this is, but if I don't laugh I might scream until my lungs give out. Thoren eyes me suspiciously before dropping a kiss on my head.

"Crazy girl. I'll be right back."

He jogs to his truck, pulling it up next to Marge, with Jake's truck following. Sirens sound in the distance as I get up and step away from Tyler, who is still slowly coming to. Shadow chooses not to follow, instead sitting and growling at the man writhing in pain.

I can't believe he flew out here to threaten me. His actions have been stupid lately, but this was monumental. Blood is still dripping from his nose and mouth, and his eye is starting to swell already. I don't feel bad for him. If Thoren hadn't come home when he did I don't know what would have happened. I rub at the tender spot on my head where a bump is already forming.

Jake looks over the whole scene before narrowing his gaze on my arm and the wince of pain as I prod at the goose egg. "I'm going to kill him," he steps forward, only to be held back by Thoren's quickly swelling hand.

"I nearly did already. We don't need to be sharing a jail cell," he jokes, but it lacks humor.

"Fuck," Jake grits out, pulling me in for a tight hug, not caring that I'm getting blood on his shirt. "I'm sorry, Lily, we'll get this taken care of." He lets me go, passing me off to Thoren's waiting arms as his boots kick up gravel on the way to Tyler. Leaning down, he gives Shadow a head scratch before saying something to Tyler, too low for me to make out. I don't miss the way Tyler cowers in on himself trying to move further from Jake.

An ambulance pulls into my driveway, followed by two police cruisers. Jake meets them, pointing over to Tyler and then to Thoren and I. The EMT's grab a gurney and rush over to Tyler's side with one officer, as the other two make their way over to me.

The first one looks a little older than us, the other looks like this is his first day on the job. The first reaches out to shake Thoren's hand, taking note of the split knuckles. "Good to see you man, sorry it's like this. Everyone okay?" he asks, his eyes roving over us, only to stop when he sees my arm.

"Hey!" he shouts toward the EMTs. "I need one of you over here."

I go to wave him off, but Thoren grips me tighter. "Let them clean you up and bandage you," he says into my hair. "That piece of shit doesn't deserve the care he is getting." The nodding heads of the cops seem inclined to agree with him. "Bobby, this is my girlfriend, Lily. Bobby and River played baseball together."

"Nice to meet you, Lily. I need to take a few photos of your arm before it's cleaned up. Then can you tell me what happened here?"

"Yes." I will tell them everything and anything to keep Thoren from getting in trouble.

"She has a restraining order against him," Thoren adds as the young kid snaps some pictures. "Pretty sure it's his rental parked out by the road there."

"That makes this a lot easier," the cop grunts, as the EMT comes over with his medical bag. "Let's get you taken care of, then we can sit down and talk."

The rest of the evening passes in a blur of activity. My arm was bandaged, and Thoren's knuckles were cleaned where they had split open on Tyler's face. I recounted everything to the police, starting from when I opened the door to when they pulled up. I might have held back a little on how badly Thoren beat Tyler, but the evidence was there.

Luckily, they seemed to agree with Thoren's use of force, and Bobby talked all about how much he respected David, who had trained him when he was a rookie. I totally forgot that he used to be an officer until that point. After taking our statements and convincing me to press charges, they left us around 6:30.

To my surprise, Jake stayed the whole time, making my discarded pie for me and cleaning up the mess. Seeing the burly tatted up man moving around my small kitchen baking for us eased some of the tension. He cut us each a slice and brought them to us on my new couch.

"Thank you," I say, taking the offered goodness. "I didn't know you could bake."

"I'm good with precise measurements. I have to be with building furniture, and it just so happens to correlate to baking," he shrugs nonchalantly. If a woman can look past his quiet and surly nature, they are going to find a real treasure with him.

"You're staying with me tonight, Lily. I need you in my home after today," Thoren says around a bite of pie. He won't find me arguing. I'm a bit shaken up and his bed sounds like exactly where I want to be.

"I can find somewhere else to go," Jake offers quietly. I look questioningly between the two of them, confused.

"Jake has a gas leak at his apartment complex and needs somewhere to stay for a bit. It's why we were on the phone and he was on his way over already. I said he could stay with me, which you can and you will," he gives Jake a pointed stare.

"Or you can stay here," I offer. "I have a change of sheets in the closet. Both options are open for you."

"Your guest room is right across from the master. No offense, but I'd rather stay here and not listen to you two fuck all night. Thanks for the offer, Lily."

"Good, now that it's settled, I'm taking my girl and going home. We're taking the pie, too," Thoren says, picking me up and throwing me over his shoulder. "Her keys are on the counter. Come over in the morning for breakfast."

With that, he grabs the pie plate in his free hand and carries me out the front door with Shadow hot on his heels.

thoren

Bros and Hoe Group Chat

RIVER ✐ :

Is Lily okay?

JAKE ▤ :

The real question is why isn't Tyler dead?

RIVER ✐ :

Yeah, what he said.

THOREN ⚒ :

She's okay, sleeping now. I think I'm more angry than her. She didn't look who was at the door before opening it.

JAKE ▤ :

My girl would have a red ass for that move.

THOREN ⚒ :

....

RIVER ✎:

Gross. Dad said he will be in the hospital for another day before being released. Need me to drive over and pay him a visit?

JAKE 🪜:

I knew there was a reason I liked you. Count me in.

THOREN 🔨:

Sit your asses down, we don't need another lawsuit on our hands.

JAKE 🪜:

Worth it

RIVER ✎:

So anyone want to tell me why the group chat name changed?

JAKE 🪜:

Nope

THOREN 🔨:

Don't know what you're talking about.

RIVER ⚾:

Fuck you very much for always leaving me out of shit.

RIVER ⚾:

...give Lily a hug from me.

The moonlight, filtering through the window, illuminates the sleeping beauty beside me, emphasizing the flutter of her lashes as she dreams with quiet breaths. There is no sleeping for me after the events of today. When I drove up and saw an unfamiliar car parked on the road, anxiety flooded my senses. It was nothing compared to the fear that followed seeing her cowering in the doorway where he had her pinned and was shaking her.

I honestly didn't think that prick had the gall to come after her, or I never would have left her alone. White hot anger coursed through me as I heard his bitter and cutting words to her. I have never dreamed of speaking to a woman that way, and hearing it come out of his pathetic mouth aimed at Lily broke something in me. Everything from then on is hazy as I acted on blind rage. All I remember is Lily's scared voice begging me to stop, and like I told her before, I will do anything she asks.

Flexing my still swollen knuckles, I relish the ache in them. I'm not a violent person, I never have been, but beating the hell out of him was cathartic. My dad called me earlier this evening to let me know Tyler had a broken nose, three stitches in his eyebrow, two on his lip, and a cracked rib. Overall, he got off lucky and I am not remotely sorry about it. Part of me wishes I let Jake have a go, but that would have landed him an overnight police stay at least. He doesn't typically start fights, but he always ends them.

Seeing the bandage on her arm as she snuggles into me cuts me. I should have kept her safe. She's mine, and I will always protect what is mine. There's no way in hell she is moving back into her place, even if I am there with her at night. I'm ordering a security system for my place first thing in the morning, something I never thought I would need out here. I didn't want her to move back out the first time, but now I don't think I can let her go, even if it's what she wants.

I know that's her cabin, and it was the symbol of her strength and perseverance when she moved here. She doesn't need to prove that to herself anymore; she is strength personified. I have seen so many changes in her in the last few months. One of the greatest ones being that she has learned strength doesn't always mean doing it all on your own. Lily has learned that leaning on others and accepting their help shows as much strength as doing it alone.

I even have the perfect plan in place so she can keep her cabin and have that reassurance to herself. Jake admitted today he was grateful for the gas leak at his apartment. Turns out he's been wanting to get out of that place for a while and he is taking this as his sign to finally move. Lily's cabin would be the perfect place for him to rent, and I would never complain about him living so close and that extra set of eyes around to make sure my girl is safe.

Around four, I give up on the pretense of trying to sleep, and decide on a gym session in the garage. I sent off a text to Jake for him to join if he's up. Unsurprisingly, he comes strolling in the garage fifteen minutes later.

"You couldn't sleep either?" I ask, putting down the dumbbell.

"I got some. It's so quiet without sharing your walls." He walks over to the squat rack and starts loading the bar with weights.

"Funny you should mention that. Want to move into Lily's place?"

He stops, the forty-five pound weight plate hanging from one hand like it weighs nothing. "She's selling? Michele said I can't buy anything if I want to be approved to get a storefront."

"You're getting a storefront? What the hell? Why didn't I know that?" I pick up the dumbbell again, starting on another round of curls. "But no, she's moving in permanently, so hers will be open to rent."

He eyes me suspiciously, but says nothing while he goes through his first set of squats. "Does she know that?"

I can't help but smirk. "She will."

He barks out a laugh, shaking his head. "Alright, you get her on board, and I'm interested."

He adds another fifty pounds to the bar and begins his next

set. I'm reminded why I stopped working out with him as he pushes through without breaking a sweat while I lift half the weight and struggle. It's after six by the time we finish and go our separate ways. I offered to make him breakfast, but his smile told me he knows exactly what my plans are for Lily, so he declined.

I snuck into the guest bathroom so my shower wouldn't wake Lily before slipping back downstairs to make her breakfast. After yesterday, my girl deserves to be treated like royalty, so I whipped up french toast with fresh berries and a side of bacon and coffee. I quietly call down Shadow to do her business and have her breakfast so I can eat with Lily in peace. After loading up a tray, I climb the stairs to find Lily playing on her phone in bed.

Her face lights up when she sees the tray full of goodies that I set on the bed in front of her. "What's all this?"

"Breakfast." I lean forward, brushing my lips over hers. "Good morning, baby."

"Good morning," she whispers against my lips before moving back and taking a slice of bacon. "If that's all it took to get breakfast in bed, I would have asked Tyler to come threaten me weeks ago."

Her snark surprises me, but the bright look in her eyes tells me she's okay. I sure as hell am not, but she's the one who matters. Biting a piece off her bacon, I smirk, "You're going to pay for that."

"I'm shaking in my boots," she quips, taking a bite of the fruit and french toast next.

I grab her chin between my thumb and finger, guiding her to look at me. "Move in with me, Lily."

I need her to see the seriousness in my face, hear the pleading in my voice. This is her home. This is where she belongs.

After last night, I expected sadness, anger, maybe even fear from her. In typical Lily fashion, she keeps me on my toes. She's all light and sass this morning, and I fall just a little bit harder.

"We talked about this. I have a cabin right next door. I'm not going to cower and hide. Was I terrified yesterday? Absolutely. It solidified something in me, though. I have let other people control my emotions and decisions for too long, and I'm not doing it anymore," she points her fork at me playfully. "So to answer your question… no."

I snatch the french toast off the fork before she can pull it back and chew it with a sinful smirk on my face. "Oh sweet Lily, you know better than to get sassy with me. I don't want you here because I think you need to hide. I want you here because I love you and this house isn't a home without you."

Her pout is adorable as she loads her fork with another bite. "I won't say the offer isn't enticing, but it's too fast."

"Do you not want to live with me?"

She taps her finger to her chin with mock exaggeration. "Hmmm," she smiles sweetly at me. "I suppose my best friend does live here. Where is Shadow, anyway?"

"The mouth on you." I move the tray to the nightstand before lunging at her. "I don't know whether to kiss you stupid, shove my cock in it to shut you up, or edge you until the only words coming out of that mouth are you begging to move in with me and to let you come."

"That one, yep. Definitely that last one," Lily giggles, pulling me down on her and smashing her lips against mine. Her tongue strokes against mine, tasting of berries and syrup. I let her think she's in control, setting the pace as her hands trace the lines of my stomach.

When delicate fingers reach into my sweats, I pull off her and grab the hem of her shirt. Yanking it up her body, I get it halfway off her arms before using it to tie her wrists together. "If you move these hands, you get spanked. Understood?"

She nods rapidly, her eyes glowing with excitement. "Yes, sir."

Blood rushes to my thickening cock at those words slipping from her mouth. I slid down the bed, happy to find her bare for me. Her chest heaves as she waits for my next move. Starting at the spot just below her ear, I suck until there is a little purple bruise before kissing my way down to the hollow of her throat. Licking my way to her collarbone, she lets out the softest whimper, encouraging me. I nip at her skin, making my way down to her pebbled nipples. Pulling one into my mouth, I pinch the other between my fingers and rub as my tongue flicks over the other.

"Will you move in with me?"

"No," comes her breathy reply. Her back arches as I bite down on her nipple, but she clamps her mouth shut. I trail my free hand down her body until it meets the heat of her center.

"So wet for me, baby," I smirk, shoving two fingers in her pussy. I continue to work her over, fucking her with my fingers while my palm rubs her clit. I alternate between her nipples, sucking one into my mouth, flicking my tongue over it, then biting down on the tender flesh.

Her breath hitches, as her body tenses on the verge of orgasm when I slip my hand from her. Her cry of frustration is music to my ears as I smile wickedly at her.

"Move in with me."

"Make me come," she snarks back.

My fingers return to her pussy as I push three fingers in this time, my thumb making quick circles around her clit. She writhes beneath me, her legs shaking as she bucks into my hand. I work her over again, bringing her right to the brink, only to pull away at the last second.

"Please baby," she begs, "Please let me come."

"You know what I need to hear."

This time I latch onto her clit, sucking and licking the swollen bud. I hold her legs wide, devouring her pussy like it was made for me. She smells like vanilla, and I swear that's what she tastes like. Her moans float around us as she grinds herself into my face. I listen for the cues that she is getting close before pulling away at the last second again.

Tears are streaming down her pink cheeks, her legs shaking and arms straining to stay in place above her head. She looks breathtaking like this, begging so sweetly for me.

"Tell me, Lily, and I'll give you exactly what you want."

"I'll move in with you," she cries. That's all I need to hear. I shuck off my sweats and ram into her in one swift movement. Her scream of pleasure echoes through the room and my whole body locks up with the feel of her hot pussy squeezing me tight.

"That's my girl," my voice is gravelly, as on edge as her. My cock has been throbbing painfully, and the only relief for it is the stunning woman beneath me.

Lily pushes on my shoulder, rolling me to my back, straddling me like a queen. I love a submissive Lily, but the one who owns her sexuality and takes what she wants… damn, she is incredible.

Her sigh of satisfaction as our thighs touch and I bottom out is met with a groan of my own. "Ride me. Take what you need from me."

Her smile is sinful as she grinds over me, rocking her hips to rub her clit with every pass. She's been on edge so long that I know it won't take much. My hands glide up her hips, squeezing her perky tits. Her head falls back, long hair flowing behind her, as a moan slips through her lips. I reach up to grip her neck to pull her face down to look at me.

"Eyes on me, baby." Her pussy clenches around me, ripples of pleasure shooting through us. I can feel my impending orgasm at the base of my spine. "Come with me, Lily."

She clamps around me, her pussy flooding me with her release as I fill her with my cum. Sitting up, I claim her mouth in a passionate kiss, caressing her lips with my own. My hands glide up and down her back, over her shoulders, and tenderly down her arms. She's still a shaky mess as I try to bring her down from the intensity of our orgasms, her body pliant and molded to mine.

Scooting to the edge of the bed, I grip her under her ass and carry her to the shower, still inside her with our release dripping out around us. I turn on the shower and hold her to me, lavishing her face and neck with kisses.

"You did so good, baby," I whisper in her ear. "Nothing is going to make me happier than seeing my two favorite girls every time I come home. At least, until the day you agree to be my wife. I love you, Lily, and I can't wait to make this our home."

After we made love against the shower wall, and then actually showered, we ate the now cold breakfast together in bed.

"Does Jake really want to move into my place?"

"Yeah, he has needed out of his apartment for a while, and your place is perfect for him. He'll be a good tenant, I promise."

"I know that," she says around a bite of french toast. "I actually like the idea of him renting it and being here. The big oaf is growing on me."

I chuckle, leaning against the headboard. "It was the dick piercing that really sold him, wasn't it?" It warms my heart that they get along so well. Lily takes the time to get to know people and seems to always find the good in them. Jake has a lot of good in him. He just hides it sometimes, but I am so glad he is showing it to her. Real friends are still so new to her, but mine will love her unconditionally.

"Definitely the dick piercing. He deserves good things, and that home has a lot of love in it for him."

The smile on my face stayed for the rest of our breakfast. I tried to keep reality at bay as long as I could, relishing in the fact that Lily was going to move in with me permanently. The afterglow of our morning was so good, even after no sleep, that I was sure nothing could ruin my day.

That was quickly squashed when Kinsley called a little after lunch, having heard about Tyler.

"Lily, I am so sorry that happened. I am so glad it wasn't worse than it was. I've been assured there is a police officer outside of his hospital room, and he'll go straight into custody upon release. I don't doubt that his wife will post bail for him, but because he violated a restraining order and assaulted you, chances are high he will remain under house arrest until the trial. My team is going to be working hard on that case, and I assure you we are aiming for the maximum five-year sentence and a large fine," Kinsley's no bullshit voice comes through the phone speaker.

"Thank you so much, Kinsley. What does this mean for the rest of the trial and everything else?"

"Nothing. Everything will remain the same. We already have the trial for the wrongful termination and the civil suit against Tyler set back to back. Now that suit will become felony charges instead."

I wish I could feel like that is enough. His wife deserves to feel Lily's wrath, too, for the way she treated her. I hope she shows at the trial so I can watch her face as her husband is sent to prison for messing with my woman.

"Okay, thank you for the call. I appreciate everything you are doing for me."

"I'm happy to help. I just wish I could have prevented this somehow. Although I'm not mad at the outcome, make sure that man of yours is icing his hand."

Lily hangs up, a wide grin splitting her face. "How is the hand today?"

I look down at my knuckles, barely swollen with a few small cuts. "Good enough to pack some bags and boxes."

"Today already?"

"Yeah baby, I meant it when I said I wanted you here. This is our home now. We can even move your new couch here. Jake doesn't need one."

She snorts a laugh. "I actually like the idea of him having purple pillows on his couch and in the bathroom. Can we leave those? He needs some color in his life."

"Whatever you want to take or leave, we will. And anything you want to change here, we will. It's you and me now."

"And Shadow, how dare you forget about our baby!" She feigns mock horror.

"Don't go talking about babies with me. I will knock you up tomorrow if you let me," I smack her ass and walk to the front door, winking at her shocked face over my shoulder. "Come on, beautiful, we have some packing to do."

CHAPTER THIRTY-ONE

Our morning coffee on the porch is still my favorite activity, despite the late September chill. Draped in a blanket, I sip my cooling coffee, watching Thoren toss the ball Shadow left beside us.

"Are we going to do this all through winter?" Thoren jokes, perched on the outdoor sofa next to me. I moved it here when I packed up my things. Jake and Thoren spent last weekend adding on a few extra feet to the deck so we could fit it with his outdoor dining set and grill. If you ask me, it was totally worth it. If you ask Jake, he's grumpy that he has to make a new one for his deck now.

"As long as it's not snowing, then yes. Maybe you can turn part of this into a covered porch, then I can do this year round. Mittens, snow jackets, and all."

His laugh is boisterous. "Anything you want, Lily. I will make it happen."

"Good, now get your butt to work before you are late."

With a chaste kiss, he heads inside, calling, "I love you" over his shoulder. Two weeks of officially living with the man and I still love watching his ass in those work pants as he leaves. I throw the ball to Shadow a few more times, finishing my coffee before retreating inside.

Andrea called yesterday to say she sent the proof copy of my book out and I should get it today. I could hardly sleep all night with a mix of nerves and excitement. Seeing the mockup of the book is not the same as holding an actual copy of all my hard work perfectly bound into a beautiful masterpiece.

I made plans to deep clean the house today until the mail comes to keep me distracted. The mail usually comes around eleven and I plan to park my bum at the mailbox until it shows. Shadow fed off my frenzied energy, trailing me through every room of the house as I did laundry, vacuumed and mopped, dusted, and even cleaned all the drawers in the fridge. I made an omelet for brunch, and then finally the clock struck eleven. I slipped into my tennis shoes and a jacket, harnessed up Shadow, and began our trek to the end of the road.

As luck would have it, the mail is waiting for us when we get there, my little package sitting right on top of it all. Without finesse, I rip it open to see the culmination of my hard work. The cover is exactly what I hoped for, perfectly done and the pages aligned. A happy tear slips free as Shadow prances around my feet.

"Do you like it too, girl? It's really pretty, huh?" I ask, holding it out for her to sniff. She gives a bark of approval before leading me back home. Tucking the book under my arm, I flip through the rest of the mail. There's a junk advertisement, and then a letter from Kinsley. I open it when I remember Andrea sent the book to Thoren's mailbox. Flipping the envelope, I see it is indeed Thoren it's addressed to.

Dread fills me, but I finish opening it anyway. Something feels off as I pull out the small stack of papers folded. Trepidation courses through my veins when I see the bill for services. *My services.*

Kinsley was never working pro bono for me. Thoren has been paying behind my back the whole time. Bile rises up in my throat at the total that is due. Is this the real reason he sold the plot of land a few weeks ago?

I know he's doing this for me, but the lie and betrayal still hurts. Shoving aside the crushing weight in my chest, I rush back to the house with Shadow. Hot tears leak from my eyes as I try to brush them away, hating I let myself get tricked by a man once again.

I know I shouldn't be putting Thoren and Tyler in the same category, but a lie is a lie. He knows how important honesty is to me. Looking around the house, all I see are walls closing in on me. I can't be here when he comes home today. I can't face him right now. I need time to work through my thoughts and feelings on this all.

Making a rash decision, I throw my book and the bill on the kitchen counter and grab my hiking backpack. I switch out my shoes for my hiking boots and head for the door. Shadow's tail whips my leg in excitement, but I can't bring her. I need some time on my own.

"Sorry, sweet girl. Mom needs to be alone for a bit, okay?" She plops her butt with the saddest eyes, so I give her a kiss, grab my keys, and head out the door.

There's only one place I want to go where I know I'll be able to clear my head and think rationally about this. Putting Marge in park, I throw on my backpack and start the hike to the waterfall. The weather is brisk, but the trees provide shelter from the nip of the wind. By the time I make it to the clearing, I am warmed up, angry, but most of all, hurt.

I feel the loss of Thoren instantly when I realize I don't have a blanket to spread out because he always brings one for us. Instead, I find a grassy spot, and plop myself down to pull out my water bottle.

The mournful whisper of the water cascading over the rocks mirrors the ache in my heart, amplifying the emptiness I feel. This is supposed to be my place to feel at peace, but today it feels anything but.

My brain is muddled with everything we have been through in the last few months. Thoren took the shattered pieces of my heart and meticulously glued them back together through words and actions. He wove pieces of his own heart in with it, forever making him a part of me.

He has brought so much joy, laughter, and love into my life. He's the reason I have been able to fight back, to stand on my own, and to take back some of the power that has been stripped from me over the years. How can he be the one who stood up for me against Tyler and my parents, and be the man who broke my trust again?

I know he wouldn't have lied unless he felt he had a good reason to. Would I have let him pay for the lawyer if he asked? Or would I have found a crappy, cheap lawyer and hoped for the best while pinching pennies? I probably could have found one that only requires payment if they win, but they wouldn't have been Kinsley. They certainly wouldn't have been someone who is as much in my corner as Thoren and my friends.

Am I overreacting, because the thing he lied about was to do something that is monumentally amazing? I hate that he lied and hid this from me, but if I really think about it, I can see both sides. I can see my right to be upset, but I can also see his justifications for keeping this from me.

When I picture my future, I see Thoren. I see slow mornings on the back porch, book signings in Seattle, Shadow chasing our kids through the yard, and weekend dinners with his parents. I want that with him more than anything, but I need *trust.* Can you have love without having trust?

The wind picks up in the clearing as I realize I have been

sitting here for over two hours. The air has taken on the wet scent of rain, and I know it's coming. I throw on my backpack for the trek back as a chill seeps through my sweatshirt. I never should have come out without checking the weather first.

Two minutes into the hike, the pitter patter of early rain surrounds me. A few rogue drops drip through the canopy the trees provide while I quicken my steps. In a matter of minutes, it turns into a torrential downpour. The trail quickly turns into slippery mud as I focus on my feet and begin a light jog.

I'm so focused on not slipping that when I take a break to catch my breath, I realize I don't think I took the turn I was supposed to. All the trees and trails look the same out here, but surely something would have stood out, notifying me of the turn I was supposed to take. I suck in a deep lung full of the damp air, before jogging on.

I continue until a trail veers to the right, and I take it, hoping it's correct. Keeping my eyes on the trail as the mud turns into puddles in spots, I keep pushing. The icy rain has soaked through my sweater and my legs are caked in mud.

I think I am almost to the next spot I need to turn, so I glance around, only to falter in my steps. My ankle twists and my feet slip out from under me. In an attempt to not fall in the puddle before me, I throw my body to the side, and that's when everything goes black.

thoren

I have had this pit in my stomach all day that something isn't right. Lily was supposed to get the proof copy of her book today and she was so excited about it. I thought she would call me or at least text me to say if it was everything she hoped for or not. Instead, it's been radio silence all day. I've chalked it up to her being on the phone with Andrea and her team talking it over, but even that doesn't feel right.

The minute the clock hits five, I am out the door and headed to my truck. A nasty storm rolled in today, and Niles and I did several drives through the campgrounds to make sure everyone was faring okay. My windshield wipers struggle to keep up with the onslaught of rain and wind, but I don't dare slow. The pit in my stomach is growing by the minute the closer I get to home.

It amplifies tenfold when I pull up to the cabin, and Lily's car is noticeably absent. I throw Freya in park and run into the house, only to find an anxious Shadow waiting at the door for me.

"Lily?" I call, checking through the house. "Lily, honey, are you home?" My feet carry me room to room, but all of them come up empty. I slip my phone from my pocket and dial her number, but she doesn't answer, so I leave a quick message. I pace the living room, trying to think where she could be, before making my way to the kitchen in search of a note she might have left.

The minute I see her book and the opened envelope on the counter, I know I've fucked up. The logo from Kinsley's firm is stamped in bold on the top of the pages, and I know that she knows. I sink onto the stool at the island, my head in my hands. I should have told her, why the fuck didn't I tell her?

The wind shifts, pelting rain into the windows, as a shiver runs through me. Lily shouldn't be out in this storm. I pull my phone back out and call Jake, but he hasn't seen or heard from her. Michele is next, but she hasn't heard from her either. She chews me out when I tell her about the bill she found, but then tells me she's getting in the car to drive around town to look for her. My parents haven't spoken to her, and neither has Amber.

Fear is pulsing through my veins as I try to deduce where she could be. I start a group text with everyone, asking them to let me know if they hear from her. By the time I change into warm dry clothes, the replies have poured in. Each and every one of them is going to drive around in this storm and look for her and her car.

With most of them in town, I head further into the woods. My gut is telling me that I know exactly where she is. I'm terrified to find out if I'm right, because if she went to our spot, she would be somewhere in the woods in the middle of a horrendous storm with no end in sight.

My heart stops as my truck pulls up to the small turn off to see Lily's car in the parking lot all alone. I pull up next to her, heart in my throat, but she isn't in her car. I try calling again and see her phone light up on her center console.

FUCK!

I dial Jake, who picks up on the second ring. "I'm still driving around, but haven't found her yet," he says gruffly.

"I found her car," comes my fearful reply. "I need you to get the SAR team together for me. All the gear for a long search through the night, the sked litter, emergency blankets, all of it. Call Niles, he was staying late at the office, tell him to pull in every volunteer. The pull off by marker 87, the one with over fifteen miles of trails."

"Thoren," Jake interrupts. "Stop talking like a robot. She's going to be okay. I'll make the call, but I'm on my way to you. Don't go off without me."

"I don't know how long she's been gone," I whisper the words I don't want to say out loud. "I'm going in now."

"Damn it, Thoren, don't you dare. Ten minutes." He hangs up to make the call to Niles. There is no way that I am waiting here if Lily is lost or hurt in these woods.

Reaching into my glove compartment, I pull out my map and a marker and scribble where I am heading first and where I think Lily will have been. I know she went to the waterfall, so that's where I am starting the search. I place it on my dash in hopes of someone seeing it. I really wish I grabbed my hiking backpack, or any of my SAR gear at the house, but I'm not turning around for it now. Grabbing the emergency flashlight from the center console, I lock up my truck and head to the trail.

Jake's truck races into the parking lot when I am five feet onto the muddy path. "Dick!" he yells out over the rain, throwing a heavy jacket on. "I knew you wouldn't wait." He jogs over to catch up with me. "Search and Rescue 101 - always go in pairs. Niles is getting the team together, and your dad and Michele are on their way. Let's go."

LILY

My head throbs with every pulse, my body shudders with uncontrollable shivers, and my ankle aches with a dull, throbbing pain. All I want is to roll over into the warmth of Thoren's arms. The sounds of the pouring rain and rolling thunder forces my eyes to flutter open as I take in the trees, ferns, and muddy forest floor around me.

My fingers press at the painful spot on my head, wincing at the tenderness there. My fear spikes when my hand comes away streaked with blood. Trying to sit up, I gently roll my ankle to see how bad I tweaked it. Pain lances up my leg with the movement, and I can feel the swelling with the tightness in that boot.

Pulling off my backpack, I dig through for any help I have for this situation. I left my phone in the car like an idiot, so I can't call for help. The emergency kit has some gauze that I press to the cut on my head, but it soaks up more water than blood. There's also a small emergency blanket at the bottom that I unwrap and drape around me.

It's getting dark, so I pull out the emergency glow stick and pop that, setting it by my side. I try to adjust myself a little further onto the wet pines and ferns instead of the muddy trail, setting my backpack against a tree trunk to use as a pillow. I could try to walk on my ankle, but with how slippery the path is, I won't get far. Huddling the best I can under the silver foil blanket, I let my eyes close again, letting sleep take me under.

THOREN

"Lily!" I swing the flashlight around the clearing again, not seeing anything that points to her being here. "Lily!"

Jake comes tramping out of the woods, his phone flashlight in hand. "She's not here. We should turn around and check the other trails."

My legs give out, my body sinking to my knees. I thought for sure Lily would be hiding here, waiting out the storm. We didn't pass her on the hike up here, and there were no signs of life, although the rain and mud would have washed away any footprints. She is somewhere out here, lost, scared, and possibly hurt, and it's all my fault.

What the hell was I thinking not telling her? It seems so trivial now, keeping such a stupid thing from her. I know I could have convinced her to let me pay. I just chose the easy way out and this is what it got me.

Lily is my everything, my true north, the one true love of my life. When we find her, I swear to god, I am going to fix this and make her my wife. She has to be okay. I try to focus on the future we are going to have; the beautiful white dress she will wear, her belly swelling with each child we will have, her black hair turning gray and accentuating her beauty.

Jake grips my shoulder hard, pulling me from my spiraling thoughts. "Get up. She needs your head on straight right now. Do you know what time she might have come out here?"

"Mail comes around eleven. If she came right away, then she has been out here for eight hours," my voice cracks on the last word.

"Then she needs us now. Come on, the rest of the crews should be out looking by now. Let's try to get back to a spot with service so we can see which trails are being searched and where they need us." He holds out his hand, helping me up and pulling me into a hug. "She's going to be okay. She has to be."

By the time we reach a spot with cell service, my phone is blowing up with messages.

DAD:

I stopped by your place and picked up Shadow.
I figured we could use all the help we can get.

MICHELE:

I have extra clothes packed for her.

NILES:

I called everyone, fifteen made it in. Your mom
set up some tents at the trailhead with hot food
and drinks, and is manning the walkie-talkies
and map with an Amber. We are in five groups
of three, and your dad is with a woman and a
dog on their own, too. We are splitting up the
trails, so join whoever you find first. There's no
back-up teams, we are all gears going. We are
going to find her tonight.

UNKNOWN NUMBER:

Hey this is Amber. Michele gave me your
number. I closed the shop early and am helping
your mom track where everyone is. I packed my
car with every blanket I own and some random
sizes of jackets from the store if anyone needs
to warm up or get dry clothes.

MOM:

I sent some extra waters and two winter coats
with your dad if you find him. I know you boys
went out without thinking. Not sure if they will fit
Jake though. Bring her home, son.

Fuck, my eyes prick with tears. I am grateful every day for
this community, but right now, I feel overwhelmed with the love
and support. All for the beautiful woman who blew into town and
tipped my world upside down with her gentle manners, kind
smile, and striking blue eyes.

I make a quick call to my mom, getting a general location of
my dad, and Jake and I make our way toward him and Michele. If
anyone can find Lily, it will be Shadow.

I know these woods and these trails well, but in the dark, with
the wind and rain still whipping around us, it's easy to get turned
around. Our boots squelch through the mud, trying to keep a
decent pace to find my dad and to keep the chill at bay. It can't be

over fifty degrees out. I keep my feet moving, trying not to think of all the things that could go wrong for Lily right now.

After another thirty minutes, I hear Shadow before I see her. Her black fur keeps her hidden in the night, but my flashlight catches her barreling for us. My dad and Michele aren't far behind her, and I am beyond relieved to see them.

"How you holding up?" my dad asks, pulling the jackets from his bag. We put them on, neither of us able to zip them up, but it's better than the sweaters Jake and I currently have.

"Not great."

"Well, let's keep moving. Shadow seemed on a mission before she heard you two behind us," Michele says, giving me a sympathetic look. The worry we are all feeling is palpable, but we keep moving, following Shadow, who keeps her nose to the ground.

Dad's radio squawks, my mom calling out for updates on the location of everyone and checking in to ensure everyone is still doing okay. Slowly, the replies come through the static, and each one that verifies they have found nothing yet adds more pressure to my chest.

My dad radios in our reply, as we continue to search through the dark. Michele keeps her flashlight trained on the path while I keep mine on Shadow, and dad and Jake search the woods on either side. It's slow going, but it's important to not miss anything, and another thirty minutes pass with no signs of Lily. My chest feels like a leaden weight, each inhale a painful reminder of the empty space her absence has created.

Shadow's sharp bark breaks through the deafening silence around us as she races into the distance. Before I can comprehend it, I am sprinting after her, hoping and praying she is leading me to Lily. Her paws stop in an instant as a small light illuminates her and a reflective surface. Shadow whines before her piercing bark continues until I am by her side.

She burrows next to the light, and that's when I see her. Lily's small body is huddled under an emergency blanket, her skin is pale, and there's dried blood on her forehead.

"She's here!" I shout behind me, falling to my knees at her side. She's cold to the touch as I try to assess her for injuries. "Lily, baby, I'm here. Open your eyes, baby. It's going to be okay. I'm here."

Her lashes flutter, struggling to stay open. "Tor-n?" she slurs. *Fucking fuck.* With her coloring and slurred speech, she's hypothermic and needs to be warmed immediately. I hear the others before I see them as they crouch around me, and my dad calls through the radio, giving our location and that we need an extraction.

I pull off the blanket, seeing her soaked clothes beneath it. Normally, these emergency heat blankets would be the right thing to use, but with a cold body and wet clothes, they can actually prevent you from getting dry and cause more harm than good.

Michele has done some SAR training in the past and is already pulling off her boots and socks and telling Jake to pull the dry clothing from her pack. "Her ankle is a mess," she says, as I carefully prod her head to find where the blood came from. I glance down to see one ankle swollen and purple, but I'm more concerned with how pale her toes look.

Finally, I feel the cut on the side of her head. Head wounds tend to bleed a lot, and it doesn't seem too bad, but a concussion is a possibility, too. I pull off her sweatshirt and shirt underneath, leaving her in just her bra and panties as Michele and I put her in the long johns, sweats, and jacket that Michele brought. Jake grabs thermal socks from the bag, handing them over without looking.

"Thank you," I mutter to Michele, knowing this small act can make a huge difference for Lily right now.

"They're coming with the sked litter. Team three packed it in and they are about a mile out," my dad interrupts. "How's she doing?"

"Lily, wake up. We're getting you out of here, but I need to know where you hurt."

Her blue eyes flutter again before remaining shut. "Head a-a-and ankle."

"She's too cold, and we are wasting time staying here. I'm carrying her to them." I delicately lift her into my arms. My dad rummages around in his backpack, pulling out a fresh emergency blanket. He drapes it around her as best as he can before nodding to me.

"We'll be right behind you."

"Give her to me," Jake says with a stern glare when I scowl at him. "They will need your help to carry her in the sked and it's a long hike back. I'm too tall to help with that, I'll throw off the balance. Let me help while I can."

I reluctantly pass her off, stroking her hair as she settles into Jake's large arms. He made the right call. With his long strides, the rest of us are practically jogging to keep up with him. I hear him whispering to her the whole time, telling her about all the people who showed up for her today, and fuck, that one act about broke me. We make it to team three in no time. They have extra emergency blankets that we wrap around Lily like a cocoon before buckling her in.

I watch her shallow breathing as my team and I carry her out, and she still can't keep her eyes open. When we finally reach the trailhead, an ambulance and EMTs are there waiting. The sight of them surrounded by all the cars, and my mom and Amber under the large tent with tables and lights set up almost brings me to my knees.

The EMTs are by our side instantly, working on transferring her to their gurney. I take in all the people standing there, a mix of fear and relief covering their faces. I have so many things I want to say, so many thanks to give. My mom shakes her head at me, tears streaming down her cheeks. "Go, we have this. We will meet you at the hospital as soon as we can."

I climb into the ambulance with Lily, the lights and sounds around me not even registering. I only have eyes for her. My heart, my future, my whole damn world, laying on the gurney next to me. I reach for her free hand across from where the paramedic works on her, stroking my thumb over her knuckles.

"We've got her now. It's going to be okay," the paramedic says in a calm and reassuring voice as he works on her IV.

She's going to be okay. She has to be okay.

CHAPTER THIRTY-THREE

thoren

The last twenty-four hours have been some of the worst of my life, starting this morning when I felt like something was wrong. When we arrived at the hospital, they rushed Lily into the ICU, where I wasn't allowed to follow. I paced the small waiting room for over an hour until Jake showed up with a change of clean and dry clothes for me. Then I paced for another hour before my parents showed up with food and coffee. It's approaching midnight now, and although I missed dinner, there is no way I would be eating.

Another hour passed before a doctor came out to update us on Lily's condition. They said she has severe hypothermia but they are gradually warming her with heated blankets and warmed IV fluids. Her head wound required stitches, but a concussion assessment was impossible due to overlapping symptoms with her severe hypothermia. Luckily, her ankle was only sprained, and the rest of her seemed to be okay.

He said protocol dictates I couldn't go back until they have her conscious and aware, but I begged with my life. The doctor allowed me five minutes to sit with her, hold her hand, and tell her how sorry I was, and how much I love her. The sight of her still pale skin squeezed that already tight noose wrapped around my chest, but I held it together until I returned to the waiting room.

The moment I stepped back through those doors and saw my mom, I lost it. I let the weight crush me, as I crumpled to the floor and let my emotions take over. My mom sat on the floor with me, holding me while I fell apart. Her soft hands stroked down my back as she assured me Lily would be okay. As the tears settled, I confessed the lie I told Lily about her lawyer, and that I was the cause of her being out in the woods alone today.

In her true motherly fashion, she scolded me for lying, then told me that today was no one's fault. She had the utmost faith that I would grovel and Lily would forgive me. Her words echoed in my mind the rest of the morning. *Couples fight honey, but a love like yours doesn't fade. It can't be suppressed or concealed, it's an unbreakable bond that lasts a lifetime.*

Jake went home to check on Shadow and get some sleep, and I sent my parents home to get some sleep as well. Michele showed up about an hour after they left, and we tried to rest on the awful chairs until the doctor came back to get me.

"She's doing okay. Her body temperature is hovering around 98 degrees, but we still have her under warming blankets. She's alert and talking, but her heart rate is still slower than we would like, so we are monitoring that. Her movements are slow still, but that is to be expected and should improve throughout the morning," her doctor says as he walks with me. "Visiting hours don't technically start until eight, so if you can keep everyone else out until then, that would be great. She asked for you, so I'm making an exception."

"Thank you, Dr. Klein," my voice is hoarse. He nods and points to her door, telling me I can go in.

The moment I step into the room, her blue eyes latch onto mine. Her lower lip wobbles, a lone tear breaking free from its confinement and trickling down her flushed cheek. *Her flushed cheeks*. I can feel my heart skip a beat as a surge of relief washes over me at seeing the color back in her complexion. The weight of her stare settles on my chest, making it difficult to breathe again. A knot forms in my stomach, tightening with each passing second.

As I approach her, my hands instinctively reach out, aching to wipe away the tear and offer comfort. "I'm so sorry, Lily. I have so many things I want to say to you, but I can't seem to think of a single one. I just need to know you're okay."

"I'm okay," her soft voice cracks, so I grab the cup from beside her to give her little sips of water. Pulling the chair as close to her bedside as I can, I slipped my hands under the blanket to hold hers. "I'm so angry. At you, at myself, at that stupid storm."

"I'm so-"

"No," she interrupts me. "It's my turn to speak now. I have a lot to say."

A smile spreads on my face at my strong woman putting me in my place. "Go ahead, baby."

"You should have never lied. You knew, Thoren. Out of everyone, you knew how important trust was to me. You knew how I felt about lies and being made a fool of. I am so mad at you for choosing to lie to me instead of trusting me to make the right choice in allowing you to help."

She's right. I know she's right, and I have nothing to rebuttal. I've known from the beginning that lying was a bad idea, but I was so sure she would be stubborn and not allow me to help.

"There's no excuse. I should have told you. I was going to tell you when you won the case, because you are going to win it. You deserve the right person fighting for you, and that person is Kinsley. I didn't want money to hold you back when I could take care of it for you."

"It wasn't your choice to make," her fingers lightly squeeze mine. "You know that, right? You see why I am upset?"

"I do. I am so sorry for lying, but I'm not sorry for making sure you are taken care of and that you get to right a wrong. I would do it over and over again. Anything to make sure you feel seen, you are heard, and you are validated. I'm not sorry for doing it, but I am sorry for lying about it. I never should have broken that trust with you."

A nurse walks in then, breaking our tense moment. "How are you doing, Lily?" she asks, taking note of the monitors.

"Tired, but okay," she says, as the nurse goes through several checks. She asks a series of questions and does a range of motion maneuver with her arms and legs.

"You're making improvements, but you will have to stay another night or two for continued monitoring. We will be in every two hours to monitor your progress, and I am going to order some soup for you this morning so that will be down in a bit. Try to rest, and hit the call button if you need anything," she smiles politely at me before stepping back out of the room.

When we are alone again, I brush the hair from her face, placing a gentle kiss on her lips. "I don't want to be another bad guy in your story, but I told you before. I will do anything to protect you, and I felt that's what I was doing."

"You have a lot of groveling to do, and you are getting every penny back when I win."

A genuine smile stretches across my face, and the tension in my chest eases, letting me take a full breath for the first time since I came home and found her missing last night. "Okay, baby, if that's what you need. Just know that every cent will go into a fund for our future. A ring for your dainty finger, your dream trip to Iceland, the wedding you've always dreamed of, and college funds for our kids."

She shakes her head, a small smile gracing her lips. "I love you. I was so scared yesterday. So scared that I was going to die out there without getting to tell you that I want it all with you. Even mad at you, it was your comfort I wanted, your arms I wanted to find solace in, and your love that gave me the strength to stand up for myself. Knowing I could get angry with you, and instead of shaming me for it, you would be proud that I am demanding the respect and honesty that I deserve. I fought so hard to stay alive so I could see your hazel eyes and tell you that you are my everything, Thoren. Good, bad, and amazing–you are it for me."

Tears prick at my eyes again, my hands cupping her face. I let the weight of her words fill me with warmth. As much as I hate the thought of her out there alone and scared, fighting to survive, I was reveling in the fact she was thinking of me. I know she never left my thoughts.

"I was scared, too. It was a bone deep fear that I wouldn't find you on time. All I could think of was how much I love you. I love the way your blue eyes shine when the morning rays hit them, and the small smile that graces your lips when you take the first inhale of your morning coffee. I love the way you tuck your legs under you for comfort, and that you hum when you load the dishwasher. I love the way you wrap around me in bed, and stand on your tiptoes to wash my hair when we shower together. I thought I might never get to see those things again, and it broke me, Lily. You are my everything. I'm just so sorry for it all."

"Come here," she whispers through tears. I carefully climb into the bed with her, avoiding her IV, as I wrap myself around her. My hands trail down her cheeks and over her arm, soaking in the feel of her safe in my arms. "You can grovel later. Right now, I just need you to hold me while I sleep, okay?"

"Okay, baby."

LILY

There's a light knock at the door before Michele's face pops around the corner. Her relief is instant when she sees me, her chin wobbling as she holds back her emotions. "Hi," she says, eyes bright with unshed tears. "I didn't wake you, did I?"

I fight back a yawn. "No, the nurses just woke me for their check. He's been zonked for about three hours now." I run my hands through Thoren's hair, his body carefully laid over me.

She pulls up the chair Thoren was in earlier, dropping a bag by her feet before grabbing my free hand in hers. "It's good to see you with some color. You gave us all a good scare, and when you're feeling better, I am going to yell at you for it."

"If it makes you feel better, I scared myself. I never expected the storm, and then I got lost and fell, and it's all a little hazy from there," I wince as Thoren twitches, hitting my ankle with his foot.

He wakes instantly, blinking as he scours my face. "Are you okay?"

"Your big body is crushing her, so no, she's not okay," Michele quips.

He slowly sits up, careful not to smush me any more, and steps off the bed. "When did you get here?"

"Just a minute ago. Go get coffee and food. You look like hell, and I've got plans for Lily."

He looks to me for confirmation that I'm okay, his eyes softening when I give him a reassuring smile. "Can I get either of you anything?" We both tell him no before he slips out of the room, promising to be back as soon as possible.

"I'm going to wash your hair. I already asked the nurse before I came in here and she's bringing a shower chair. I brought my good shower supplies and stopped by your place to get you some fresh clothes. While I do this, you're going to tell me exactly what's been going on. Deal?"

A lump forms in my throat as I take in my beautiful friend. I don't know what I did to deserve a woman like her in my life, but I will be eternally grateful. She helps me out of bed and into the shower, leaving my hospital gown on so I have some privacy. Michele takes her time as she carefully and meticulously washes the mud from my hair while avoiding my stitches. She even helps me wash my body when I struggle to do it on my own.

"He lied to me," I confess while her fingers stroke through my hair, rinsing out the conditioner. "He has been paying for the lawyer the whole time and didn't tell me."

Michele's hands pause a moment before continuing. "Did he tell you why he lied?"

"He didn't have to. I can put two and two together. I know I have been stubborn about wanting to do as much as possible on my own, especially when you guys first found out about Tyler. He explained that he hated lying but he would do anything for me, including make sure I have the best people fighting for me, and that meant making sure I had Kinsley."

She turns off the shower, wringing out my hair before helping me get out and into the fresh clothes she brought. I step out of the bathroom in baggy sweats, cozy socks that aren't too tight on my ankle, and a loose shirt that won't interfere with my IV. Just when I think Michele has gone above and beyond, she sits me on the bed sideways so she can brush and braid my hair.

"I have to be honest, and it's okay if you're mad at me," she starts again as she parts my hair. "I knew about Kinsley. I told him so many times to tell you, but he was scared you would fire her and go with someone cheaper."

I take a deep breath, letting the information settle. I want to be mad, I feel like I should be mad, but I'm not. I could have died yesterday. If Thoren and his team had waited the six hours to verify that I was lost, or Shadow hadn't been out there helping, I would have died. It makes things like this seem trivial.

When I step back and look at it from an outsider's perspective, Thoren went out of his way to spend his money on something that was important to me. I can be mad at the lie, but being upset about him putting such a high value on my justice and feelings is just stupid. Thoren has shown time and time again that he is going to be by my side through it all. That I am his number one priority in life. It's a heady feeling standing in the glow of his love.

I grab her wrist after she ties off the braid, pulling her down so I can see her. "Don't yell at me for almost dying and we are even."

She barks a surprised laugh, wrapping me in a hug, "Deal."

Thoren makes it back with an army in tow, each one with their hands full. "I got you some tea. The nurse said it would be okay," he says, handing me a cup from his tray, before giving another to Michele and taking the last for himself. "You look beautiful," he whispers, dropping a kiss on my forehead.

"It's good to see you up," Evelyn says, pushing him out of the way to hug me. "I didn't think we were allowed to bring anything in the ICU, but I guess River knows the tricks. The basket is from him."

David gingerly places a basket on my lap, giving my shoulder a squeeze. I peek through the gift, seeing fuzzy socks, a thick robe, some newly released romance books, a candle, and some lotion. There's a bulky envelope slipped in the middle, so I grab it out.

Thought these might be helpful for you in the future. Glad you're okay.

—Riv

I dump the contents to find a compass and a bumper sticker

that says 'Support Search and Rescue: Get Lost'. Chuckling, I slip the items back into the basket and place it on the table next to me. He is a good and kind man, but also kind of an ass, and I can't help but love him for it.

"Jake was going to come check on you, but Shadow is an anxious mess right now, so he is staying with her instead," Thoren says, tucking me back under all the blankets before wrapping himself around me again. "She's the one who found you first, and I think it's killing her not knowing you're okay. Jake said he snuck over to our house and had to steal one of your shirts to calm her."

He pulls his phone from his pocket, scrolling to the text thread to Jake. There's a photo of Shadow snuggled on the couch, my shirt under her head.

David speaks up from his spot on the wall, laughing lightly. "She tried to follow you into the ambulance. It took both Jake and I to hold her back. That dog is as much yours as Thoren's."

"Damn straight. Lily's her mom," Thoren says proudly. "I like the sound of that. Can we come back here in nine months to make you a real mom?"

My wide eyes turn to him, beaming at the casual drop of wanting to get me pregnant.

"That's our cue," Evelyn says, patting my leg. "We just wanted to see you and drop off River's gift. The fridge and freezer will be stocked with meals when you get home. If you need anything else, you just call, dear. Oh, and I will make an excellent grandma."

She walks out of the room completely nonchalant, as David makes his way over. He drops a kiss on the top of my head. "Glad you're doing okay. I'd be a good grandpa, too, in case you were wondering." He follows his wife out, and I turn to look at Thoren, whose smile is even wider somehow.

Michele puts her hands up when I look at her. "I'm staying

out of this. Thoren, I expect expert level groveling. Lily, rest up and then put that man to work. I'm around if you guys need anything."

My nurse comes in to bring me soup, and Michele clears out her things, promising to stop by tomorrow morning again. Thoren feeds me each sip slowly, despite my protest, then snuggles right back into bed with me to catch up on sleep. My body is utterly exhausted, the shower having used every ounce of energy I had. I soak in Thoren's body heat, and drift off to sleep with him.

lily

"You know they said I could walk, right?" I ask, as Thoren carries me from the truck bridal style.

"Yep, doesn't mean you have to. That ankle is still bruised, and I like carrying you. I get to practice for when I do this with you in a white dress." The minute he pushes the front door open, Shadow launches herself at us, jumping up to lick me while whining.

He rushes me to the couch, gently setting me on it. Shadow is at my side immediately, kissing my face with fervor. "Gentle," Thoren tells her, and she lays down, plopping her head into my lap.

"I missed you, too, girl," I tell her as she rolls onto her back to look up at me. "Thank you for finding me."

Thoren walks out, giving us a moment, before coming back in with arms full of flowers. "We have a lot of these in the kitchen," he says, putting three vases on the coffee table. "These three are from Andrea, River, and Amber. I really like her, by the way. There's four more in the kitchen from the SAR team, Michele, my parents, and even Jake."

"There are also these." He hands me some get well soon

cards, and on the bottom of it all is the proof copy of my book. He kneels in front of the couch, hands sliding up my legs. "I want you to know that I am so proud of you. This book is incredible. You are incredible. I am so sorry that you didn't get to celebrate it because of my stupid shit."

"You read it?" my voice squeaks out.

"Michele saw it on the counter when she grabbed your clothes and brought it. I read it every time you slept." I lean forward, smoothing my lips over his. There are no reservations left when it comes to this man. He has consumed me, and I am his.

His rough fingers stroke my cheeks when I pull back. "Thank you. We can celebrate the release instead." My stomach rumbles, clearly unsatisfied with the hospital food of the last few days. "Will you make us dinner?"

"Absolutely. Give our girl some more love," he says, rubbing Shadow's belly as he places the cards and book on the table before heading to the kitchen.

It's good to finally be home. I spent two more nights at the hospital because movement was still slow going for a while. My concussion is manageable, and I just need to be careful on my ankle for another week. Overall, I am beyond lucky that things aren't worse. I didn't realize how close I was to death until the doctor laid it all out for me, scolding me for putting the emergency blanket over my wet and cold clothes. At least I know for next time. *God, I hope there is no next time.*

Michele came back to visit every morning, and Amber even stopped by on her way to see Jana. I had Thoren text my parents to let them know what had happened, and a small part of me hoped that they would fly out, but they didn't. They didn't even call, instead texting a simple 'glad you're okay'. That hurt more than I want to admit, but I am coming to terms that they will never be the parents I want them to be.

If my brush with death wasn't enough to warrant a phone call, then nothing will be able to mend what's broken. I won't fight for people that don't want to fight for me. I spent too long trying to please others that didn't see me. For months now, I have been working towards being confident in who I am and not accepting less than I deserve.

I'm learning that family isn't necessarily the people that you share your DNA with, but those that choose to be a part of your life. The love I have from my family here is more than my love-starved heart could have ever hoped for.

It's that love that has had my head spinning these last few days. The only thought that ran through my head while I laid on the cold forest floor was that I still had things I wanted to do with my life. I saw visions of my white dress with Thoren waiting for me at the end of the aisle. His hands latched onto mine, smiling brightly, as he encouraged me to give one more good push. His soft voice singing to our child as he danced around the kitchen. His legs wrapped around my body as I nestled back onto his chest, both of us watching our little boys and Shadow play in the water at our spot.

"Chicken enchiladas, shepherd's pie, or lasagna for dinner tonight?" Thoren calls from the kitchen, bringing me back to reality.

"Lasagna sounds incredible. Did your mom make all those meals?"

"Those are just the first ones available. We won't have to cook dinner for weeks with all this food," he jokes, taking a seat on the couch next to me. "Want to pick a movie while the oven heats?"

"No, I want to talk to you about something." I turn to face him as best as possible without moving and upsetting Shadow.

"I don't like the sound of that. What's going on, baby?"

"Did you mean what you said in the hospital? That I am your everything and you see your future with me?"

"Lily, you are my sun, moon, and stars. The brightest spot in my days, the one I look forward to seeing every night, and the one I have wished for all my life, and have finally found. Yes, I meant every word of it," his hands clasp mine, his eyes radiating sincerity.

There is no more time for fear in my life. I have a second chance and I am jumping in with both feet. He is the one my soul longs for, and I want to start our future now.

"I want to have your baby," I blurt. "When I was out there alone in the woods, all I could think of was my future with you. Mad as hell at you and your dumb lie, it was still your heart I wanted to make my home in. I know it's soon, and crazy, and we aren't even engaged and life has been throwing us curve balls… but I love you, Thoren James, and I want to have your baby."

He sits stock still, unblinking, his mouth opening, then closing again. I can feel the sweat roll down my neck, anxiety taking over. He isn't ready. His comments and jokes have been just that, jokes.

He shakes off his shocked face, wraps his arms around me and picks me up, spinning me in a circle. He peppers kisses across my face before gently setting me on my feet. He leans back to look me in the eyes, his glassy and filled with happiness. "You want to have my babies?"

"I do."

I'm picked right back up as I wrap my legs around his waist. Shadow huffs behind us, left out again, as Thoren barrels up the stairs. "You can't say those two words to me baby," he breathes into my neck, "They make my dick hard coming from your sweet mouth."

"I thought you were heating up our dinner?" I ask, a little breathless as he lays me on the bed, climbing on top.

He lifts my shirt, kissing his way from my hip bone to the

bottom of my bra, flicking his tongue over the fabric covering my peeked nipple. "That's on pause," he pulls down the cup, wrapping his warm lips over the pebbled bud. "I'm going to put a baby in you first."

I huff a laugh, sucking in a sharp breath when his teeth clamp down. "A baby before dinner, huh?"

"Baby, your perfect little pussy will be dripping with my cum every day until there's a positive on a stick." He lowers my other bra cup, licking his way to the other nipple. "Probably every day after, too."

Achingly slow, he strips us both of our clothes, his hands gliding across my skin with reverence. His lips follow his hands, kissing every inch of exposed skin. He settles himself over me, one hand trailing down my stomach to find me ready for him.

"You're soaked for me," he whispers, one finger slipping into me easily.

"Please don't tease me, Thoren. I need you." My fingers grip his biceps, my back arching as he strokes just the right spot.

"You know I'll give you anything you ask for," he removes his finger, bringing it to my lips, tracing it over them. Lining himself up, he takes my lip in a searing kiss as he pushes into me. He licks and sucks on my lips, tasting every drop of me that he painted there. He circles his hips, stretching me out to take him.

"You take my cock so well, princess." He sits on his knees, holding me spread wide for him. His thrusts are slow and even, angled the way I need him. His hazel eyes watch me intently, sparkling with unadulterated desire, showing me every nuance of his emotions. He keeps the rhythm steady, building us up gradually. Large hands graze up my thighs, one of them moving up to pinch and pluck my nipples, the thumb of his other circling my clit with delicious pressure.

"I love you," I cry out, as he replaces his fingers on my breast with his mouth.

He moves up to take my mouth, never stopping his thumb from keeping me right on edge. His soft lips part mine, his stubble tickling my cheeks. Thoren kisses me as slowly and steadily as he's fucking me, driving me wild. He's showing me he's here to be my constant. To be my steady rock in the rushing river, redirecting the pain and onslaught of the outside world. His tongue swirls around mine before retreating to kiss up my jaw line.

"I love you," he breathes into my ear. His hips pick up the pace, his thumb circling faster as his breathing grows ragged. My sensitive nipples glide over the smattering of hair on his chest, bringing my orgasm to the edge. "Come with me, baby. Fall apart with me so I can stitch us back together."

His teeth clamp down on the sensitive spot below my ear, setting off my orgasm as I shatter around him. Thoren grunts in my ear as his hips falter and he fills me with hot bursts of cum. Our sweat slicked bodies stick together as he lies on top of me, catching his breath. Aftershocks of my orgasm skitter through me as he sits up and pulls out of me.

I close my legs on instinct, but his calloused hands pull my thighs apart, watching as his cum drips from me. His eyes meet mine as he reaches down and uses two fingers to shove it back inside. Tingles of heat travel through me as he watches me with a fire in his eyes.

"Such a good girl, not wasting a drop." He places a featherlight kiss on my nose before covering me up with the blankets. He doesn't bother cleaning up, throwing on sweats while smirking when he notices my eyes glued to his biteable ass. "Stay there and make our baby, I'll be back with food."

I snuggle under the blankets, soaking in the soft feel of them against my skin, laced in Thoren's amber scent. It's such a stark contrast from the sterile, scratchy blankets I had in the hospital. The comforts and care that Thoren put into this home, our home, astounds me. He put together every piece of this with a family in mind, and I get to be part of that family.

Shadow comes bounding up the stairs, jumping onto the bed, curling into my side. Her fur is cold from the crisp night air, but her tongue is hot as she licks my hand. I missed her while I was in the hospital. I don't know how to communicate to her how grateful I am to have her. She bit Tyler when he hurt me, she found me in the woods, and she has been the best little wing woman between Thoren and I. I rub her ears, kissing her soft nose, and breathe in her stinky dog breath. I wouldn't trade it for anything.

Heavy footfalls trudge up the stairs as Thoren pops into the room with a tray of food. "This looks oddly familiar. Am I about to get edged again?"

His eyes dance with mirth, "That mouth of yours, Lily." He sets the tray on my lap, crawling in bed next to me as he grabs his plate of lasagna. "So I thought of something while I was downstairs."

"Yeah?" I reply, blowing on a steamy bite of my dinner.

"Can you even get pregnant right now? Aren't you on birth control?" he asks before shoving a bite in his mouth.

"I haven't taken it for the last three nights since I was in the hospital. I was thinking I would just stop altogether." I take a bite of the lasagna, groaning at how cheesy and delicious it is. "I might keep you around just to have access to your mom's food."

He nudges my shoulder. "Keep making those noises and I don't care why you stick around, as long as you do."

"Dick," I mutter, taking another bite.

"Lily James, did you just call me a dick?! I don't think I've ever heard you swear," he mocks, one hand over his chest.

"Oh shut it, I have to balance you out somehow. Did you just call me Lily James?"

His eyes light with mischief. "Has a nice ring to it, doesn't it?"

We eat the rest of our dinner, passing playful quips back and forth. Thoren takes the dishes downstairs, so I make my way to the shower. Standing for long periods is still uncomfortable on my tender ankle, but I need to get the feel of the hospital off of me. Thoren joins me halfway through, demanding I sit as he finishes washing my hair for me. He rushes through his own shower, stepping out first to get my towel and dry me off.

Once I'm dry, he wraps me in the fluffy robe from River and sets me on the counter. He takes out my blow dryer, spending the next fifteen minutes meticulously drying every strand of hair. "I don't want you getting cold," he says when I ask why he insisted on doing it. Butterflies take flight in my stomach over his gentle touch and insistence on taking care of me.

We crawl back into bed together, snuggling under the blankets, his fingers combing through my hair. There's one thing that has been niggling at me for a few days, so I ask, "Did you sell your land for me?"

"Not entirely," he admits. "The money will help with paying for Kinsley, yes. But it will also take care of things for us for a while. I own a lot of land, Lily, and it seems selfish to keep it all to myself. Paying for Kinsley was just the thing to get the ball rolling in this case."

The way he lays it flat out for me is both a stab and a balm to my heart. I asked for honesty, even if he thinks it will hurt me and he is giving it to me. It bothers me that he is giving up something he carefully invested in for me.

"I wish you could take it back. I'll find a way to pay for Kinsley, even if we lose the case. I could do some signing tours to bring in some money. I never wanted to before because traveling alone never appealed to me."

"It's okay, baby. I'm not upset about it. I would sell it all to take care of you. Sleep now, you still need to rest. We don't have anything to worry about."

I close my eyes, breathing in his warm skin beneath me, feeling Shadow stretch out near my legs, and I truly feel it.

This is happiness.

This is home.

Everything is going to be okay.

CHAPTER THIRTY-FIVE

Six Weeks Later

The Karma Crew group chat

MICHELE:

Bags are packed, mission is a go.

JAKE:

We're wearing black, right? Because we're
going to bury them.

THOREN:

Clever, I like it. I'm in.

RIVER:

I like the crew name. Can we name Tyler
something too? Tiny dick Tyler?

MICHELE:

Tyler the twat?

JAKE:

Tyler the taint.

THOREN:

Terrible Tyler the tool?

RIVER:

We'll keep thinking.

LILY:

I love you guys. See you soon.

The last month and a half has flown by. I spent that first week at home hiding out from the world, much to Shadow's pleasure. Michele finally showed up the next Saturday and dragged me out to get dinner and drinks with her and Amber. It's a small town, and word travels fast, so I had a lot of stares, but it was worth it. We laughed until we cried as they caught me up on their lives.

It was the jumpstart I needed to get my act together. I focused on starting my next novel while Andrea and my team worked on marketing for the first one. Even though everything on my end was complete, the book release wasn't until the middle of December. I decided against a signing tour, despite Andrea's begging. Once the series is complete, I will do one.

For now, I want to focus on the next novel and spend my time doing things I love. I have spent so much of my life doing things for others that it almost feels selfish living for myself. Thoren tries to shut down those thoughts, asking me every morning 'What would make your heart happy today?' and encouraging me to do exactly that. I have spent so much time with Amber and Michele that I now have a writing station at the boutique and Michele's office. I'm living my dream every day and crawling into Thoren's waiting arms every night.

There's only three items left on the list of things that would make my heart happy, and one of those things is getting taken care of this week. When we started packing for the trip to Phoenix for the trial, I wasn't surprised when Thoren said he would book the hotel. I was surprised when I heard him book four rooms. River, Jake, and Michele all refused to stay home in case I needed extra support. I still don't know what I did to deserve these people in my life.

Across the plane aisle, Jake and Michele are bickering over who gets to use the armrest. Life is more fun with them in it, and their antics keep my anxiety from spiraling. Thoren brushes his thumb over my knuckles absentmindedly as he reads my first ever written novel.

"How are you feeling?" he asks, putting the book down.

"Good, all things considered. Having you all with me means more than words can express." Win or lose, justice served or not, I have my family behind me. The family that I chose, or more accurately, the family that chose me. At the end of this, that's what matters. I can hope that justice is served on all accounts, but in three days, I will be back on this plane heading home with the love and support of these people. A life I fall more in love with every day.

"We've got you. Always." His lips drop to my forehead, lingering a moment. Picking the book back up, he continues to read.

The flight passes quickly, as does our drive to the hotel. My mind isn't focused on my surroundings as much as seeing Tyler again tomorrow. We get checked in, waiting on River, who flies in later this evening. The decision is made to go out to dinner and explore the city before the first trial tomorrow.

I slip on some black skinny jeans with a hunter green sweater, layered with knee-high boots, keeping it casual but stylish. Thoren steps out of the bathroom, and my mouth instantly waters. He's wearing dark jeans and a cream-colored henley underneath a navy jacket with brown boots. His trimmed stubble is neat, his hair mussed on top, and his signature smirk pointed right at me. He looks like my every fantasy wrapped into one, and I suddenly have no desire to leave the hotel.

"Come on," Thoren chuckles, handing me my purse and opening the door. "I know that look, and if we don't leave now, then we never will."

"Room service sounds amazing," I pout as I walk past him to find our trio already in the hall, all giving me a knowing look.

My cheeks heat, but River doesn't let my embarrassment stop him. He scoops me in a hug, swinging me around. "I missed you! The guys have been asking about you."

"Stop it!" I slap his chest as he puts me down to the disapproving growl of the man behind me. "Don't poke the bear."

"But it's so fun," he whines, pulling Thoren for a hug, too. I link arms with Michele, leading the way to the elevator. She looks stunning in black leggings, a tight scoop neck sweater, and a long jacket overtop.

Behind us is a pensive Jake in his typical black boots, dark jeans, black tee, and, surprisingly, a brown jacket. "You can walk with us, since the wonder twins are in their own land," I offer, Thoren and River walking behind him, lost in an animated conversation.

"They even dressed alike." Jake rolls his eyes, looming over Michele and I. I look back again to see River also donning a henley and brown boots.

"They're so cute," Michele chuckles as we step into the elevator. "So, where are we heading?"

"Hear me out," I start, because this will be hit or miss. "I'm a comfort food girl. There's a grilled cheese place not far from here. It's the second most amazing thing I've ever put in my mouth."

"What's the first?"

"Hell yes."

"I'm in," River, Thoren, and Jake all answer simultaneously.

I stand smiling, as River groans. "Gross. I'm in for the grilled cheese. Can I invite Kinsley?"

Two hours later, we are all a little wine drunk at Cheddar Charm, our stomachs and hearts full. Our round table is filled with empty plates and loud laughter. My anxiety over tomorrow is all but forgotten with Kinsley's insistence that she and her team feel confident, and my friends constantly veering the topic to lighter things. Jake and River have been trying to convince us all to get matching tattoos, but I'm not sold.

"How about a picture of us all instead?" Thoren suggests, stopping a waiter to grab one for us.

As he sends the photo to us all, my mind wanders to how different my life has turned out from six months ago. I used to come here for dinner, but I was always alone. I would sit at a small table for two, often in the corner and out of sight, eating my grilled cheese in silence as chatter and laughter rang out around me. I felt isolated, a part of me wondering if that's what life would always be like.

I thought city life fostered this community of being alone. That despite everyone living so close together, no one talked to each other, always rushing from one thing to the next. Every friendship and interaction seemed superficial, and that was just the reality of life as an adult. Looking at my friends around the table, I see how wrong I was. You can have real and genuine friends anywhere. You just need to find your people.

I found mine.

River picks up the tab, then we all head back toward the hotel as Kinsley heads to hers. Thoren lifts our joined hands, trailing kisses over my knuckles. "Ready for tomorrow?"

"Yeah, I am."

"Good. We will be right behind you the whole time. I also got you something to wear, so if at any point you need to remember you're not alone, you can look down at this." He pulls a long thin box from his pocket and hands it to me.

I take the box and pop it open, my feet stopping in the middle of the sidewalk. Inside is a beautiful bracelet with a dainty chain, and in the center is a purple amethyst gem with an emerald on either side.

"It's our birthstones," he says, taking it from the box and fastening it around my wrist. "I will always protect you and keep you safe, and I will always be by your side."

Tears sting as I take in the visual representation of his love. Words feel heavy in my throat, unable to come out in a way that I can express how much this means to me.

"I know," he says, kissing my forehead, as he slips the box back in his pocket and takes my hand to keep walking. "I love you, too."

"I love you," I murmur, my voice thick with emotion.

"Love you all, too," Michele calls from behind us. "Except for Vanessa, I don't like her." Her eyes trail over her shoulder where River is arguing with someone on the phone.

"What's going on?" Thoren asks.

"He posted that picture of us at dinner on his social media. She doesn't like that he was sitting by Kinsley," Jake snickers.

I didn't get the best feelings about her when we met, but it's not my relationship, so I keep my mouth shut. My eyes travel back down to my wrist, the stunning bracelet glowing in the lights of the shops we pass. I feel bad for River, but nothing can ruin this night. Not even the looming trial in the morning.

Kinsley leans over, touching the bracelet on my wrist. "This is beautiful."

"Thank you." I smile as I look over my shoulder to find Thoren's eyes already on me.

The first trial was not as scary as I thought it would be. Kinsley has been ensuring me for months that she will take care of me, but a part of me was still worried. My manager and the HR representative that let me go were called in and both of them defended me. They claimed I had a stellar performance, never did anything wrong, and were blindsided by my termination. That, coupled with the emails and texts that were discovered where Tyler blatantly asked for me to be fired because 'my wife doesn't want me working with my whore', put the nails in their coffin.

Kinsley brought in a woman during the trial that had been terminated without warning two years prior. She recounted how she had been with the COO of the company, despite the man being married and her direct supervisor. Tyler had caught her and the man together, and she was let go the next day. The COO was questioned and admitted to letting me go, due to Tyler's insistence and blackmail.

The case only took a few hours, and the judge called us all back in to deliver the decision. Tyler wasn't here for this case, which made it a little easier, but I will have to face him tomorrow. The jury walked back in, and Kinsley nudged for me to stand with her as they took their seats. She grabbed my hand in hers, giving it a light squeeze as the judge read out the decision. The ringing in my ears and loud beats of my heart prevented me from hearing much outside of Michele's "damn right" behind me.

I turn to a smiling Kinsley as she pulls me in for a hug. "You did it. They awarded you two million!"

I hug her back, tears of validation lining my eyes. It's not about the money, it's about the justice, and the stuck up men who think they can play women like puppets. I feel Thoren's hand at my back as I turn to his embrace over the half wall behind me.

"I'm so proud of you, baby. One more trial and you are free."

"I'm paying you back now."

His laugh is loud and so full of ease. One hurdle done, one more to go.

The steps of the courthouse seem more daunting today, but I climb them anyway. Thoren's hand is at my back, and Michele is at my side, the two hulking figures of Jake and River taking up the rear. They weren't kidding about the outfits either, all of us dressed in head to toe black. I know we look intimidating, and as we enter the courtroom, all eyes turn to us.

Tyler's wife sits in the front row, directly behind him, a deadly scowl on her face. Tyler looks between all of us, and when his eyes land on Jake, he cowers into his seat. I never asked what he said to him the day Thoren beat him, but now I kind of want to know.

"Did we ever decide on his nickname?" River asks, not too quietly, as they take their seats behind Kinsley and I.

"Toxic trash Tyler," Jake responds.

"I've just been referring to him as a little bitch," a voice I know well calls from behind me. I spin to see Andrea sitting down next to Michele.

I jump from my seat and lean over the partition to give her a hug. "I didn't think you could make it!" Per her request, I have been keeping her informed of everything. She has two authors launching books this week and is swamped with marketing and signings with them.

"I can't stay more than an hour, but I wanted you to know I am here. You've got this. Kick his ass. Again."

Kinsley tries to cover her snort as we rise for the judge to enter. This trial is a little different from yesterday, and I find myself paying more attention. Tyler and I are both called to the stand, but most of the talking comes from Kinsley. Tyler's lawyers can only say so much in defense when he violated a restraining order and assaulted me.

Kinsley presses for five years minimum for jail time on felony charges, as well as half a million in damages. Throughout the trial, I feel eyes on me, and am surprised to find they belong to Tyler's wife, Angela. If looks could kill, I would be dead. I still don't understand her hate and anger towards me, but I let it go.

At close to one, the jury is dismissed to deliberate, and we are free to leave. Andrea slipped out and texted me to keep her informed and that she loves me. That she made it at all means so much to me. Kinsley told us not to go far because she doesn't see this taking long, so we all find a deli down the street for lunch. It's a quiet meal, all of us in our heads, anxiously awaiting the results.

I lean over to Jake, whispering so the others don't hear, "What did you say to Tyler?"

He smirks, a twinkle of mirth in his eyes. "I don't know what you're talking about." I chuckle, taking another bite of my sandwich. I'll let him keep his secret for now, only because it was glorious to see the fear of god on Tyler's face earlier.

"Thank you," I mutter, and he nods, then goes back to his meal.

"It's time," River says, looking at his phone. "They're ready for us."

We all walk back to the courthouse, but Michele and I veer off to use the restroom before we go in. I'm alone at the sink when I hear the door open, and Angela walks in. She heads straight for me, and I freeze, transported back to the bathroom with her at the work party.

"I put up with his blatant cheating and having to share with a little skank like yourself. His money is mine, and you don't deserve a damn cent of it. I deserve the life I have been living in the house I have been in. How dare you try to take it from me," she seethes.

All of my sympathy and empathy fly out the window for this woman. "You deserve the miserable life you've been living with a cheating husband," I tell her as I turn and dry my hands. Michele is now at the sink next to me, calmly washing her hands. We don't give her another ounce of attention, which seems to really piss her off. She harrumphs and turns to stalk off, but Michele kicks her foot out lightning fast, breaking the heel of her stiletto.

She flies forward at the unbalance, bashing her face on the wall in front of her, crying out. Michele looks down at her, blood dripping from under her nose where she cradles it, down to her broken shoe.

Continuing in a calm manner, Michele grabs some paper towels and tosses them on her. "You really should be careful in heels like that. They break so easily."

She takes my hand, leading me out of the bathroom and tells a security member standing further down the hall that a woman broke her heel and fell in the bathroom and might need help. I follow her in stunned silence as she leads us into the courtroom. My mouth opens and closes a few times, unsure of what to say, before I pull her into a tight hug. "I love you."

"You better. I wanted to smash her face in, but orange really isn't my color. I know you weren't going to dole out the punishment she deserves. It's not assault if I didn't touch her," she winks, then takes her place next to Jake while I take mine next to Kinsley.

Thoren leans up, "Are you okay?"

I think it through, and no matter the outcome here, I am. Maybe extra okay when I see Tyler and his wife walk back in to take their respective seats, her limping on her broken heel with gauze held under her nose. "Yeah, baby. I'm okay."

We all stand as the judge and jury make their way back into

the room. My fingers play with the bracelet around my wrist as I smile over my shoulder at Thoren. My constant. My steady. My everything.

I keep my eyes on him as the judge reads out the deliberation, as both our smiles grow. Tyler will go to prison for four years, with the possibility of parole after three. He will also pay me the entire half a million dollars. It's an absolute win, but suddenly I don't even care.

All I want is to go back home, and have mundane days with Thoren and Shadow in our home as we follow our dreams and build our family. I got justice, but more than that, I got everything I ever wanted in the people seated behind me.

CHAPTER THIRTY-SIX

thoren

Three Weeks Later

"I'm putting the extra drinks outside," River hollers as he carries the beer and wine to the back door.

"Why?"

"Fridge is full, and the snow will keep them cold. Why didn't you pick up another cooler?"

I shot a glare at him. "I thought the small one and the fridge would be fine. I just wanted a nice celebration for Lily."

Today is the official release day for Lily's book and after all of her hard work, I want her to be celebrated. It's a huge accomplishment, and I can't wait to top my celebrations with each new book release.

Michele and Amber picked up Lily earlier to get massages and have their nails done. I told them I would need at least three hours to set up, and they were on it. River and Vanessa drove over as a surprise as well, and are helping me decorate the house. It's a little tacky, but I don't care.

I bought balloons, flowers, alcohol, and a slew of snacks. Jake is smoking a pork butt, and Vanessa is helping to decorate. I'm still not sure how I feel about her, but she's been kind and helpful, so maybe there's hope for her after all.

I made a display of all of Lily's books on the table and had Andrea send me enough copies of her newest one for everyone to take one home. I tried to get her out here as well for the party, but she couldn't make it. I only met her for a moment at the trial, but her genuine love for Lily made a lasting impression on me. We have all of her closest friends coming, a few of my coworkers, and my family. It's going to be a full house, definitely the most people I have had here at one time, and it's everything I envisioned for this home.

My phone pings in my pocket with a text from Michele alerting me they should be here in ten minutes. I take a moment to look around the house, my parents setting up snacks in the kitchen, River and Vanessa sitting on the couch, co-workers and friends mingling around, even Lily's nurse came.

Jake steps in from the deck, tray of meat in his hands. "Do you want this out now?"

"Yeah, she will be here in a minute. Thank you for helping. I still have a lot to make up for."

He shakes his head, chuckling, "That you do. Could have lost her, though, so you're doing okay." He puts the tray down, giving my mom a squeeze on his way past. "I'm not drinking in case anyone needs a ride home. I'm not sure how bad the snow will get tonight, so I'll have my truck ready in case."

"She's here," River yells from the living room. I know all the cars outside kind of give away the surprise, but we all stand anyway.

Shadow is the first to jump excitedly on her when the door opens, unsure of the occasion but knowing something is happening. Lily's smile is wide as she pets our girl. "Hi everyone, what's going on?" I step up to her, winking at her rosy cheeks.

"Happy release day, baby. We all wanted to show our support, and tell you how proud of you we are. This book is going to be a huge success and we can't wait to watch your career continue to grow. You are incredible, Lily, and we want to celebrate you today."

Her blue eyes shine, her chin quivering with emotion, "Thank you," she whispers before facing the room. "Thank you all so much for doing this. It means a lot."

I wrap her in a tight hug, letting my lips meet her ear. "I am so damn proud of you, baby."

She's quickly pulled from my arms, with River stepping in like the pushy asshole he is. He makes a big show of smacking a kiss to her cheek before letting the rest of the room congratulate her. We stand side by side, watching everyone fawn over my girl like she deserves. Her smile never fades as she takes in each and every person who showed up for her.

"When are you making her family?"

I glance at my brother, taking in the soft smile he wears as he watches my mom wrap Lily in a tight embrace. "Soon," I murmur. "Let's be honest, she's already family. I'll just be making it official. You going to be joining that club anytime soon?"

We both take in Vanessa, sitting alone on the couch, scrolling through her phone. "Nah, not soon. I'm going to get some food," he slaps my shoulder before making his way to the kitchen.

I stay where I am, taking it all in. This is everything I could have ever hoped for. As the sun dips below the horizon, its fiery glow illuminates the falling snow, casting long streaks of light through the windows. The kitchen island filled with food, the mix of laughter and conversation radiating around the home.

I know as the host I should mingle, but I'm rooted to the spot, watching everything unfold. My mom and Amber are huddled in the kitchen, their smiles watery as they focus only on each other. Michele, the constant life of the party, is moving from one person to the next, taking care of the hosting for me. My dad, River, and

Jake are all clearly talking about River's season. I don't miss the heated looks Jake has been giving Amber, but I'm not entirely sure they're friendly. Finally, Lily makes her way back to my side, plate of food in hand.

"I can't believe you did this for me. Thank you." She takes it all in with me. "I can't believe they all showed up for me."

"Believe it, baby. Andrea was really upset she couldn't make it. She was happy to make sure I got enough copies of your book though, and the flowers on the table are from her." I steal a chip from her plate, popping it in my mouth. "We are all so proud of you, but no one more than me. It has been my greatest joy getting to watch you embrace your passions. You have stepped into your own in the last few months. Watching your confidence soar and the way you have overcome your past has made me the happiest man. Getting to be a part of that journey is more than I deserve, but I will try every day to earn it. Happy release day, baby."

I mean every word of it, seeing her embrace her accomplishments has been so incredible. She is still her humble and reserved self, but every day she steps a little further out of her shell. She's no longer afraid to state what she wants and to go after it. I can see the pieces of herself that she hid away making their way back to the surface, and I do everything I can to coax more of her out.

Lily has captivated me from day one, but the more I learn about her, the more I see her feisty side and goofy side, the harder I fall. Her beauty is just as striking and only accentuated by everything that is *her.* Like the way her nose scrunches every time she has to put a bra on, not that I can blame her, I hate those pesky things, too. Or the way her eyes glass over at the end of every romance novel she reads when the couple gets their happily ever after. The way her hairstyles match her moods, and how her fingers rub together when she is anxious.

She is getting more comfortable expressing herself not only in the way she speaks, but also in the way she dresses. She didn't own a single black shirt when she moved here. With no one telling her it isn't a feminine color, she is able to embrace her own mixed style. I think she looks beautiful in everything, but I'm partial to when she wears one of my shirts… and nothing else.

As the evening carries on, people slowly trickle out with a copy of Lily's book that she took the time to sign and write nice notes in. The snow hasn't let up, piling up in the dark evening. River insists on driving my parents home so we say our goodbyes, promising to show tomorrow for brunch at their house. After the front door shuts, it's just Michele, Amber, Jake, Lily, and I. Shadow is fast asleep on her back in front of the fireplace enjoying the warmth on her belly.

Lily takes a seat on the couch next to me, leaning on my shoulder. Her eyes rove over Amber who is sitting on the floor next to Shadow, an amber liquid in her glass, as she takes small sips. "I'm worried about her," she says in my ear. "Something happened this morning that she's trying to hide, but I can tell she's struggling."

Amber swirls her glass before taking the rest back in one large sip. Her eyes look desolate, a pain far beyond just being sad written in them. "My mom said Jana was doing okay yesterday."

"Yeah, it's not her. I just don't know what it is, and when I tried asking, she said it was my day and not to worry," she chews on her bottom lip, looking up at me.

"But you wouldn't be you if you didn't worry about others." I brush my lips across her forehead. "I'll make sure Jake gets her home safe, okay?"

"My body is happy," Michele claims from where she's sprawled on the floor.

"Why is everyone on the floor?" I ask, looking around. At least Jake is in a chair. "I have furniture, you know?"

"Nahhh, the floor is nice. After getting a total rub down today, then filling myself with alcohol, I am happy right where I am," Michele slurs.

"You ladies want to stay here? I make a mean hangover breakfast."

Amber's eyes go wide as she looks at Michele. "I have to open in the morning!"

"I'll take you home," Jake's eyes bore into her. "My truck is used to the snow and I'm sober."

A light flush takes over Amber's cheeks as she takes him in before quickly turning away with a muttered "thanks" that is met with Jake's signature smirk. Lily and I's gazes meet as she turns further into me to hide her giggle.

Michele pushes herself off the floor, pointing between me and Lily. "I'm a really heavy sleeper, but I need like an hour to fall asleep. Please keep the fucking until after…" she squints down at her phone, "ten thirty. And not a moment before!"

With that, she grabs a water from my fridge and ascends the stairs. "Good night," she calls before slamming a door shut.

"I think that's our cue," Amber says quietly, also moving to a stand, but swaying on her feet. Jake is by her side in an instant, holding her steady.

"Do you have a purse or anything?" he asks gently.

"I've got it all," Lily says, pulling out a jacket and purse from the front closet. "Get her home safely, please. If the roads are too bad, stay with your parents. Either way, please let us know when you get somewhere safe for the night." She pats Jake's chest before helping her friend into her jacket.

"You okay taking her home?" I mutter to Jake.

"Girl's smashed at her friend's celebration." He rolls his eyes, watching Amber and Lily say goodbye with annoyance radiating off him. "I'm not thrilled, but you know I'll make sure she gets home safe."

We watch Jake practically carry her to his truck, Lily shaking her head the whole time. "I'm calling it now. They're ending up together." I pull her into me, thrilled to finally have her all to myself again… kind of. "Thank you, again. I've never celebrated a release before, and it really means a lot to me that you did this. I love you."

"I would do anything for you, baby. Anything. Now go crawl your sweet ass in the tub while I clean up. I have plans for you tonight, but I have another forty minutes to kill," I wink as I smack her ass. Her giggles follow her up the steps as I watch her go and damn, I love the sound of it. I hope to hear her laughter in our home every day for the rest of our lives.

lily

Two Weeks Later - Christmas Day

Warmth spreads through me, as prickles of awareness touch my senses. My eyes flutter open, orienting myself to the pinks of the morning light peeking through the curtains. It's too early, but as another wave of pleasure rocks through me, I realize exactly why I'm awake. Thoren's mouth latches around my clit, sucking it into his mouth as he pushes my thighs further apart.

Reaching below the blankets, my fingers tangle through his hair, holding him to me. He growls, doubling his efforts as one of his hands trails up my thigh to my aching center. He swirls one finger around my entrance before pushing in, stroking it against the spot that makes me see stars.

I pull the blankets off me, wanting to watch as he devours me for breakfast. His hazel eyes fix on mine, the green glinting when he winks. His tongue swirls around and around, driving me closer to climax.

"Don't stop," I pant out as he adds a second finger. His teeth come out to play, lightly scraping over my sensitive nerves before he sucks my clit hard again. I shatter around him, my hands clenched tightly in his hair, holding him to me as I ride out my orgasm. When my body slumps onto the bed, he kisses his way up until his lips cover mine.

"Merry Christmas," he whispers against my lips. I kiss along his bottom lip before slipping my tongue inside. He groans his approval, deepening the kiss as his hands spear into my hair. His hard dick rubs against my pussy, soaking himself in my cum. Reaching down, I line him up to slide inside.

Our moans come in unison as his thick cock stretches me, filling me completely in one thrust. I shift my hips, rolling us so I am on top. I love waking up to his tongue inside me, but he loves watching me ride him, and on Christmas, the least I can do is oblige. I rock my hips over him, rubbing my clit against him with every back-and-forth motion.

"Fuck, baby, you look so pretty riding me." One rough hand grips my hip tight, the other drawing small circles on my already sensitive clit. My head falls back, focusing on the feel of his hands on me as I rock on his hard cock.

"I'm so… close.." I moan as he doubles his efforts, guiding me over him faster. The deep ache inside explodes through me as my pussy clamps down on him like a vise. Thoren's deep grunts follow my cries of pleasure as his cock pulses, spilling himself in me. He pulls me down, burying his head in my neck, as his fingers skate down my back.

"Merry Christmas, baby."

Thoren rolled us to the side, letting his spent dick fall from me. It's quickly replaced by his fingers as he pushes his cum back in me with a wicked smirk on his lips. "Does this count as a Christmas gift?"

I choke on a laugh. "We promised only two gifts, so I should be mad if this is one of them, but I'm not. I'll take this gift any day."

Satisfied his cum is back inside me, he climbs out of bed. "I think I have proven I will fuck you every day of your life," he calls over his shoulder as he turns on the shower. "Get your sweet ass in here, I am excited for gifts!"

I happily follow him in, soaking in the feel of the hot water. I thought the honeymoon phase of our relationship would have faded by now, but it is far from it. We love to shower together, taking the time to wash each other. Even out of the shower, we still love to cook together, watch shows and read together, spend every moment we can tucked into each other's arms.

I have been off birth control since the hospital, but I haven't had a positive test yet. As much as I want to build a family with him, I know he isn't going anywhere and we have our whole lives ahead of us to have babies. Until then, I will continue to enjoy trying, because holy cow does he make it fun. I love that he can be sweet like this morning, but if I push him enough, he will bend me over and make it rough in the most delicious of ways.

"Whatcha thinking about over there?" his deep voice rumbles against my back as his nose runs along my neck. "You just got the prettiest flush."

"Nothing," my denial sounds weak. "Present time."

I turn off the shower, and we step out, getting our towels. "Christmas pajamas only," he tells me sternly as he moves to the bedroom to get dressed. "We are looking like a family in our matching jammies when we go to my parents later. I also might have bought some for Shadow."

He holds up dog pajamas that match the ones we have, and I am instantly in love. The pup in question is eyeing us warily, but she is going to look adorable in them. The three of us dress in our matching reindeer pajamas before heading downstairs. We agreed on two gifts each, one big and one small. Not that money is an issue, but something about it felt special. Plus, he warned me we would get spoiled when we went to brunch at his parents later. Something about River not believing in budgets.

Thoren lights a fire as I let Shadow out and start the coffee. The snow is piled high outside, a glistening white blanket, but thankfully no more is falling. I knew living in the mountains meant snowy winters, but I wasn't prepared for multiple feet of snow. It is so serene, and I don't find myself hating it. I usher Shadow back in, wiping down her paws and sending her to the rug in front of the fireplace to dry her pajamas.

"Shadow's first?" I ask, passing Thoren a mug as we sit in front of the Christmas tree, one we cut down and decorated together while blasting Christmas music.

He pulls out the two wrapped presents for her, each of us helping her unwrap one. The first one is a new bag of bones which she quickly dismisses for the new purple dragon. Hers had a hole in it and we had to throw it away. She's been moping ever since, but her ears perk up when she spots the new one.

"Our turn, big ones first," Thoren declares. We both get up to retrieve our hidden gifts. Apparently, neither of us trusted the other not to snoop. We sit back down with an envelope in hand, as we stare at each other wide eyed. "We said big gifts, Lily," he says accusingly,

"You literally have an envelope in your hand, too, dummy." I hand him mine, my anxiety spiking. "You first."

With careful fingers, he opens the envelope and pulls out the small packet of folded papers. It's not the official documents, those are hidden in the safe upstairs, but I made copies for this. I watch his face carefully, as his expression morphs from confusion to surprise.

"I really hated that you sold land for me, so I bought you some more. Specifically, the rest of the land and the other cabin on our lane. The owners took some convincing, but we reached an agreement. I thought we could rent it out or renovate it. Maybe as your parents get older, we can convince them to move in there so we can keep a closer eye on your mom."

Thoren looks up at me with glassy eyes and the softest expression. "You bought us a cabin to take care of my parents?"

I nod, my throat thick with emotion. I may not have my parents around, but David and Evelyn have taken me in with no questions asked and shown up for me constantly. Of course I want them close to us and want to show them an ounce of the kindness they have shown me.

Thoren pulls me into his lap, kissing me deep. "It will take a miracle to get them out of their home, but I love it. I love it so much and I love you. Thank you, baby. This is amazing and so thoughtful."

"Good," I croak, "Because my next gift is not nearly as thoughtful."

He places me next to him, turning me sideways so he can see my face. "Your turn."

I take the envelope from him, pulling open the tab and taking out the papers inside. My hands shake as I read the itinerary for a trip for two to Iceland next month. It is a week-long trip with hotels and activities all planned out for us. It is even better than the trip I dreamed of.

I turn to find him kneeling beside me on one knee, a small black box in his hands. His smile is nervous, but the glint in his eye shows pure love.

"Lily, I know we are doing this all sorts of backwards, sideways and upside-down, but I wouldn't have it any other way. From the moment you walked into my life, you have captivated me, heart and soul. You are the reason my sun rises in the morning. The reason the flowers around me bloom, the leaves turn, and the rain falls. You are the reason my life makes sense and has purpose. Without you, I can't breathe, I can't think. You are my reason for everything, Lily. With you by my side, I have felt true peace. I want to spend the rest of my days making you feel that, too. Marry me, Lily Wilks."

With tears streaming down my face, I tackle him, wrapping my arms around his neck. "Yes, Thoren, yes!" His arms hold me tight as I try to pull myself together. I finally pull back to take in the ring, causing more tears to fall.

Inside the small box is an oval diamond with purple gems along the band. It's dainty and shiny, something I would have picked for myself. His hands tremble slightly as he slides the ring onto my finger before bringing it to his lips.

"It looks perfect on you, Lily James," he muses, as he pulls me into his lap again. "I know the honeymoon is supposed to come after the wedding, but we've done everything else backwards; living together, trying for a baby, so I just thought we could do this the same."

"I love you so much, Thoren James. You have shown me every day what true love looks like. You make my life bigger and brighter just by being in it. I can't wait to be your wife."

I kiss him deep, letting him feel the strength of my love. "But I kind of hate you right now. This really puts my other gift to shame." I already struggled with what to get him, but went practical. I'm a practical person, and he has mentioned needing a new one of these a few times over the last month. I felt fine about the gift until now.

"Hand it over, baby."

I pull the box from where I was sitting and place it in front of him. I watch as he rips open the wrapping, opening the box to pull out a new axe.

"This is exactly what I needed," he says, inspecting it like a prized treasure.

"It's no ring," I grumble under my breath. His laugh is hearty as he puts down the axe and squeezes me tighter. "It was a selfish gift, really. I like sitting on the porch while you chop wood."

"You just agreed to be my wife. There is no gift on this planet that can top that," he nips at my ear. "But if it's a close second, it's you letting me bend you over the stump again," he smirks. "Now you get to plan the wedding of your dreams."

"The wedding of my dreams is right here, in our backyard, surrounded by our friends and family, and the prettiest flowers around." I never really wanted a big wedding. I didn't have a whole huge list of family and friends that I want to attend, and I want the day to be about Thoren and I. A beautiful white dress on a warm spring day in the place that we love sounds like a dream.

"That sounds perfect, baby. Come on, let's go tell the family."

thoren

EPILOGUE

April 25th

River pulls up to the house in my truck, a wide smile on his face. He steps out, throwing my keys to me before walking around to the bed. "Go figure, mom had them all prepped and cut in buckets. When is the flower lady going to be here?"

"She's been here for an hour. Do you think Lily will like the surprise?" The truck bed has six large black buckets filled with freshly cut lilacs for the florist to add into the flowers Lily already picked out.

When I discovered Lily loved lilacs last summer, I asked my mom if I could plant some extra bushes along the edge of their property. I had plans to bring Lily a fresh bouquet of them every day this spring before replanting them here, but this worked out better.

Lily asked for so little for this wedding, that it almost broke my heart, until I realized that's just who she is. She's a quiet love and quiet strength. She doesn't need a big show of things, but I want to give it to her anyway. I agreed to the backyard wedding that she wanted, but what she doesn't know is that there will be a few added surprises.

She stayed in our new cabin last night with Amber and Michele, and they are going to keep her there getting ready and pampered until the ceremony. It gave me the perfect time to set up all the extras. I ordered a large white tent with a dance floor for the side of the yard that was set up last night and hired some ladies from in town to decorate it this morning.

River and I each grab two of the buckets of lilacs, bringing them to the clearing behind the cabin where the chairs are set up around a makeshift aisle with a wooden arch at the center. Lily wanted the color scheme to be 'the sunrises we watch together' and the decorators delivered. There's mild hues of pink, yellow, and orange flowers along the aisle, and these lilacs will be the perfect addition.

The florist claps her hands as we set down the buckets for her. "These will be perfect for the bouquet! I am going to pair them with white roses," she exclaims happily, so I leave her to it.

River and I make our way to the tent to check on the progress there. Lily thinks we had picnic tables delivered, but instead I have one long table to seat everyone for dinner. It's decorated with nice dinnerware and signs for each guest. She used cuts of wood from the surrounding woods as bases for her centerpieces, which featured stacked books and candles, to incorporate things we love.

In one corner, I set up an open bar, and the other has a small DJ table beside the dance floor. The decorators hung twinkling lights and swaths of colored fabric around the ceiling. It's so much better than I could have imagined.

"I think you nailed it," River slaps my back as he takes it all in. "Did you get her a gift?"

"Yeah, it's in the cabin. I need to have it delivered soon, and then I need to shower and get ready. You got your suit and speech ready?" Lily wanted to include my family as much as possible in the wedding, so we asked River to get ordained to be our minister. As much as I want my brother to be part of this day, I would be lying if I said I wasn't a little scared of what might come out of his mouth up there.

"Oooh, give it to me. I'll deliver it. Then I'll be right behind you getting ready. Don't worry, little bro, I've got everything handled."

His smirk is exactly why I am worried, but I lead him inside to get the gift. Jake steps in the front door as we step in the back, his suit bag hanging over his shoulder. Lily and I decided to not do bridesmaids and groomsmen since our wedding is so small. However, we did have Michele and Amber wear pink dresses, and River and Jake will both be rocking pink bow ties.

"Happy wedding day, man." Jake says as he gives me a hug, then heads to the guest room to put his suit on the bed. I give the gift bag to River, who calls Shadow to follow him.

"Don't let her roll in anything," I call over my shoulder, as I head up the stairs to shower and get ready. "She was groomed yesterday, and she needs to look nice as our flower girl."

I strip in my room, climbing into the shower. I can't believe the day is finally here. Today, I make Lily my wife. My happily ever after will walk down the aisle and promise to love and cherish me for the rest of her days. Today is the first day of the rest of my life.

Lily

"Knock knock," River calls out as he pokes his head in the front door. "Can I come in?"

Shadow pushes past him, running straight for me. Her furry tail creates a wind tunnel it's wagging so fast. "All clear. What are you doing here?"

He steps in, taking in the mess of hair and makeup products spread out on the kitchen table. When I bought this place, they agreed to leave it furnished, which came in handy with us girls having spent last night here, as well as giving us a place to get ready today.

"I brought you a gift from your boo," he says, handing me a small bag. "You look stunning, Lily. Can I see the dress?"

I take the bag and nod to the stairs. Michele is putting the finishing touches on my hair, which is a half updo with big Hollywood curls. My makeup is complete, as are the girls' and Amber is upstairs getting dressed first to bring Thoren my gift. I got him socks with Shadow's face on them in case he gets 'cold feet.' I also got him a new watch that is custom made with wood from a tree in our favorite clearing by our waterfall. "Thanks Riv. The photographer has it upstairs taking pictures of it. If you promise not to spoil it, you can take a peek."

I swear he giggles like a schoolgirl as he bounds up the steps. I pull out the tissue seeing a small card that I will read when Michele isn't looking over my shoulder. There's a black velvet box at the bottom encasing the most stunning necklace. It has a gold chain with vines and flowers in the center. The vines have his green birthstone in them, and the flowers have a mix of diamonds and purple amethysts. My fingers trail over it, tears springing to my eyes.

"It will look great with your dress, and it matches your ring and bracelet."

I turn to my best friend, my smile watery. "He's incredible. Am I all done?"

"You are. Let's go kick Riv out and get dressed. We are a little behind the photographer's schedule."

We pass Amber on the stairs, followed by River, who insists on going with her to see what's in the gift. They take a very reluctant-to-leave Shadow so I can get my dress on and take photos.

Before I get too far, River grabs my hand, giving it a squeeze.

"He's going to cry, but in that dress, there won't be a dry eye in the house. Welcome to the family, Lil."

I blink back the tears that form again, giving him a small smile. I can't say anything back or all my makeup will be useless. I called my parents last month after not speaking to them since the day Thoren hung up on them. The call went okay, but they said they couldn't make it out for the wedding because they already had a trip planned. There were no apologies, no congratulations, no effort at all from them. While it hurts, I have learned to embrace the family I do have. The incredible James family that welcomed me with open arms and fiercely loves me. Andrea even made it out for the wedding, flying in early this morning. My family is here; they just look a little different.

The photographer pulls my dress from its spot on the window and lays it out for me. The dress is a white silk chiffon with a sweetheart neckline and thin straps. It's a mermaid style with a low back and long train. There's lace along the edges that adds a touch of feminine beauty to it. Honestly, it's probably too fancy for our setting, but I fell in love and couldn't leave the store without it.

With the dress on, I sit on the bed and read Thoren's letter. There's no stopping the tears that fall now, but I blot with a tissue as I make it through. In less than an hour, I get to call him my husband, and it is beyond my wildest dreams. His kindness and warmth, his generous and giving spirit, his heart that is woven into mine. I woke up knowing this was going to be the best day ever. When I snuck to the bathroom earlier and the little blue lines popped up, I knew it was going to be even better than I imagined.

When I step out of the primary bedroom, Michele and Amber are standing there waiting.

"Holy shit."

"You are the most beautiful bride."

The three of us head outside for photos before the ceremony.

David and Evelyn make their way over, both tearing up when they catch sight of me. This is now the third time this wedding has made them cry. The first was when we showed up Christmas morning to tell them we were engaged, followed a few weeks later when I asked David if he would walk me down the aisle and Evelyn if she would be the flower girl with Shadow. It might be a silly thing, but she was beyond honored. They both were.

The girls leave us to take their seats as we make our way into our cabin, where I will walk out from the back door. Evelyn and Shadow slip through first, leaving me and David alone until we get the signal.

He grabs my hands in his, his chin trembling. "I thought when I had sons, that they would be my greatest pride in life. And they are, but adding you to our family, and watching Thoren be seen and valued for exactly who he is; watching you love him as deeply and truly as we do… Lily, it has been the greatest joy. I'm so proud to call you part of our family."

"Damn it, David," I croak as a tear breaks free and trails down my cheek. "You aren't supposed to make me cry right before walking down the aisle."

His laugh booms as he pulls out a handkerchief and gently taps my cheek. "You are supposed to be the one person in this family who doesn't swear. Ah, to hell with it. Let's get you fucking married."

Thoren is waiting under the arch for me, his hair in that effortlessly messy but styled look I love. His beard is neatly trimmed, and his black suit is tailored to perfection, hugging his thick thighs and snug over his broad shoulders. He looks absolutely edible, and he's all mine. When our eyes finally catch, I see the glassy sheen as he takes me in. He mouths 'I love you' with a wink, causing my heart to beat out of my chest.

He takes me from his dad, his eyes trailing down my dress

and back up. "You look stunning. I can't believe I get to marry you," he whispers.

"I love you, handsome. Let's make this official."

River starts the ceremony, thanking everyone for coming out and celebrating us. Surprisingly, he keeps the entire speech appropriate, with humor mixed in. I block out parts of it, too focused on the man in front of me. Thoren's thumbs stroke over my knuckles as his eyes stay locked on mine. Our gazes tell each other every emotion we are feeling at finally getting to this day.

We say our vows, promising our lives to each other. Lives that I know will be filled with love, happiness, family, and adventures.

River finally tells Thoren that he may kiss his bride, and as his lips come in to meet mine, I whisper against his, "I'm pregnant."

bonus:

WEDDING DAY LETTERS

My dearest Lily Kim Wilks,

Today is the day you become Lily Kim James, and I become the happiest man on earth. I wish I had the words to explain to you exactly how I am feeling, but that is your area of expertise. All I can tell you is that, with you, I feel complete. Every tattered part of me is now entwined with every broken piece of you, and together, we are whole. I've never felt so cared for more than how you care for me. Every morning, I rush to wake to see your beautiful face, and every night I close my eyes to dream of you. The light of your love is like the sun, nurturing and shining on everything around you. Shadow is the luckiest dog in the world to have you as her mom, and I can only imagine how that love will transfer to our children. I can't wait to have kids with you, Lily. To see your belly filled with our child. To hold your hand through every step, and to watch them come into the world and into our arms. You were meant to be a mom, and I will try with everything in me to be the best dad. Our family is growing today, baby, as you take my last name. Soon, it will grow again, I can feel it in my bones. I'll swing my hammer every day until that stick has two lines. (Don't laugh, I worked hard on that line, and my dick is proud of it.)

You don't know this, but I had your bracelet, ring and this necklace all made at the same time. I knew within two months of meeting you that you were the woman I wanted to spend the rest of my life with. Each part of this gift was strategic and symbolic. I see you in the flowers of this necklace, growing and bringing beauty and joy to those around you. You have so much strength in you, Lily. Despite everything, you shine and keep moving forward. It is my honor to get to grow with you for the rest of our lives.

I love you, Lily James. I'll be waiting.

Thoren

My love,

Thoren, today my heart is so full. Full of love, happiness, and an overwhelming sense of peace. I knew you were special when you took the time to get to know me, and waited for me to be ready for your heart. Your love and devotion to family astounds me. Your strength, while being gentle, your fierce protectiveness, while being my best friend. You are the person I want to dive headfirst into life with. When I plan an adventure, it's you I want holding the map... partially because I'm clearly bad with directions. I want to plunge into the cold waters of the future with you because it looks bigger and brighter by your side. There is no greater man in the world than you and no place I would rather be than with you. On this day, you become a husband and I become a wife, and I already know it is something we will both excel at. Loving you is the easiest thing I have ever done. The day we get the honor of becoming parents will be the only feeling that could top this absolute elation I feel. My life was so empty before you, and you have made sure to fill it with friends, laughter, family, and more love than I thought imaginable. My life is richer with you in it, Thoren James.

I got you socks with Shadow on them in case of cold feet, and so she can remain at our side where she belongs. The watch is made from a fir tree that was taken from our favorite clearing in the woods. I hope as you carry it with you, it always brings the sense of serenity we feel there. There is a small heart engraved in the back because you carry my heart with you, Thoren. It only beats for you, much like that watch.

I love you. See you soon. I'll be the one in white.

Lily

acknowledgments

Writing this book was such a mix of feelings. I worried after my first book that I wouldn't be able to do it again. Imposter syndrome ran strong that I was a 'one hit wonder' but with my novel. When I sat down to write this book, the words poured out of me, erasing that doubt. I love these characters and can't wait to share this whole series with you all. I hope that Thoren and Lily touched your heart in the same healing way they touched mine.

Thank you to my alpha readers: Ashley, Emily, and Jenn. You three walked through this story with me and watched me pour my heart into it. It was such a joy having you three watch these characters come to life with me. Your feedback and encouragement meant the world to me on the hard days.

My beta readers: Alyssa, Alicia, Amanda, Casey, Lazarra and Sarah. (Apparently I have a thing for A-names) thank you for taking the time to read this and give me feedback. Your excitement and love for this story fueled my soul.

These two groups of amazing women mean the world to me for taking a chance on me and believing in me on the days I didn't believe in myself.

To my husband and daughter, thank you for your ongoing support. Mr. Lane, you push me and encourage me to take on every opportunity. B, I love your excitement over every little win that I have. You're the hype girl everyone needs in their corner and I'm glad you're in mine. I love you both dearly.

To Kristin, my cover artist, you did it again! Your skill is unmatched and you are a true joy to work with.

To Sara, my editor and friend, THANK YOU. Thank you for rushing when I throw crazy things at you. For talking through every issue I face, and being my sounding board through so much. Your belief in me, encouragement, and passion for my success is everything I have needed and more.

To you, my readers, I am eternally grateful. This dream of mine could never be a reality without your support. I hope to continually bring you swoon worthy stories that touch your heart.

Coming next in the Wanderland Series:
Jake and Amber's story

Etta Lane is a married mother who loves to read spicy romance as much as she loves to write it. She loves the outdoors, adventures, and game nights with friends. When she isn't reading or writing, you can find her spending time with her family or Facetiming her sister.

connect with etta

Instagram: @ettalane.author
Facebook: Etta Lane
TikTok: @etta.lane.author
Facebook Reader Group: Etta Lane's Reader Group
Email: ettalanewrites@gmail.com